The Girl Next Door

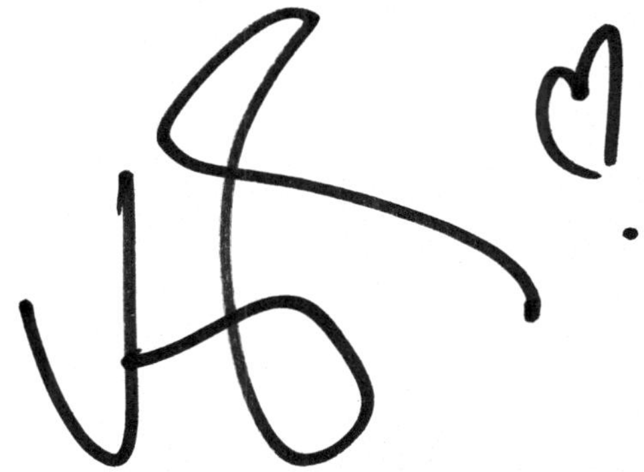

Katherine Nightingale

Second Edition

DEDICATION

To my family who has had patience with me while spending time on this adventure. My dear friends who have helped not only in supportive ways, but have also been my editors. My extended family that always supports whatever crazy escapade I begin.

To my beautiful, rebellious Luke.

Robert, the pillar that stands strong.

Gale, for your genuine motherly love.

CHAPTER 1

"Hey- You need any help today?" As I turned around, I noticed my neighbor Austin was shadowing me from the sun. He was seventeen years old, sculpted from being a football quarterback, and hair from a Greek God, even though you couldn't see it completely from the hat being worn on backward.

"Yes, I could."

"Great, where do you want me to start?"

I pointed over to a huge pile of limestones that I just had delivered and showed him where I wanted them around each flower bed. After he got started, I went back to pulling weeds and redesigning flower beds. The sun was clearly starting to fade I decided it was time to go in for the night. I walked over to Austin and asked if he was ready to call it quits and have a cold drink. He smiled and said,

"Sure, let me pick this stuff up and I'll be in." I went back to my area, picked up my tools and headed for the house. Austin wasn't long after, I think quitting and getting a cold drink was a very welcomed thought.

"Lemonade?"

"Yeah, that'd be awesome!" he said.

I poured a glass for him and me and handed it to him. By this point of the day, he had lost his shirt and was now using it as a towel to remove the sweat from his glistening body. Summers in the Midwest can be so hot and miserable that even removing your own skin won't give you any relief. He downed his glass before I even got a sip of mine.

"More?"

"Please." I could smell the fading cologne/deodorant masked by the odor of sweat, fresh air, and grass. I could feel the heat from the sun still radiating off his body, and knew that the air conditioning in the house, cold drink, and shirtless top hadn't cool him off yet.

"Thank you for all the help today. It would have taken me forever by myself."

"No problem. I like to work outside and it's good to keep in shape for the team."

"Yea, I guess I don't need to go to the gym tonight either. Can I give you anything for all the help?"

Austin paused for a moment, set his glass down on the counter behind me, and locked eyes. He had brilliant evergreen eyes that were hard to avoid. You could see the speckles of gold shimmer like rays of sun dancing on water. His arm was resting on the counter and touching my lower back. Keeping his eyes locked on me he leaned in and pressed his lips against mine. I knew that this was wrong on so many levels, his age, my age, and being a lawyer- a damn good one- I let all rational leave my mind. I wanted this, I needed this. I succumb to the kiss developing deeper into his. Feeling his chest press against mine, made me realize that my heart was beating harder than I was aware. He ended the kiss softly by pulling back, I caught my breath, I opened my eyes, looked at a perfect white-toothed smile, carved cheekbones that extended to his stubbled defined jawbone that had been marked by the sun as well.

"No. Thank you for the drinks." He backed away, grabbed his shirt off the counter and headed for the door. Before he left he turned back, gave one more smile and pushed the screen door open and disappeared.

It took me a moment to gather my thoughts, clear my head, and come back to reality. I figured a cool shower would help me gain self-control and figure out what the hell just happened. As I was letting the cool water rain down on me I was replaying the details of what just happened, going back and forth on right from wrong, "yeah, he's only seventeen" I told myself, "but you're only twenty-three. He kissed you…. but you kissed back. It was hot, and obviously too much sun, you weren't thinking clearly. How could you think clearly, he is gorgeous?! And you aren't horrible to look either." I wasn't. I am 5'6 and 126 pounds. I go to the gym at least 3 times a week to blow off crap from the office and to stay fit. I have a personal Krav Maga coach to help me stay safe being a young single woman. So, Yeah- why wouldn't he want to kiss me I'm frikin' hot!!I shook my head and thought this is ridiculous, maybe I should go to the gym anyway and work whatever this is off. I stepped out of the shower, dried off, found my workout clothes, and got dressed. After making a protein drink for my 'dinner', I grabbed my iPod, headphones, towel, and gym bag and headed to the car. Backing out of the driveway, I paused and stared at the rearview mirror and noticed Austin's car was in the driveway but the garage door was shut and I felt my heart skip for a second. "Oh, for the love of God- this is insane!!" I thought and continued in reverse, put it in drive and headed for the gym.

I was in luck when I got to the gym, my trainer/coach was there and I knew I would be in for a solid ass-kicking workout if I was up for it, and I totally was. It seemed that all the muggy work outside didn't faze me a bit. This pent-up lust I was having seemed to trump anything else and I knew I needed to burn it out of my system.

"Hi, Ellie- what are you doing here tonight?"

"Just needing a little motivation and head clearing, Rick."

"Well let's get to it! Go start on stretches, push-ups, abs, then bag. What do you want to hear?"

"Something intense and extreme!" I replied.

As I was wrapping my wrists guards with the tape, I heard the familiar intro to AC/DC's Thunderstruck- Oh yeah, this was going to be a good workout.

Laying on the mat, my back enjoying the cool plastic feeling, trying to slow my breath, Rick says;

"You haven't been that intense in a long time, what's got into you? A bad case at work?"

"No, I guess I just have a lot to burn off." I replied, knowing that this was true, but not in the same meaning as Rick thought.

"Well, go drink your 'dinner', hit the shower and I will catch you later."

"Thanks for kicking my ass, Rick!"

"Thanks for letting me!!"

As I rolled over to push myself up off the mat, I felt the workout. Could have been the entire day overdone a little, but most everything hurt. I went to the gym's fridge, grabbed my 'dinner', and guzzled it down. I guess I was hungrier than I thought. I took a shower because I hated 'gym smell' in my car, and headed back to the house. I was exhausted. The workout apparently is what I needed to clear my emotions. I hardly thought about the events of the day. I just tried to focus on driving home and going to bed without an accident. Even passing Austin's house didn't faze me. It was 2 a.m. and I just wanted to crawl into my 1800 thread count sheets after taking some Advil.

The week went by, as usual, not a thought was given to the event that occurred. I had a really large case and I spent several hours preparing and going to testimonials and when I wasn't at work, I was at the gym beating the crap out of the heavy bag because it was that or the case. I found releasing my frustration cleared my mind to think of new scenarios for the case at hand. Being single and determined I spent more hours in my office than my fellow partners at the firm. I didn't have the family to rush home too or the pissed off spouse that expected me home to make or eat dinner. I could come and go as I pleased. As I drove onto my street, I noticed there were about three cars around Austin's driveway with about five guys shooting baskets. Most of them were without shirts on, Austin is one. Man, did he look good. He was sweating from the game in the humid weather and gleaming in the sun. The enthralling game they were in, he didn't even notice I had driven in, which was fine by me. He was seventeen and I completely needed to stay out of that situation. I stepped out of my car and was bending over in my almost too short business suit getting my briefcase and paperwork out of the back seat when I heard the familiar sound of a basketball bouncing my way. I looked up and saw a pretty saturated boy -man coming up after it with a huge smile on his face. I caught the ball with my stiletto where I purposely held down the ball. "Two can play this game", I thought because I am wearing one of my 'hotter' outfits. Austin bent down to grab the ball under my $300.00 Louboutin shoe and ended up kneeling because I didn't relinquish the ball. He looked up at me, first to check me out, which felt awesome, but then to try and stare me down with his charm. "I'm a lawyer," I thought, that's not going to work. But it only took one sentence to completely knock me off my guard.

"You know I'm not sorry." He said.

"Not sorry for what?" I replied, trying to act as smug and nonchalant as I could muster. I go up against the biggest corporations and have some of the richest clients in the world and they expect me to hold their lives in their hands, but yet this kid -YEAH- kid says one sentence and I turn into a high schooler again….

"For the kiss." I just stared at him, forgetting about the ball under my foot, released it without my admission and he swept it up. He stood up and stuck it under his arm and said, "I would and will do it again."

"Oh, you think?" Is all I could manage to say being thrown completely off. He turned to join his friends then turned his head back and with a wink said, "you look very nice by the way." I went in the house flushed and bewildered by the 'I would and will do it again', statement. What did he mean by that? Again? There won't be an 'again'. There can't be an 'again'. I could lose my license, job, jail time…. Humph, and I blew it off or at least tried too, but the heckling from the guys to each other was a distraction that peeked my interest. I wasn't too much older than them so watching them play wasn't totally wrong and one kiss, just one kiss was not going to get me in trouble. These are the things I kept telling myself while I watched the game. I forced myself to leave the game and go change. I am going to change for the gym, and look over some new testimonials and head out. That will distract me. No more silly flirtations and daydreaming. By the time I finished the paperwork, the sun was starting to set. I was tired of being inactive so I decided to head out to the gym. As I shut my door, I heard a solo basketball echo from across the street. No more heckling or laughter, just a single player shooting hoops. I stood behind my car watching when Austin looked up and yelled over, "Ya wanna shoot some?" I thought for a moment and then told myself, "What the hell? Why not."

When I walked over across the street, I said snarky, "You think you can keep your eyes on the ball?"

"I'll do my best", and with that sunk a shot without even trying. Wow, this is going to be hard I thought. It was a pretty fair fight, even though I wasn't the worst basketball player on the planet. There was a lot of trash talk and bumps and touching. Every time we connected there was a charge of electricity surge my skin straight to my heart. I wondered if he felt that way too or was just a horney teenager? Almost complete dark, the score was 20 -17 and I barely could see the hoop. Austin's mom yelled out the door that dinner was ready and caused our game to end.

"Be right there mom." He yelled back.

"See, I told you I'd win." He said cockily.

"Not by much" I informed him. I stood there a little confused on what to do next. Should I wait and see if he was going to kiss me again or kiss him or what? I really was confused. This was not my typical 'play'. I was always in charge, in control. I decided to call it a night and quit playing my mental game, so I turned to head back to my house while saying, “thanks for the game.”

“No problem.” He said while he watched me leave.

“Enjoy your dinner.”

“Bye.”

….and I walked home. Nothing. He did nothing. I did nothing. What the hell??? When I got back inside, I went to the bathroom, started the water for a shower, picked out comfortable clothes and stepped into the shower. The game was fun. If nothing came of it, it was fun. I attempted to wash, literally, away from the feelings or thoughts I was having and continue with my night.

I was in the kitchen starting my chicken breast salad, and potato I had prepared the day before when there was a knock on my door. I never had company so it was a little concerning on who could be coming over at night. I apprehensively opened the door to see Austin standing there. I opened it further and he stepped in. “I think you forgot something earlier.” He stated as he grabbed me by the waist and pulled me into him. He wrapped both large hands around the back of my head pulling me into a very intended passionate kiss. I melted into him before I even had time to think. He shut the door with his foot without his lips leaving mine and we slammed our bodies up against the closed door. This time I was taking charge. If this was going to happen, I was going to show this ‘boy” how to be treated like a man. I pressed up against him caressing him with my hands showing no relentlessness to him with my mouth or actions. He didn’t withdraw from me in any manner. His tongue was invading my mouth while his hands were moving instinctively all over my body. With every touch, there was that 'charge' again that raced to my heart which caused me to want him even more. I moved my mouth away from his by nibbling his jaw up to his ear. I circled his ear with my tongue, where he naturally moaned.

"You like when I do that?" I asked.

He turned his hips towards me and the answer was obviously 'yes' as he pressed his very erect self into my pelvic bone. It wasn't hard to notice because he was wearing very loose basketball shorts. Then I returned with a moan and he smiled and said, "Do you like that?" He picked me up, where I wrapped my legs around his waist and he walked us to the couch. He laid me down very gentle, kneeled next to the couch and lifted up my shirt and with the softest kisses, started kissing my belly button. Holy Hell does he know that this is a direct connection to my g-spot?? I moaned with a sort of giggle and he looked up and smiled. I placed my fingers in his thick curly brown hair and he proceeded to move a little further up. His lips graced the bottom of my right rib, then my left slowly working his way up to my breast. Being that I wasn't expecting company I wasn't wearing a bra, which was working out pretty well at the moment. As his tongue swirled around my hardening nipple, his right hand made work of my right nipple by slowly pinching and tugging on it. With this pattern, it didn't take long for me to reach climax and arch my back while expressing gratification and relaxation. When I returned back to a normal position regaining self-control, I opened my eyes to see him staring at me with an accomplished smile. I smiled back and said,

"Thank you. Your turn."

He looked a little confused while I sat up on the couch, patted the seat next to me where he proceeded to join me. I got on the floor, kneeled between his legs and pulled down his shorts. He figured out what I was doing and lifted his pelvis to make it easier for me to gain access to his still erected penis. I softly placed my hand around him at the base and started stroking firm yet gentle. He put his head back and gave a slight long-awaited moan deep in his throat. While my hand was stroking his cock, my other hand was massaging his balls. I placed my mouth on his tip where I teased him with my teeth. A louder moan came so I guarded my teeth with my lips and rammed him down my throat completely engulfing his erection in my mouth. He let out a loud inhaled moan, and I did it again. Up and down, sucking, and caressing him with my tongue, making this the best blowjob this guy will ever have. After a few thrusts with my mouth, he said, "I'm going to cum." Without stopping I went harder and fast as to give him permission to release in my mouth. I felt the warmth and tasted the saltiness and felt the tension diminish. He raised his head, pulled me up on the couch, laid on top of me and kissed me fervently. He looked at me and said, "that was amazing."

"I couldn't agree more," I said. We kissed a few more minutes and when things started to get heated again, he said, "I really should go." I gave him a childish pout but loosened my grip and he stood and pulled up his shorts. I stood from the couch and realized I was completely wet and was a little relieved that he was unaware of this. He pulled me into one last embraced kissed me and said, "thank you again. That was my first blowjob, and not that I have anything to compare it too, it was incredible."

"You didn't do so bad yourself," I said with a grin.

"Just naturally gifted I guess." And I stared at him with a jaw dropped expression, and we both laughed. I walked him to the door; he kissed my cheek and I told him to sleep well. "I don't see how I won't be able to after that." He claimed and I really couldn't argue that point.

I shut the door but proceeded to watch him walk into the dark.

CHAPTER 2

The next day I had to fly to New York to work on a case for a high-profile client. I realized I didn't even have his number to call and let him know I was heading out of town. I packed up my bags and prepared for my client's needs. A break will do some good to wrap my head around this forming relationship.

I arrived at LaGuardia International Airport Monday morning where a man in a black suit was waiting for me at the end of the stairs. The flight crew was removing my bags from the undercarriage as he led me to a black Lincoln. They promptly loaded the trunk full of my luggage and we pulled off the tarmac. I turned Airplane mode off my cell, where messages, emails, and texts started streaming in. I had several from the office, one from my parents telling me to be safe in the city, and texts from the pharmacy telling me I had a prescription filled. I answered emails while we drove to the client's office. We arrived at his very large office - 89 stories high, which still amazes me coming from a small town in the Midwest how anyone could even engineer such a structure. I grabbed my briefcase, strapped on my purse, and held my cell in my hand and walked comfortably into the building. This I knew. This was my playing ground.

Austin – Austin was new territory completely. We weren't that far off in age, but the law treats it like it's a hundred years apart. Because I am *so much* older than that 'eighteen' year old mark, I must be so more knowledgeable and wiser and know all these things that would corrupt his well-being. That's when I realized that at this time, in this society, with the access to all the media that is available, I am not corrupting anything. I definitely didn't force anything on him and one year away from eighteen, not even one year, for that matter, was not going to make that big of a difference mentally for the sexual consent. There! My inside lawyer had made her defense!

"Ellie." A familiar voice boomed. The very well-dressed man dripping in an expensive silk suit came towards me with a huge smile on his face and his hand extended. I greeted him back with my other hand which turned into a partial hug. He was richer than God, had his ways with the ladies back in the day, but was always respectful of me and treated me like a lawyer that saved his back-side. Besides, he probably knew that not only could I destroy him professionally, but physically as well, being that he was in his early seventies.

"Miachal" I said gracefully. "How are you?"

"Now that I see you, very fine."

"Shall we get to it?"

"Always business with you. Would you like a coffee or a massage before we get 'dirty'? You're going to be here awhile."

"I'll take a 20-oz. salted caramel latte with 3 yellow packets, low-fat cream, and no massage, -at least not right now." I said with a smile. "I need to work up a good stressful butt kicking before I enjoy such a treat. Besides you haven't pissed me off *yet*."

"Give it time my dear." Miachal gave my order to some intern standing at attention next to him like she didn't hear what I had just said.

"Do you want any substance? Bagel, eggs, steak?"

"No thank you, just the latté will be sufficient."

"GO!" He barked at the intern. "And it better be hot when you return!"

"You really need to treat those interns better." I lectured.

"They're young and stupid." He replied.

"Miachal, I am not that much older, if not the same age."

"Yes, my dear, but you have something they don't and that is charisma! You are beautiful and I truly believe the smartest woman on this planet, after my wife of course." He smiled.

"Nice save, Mia."

"You know you really should eat, we have a pretty busy day."

"First off, don't worry, I will let you buy me a ridiculously expensive lunch later. Second, I have gone over all your files and I am very well aware of how busy I will be with your day. Third, you are going to show me to my office, and not hover over me like a protective mother hen. I will call you in or schedule time with your 'grunts' when I need you."

"As you wish. You know best as always. We are also meeting up with the Mrs. tonight for drinks and dinner. I have a young fellow interested in working on some of my projects I would like you to engage with."

"Seriously Mia? Are you setting me up? I'm your lawyer for God's sake! A very important lifeline so-to-speak."

"Just drinks sweetheart, not a royal engagement." And he turned, grabbed the latte from the heavy panting intern that had returned, and told her to show me to my office. I hated when he called me 'sweetheart'. Gave me the willies. Men in power often use words like that when they feel inferior and I would have to make a mental note to address this – but at a later time, I have work to do.

My office was enormous, bigger than some apartments I was looking down on. Windows from ceiling to floor, left to right. But I told Mia in the past that I didn't like that feeling, so he put beautiful sheers with a valance to separate the illusion. I also prefer oak vs. dark wood, so instead of the office furniture being dark mahogany, which I felt too serious, confining and depressing, it was a medium oak. It had all the necessities plus extras, a very comfortable couch, that not on more than one occasion I thought about taking home. And I know it would only take one word, and I would come home and find an exact duplicate, not only at my house but completely set up for me. There is a large conference table that at first, I thought was stupid, but does turn out useful when I need to spread out charts, files, and other paperwork to explain things to Mia. Of course, my desk, credenza, beautiful floor lamps with that ambient lighting, along with desk lamps. I told Mia, I don't want overhead fluorescents- they looked crappy and hurt my eyes. "You will be a difficult wife someday young lady." He told me when I gave him this request. Next to my office was a private bathroom with all the luxuries from a five-star hotel. For that matter, I don't even know why I stay at one.

I set up my laptop, pulled the files that I carried out of the briefcase and set them on the table, sipped my latte and sat down adjusting my mind to get prepared for all the topics, situations, and new adventures Mia would throw at me. I glanced at the clock on the computer, 10:23. My mind drifted to home. Was he still sleeping? I really wanted to tell him I was out of town. But what if he didn't care? What if I was putting more thought into this? Oh, this is frustrating! I need to focus on my work, not this crap! Maybe, if I send him a text, I will be able to focus on my job. J-O-B Ellie! The reason you're here!!! I had his mother's phone number so I thought I would shoot her a text asking for Austin's cell number, being out of town maybe he could do some stuff around my house for me?

"Hey, Chelsea – this is Ellie, your neighbor. I'm in NY on business. Could you give me Austin's cell number, I would like to ask him if he could do some things around my house, mail, and stuff while I'm out of town?" …. and send. Why is my heart racing? My palms are even wet! What the…?!? I rolled my eyes and thought, it's just a stupid number. I put my phone down and decided to dive into Mia's newest mergers. My mind was completely engulfed in legal babble and notes when a 'ping melody' came across my cell. My heart leaped and I think I may have jumped a little like an explosion just went off.

"Hey, sure! Wow NY! He's at work now so he may not reply right away. I'll remind him later to check his cell. Be safe in the big city LOL"

"Thanks. I'll try." And Chelsea gave me his number. Work? What work? He has a job? Wow, I really don't know anything about him. Then I started thinking, what did I know? Besides his looks and athletic abilities, nothing. He may have a girlfriend for all I know. Well, they obviously haven't gotten that far because he said I was his first blowjob. Maybe he was just testing the 'waters' with me before he could impress her?

"Ms. Ellie?" A weak voice squeaked in my doorway. I jumped again, startled and pulled from this inner dialogue I was having while staring at my phone. I looked up to see 'Intern 1' in my doorway.

"Mr. Williams wants to know if you are ready for your 'ridiculously expensive lunch' yet?" I looked at the clock on the monitor again, 11:30. Damn.

"Yes, I'll wrap this up and I will be there in 15."

"I'll tell Mr. Williams you'll meet him in the foyer in 15." I rolled my eyes, and thought "thank you parrot, maybe they really are stupid."

I organized the papers, locked my laptop, grabbed my purse, looked for my cell phone, which was in my hand, obviously still befuddled, and walked out the office door. I locked the door behind me because you never know who's working for who at this level. As I walked into the foyer, Mia was standing patiently waiting. It was 11:45 and I was on time as always. I knew never to let this man wait. And not to give it away I was starting to become famished. If he found out he would never let me hear the end of it.

"Terrace?" He said.

"As always. Mr. Williams." I said with a slight giggle but a straight face.

"Ahh, you are such a delight, Miss Ellie."

We walked to the elevator, he pressed 'B' for the basement and the elevator doors opened revealing brass and glass reflecting our silhouettes.

"After you." And he placed his hand on my lower back and led me in.

"Hold my calls and reschedule any meetings until further notice. Only allow my wife to get through." He ordered through the opening. And as on cue, the doors closed. "Get anything accomplished?"

"Why yes, I did, as a matter of fact. You have been a busy man these past months. Are you trying to take over the world?

"Not the world, maybe just Manhattan."

"Manhattan, you already own most of Manhattan."

"OK then, New York and maybe some of the Eastern Hemisphere."

We walked to the waiting black Lincoln where a man in a grey suit greeted us, holding the door. "Ladies first," Mia stated, standing back letting me crawl through the door. He followed and we were heading out of the dark basement structure.

Lunch was a usual location, 'The Terrace'. A high-end restaurant with table clothes, linen napkins and a personal waitstaff for each table. Sometimes the chef would personally serve Mia and Mia liked his ass kissed in this manner. He was a man of money and didn't mind people respecting that quality. He was just as kind of reciprocating their efforts.

"Welcome back Mr. Williams."

"Thank you, André. You remember Miss Ellie?"

"Yes, of course, how nice to see you again Ms., Would you like a glass of Inniskillin?"

"Not this early André, just a peach lemonade. I need to keep my brain sharp for Mr. Williams here." I smiled at his expressionless face.

"Yes, Ms. And for you sir?"

"My usual André."

"Yes, Sir."

"Well, I see André is as pleasant as usual," I said smiling. Mia smiled back, "Yes, his usual charming self. He gets the job done efficiently and proper and you really can't ask for anything other than that."

"Well, I'm just glad he's not my doctor, must have ice cold hands!" and we both got a chuckle out that. André brought our drinks and some garlic bread with fancy spreads and took our orders. I chose my regular filet mignon salad, medium-well, substitute the gorgonzola crumbles with sharp cheddar and ranch instead of red wine vinaigrette. Mia ordered his usual Lobster Thermidor, crisp green beans, and yellow potatoes - not grungy Idaho. "Skins too thick for lobster. You have an Idaho with a hardy steak or in a stew." He would say if you asked. We talked about our lives from where we left off from the last visit. Grandkids, elite parties that he hated, and his wife and all her charity work. We don't 'talk business' over lunch, even though it was a business lunch. "Sours the stomach." Mia would say.

"Grandkids are growing like a weed. Oldest boy Carter going into a championship soccer match and Bella is in her second year of Ballet." Mia pulled pictures from his wallet.

"You should really use your phone, Mia; you can store a lot more pics and show them off better."

"Phones are too complicated as it is, they should just be for calling. I wouldn't have one if I had a choice, but all the smart people in my life, like you, insist on me having one. Besides, my wife wants to know she can get ahold of me at any time."

"Very true."

Our meals came and the conversation turned silent as we focused on eating. After our meals, and the bill was paid, we went briefly over what I had worked on this morning and my feelings on his affairs.

I was interrupted by a vibrating sensation in my pocket. When I had a second to break eye contact with Mia, I checked my screen.

"Hey stranger – mom said you needed to ask me something."

My heart stopped, with a lurch, I completely forgot to text Austin. Crap.

"Oh – this is Austin btw"

"Ellie... Ellie…"

"Hmm? What? Sorry, Mia."

"Everything OK?"

"Oh yeah, just an unexpected text. No biggie."

"No biggie? You've been staring at your phone like you've seen a ghost!"

"Sorry, just a surprise. Where were we?"

Mia and I picked up from his new proposal, "I'm glad you're sitting for this because I haven't run it past anyone yet, well, I have enlightened the Mrs." This piqued my curiosity. I raised my eyebrows in a 'bring-it-on' manner.

"I want to run."

"OK, for the NYC Marathon?"

"No, for President."

Thank God, I didn't have anything in my mouth or I would have ended up spitting it clear across the room!

"For the United States of America?" I proclaimed flabbergasted.

"Yes, young lady. Why is that so hard to fathom?"

"It's not." I paused. "It's just going to take some getting use too," I said truthfully. "But what does this have to do with me?"

"I want you to be on my side. Team."

"Wow, Mia. That is something I am going to have to wrap my head around. That is a whole new ballgame, as you would call it."

"I understand. And they're a lot of details to go over, and I wouldn't expect for you to even come onboard fully until I win. So, that should give you enough time to think it over and decide what you want to do."

"And if you don't?"

"Don't what?"

"Win. What happens?"

"With what Eli? Me? You? What? Listen, we will stay on track until there's a call for a change. We will stay on the same course until there is a need to turn. I wanted to bring you in on this you understand why my investments, businesses, and life patterns change. You will remain doing what you do, until you decide if a decision is needed to come onboard a different way."

"Not saying I won't join you or… will… just what if I don't join you?"

"I really don't have all the details as of yet Ellie, I just came up with this idea because I don't like who our leader is now and I think I can make a change in this world. If you became my legal advisor, my right-hand ma-, err, lady counsel, doors will open for you on so many levels. Not trying to sway you one way or the other, of course."

"Of course."

"I wanted to prepare you for the idea, and tell you I'm serious about this new venture."

"Thank you for confiding in me Mia. I am honored you would even consider me for a position like that. I will defiantly take the time from the campaign to consider all my options and make the decision when the time calls. In the meantime, I will just continue as your legal counsel in the role I have been 'playing' thus far."

"Sounds like a smart business plan to me. As I knew it would."

We left the table; Mia escorted me out the held door and into the prepared Lincoln. I returned to my office, the quiet sanctuary trying to wrap my head around this proposition that just completely blew me out of the water. What is happening? First Austin and now this – Oh crap – Austin's text. I grabbed my cell from my purse, lit the screen and the text app was still open. I stared at the message he sent me;

"Hey stranger – mom said you needed to ask me something."

"Oh – this is Austin btw ;)"

I reverted to a 'squirrely' high school girl again and the winky emoji reminded me of when he turned around and winked at me and said, "you look very nice by the way." My heart flutter and I felt my cheeks grow warm. I just stared at the phone in my hand with my thumb hovering over the keypad like I had never used one before. I had no idea what to write. I had no idea what to say. I was a complete blank. "Come on Ellie, just say hi or something." I thought.

"Hi. Sorry I was in a meeting. I wanted to let you know that I am in NY for business. In case you ……." In case you what Ellie? Come on, type. You throw tax evaders away for years and negotiate world changing deals, yet you can't type a single text? …In case you cared…, in case you WONDERED…, in case you…, so you wouldn't… be concerned... Yeah, that's it!

"Hi. Sorry I was in a meeting. I wanted to let you know that I am in NY for business. So, you wouldn't be concerned if you didn't see me around."

Strangely, I put my phone down, closed my eyes, and took a breath like I had just made the hardest deal of my life and I was waiting for the judge to return the verdict. *PING*

"Thanks for that. I would have wondered if I caused you to leave town or something. LOL"

"Well, I realized I didn't even have your number *blush*, to let you know, so I had to go through your mom. Sorry."

"No worries. I'm glad you did."

This was becoming easier. This conversation texting thing.

"I have a busy afternoon can I talk later?"

"Yeah, sure NP. When EvR you get time."

"Thanks, talk soon."

I wasn't used to the shorthand texting word so it took a minute for me to understand his meaning. I pulled out my files, turned on my computer again and started to go over new business when I picked up my cell and typed;

"Do you have a girlfriend?"

What happened to work Ellie? Good Lord! Let's just put that out there, shall we??? I think I'm losing my mind. I shook my head and closed my eyes trying to figure out how to undo my last text.

PING

"WHAT??? Why would you even think that????"

PING

"WHY? WHAT? I don't even know how to respond to that?"

Austin was shouting, at least I think he was by the font. OH, CRAP!!!! He's mad… well maybe, hard to tell in a text, right?

"I don't know honestly. This is new to me. I deal with black and white… and grey? I just don't do 'grey'."

"Well for one, this isn't 'grey'. No, I don't have a gf. Why on earth would I have done what we did if I had one? I'm not one of 'those guys. Do you have a BF?"

What?? Whoa! Well, I guess that's fair I did just drop a huge one on him…

"No. I do not have a BF. I'm not "One of those kinds" either"

"Well, that's good, now can we stop this weird shit? I thought you had a busy day, lawyer lady?"

"I do, just can't seem to focus on work at the moment."

"Why? Something on UR mind?"

"Yeah, can't seem to shake this stupid smile. Can't figure out why. But I really do need to focus before I release 10 million dollars to the wrong person. Might get in a bit of trouble for that. I will try and call or txt when am done. We are going out for drinks/dinner tonight so might be late."

There was a long pause.

"10 MILLION DOLLARS???WTF??? If you need to find it a home, I will gladly give you my act #. I will wait up. Bye."

That reminded me, I wanted to ask him about his job. What job? But that would have to wait for later. I really needed to focus on work.

At 5:30 my alarm buzzed on my phone reminding me I needed to get ready for our 'dinner with the Mrs.' tonight. I closed files down, put paperwork in order, made a mental note of where I left things. I stood up, stretched, glanced at the window realizing the sun was suspended lower in the sky. I went to the garment bag hanging on the coat rack in the corner, unzipped it, took out my dinner dress and heals, went into my very nice bathroom and prepared myself. At 6:15 sharp there was a knock on the office door.

"Come in," I said.

Mia opened the door and said, "If I weren't a married man Eli— You ready to go?"

"Thanks, yes. And you are." I winked at him.

I grabbed my purse, cell, and keys. I shut the door, turned around and locked it. Glanced up at Mia who smiled and directed me to the foyer.

"Are we meeting Angelica or is she downstairs?"

"We are meeting her. She had some gallery affair today and

was on the other side of town. She is so excited to see you! She absolutely adores you!" I felt my cheeks warm. This woman was old enough to be my mom and Mia, my grandfather. Just weird.

"I enjoy seeing her as well," I replied. "It's nice to spend the evening with such a diverse and intelligent woman."

"I think she feels the same way."

CHAPTER 3

As we waited for Angelica at the restaurant's bar, a young man approximately my age approached Mia. He placed his left hand on Mia's shoulder and when Mia turned around, shook with his right. This must be the man that I was told to 'engage' with. Mia, standing, turned towards me and with a big, no, huge smile said, "Colin, this is Ellie. The most brilliant woman you will ever come into contact with." Holy Hell Mia, how am I supposed to live up to that introduction?

"Ellie, this is Colin. The gentleman I told you was interested in some of my business 'adventures' so-to-speak." And he winked and never lost his smile. I reached out to shake his hand and he pulled my hand to his lips and gave it a brief kiss.

"It is nice to meet you. I don't come across such a beautiful and apparently the most brilliant women every day."

OKAY, what is going on? I think I was kicked in the head when Rick and I were working out and I am in some kind of euphoric dream lying unconscious in a hospital bed. That must be what is going on because life is being insane at the moment!

As my cheeks fill with heat – again – I mustered up enough to say, "Thank you, Mia is being too kind."

"Well, Miachal or 'Mia', as you call him, must be correct about your brilliance, because he is dead-on about your beauty. You are gorgeous!"

"Ok stop now, Colin." Mia found his voice. "You're embarrassing the girl."

"Thank you. Colin." Is all I barely could manage out. Colin wasn't bad to look at either. He really could have passed for an Abercrombie and Fitch model. He stood about 6'2 and had a chiseled jaw. He was cleanly shaven and a very proper but current hairstyle. Dirty blonde hair and spent some time in the sun, if I were to guess, on his family's sailboat or playing Polo. His eyes were a brilliant blue and he had perfect teeth which probably caused a perfect penny. He wore a suit jacket with an open buttoned shirt, no tie. Khakis with a leather belt and brown leather shoes that probably cost more than my first paycheck. The bartender came over to us from the other side of the counter and asked, "Sir, what will you be having this evening?"

"Martini - Dirty."

"Yes, sir- coming right up."

I was not surprised that he knew how to order a drink. I would not be surprised at almost *anything* this man can do. He obviously knows his way around A LOT of areas, women being one.

Angelica came bouncing in and Mia had an awareness of her presences. He turned around and with open arms boasted, “There’s my Angle!!”

“Oh, hello darling!” She claimed back. If he does become President, I can’t imagine a more attractive or sophisticated First Lady. She is the pinnacle of New York high-society. She is a very slender woman, wearing a black Armani Collezioni suit, manicured nails, holding a black clutch. Black stilettos probably Louie or Manolo, and a diamond pendant at least 3 ct. that pops against the black. Her hair is in an up-do loose pony-tail with curls covering the clip and very lifted bangs that look like a wave coming onto the shore. Her hair has hints of grey that is hidden by highlights that resembles Hickory wood, a little blonde, a little walnut, a mix sorts of blondes. After her embrace with Mia she came over to me and gave me a motherly-hug that says, ‘you don’t come home to visit nearly enough’ and kissed both cheeks. “Ellie, it is so wonderful to see my girl again!!”

“Hello, Mrs. Williams.”

“Mrs. Williams? You know better G-G Please!”

“Alright, I’m sorry, G-G.”

She just stared at me and petted my cheek. “You just get more beautiful every time I see you!! I just can’t wait to find out what you have been doing these past months!” She beamed.

The maître d’ came up to us and signaled for us to follow.

"Your table is this way sir," He stated to Mia. Mia stepped aside, GG and I arm in arm lead the way behind the maître d' with Collin and Mia following. The head waiter was standing waiting for GG, he pulled the chair out for her, grabbed her napkin off the table, an indicated that he would like to place it on her lap. She nodded and accepted the offer. Then he came over to me and continued this around the table. Once we were all seated, we place our drink order, again. "Should I order us a bottle of Dom?" Mia asked. I looked around and nobody seemed to be interested at the moment.

"Not at this moment darling." GG seemed to pick up on the fact no one was jumping at this offer.

"I know I am usually an ice wine drinker, but tonight I am in the mood for a Chateau Dereszla Tokaji. 2007 if you have it." I stated. I know how to 'play' with these people in their world, even if this isn't how I currently live or was raised.

"I'll see if we have that in our reserves Ms." And he took the rest of the orders. When he turned and left, GG started in on my life and all the activities that have kept me busy. Mia and Colin were in a conversation and I started, "…not much really. I stay pretty busy at the firm. I do enjoy the gym and try to get in as often as possible. I have a Krav Maga coach who not only keeps me fit but safe as well."

"Well, you can't be too safe being a girl alone in the world. You need all the protection you can get. And I would say the gym is treating you well. How is the office? Are the partners being fair?

You know, my husband can move the earth for you if you want to go somewhere else."

"Oh, thank you GG, I am happy there at the moment. I know Mia would help if I need it, but they are treating me good.
Your husband is a good client and they know he is on 'my side' so they don't want to piss me off." I said smiling.

"So, are there any young men in your life? A lady can be independent but have some fun on the side!!" She exclaimed, with a lit-up devilish smile, showing her perfect white teeth. With these words, Colin's ears perked up and his attention turned to GG's confrontation breaking eye contact with Mia. Oh Shit! What do I say to that?
'Why yes, I'm engaging in a relationship with my seventeen-year-old neighbor boy who is showing awesome signs of being phenomenal in bed because he makes me have an orgasm by tweaking my nipples??'

"Um, I really haven't had time to even try to find anyone at the moment." Which wasn't a complete lie, I am busy and I didn't go out looking for Austin, it just kind of came about.

"Oh honey, a girl has to release her frustrations every so often if you understand my meaning."

"Angel, please stop badgering the girl," Mia said, apparently as uncomfortable with her last statement as I was. Colin was staring at me with a smile at this point biting his lip and the waiter showed up just in time with our drinks. Thank God! I needed to take a drink after that! Would it be too obvious if I downed the entire glass, due to a very awkward and embarrassing situation??? Because of GG's revealing discovery of me being single, Colin hung on every word that was said.

"You know, a Fortune 500 top young entrepreneur is sitting across from you miss Ellie." A proud father-like Mia boasted.

"And since when do you give a shit about what Fortune or any other company has to say about anything?" Wine starting to talk more than I was, or rather bringing out the harder side of 'Ellie'.

"Well, I usually don't, but since this young man is interested in doing business ventures with me, I think it is an important fact to state."

I just rolled my eyes. I had enough of being set up and criticized for being single.

"It's getting late Mia, and I have to be in the office early. We have a lot of paperwork to get through tomorrow, and I have to set up new legal docs for your 'new adventures'."

"Do you really have to go?" GG asked.

"I second that." Interjected Colin. Like at this point I gave two shits about what Mr. ass kissing model had to say.

"I really should, don't forget I flew in today as well as worked with Mr. Man over there."

"That's true. Please, let's get together again before you leave town. I don't get to spend enough time with you. It seems my husband keeps you all to himself." GG practically pouting.

"Yes, he is quite the selfish bartered." I smiled at Mia.

"I'll walk you out and hail a cab for you." Colin offered.

"No. I mean you can walk her out if you want, but she can take the Lincoln. The driver knows where she's staying." Mia asserted. As I stood to walk out, I felt the wine rear her head. Guess I had a little extra tonight, but dinner was intense. Everyone stood with me and GG gave me that all too familiar 'motherly-hug", Mia gave me a quick squeeze, "See you in the office tomorrow." And Colin took his cue, and escorted me to the front door, placing his hand on my lower back. Single or not, I am NOT interested in this player, but I didn't want to cause a scene.

"How long will you be in town for?" He asked.

"As long as it takes to get the jobs done," I replied curtly.

"Well, can I call you later and maybe take you to dinner?"

"I don't know. I really am not interested in any relationships at this time Colin, and I don't even live here so…."

"It's just dinner and drinks, Ellie, not asking for your hand in marriage."

Wow, did he just say that? Pompous Ass!

"Well, when you put it that way, No. Here's the car. Thank you for walking me out. Have a good rest of your evening. Oh, it was nice to meet you by the way." I got in the waiting car and was so grateful that this night was over.

Back at the hotel room, I noticed that my luggage had already been placed in my room. Turn down service came, and a bottle of Dom was on the desk with a note, "I look forward to working with you, Mia." Well, that was nice, usual, but nice. I opened my suitcase, took out my PJ's, and crawled into bed. Man did this feel good. I stretched out trying to forget about Colin and all of GG's ridiculous motherly advice tonight. I looked at the clock, 11:12, is it too late to call? He said he'd wait up… That's odd I thought, the first thing I think of after a long ass day is to pick up the phone and call him? I shook my head and hit the text feature, where I pressed the phone icon to call him.

"Hi," a sultry voice answered.

"Is it too late?"

"No. I told you I'd wait up."

"What made you think I would call?"

"You said you would, so why wouldn't I believe you?"

"OK."

"So how was your fancy dinner?"

"Long!" I really wanted to tell him all the gory details about Colin and GG's comments, but thought better of it.

"What do you mean LONG?"

"You know, just a lot of talking about boring lawyer stuff with stuffy people talking about the Market and how successful they are."

"So, this is the highlight of your night? Is that what you're saying?" He said with a cocky giggle.

"Yeah- I guess that's what I'm saying. How are you?"

"Better now." I felt my heart constrict and my throat tighten.

"Really? Why?" Trying to act coy.

"Because I am talking to you. It's nice to hear your voice. I'm just sorry I can't see your face at the same time."

"You don't want to see my face… it's all blotchy and tired from the day."

"I'm sure it's just as beautiful as I saw it the last time."

"Well, you're sure full of it tonight."

"Just stating the truth."

"How was your day?"

"Uneventful. Went for a run. Worked. Came home. Watched TV, waited for you to call. 'Bout it."

"Speaking of work, you have a job?"

"Yup, I work at the local landscaping company in town. Keeps me in shape for the team."

"So, when you helped me the other day you really meant what you said, you like to work outside?"

"You really don't believe anything, do you? Must be the 'lawyer' inside of you."

"Yeah, must be. I'll work on that. You went for a run?"

"I try to run sometime every day, but mostly in the morning. It's cooler out and it gets my mind and body prepared for the day ahead."

"I like to run too. When I get home, you want to go together… for a run?"

"That's sound awesome. But be prepared."

"For what?"

"I might leave you behind." With that, I giggled.

"Alright, I'll keep that in mind. But it will be your loss."

"Loss of what?"

"That's just something you'll have to find out if you don't play fair."

"Oh, looks who's not playing fair now?"

I smiled. I liked the way this conversation was going. I felt comfortable with him. Unlike Colin. Man - he made my skin crawl. So arrogant!

"I really enjoyed the other night. Completely unexpected, but…"

"…But what?"

"But I don't know, I just really enjoyed you."

"You really are new to this aren't you?"

"Aren't you?"

"I told you I was. Again…. Trust."

"Sorry, work in progress."

"I had a really nice time and I hope to again."

"Me too." I felt warm all over and giddy. I also felt tired from the long day but didn't want to end the conversation.

"Do you work tomorrow?"

"Yep. 8-4."

"I'll call tomorrow. I don't know what I have on my plate exactly, however. Night"

"I'll answer."

"Have a good sleep."

"I will now."

"Night." Not wanting to hang up the phone.

"You said that already, Night." I pressed the phone icon and stared at my phone. The screen changed from 'dialed' to 12:02 AM. I have to go to sleep. I tried to settle my thoughts down, but now I was too restless. Maybe a shower will help. I went into the bathroom, disrobed, turned on the hot water, found Lavender body wash, and attempted to relax away my day. It seemed to work. I dried off, redressed and crawled into bed and fell hard asleep.

My alarm startled me away. 4:45, man, that night went by fast. I got out of bed, peed, and changed into my exercise clothes. I grabbed my cell, and put my wireless BOSE headphones in my ears, and put my hair back in a ponytail. I went to the floor with the exercise equipment, did a little stretch, stepped on the sides and started it up. While it was warming up, I clicked the 'note' icon on my phone, picked my 'run' playlist, and started at a steady pace. I sped up the treadmill and three miles later, slowed it down. I had enough for the morning of the run and man-bashing music. I waited for it to slow to a complete stop, just off, did some more stretching, and went back to my room for a shower and ready for work. On my way to the room, I stopped at the front and told them I would like the car in 1 hour, held up my cell and hit the messenger icon.

> "Just finished my run. Hope you have a nice morning and a great day. Talk later. Eli~"

After I was dressed and ready for the office, I grabbed my briefcase which housed my laptop, cell phone, and room key/card, and went to the lobby for something to eat. A woman addressed me at the restaurant entryway and led me over to a table. I ordered a coffee and asiago cheese bagel, lightly toasted, with regular cream cheese. Because it not being a complex order it came rather quickly. I finished the bagel, asked for a refill in a 'to go' cup and headed to the lobby. While waiting for the Lincoln, I went through some late-night emails, mainly ideas from Mia after he got home and couldn't sleep like me. The driver pulled up at exactly one hour to the time given, parked the car, and held the door for me as I crawled in. It's not customary to greet your driver in New York, but being a Midwest girl, and feeling a little happier this morning, I said, "Good Morning sir. Thank you for holding the door and driving me today."

"You're welcome." Came from the front without a glance or recognition my way. "Typical behavior", I thought.

There wasn't anyone in the office when I arrived. I went to my desk, and set up for the day, arranging my files, booting up my laptop, and enjoying the quiet before the hectic day started. A quiet knock came from my door and I yelled to come in. 'Intern 1' uneasily approached my desk holding a cup of coffee. "20-oz. salted caramel latte with 3 yellow packets, low-fat cream?" OK- Maybe this one has potential.

"Yes. Thank you." I reached for the cup and noticed a slight shake of the hand. "Do I make you nervous?"

"Um, a little I guess."

"Can I give you a bit of advice?"

"Sure."

"I'm not much older than you, OK. I worked very hard to

get where I am today, yes, I went to a private and Ivy League school, but that wasn't handed to me. You need to take charge of you! Do you know how to do your job?"

"Yes."

"Is there anything you don't know how to do in your position?"

"No."

"Are you overqualified for your position?" The intern paused, not wanting to sound arrogant or conceited. "It's Okay to be, I'm just trying to get to a point."

"Yes."

"So, let me get this straight, you know more than you need to, and very competent for this job, but yet you Mouse around here and get barked at all day?"

With a more confident smile, she said, "Yes. I guess I do."

"Then stop. Do your job and when it's done, do more. When Mia 'barks' at you, correct him. He can take it trust me. Do it respectfully, but tell him that he doesn't need to speak that way and you would be glad to complete his request when he modifies his language. Now remember he is the boss, and he is male so you will have to be careful of his ego. Once he changes, which he will, and you've accomplished your duty, go ask for something more challenging. What is your degree in?"

"Marketing and Research."

"You need to show him you can do more, ask to run numbers for him."

"Thank you."

"If anything, I've learned is that if you don't stand up for yourself, you will be stood on." Wow, I was on a roll today.... Bring me my soapbox!

PING

"Thank you. I will take your advice and try harder."

"Do you have a name?

She blushed, "Jane. My name is Jane."

"It's nice to meet you - Jane. I can stop calling you 'Intern 1' now. I glanced at my phone, '1 Message'. I opened up my messenger app and got that constricted giggle in my throat.

"I have to take this Jane." Who was still standing there staring at me. Hopefully, that reaction was completely internal and me acting like a stupid girl didn't surface.

"Sorry." And she walked out the door.

"Please close my door – Jane."

"Good morning beautiful! I'm headed out for my run now."

"What are you listening to on your run?"

"A little of this and that, mixed playlist."

"May I recommend AC/DC Thunderstruck? Seems to get the blood moving"

"Thanks, I'll add it to my list. How far d'ya go?"

"Only 3 miles. Had to get in the office early."

"HA! I'll top that in the first ½ hour. LOL What's on your playlist?

"Mainly, angry girls bashing men.... Seems to get my blood moving. LOL"

"Nice – may I recommend the Rocky theme song? Not so 'man-hating'. We're not all bad."

"I know. In the business world, I have to "Stay ANGRY." "LOL"

"You're in a good mood this morning."

"I had a nice conversation with this guy last night that helped me have a wonderful sleep."

"Hmmm, sounds like that guy is magical!"

"Oh, in so many ways!" and I squeezed my thighs together trying to calm my breathing and control my pulse.

"Yeah, that's strange, I talked to a pretty amazing woman last night that had the same effect"

"You better get running. I'll talk later."

"K- Later~"

My cheekbones actually hurt from smiling so much. How can a text conversation have this effect on me? I still don't know this boy… man… whatever he is? Boy-man? Ugh, that's just complicated.

"Morning!" My door swung open. Mia was standing bright and cheerful in the doorway.

"Good morning, Sir. Have you heard of knocking?"

"Knocking, for what? This is my building!"

"I am completely aware that this is your building, but I might have been on the phone with Asia and because of your intrusive announcement, I could have lost you millions of dollars!!"

"Did you?"

"No."

"So then, no harm, no foul."

I just stared at him, not in the mood to put up with his omnipotent attitude.

"Did you receive my emails?"

"Yes. I made the revisions already and after you take a look, I will print up the docs and submit them."

"Sounds good. Lunch today?

"Sure. Let me get through this stuff, I'll call you in a bit and we can start going over details."

"OK Young lady. Talk to you soon."

He turned and walked out the door. "You could shut my door," I mumbled under my breath. I stood up, walked over and started to shut my door. I noticed Jane watching how I interacted with Mia.

"See, respectful control." I smiled at her. She smiled back. I shut my door.

By the end of two weeks, I was anxious to get home. I was tired of the hotel room and the monotony that progressed throughout the weeks in the office. My relationship with Austin was growing exponentially with every passing day and I had a yearning to see him in person. I wanted to smell him and feel his warmth, touch his skin, feel that fire that comes between us. I want that mind-numbing passion that devours you and you can't think clearly because of the heat and raw emotional depletion. That's it. I'm going home. Maybe for the wrong reasons, but there isn't anything that I cannot get done at the office at home, that I can't get done here. We have gone over all the current materials, and I have written up propositions for the new enterprises. I am on board with all the current projects and future endeavors that he is planning. I packed up my things, grabbed my case and belongings, and locked the door. I went into Mia's office and told him of my plan. I ask if the jet could take me back this afternoon.

"Sure." He said, and he stood to give me a profession hug good-bye.

"I will be in touch after I land."

"Why don't you take the night off? You've been completely consumed here for two weeks."

"Sounds good. I'm confident that everything that needs to be in order is, and all the new material will work out just as planned."

"No worries. You're my number one girl. The car will take you back, then to the airport."

"Thank you, Mia." I gave him a kiss on the cheek, turned and walked out the door. My heart was leaping and I couldn't stop the stupid smile that was radiating across my face.

CHAPTER 4

The wheels touched down on the tarmac and a sense of release washed over me. I was glad to be home, not only for Austin, but I don't fit into the New York City life. The jet pulled into the gate and by the time I had gotten to the jet bridge, my luggage was waiting for me. "Money moves quickly" I thought. "Do you want me to call someone for you Ms." The flight attendant asked.

"No thank you, I can manage." I smiled politely, grabbed my suitcase, balanced my briefcase and garment bag on top and started walking to my car.

5:25 was on the center console of my car when I pulled onto my street. As I approached Austin's house, my heart sank, his car was not in the driveway. I pulled into my garage and shut the door. I unloaded my car into the house and stood in the kitchen adrift. I don't know what I was expecting. Him bounding up to me with flowers stating that he's been pacing back and forth until I returned?? I didn't even tell him I was coming home. I seriously think I have lost my mind. I decided to go change into my gym clothes and see if I could get in a work out with Rick. Maybe a good grueling workout would kick this out of me. Pining for what? A boy? Please.

After I changed, I sent a quick text,

"Hey – watcha doin'?"

No answer, hmm. Must be busy. More reason to kick the shit out of something.

"Hey, long time no see!" Rick looked up with a smile.

"Just got in from New York."

"Ohh Fun place!"

"No Business. You got any time for me?"

"Yeah, let's go. Warm-ups - GO!"

An hour of holds, throws, punches, and pins burned out some of the apprehensive tension but I still wanted to burn off sensual tension. I thanked Rick, told him I would be back in and that I didn't have plans on going anywhere anytime soon. He was glad, "Anytime I get to kick a hot girl's ass is a good time for me!! And you pay me to knock you to the ground and roll around with you!" I laughed, "Most people would call that pimping I think!" He smiled, "I'll be your daddy!" Before this conversation grew worse, I decided to leave. I got in my car and checked my phone and it said '1 Message' on the display. A little number 1 circled over the messaging icon confirmed it. I tapped on the icon and read,

"Football practice. Be home around 7."

Seven, I looked at the phone 7:31. My heart soared. I headed to the house for a shower. This time when I pulled onto the road, his car was parked in his usual spot on the driveway. I pulled into the garage and shut the door. I was shaking with exhilaration. I hurried into the house to take a quick shower. He's home!! I couldn't wait. I looked through my closet, I wanted to find something revealing, but proper as well. I dabbed a little perfume on my neck, in my cleavage, and behind my ears. I found a double pink and grey tank-top that was low cut and a black push-up bra. I grabbed a matching thong and I put on my ripped shorts, where the pockets stuck out through the front and were frayed all around. I put my hair up in a messy half twist up-do with trundles hanging down. I put on my converse without socks, a little gold glitter gloss and a very thin line of eyeliner. I didn't want to look like I 'tried' to look hot, but if I was truthful, I wouldn't say no to me. I stepped outside, took a deep, no HUGE breath and started across the street. 'Holy crap – let's try not to fall over miss weak legs!!' My mission: get my mail. That sounded good. I went to the front door and rang the bell. Chelsea came to the door.

"Hi, you're back!"

"Yes. So glad to be back!"

"Come in. Austin is in the shower. He just got home from practice." As I was standing in the doorway Austin's younger brother Max came into the living room. His jaw dropped and he had an embarrassed smile. 'Oh yeah!! That was the reaction I was looking for!'

"So how was the big city?"

"Busy. Not a huge fan of the city. Too busy for me, people coming and going and so rude! I mainly just worked at the office and crashed at the hotel at night. Not as luxurious as people think."

"Did you have any fun? See any shows?

"No shows, I did have a couple of nice dinners and such…." And my voice trailed off.

"I don't know where Austin put your mail, do you have a minute? He shouldn't be much longer."

"Sure, I don't have any plans. Just got home."

A few minutes later a very defined, sculpted, golden sun-kissed frame came around the corner of the hallway into the living room. He had loose shorts draping off of his chiseled pelvis which exposed the waistband of his underwear. He had the towel around his shoulders and his very distinguished bicep was drying the water from his hair. I think - that I am pretty positive - that it is against the law of nature to look this good. He looked at me and beamed. He quickly glanced at his mom, then his brother, who gave him a smirk like some unwritten communication between brothers or boys - I couldn't tell.

"Welcome back."

"Thank you. I came over to get my mail."

"Sure thing, gimme a sec."

He turned went down the hallway and came back with a hand full of envelopes. "Wow, who knew I was so popular? Thank you again, I can't believe I forgot to put a hold on my mail." I looked at his mom, I didn't want to linger on him for too long for fear that I would instantaneously combust, or it'd be a dead giveaway of my feelings.

"Anytime," Chelsea said.

I turned to walk out the door, "Let me walk you out." Austin grabbed the door handle to hold it open for me.

"Thank you."

I was grateful to see that the sun was gone, but enough light left in the sky that we could still see each other, it would be hard to identify us in the driveway of cars passing by. As we turned the corner, being blocked by the garage, Austin grabbed me by the waist and pulled me towards him.

"Why didn't you tell me you were coming home?"

"I wanted it to be a surprise. SURPRISE!"

Austin smiled, put both hands on the back of my head and pulled me into a very deep kiss. I was having trouble feeling my legs and hoped that they would continue to hold me up and that my brain would continue to work and tell them to do so. When our lips parted, we were both breathing heavy.

"I like my surprise. And I must say you look SO unbelievably hot!! I really like this outfit."

"Thank you."

"You're very welcome."

He placed his right hand on my waist and with his left, took the mail out of my hand and dropped it to the ground. He placed his open hand on the other side of my waist and pulled me tight up against him where I felt his growing erection. He started kissing my collarbone, while moving his hands down my ass, squeezing gently as they moved. “You smell SOOOO good.” He said with his lips muffled in my neck. The movement of his lips talking caused shockwave throughout my body. I placed my hands on his chest slowly identifying each individual pectoral muscle. I kissed him soft and gentle on his chest, which was smooth and had a soft covering of curly brown hair.

“I missed you.” He said while moving his lips across my jaw bone towards my ear.

“Why do you think I came home?”

He stopped and looked at me eye to eye. “Really?”

“Really. I missed you too. I wanted to see you. I wanted to do… to do this.”

“Me too.”

I took a step back and pulled away a little. He looked taken aback.

“Do you think that’s normal?”

“What?”

“To miss each other so soon?”

“I don’t know about normal or not, but I know that’s what I was feeling. I enjoyed talking to you on the phone, but after every conversation ended I felt I wanted more. Is that ‘normal’ or ‘wrong’? I don’t know”

“That’s exactly how I was feeling. As the time was going on I was aching to see you and feel you. I couldn't stare at the New York crew anymore. I wanted to be with you. But we do, not tonight, need to have a serious conversation."

"Alright, but not tonight?" he repeated.

I kissed him, forcing his mouth open with mine and exploring his mouth with my tongue. Damn, letting him go tonight is going to be difficult, but his family is going to get suspicious if we're out here much longer.

"Your family is going to start wondering if you don't head back in."

"I know, but I don't want to let go."

"I completely agree."

"I *want* to slowly peel you out of every piece of clothing and go exploring with my lips starting at your toes and working my way up. Who knows what treasures I may find."

"You need to stop before I put all sensibility aside and take you up on that offer." He kissed me one last time, slowly pulled away having our foreheads be the last thing touching, and gave a little bounce to adjust his erection while readjusting himself. I bent down and picked up my mail. "Man, you have a nice ass!" he grabbed it. I grabbed his penis, and said, "This isn't so bad either, but you better calm down or you're going to have some unique explaining to do." He laughed.

"Good point, but I don't want you to stop because that feels awesome!" I let go and gave him a fastidious look, which I'm not positive he could see by now.

"Go for a run tomorrow?"

"Only if you think you can keep up," I said with a giggle. He pulled me by the waist one more time kissed me on the nose and said, "6 AM".

"6 AM. Night."

I walked across the street to my house feeling his eyes on me the entire way. I turned to wave and disappeared into the darkness of the garage.

The next morning, I rolled over and stretched. It was nice to be back in my bed, but it was nicer because in about a half hour I was going to see him and run, two of my favorite activities at the moment. That thought made me smile. I got out of bed, did another stretch, went pee, and changed into running shorts and a sports bra. I loved sports bras because they boosted my chest bigger than normal. In the kitchen, I grabbed a water bottle and prepared my smoothie for after the run. I took a towel from my gym bag wrapped it around my shoulders, strapped my phone with the elastic armband on my bicep, and put my socks and shoes on. I secured my hair in a tight pony-tail almost on the top of my head. I was ready to go! I watched out the kitchen window for some movement across the street. 5:58 Austin exited the side door of his garage. I left my house and did some stretches while I waited for him to approach.

"Morning beautiful."

"Hi. Morning." I said with a grunt as I was pulling on my calf to give it flexibility.

"I could watch you do that all day." He said with a smirk.

"Oh, yea? Wouldn't get very far in a run then…"

"Fine by me." He smiled showing his perfect teeth. "You expecting a call?" and he nodded at my phone strapped to my arm.

"Oh sorry, habit." I slid the phone off my arm and said,

"I'll be right back."

I jogged into the garage, where I tossed the phone on top of the car's trunk and ran back down the driveway. "Ready?"

"As I'll ever be." He said while pulling on his hamstring. It was cool but already humid. We started off at a natural pace.

"How far do you want to run today?"

"I have to get into the office sometime this morning so I'm open. You working today?"

"Yeah, I have to be in at 7:30."

"Alright how about five times around the sub, then a warm down walk?"

"Sounds good."

Three miles later we slowed our pace. Austin reached over and grabbed my hand. He looked over at me and smiled. I liked the way his hand felt in mine. Around the bend, near a wooded area, he pulled me over by the brush, leaned me up against an old willow tree and pressed his lips to mine. I kissed back, putting my hands on his waist. I'm sure my heart monitor was going nuts! Even though I was very wet and sticky from the humidity and run, I was still enraptured at this moment.

"You're going to be late if we keep this up."

"I know…." And almost a pouty lip he trailed off, he pulled back. He grabbed my hand and kissed the back of my knuckles. We headed out of the brush and I nervously looked out onto the street. With that nervous reaction, I thought, "now is the time to have 'the conversation'".

"Austin," I said nervously.

"Yeah."

"I think we should talk." He looked at me troubled. "It's not bad, you don't need to be scared, OK?"

"Uh huh?" Sounding unconvinced.

"I have defiantly developed feelings for you, which I think, err... hope you have for me as well."

"You can't tell?" he sounded almost wounded.

"I can." I smiled, but I had to say this because my career depended on it more than a silly love affair.

"But I need to get this out even though it's very hard for me OK?"

"So, how is this not bad?"

"It's not – I hope. Here goes, I want to continue seeing you. I have really enjoyed our time together and I want to get to know you even better, however…" he stopped and faced me in the middle of the road. "But I am five years older and being that it's not a huge difference in age, the law doesn't quite see it that way. Being you're a 'minor', I could lose my license, my job, go to jail for being with you. If anyone found out what we've done so far I could be prosecuted for child molestation."

"Do I look molested to you?"

"That's not the point. If your parents wanted to they could and it doesn't matter at your age right now if you 'look' or not, the court can state that I manipulated your innocents and took advantage of your youth." Austin started to laugh.

"It's not funny. I'm being serious." He attempted to stop and through a choked muted snort, "I know."

"So, what I'm saying is we have to lay low. Like, how I acted when I picked up the mail. 'Just the neighbor.' Just until you turn eighteen." Then an ugly thought crossed my mind that made me cold, 'if we make it that long'.

"So, what you're saying is you want to keep dating, we just have to keep it secret until I'm eighteen?" Dating? Wow, I didn't look at it that way but…

"Yes, if that's ok with you?" My heart was in my throat and I felt a little sick that he wasn't going to like that offer.

"What do you mean 'if that's ok'? Of course, it's ok! I mean, I want to show you to all my friends and do stuff, but I don't want to put you in harm's way. It's only four months, right?"

"Yeah, I guess, but you know you can't talk about it to anyone. Not Max, or any friends at school, you get that right?"

"I understand, it sucks, but I get it."

"So, dating huh?"

He smiled, and we started walking hand in hand again.

"Yeah dating. Is this, ok?" He lifted our hands up in the air.

"Not by the house, OK?"

"OK."

"So, what is 'dating' to you? I asked him.

"You know, you're my girl." MY GIRL? Holy shit. I felt my throat tighten and constrict my air flow and my cheeks get internally warm.

"Exclusively? I mean, um, well you know."

"Yes, secretly exclusive", he laughed. "So, let me ask you something now."

"Anything."

"What if a really good-looking lawyer guy asks you out for dinner? What will you say?

"Oh, like in New York?

His job dropped. I smiled. "Yeah, I had a guy ask if he could see me again after our business meeting, but I told him I wasn't interested."

"Really?"

"Yeah. I wasn't interested… in him." I smiled. Austin looked around, bent down, picked me up over his shoulder and smacked my ass and started to run. I laughed as I bounced like a log on his shoulder along the road. He carried me almost all the way back to the house. He put me down and gave me a kiss on the cheek. We started walking side by side. Not holding hands.

"What if a hot cheerleader makes a pass at you or wants you to call or whatever? I mean it's going to look odd with 'the guys' if you're not interested, right?"

"Not really. And I really don't care what they think. Don't worry about any of the girls at school. I mean, you are so much *more* in every way, like supermodel hot, intelligent, and mature." I blushed again and felt embarrassed because I didn't see myself in that way. I mean I know I'm smart and attractive, but I work hard at both. When we approached the houses, I looked at him, want to give him a kiss goodbye, but knew better of it.

"Have a good day at work." I smiled.

"You too. I have practice tonight until 6:30. Might go out after with the guys."

"OK. I might hit the gym after work, but I don't know what time after work will be." I waved slightly and walked toward my house. When I got into the garage, I grabbed my cell off the trunk, and sent him a quick text,

"You know I wanted to kiss you bye. So, take this as my kiss."

"Me too. XO"

When I got in the house, I took my smoothie out of the fridge and started drinking it as I got ready for the shower. I picked out my outfit for the day. I finished my 'breakfast' and stepped into the shower. The warm water felt good washing off the sweat. I was sad though because it also washed off his sent. That sent that was intoxicating. I finished my shower and proceeded to get ready for work.

The next few weeks were pretty routine, runs in the morning, make out sessions after. We were really getting to know each other, even though he was good at sports, primarily football, he wanted to go to New York University to be a doctor of Sports Medicine. The ultimate goal was to work with a professional team and travel with them. I wanted to tell him that there was a potential that I would be working in Washington D.C. but that wasn't confirmed yet and was confidential. I didn't like being able to share this with him, but it came with the job. Just like my clients, I couldn't tell him about any cases until they were closed. Most cases were boring and not worth sharing. I found out that I was his first girlfriend, he had taken girls out to dances and events but nothing serious. He does have a really close girl, best friend, Jessica – 'Jess' he calls her. They have been together since kindergarten. When he talked about her, I could tell he did really just look at her as a "sister"-friend, but just 'reading' into his stories, I would guess she would want more. Who could blame her? He is quite a catch, very companionate, loyal, hot as hell, and very intelligent. I tried not to get jealous when he talked about antidotes that they did together and knowing that she was about to spend eight-plus hours with him a day made me uncomfortable. I kept my feelings on the topic private and focused on the fact that he was obsessed with me. We talked about my past with boyfriends and sexual encounters. I told him when and how I lost my virginity, senior year to a football player. This made us laugh because of the irony, not that we had slept together – yet. It was becoming difficult to cease, for I knew what it was like to go further and once the build-up starts, I craved more. I'm sure he did too, but it was just too soon to get into that aspect of the relationship. I was surprised that I hadn't seen her over, but then again, when he did have friends over, I stayed away. It was easier not having to explain why the 'neighbor' was there.

One evening after I drove in from work there was a basketball game underway in the driveway. More guys than usual and a couple girls –girls - were sitting in the grass watching them play! My inner teenage drama queen came out and I immediately wondered if one of them was 'Jess'. I tried to calm, by convincing myself that they were with the other guys, but I still started fixated.

"DUCK JESS!!!" One of the guys yelled as the ball went flying past the hoop and the blonde-hair girl squealed and moved out of the way with a screech.

"Watch it ASS!" she shouted back and I saw Austin run after the ball. They were talking for a moment and knowing him, he was checking to make sure she was fine but it pissed me off when she put her hand on his peck and laughed! I went in the house changed into a sports bra, one of my sexier-strappy ones, sweatpants rolled down to my hips showing my defined abs, ankle socks and Nikes. I put my hair in a messy pony-tail, grabbed my water bottle and gym bag. I put a tee shirt inside the bag that I would put on at the gym because I didn't want to attract guys there, I was just trying to make my point here. This was one of Austin's favorite outfits. I was going to remind him 'where is bread is buttered'. Yeah - full on inner teenager coming out. I threw my bag in the car and slowly walked down the driveway watching them play. I caught Austin's eye, where he stopped mid-bounce and stared at me. He smiled and I smirked at him. "YA-You have stupid girls over." I thought to myself. With his delaying the game, some of the other guys stopped and noticed me walking to the box. One of the boys let out a wolf howl and there was laughter and 'guy banter' with chest slaps and shoving. "Point made!!" I felt a sense of accomplishment, a completely absurd, immature sense accomplishment, however. I got in my car after looking through the mail and pretending I didn't notice all the commotion that was taking place behind me and headed for the gym. Once at the gym I put on my baggy tee shirt. I really needed to kick the shit out of something, Rick was working with another person so I just worked on my own.

When I got home, Austin was sitting in a chair outside, some of the guys were still around shooting hoops or sitting talking. No girls. I pulled into my garage and immediately closed the door. I had just about gotten in the house when the front door had a knock. I went to the door and was surprised to see Austin standing there. He had left his friends and walked or ran over.

"Nice show earlier." He said with a fixed face. Wow, he must be mad.

"What? I was just going to the mailbox before I hit the gym." I explained. He adamantly walked his way through the door and said, "What do you mean 'What?'' You know exactly what you were doing."

"And apparently it worked." I looked at him straight in the eyes not faltering.

"Yeah, apparently." He said shortly.

"Don't you have friends to get back too?" I curtly snapped. Austin reached over and lifted me up. I naturally wrapped my legs around his waist and he pressed his lips against mine. He was heated, he pried my lips open with his and intensely kissed me ravaging my tongue unveiling deeper and with meaning. I grabbed his hair with my hands making fists and pulling softly. He groaned and if even possibly became more engulfed in our kiss. He walked over to the couch, laid me down where I unwrapped my legs. He slid his hands down my sweats and under my panties. Found my clitoris without hesitation and stuck his finger up my vagina. I arched my back with the sensation, and let out a moan. Man, that feels good! He had lifted my tee shirt and yanked up my sports bra and was sucking on my nipples that were extended due to the excitement. It didn't take long before I felt my built up. I buried my head in his shoulder and as I started to orgasm, I bit down on his neck. As he felt me tighten before my release, he started moving his hand faster in and out while rubbing my clitoris. I came on his fingers while convulsing under his touch. My muscles relaxed and when I looked up at him, he said, "There's no reason to be jealous."

"Me?" I said coyly. "I was going to take a shower, want to join?" Knowing his friends were waiting and he couldn't and the thought would just antagonize him.

"You're not playing very nice today."

"Me?" I said again with a devilish smile. He removed his hand and I pulled my bra and top back down to normal positions.

"I wore this tee to the gym, just so you know."

"I was hoping you would say that." He got up from off of me, took my hands and helped me off the couch. Pulled me close and brushed his lips against mine. No hard-passionate kiss, just very soft and sensual.

"I have to get back."

"I know. What did you tell them anyway?"

"Nothing, just said, "be right back" and I came over."

"Nice."

"Hey – you wanted ambiguity and then you come and pull a stunt like that!"

"All I did was walk out and get my mail," I said with a sardonic look. He kissed my nose and turned and went out the door. I watch him jog away back to his friends who didn't even seem to notice he was gone.

CHAPTER 5

I had to run out of town for another client's needs. This wasn't as high-profile, so no fancy private jet flying me around, but I at least was in first class. This trip was to sunny Napa Valley in Napa County. The client wanted to purchase some more land and expand his company internationally so it wasn't 'open – ended' on the time frame. I would be out on Monday, and return Friday. California was a much more relaxed environment and most meetings and exchanges were done with wine. -nice perk! It was the first week of school for Austin and because we were secret, it's not like I could give regards to him having a good day. I sent him a text,

"Have a good first day. Play nice with the other children… But not TOO nice"

"Thank you, I will try. Mundane and redundant is always the first week. I will be nice, but only TOO nice to you!"

"I miss you already."

"I'd rather be running right now. *WINK*"

"Me too. Talk later. Don't forget – time difference."

"XO"

I wanted to get him a special something for his first day of senior year, but nothing fit. Teddy bears, hats, key chains… and then I thought of an idea. I would give him a key to my place. That's perfect. After one of my long days at the vineyard, I stopped by a local hardware store and had a copy of my house key duplicated. The next day I found a fitting key chain that said, "Shhhh *California*" on it. I picked up a little box and had it wrapped. I was excited about the gift. We texted and called throughout the week, but with the time difference and schedules, we were more miss than hit. He had practice and then homework, and I didn't want to call too late and make him tired for school or football. It was frustrating but do-able being I was only going to be gone for a week.

We were closer now than we were for the New York trip so I sent him a message,

"On the plane now. Be home in about 5 hours. :-("

"What's the sad face for? You don't want to come home?"

"No, I do!!! I can't wait to see you; sad face is for LONG ASS flight!!"

"I want to see you too and kiss your beautiful face. I MISS U!!!"

"Closing doors – gotta go. Miss you too XO"

I turned Airplane Mode on my phone. I got home late on Friday evening. His car was in the driveway.

"Home."

"Good, I was starting to get worried. I wish I could come over."

"Meeeee toooooo."

"I can't come up with any reason I need to leave the house at this hour."

"I totally understand. I'm just going to take a shower and go to bed."

"HMMMM a shower you say?"

"Yes, I did."

"Where are you going to wash?"

"Yeah... we're not doing this." I typed and physically rolled my eyes.

"Not tonight... I'm sorry. Too tired."

"LOL OK. Get some rest. I'll call after practice in the afternoon."

"Sounds good."

"SHIT!! – I forgot I am working at the Garden House tomorrow. I'm sorry hun."

"It's fine. Ice cream date after?"

"Sounds AWESOME!!!"

"Night."

"XOXO"

Even though I felt a little sad that I was going to have to wait ALL day to see him, I could occupy my day with things that needed to get done. I had a suitcase of laundry, a house to tidy, and paperwork to get ready for the office on Monday. When I looked at the clock from my daily undertakings, I was surprised that it read 7:02. I hadn't heard from Austin all day. That's odd. I started to get worried, it's not like him not to say something throughout the day.

I looked over at his house and his car was there.

"Hey did you forget about our ice cream date?"

"No. Just got home and moms pissed – forgot to tell her I was working today and left my cell in the car. She thought I was laying in the hospital with a concussion from practice."

I didn't want to admit the thought had crossed my mind too. Two mothers were a bit much and I was DEFINITELY not a mother to him nor I was I ever going to be.

"You want to reschedule?"

"No, just give me a few to calm her down and smooth things over." I decided to go to the ice cream place and wait instead of pacing at the house wondering how much trouble he was actually in. I grabbed his present and put it in my purse. I changed into a more appealing outfit and dabbed on some perfume. A little eyeliner and glittery gloss. I didn't wait long before he drove up. He got out of his car and didn't look very happy. Even the sight of me didn't change his appearance. Wow, this must be bad, I thought.

"Hi." I said with a lift on the 'I' parts.

"Hi." He said flatly.

"That bad?"

"She can be a royal bitch sometimes!" Woah- I have never heard him talk about another person in that manner let alone his mother….

"What in the world Austin?" Shock coming from my mouth and expression.

"I'm sorry, hun. She just pisses me off with her comments,

like "Mature people call and let people who ***CARE*** about them, that they are OK!" He stressed they -are - OK. "Maybe you're not ready to have the responsibility for a car if we don't know where you are."

"I'm sorry." I gave him a sad face.

"I *was* being responsible. I was at FUCKING WORK!!!" This is bad. I don't think I had ever seen him this angry. Kind of nice in a way messed up way, that he's 'normal' instead of this robot God that does everything in every way perfect. I totally didn't know what to say but if this was a true open relationship, I would just say what I felt.

"I am just going to say what I feel, OK?"

"Yea - K"

"I'm not … um… she was just scared."

"Oh brother." He rolled his eyes.

"Listen, I was kind of on the same wavelength." He looked at me,

"What?"

"I'm not mad, I was just concerned because it's not like you to say anything for an entire day… and…" When I voiced my concern, he seemed to relax.

"I'm sorry. I really just left my phone in the car and was concentrating at work. I was thinking about ice cream and the plays from practice.

I really didn't mean to scare you or anyone else."

"I'm fine." I smiled and he smiled back. "Ice cream?" I tilted my head sideways like a puppy that is confused on what you are saying.

"Sounds good. What sounds better is me licking it off of you!!" He grinned.

"You're being bad now, mister." It was hard to keep my distance, but we were in public and you can't be too careful. You never know who may see us and if it got reported to his parents, we could say we just ran into each other.

I decided on a cone that way I could taunt him with seductive behavior. It worked! Several times he choked on his ice cream and told me to "stop it" or "knock it off". I was thoroughly enjoying this.

We were sitting on the side of the building, not in direct sight of anyone. After we finished our ice cream, Austin said, "Listen, I'm sorry I was just angry. I wanted to tell you that you look nice. Hot, actually."

"Thank you. It's fine. That's why I go to the gym, not to look 'hot', to go blow off shit from work."

"Really?"

"Yea – I study Krav Maga at the gym in town. You should come sometime."

"So, you can kick my ass?"

"If that's what happens." I laughed.

I looked serious and he stopped laughing. "I got you, well made you… I have a present for you.

For the first day of your senior year."

"You didn't have to do that."

"I know. But it has multiple purposes."

"You have me completely intrigued." He said with a crooked smile.

"It's not like that. Here." I reached into my purse and pulled out a little box.

He looked at the box, then looked at me. Obviously, not what he was expecting. He opened the box and pulled out the key on the keychain.

"A key?"

"Well, I said it had multiple purposes. A key to my house. That way you can come and go whenever you please. If you need a quiet place to study or watch the game or whatever, it's yours."

"And the second?"

"My heart." He looked lost on that one. Even though he was very sensitive and intelligent, he was also young and male.

"My heart, I'm giving you a 'key to my heart', I paused to let it sink in.

"I don't know what to say." That wasn't the reaction I was going for. In fact, I'm not really sure what the reaction I was expecting.

He turned the key over in his hand several times staring at it.

"Mine too." He finally said extremely softly…

"Everything ok?" I asked apprehensively. "I didn't overstep, did I? You're not… I didn't scare you, did I?" Public or no public, he grabbed the back of my head and pulled my head to his where he kissed me, tenderly and gently.

"It's the best gift ever. And I said, Mine too, you have my heart as well." My heart constricted and even though I loved the kiss, it was in public, I was still nervous. It was pretty far into dusk and no one was on that side of the building. I reached over and caressed his knee. I put my head on his shoulder and he held my hand.

The next week was very busy on both sides. If Austin worked out or ran, it was with the guys on the team and when he wasn't in school, he was on the field practicing. My schedule was just as busy. I had a lot of cases to work on and some very mind-numbing, so I would go to the gym. I would get home very late, too late even to call. I would just send a text, "Home. 2:00 AM. Hope you had a good day. XO"

One night I came home from work and there were a dozen roses on my kitchen counter with a note,

Sorry we keep missing each other. Hope you had a good day.

P.S. I put my key to use.

P.P.S. First game is on Friday against Northern.

Will you come 6 pm?

Love,

Austin

XO

I blushed and smelled the roses. They were beautiful.

I responded via text,

"Yes, I see you put your key to good use. I miss you too. I did have a good day, but not in the way you think. Just productive, not fun. I have to be in court for the rest of the week. Will be hard to talk. Sorry. Love, Eli. P.S. Thank you for the roses, they're beautiful!! OOO P.P.S. Yes. I will be at your game. 6 pm"

The court was rigorous, a lot of going back and forth with opposing sides and brain exertion. You had to be one step ahead of what everyone was thinking. I found it exhilarating but by the end of the day, I was too pumped to relax so I would go to the gym and workout. Sometimes I would just run on the treadmill at home to burn the energy I had from arguing or winning my point. Friday finally arrived and I set my alarm to leave the office at 4:00 PM. I set another alarm on my phone to leave the house at 5:00 PM. I was grateful that we were done delegating by 1 in the afternoon and it would be easy for me to wrap things up at the office and be out by 4. I was just finishing up the last document when my cell phone chimed that it was 4:00 PM. I shut down my computer, organized my files, picked up my cell, purse, and keys and headed home. I noticed while walking to my car that the temperature dropped and it was going to be a cool if not chilly night.

When I got home, I went to my closet and found a navy-blue oxford shirt and an extra bulky ivory fisherman's sweater. I chose my dark blue jeans that were form-fitting, big thick socks and my brown Muk Luks Patti boots. I touched up my makeup from the long days wear, and put my hair in a half-bun, half up to stay out of my face, half down to keep my neck warm. I was surprised how quickly I was dressed.

I had just enough time to grab a bite and run out the door.

I pulled into the parking lot of the opposing school which was full of animated and energized people ready for the game. I got out, took the fleece blanket that I brought to sit on and hoped that I would remember where I parked the car. I followed the crowd in, paid for my ticket, found the 'correct' side and while I made my way to the second row of bleachers, spotted Austin's family. I avoided them by walking next to a very spirited group and found my seat all the way down near the end. They didn't see me because they were talking and enjoying a group of parents and friends. I thought Max might spot me as he looked bored hanging out with parents not friends, but apparently was really bored so much he didn't notice me either. The cheerleaders came out first revving up the crowd and one of the first girls to stand out was a platinum blonde; a pony-tail on the top of her head with school color ribbons intertwined. "She's a frickin' cheerleader? Are you kidding me?" With that thought, I flashed back to our run where I asked if a hot cheerleader made a move on him… Why didn't he tell me she was? Maybe she just joined the team and wasn't when I asked. Or maybe it was too new in the relationship to mention that part. "This is just wonderful," I thought. She couldn't be a fat cheerleader either, the ones that get picked just because they didn't have enough try-outs and had to pick her. Oh no, she was gorgeous. Long legs, tall, blonde, tan, and beautiful features. From where I was sitting, she looked as though she had perfect teeth as well. I reminded myself that he's known her for twelve years and "not to be jealous" his words exactly. I calmed down at the thought that if they were supposed to be together, they would have by now.

The players ran out onto the field and the crowd jumped to their feet. Everyone was going nuts, the cheerleaders were high kicking and jumping, the crowd was up and screaming, and some players were stretching while others were just as excited as the crowd. I spotted Austin, although a little difficult from the blur of uniforms, he was one of the players that looked more serious and stretching. He turned around to scan the crowd. He found me after a few moments after waving to his parents and smiled. I smiled back but did not wave. Even completely covered in his uniform he looked good. The pants showed off his ass quite nicely and that made my heart constrict. Right as the last play was made, and the whistle blew I stood up among the crowd to stretch. His team had won their first game. I stood on the field so he could see I stayed for the entire thing, but I was uneasy about being spotted. There was no reasonable explanation why I would be at a high school football game. The team congratulated each other and started to break. Austin started to run up to his parents, who were now on the field with several others when Jess grabbed him and gave him a huge hug. He hugged her back, said a couple of things that I couldn't make out and went over to his parents. Man, she can make my blood boil! Austin was facing the bleacher and his parent's back were towards me – easy escape. I walked past them where I caught Austin's eye. I winked and he smiled never leading on to them I was there. I walked to my car where I understood why I was getting jealous. I wanted him to run up to me and hug me, and because he can't … Jess. I knew I had 'his heart', but it still was hard. I drove home and decided I would watch a movie, which I hadn't done in forever, and just enjoy the rest of the night. I lit some candles, changed into flannel pants with a tank top, let my hair down, and curled into the couch. About an hour into my movie my phone gave off a familiar *PING*.

"You still up?"

"Yes. Just watching a movie". I was confused about my feelings, still pissed, but more at myself than at him. I didn't want to share him, but because of the damn rules and laws…had too.

"You want company?"

"Sure, but how?"

There was no answer, but instead a knock on the door. I moved the blanket I was curled under in and answered the door.

"Hi". He said.

"Hi." I opened the door wider so he could come in. He smelled awesome. Freshly showered. His hair was still a little damp and he had used a body wash that was intoxicating.

He wrapped his arms around me and hugged me tightly. He loosened his grip, looked down and gave me a sensitive kiss.

"Thank you for coming to my game tonight."

"You're welcome. I told you I would be there."

"You looked absolutely stunning, like a model walking right

off the page of a magazine. I mean you always look beautiful, but it took everything in my control to not just run up to you and say, "fuck the law!"

"Well, I'm glad you didn't, but on the same account wish you had." I half smiled, hoping not to give away my 'Jess jealousy'.

"What-cha watching?"

"Just a 'chick-flick'."

"May I join you?"

"If you want." I took his hand, and we walked over to the couch. The dent from where I was sitting was still there. He sat down and pull me next to him. I reached over, picked the blanket off the floor, and covered us. He put his arm around me and I snuggled into him. He stroked my hair with his hand and I closed my eyes enjoying his being. I wasn't even watching the movie anymore. I shut the movie off with the remote and he repositioned me with the back of my head on his lap. We were sitting in a candle-lit room, quiet, just enjoying each other's company. "I enjoyed your game tonight," I said while he caressed my forehead. My eyes were closed, but I could still feel his intense stare at me. He didn't talk, he just sat there running his fingers through my hair. "If you keep this up," I said lethargic, "I will fall asleep on you."

"Fine by me. I could stare at you all night."

"By the way, how did you get to come over tonight?"

"I told my parents I was going out to celebrate with some guys on the team. I parked down the sub in that house that's for sale.

mom was already in bed, and dad was falling asleep in his chair. He said, "be home by 1".

"MMM -HMM" I said lifelessly. We sat for quite a while in the glow when I turned my head towards his stomach and gave him a kiss. He stopped rubbing my head. I scooted up and he bent over and kissed my forehead. He moved down to my nose and found my lips. He nibbled on my upper lip lightly and I giggled. I bit down a little harder on his bottom lip and it progressed into a passionate elongated kiss. He was holding my bra-less breast and massaging the nipple which made me tingle and get wet. I moaned in his mouth and was ready to lose everything into him. His phone buzzed in his pocket that startled me. "Ten-minute warning." He claimed. I pouted and he said "Sorry. I know it sucks."

"I wouldn't trade this time tonight for anything. It's been wonderful. Don't be sorry." He kissed me again and then I sat up next to him trying to get my bearings.

"Can I talk to you about something?" He said, very cautiously.

"Sure, anything, you know that."

He turned and faced me, pulling his leg up in a bent position on the couch. He intertwined our fingers, and I could tell whatever it was he was about to tell me, was something he wasn't comfortable with. That made me uneasy.

"You know next week is another game, right?"

"Yes."

"Well, it's not just any game, it's homecoming. The homecoming game."

"Uh huh." I looked at him confused.

"You know, I want you to go more than *anything* in the world, right?"

"I guess so." Now concerned that I didn't know where he was going with this because either outcome wasn't good.

"I know you can't for obvious reasons, but being my senior year, I kind of would like to go."

"Okay…"

"So, me and some other guys were talking about going and they asked who I was bringing if I was even going. I told them I didn't know on either count yet. But it got me thinking. I was wondering…" He was rapidly moving his hand in mine and very uncomfortable now. "Was wondering if you would be Okay if I took Jess?" I sat up very erect. Still held his hand, but all the cuddle was gone. I felt a little sick. "What the hell?" I thought.

"Are you mad?" He asked.

"No." I just sat there stiff.

"You aren't moving. You aren't saying anything. You're not-"

"Rationalizing. I'm rationalizing the situation. That's what us *lawyers* do." I said a little more condescending than I meant to. "I know I can't go with you, and that physically kills me." I was looking him straight in the eyes and trying with everything not to cry.

"I SWEAR to you, it's like I'm taking my sister. She is just a friend and she might not even say yes. I didn't want to ask without talking to you first." I let go of his hand, put both feet on the floor, placed my elbows on my knees and covered my face with my hands. “This is the shit I HATE about relationships,” I thought. He started to rub my back and I shrugged him off.

“Please don’t be mad. This is a very difficult position for me too. I want you there.” He grabbed my hands, pulled them away from my buried face, turned my chin to face him with his hand and said, “I WANT you. Not her.” I just stared at him blankly, still trying to hold back tears.

“Man, Austin.” I paused because I literally did not know what to say. I didn’t even know which emotion I was feeling because they were all swarming around me like a bunch of gnats. “I don’t want to take anything away from you, I want you to be able to look back and say, “I had one hell of a senior year.” So, I give you my blessing, ‘so to speak’, to ask her to the dance.”

“I don’t know if I should thank you or what?”

“You don’t need to thank me. I DO trust you. It’s just a difficult situation like you said.”

“I know this is really poor timing, but I have to go. If I’m late I won’t be allowed to come over for a very long time.”

“I understand.” We both stood from the couch and walked to the door. We kissed, but not passionately. “I’ll call you tomorrow? He said as he turned to the door.

“OK. Night.”

“Night.”

I watch him descend into the dark, and I shut the door.

This was not how I envisioned tonight going, or ending for that matter.

CHAPTER 6

I didn't sleep well at all that night. I kept going over everything that was said, every emotion I was feeling and I decided that I needed to look at this as a 'lawyer', not an overreacted woman and that was exactly what I was doing, overreacting. As a 'lawyer', I knew the law. Unless I was willing to lose everything - then the facts are simple; he is a minor. Black and white, plain and simple. Let him go to the dance and have fun with his friends, "FRIENDS Ellie". I told myself. Even if she wants more, he doesn't and you have to have a strong line of trust. I needed to talk to him, I was going to have to go to his work today. I sent him a text,

"You working today?"

"After practice. Getting ready now."

"What time?"

"1-7."

…and nothing. That must have been the shortest conversation we have ever had. I will clear things up this afternoon. I made a protein breakfast drink, changed into my gym clothes, put my hair up, and headed out. I was feeling defeated so I didn't know how productive I would be. When I arrived at the gym, I met Rick in the parking lot. "Hey there!" he said uplifted.

"Hi," I said monotone.

"Um, that's not my usual Ellie, what's up?"

"Nothing…everything…"

"You want to work it out?"

"I will try. Got in a misunderstanding, argument, something like that…" and I waved my hands in the air like I was fanning smoke away from me. "… with someone I care about."

"You'll fix it. Come on. Warm-ups."

I think this session was one of the hardest so far. Almost back to the beginning when I was just learning.

"Your head is just not in the game today girl," Rick said while doing a choke-hold on me from behind.

"I know." I bent down, spread my legs, flipped him over my shoulder and did a sweep, which knocked him on his butt.

"Nice, but not nice enough." He did a back handspring and up got back up on his feet, and with his left arm swung, which I blocked,

but his right caught me square in the cheekbone. Immediately I covered my face, turned around and kicked him right behind the right knee and he fell to the floor. I was standing over him in defeat and pain. "Hey, you, ok?" He said.

"Yeah – hurts like hell, but I'll be fine."

"See what happens when you are off. Good thing I wasn't *trying* to hurt you or it would be a lot worse. Your bleeding, let's get that cleaned up."

We went into the office where they kept a first aid kit. Rick put antiseptic ointment on my gash, , and butterflied bandaged it. "I clocked you good." He said with a chuckle. "You're gonna have a nice shiner in a day."

"Thanks." I smiled then cringed. "Yup, that's gonna hurt." I thought "I'm going home and ice it"

"Sounds good. Sorry."

"It's fine. My fault, but next session I will knock you on your ass you so hard you won't sit down for a week!"

"Yeah? Bring it! If it helps any, I think I may have to ice my knee. That what quite a kick!"

"Ouch – quit making me smile dick!" I tried to pull my face down into a frown with my hand. I left the office, got in my car and headed home. Boy, I am getting a headache. When I got home, I took some Tylenol, grabbed an ice pack from the freezer, a dishcloth to wrap it in and laid on the couch. I placed the wrapped ice pack on my cheek and closed my eyes. After a few, the Tylenol was helping and my cheek was numb, the ice pack woke me up when it slid off my face. I didn't realize I had fallen asleep. "I wonder what time it is?" I got up and looked at my phone, 12:40. I went to my bedroom to change. Nothing fancy, I threw on some shorts, and a fitted tee and looked in the mirror. "Oh yeah, this is going to be fun to explain!!" My stomach was grumbling but my jaw wasn't going to allow me to chew anything at the moment. "I'll stop at the deli in town and grab some soup after I talk to Austin." I slid on my sandals, got my keys but couldn't find my purse. I checked the car and I had left it on the seat. I crawled in and headed for the Green Thumb.

His car wasn't in the driveway yet, so I waited. It was a small location, but busy today so no one paid much attention to me. I saw in my rearview mirror as he pulled up and he parked over on the side where the employees must park. 12:55 was on my clock, which didn't leave much time to say what I needed to. I got out of my car and started walking towards him. He was getting out of his car when I approached him. He stood up, took one look, and with a shocked face said, "Holy Hell, what the Fuck happened?" He reached over to grace my cheek and I flinched. "Are you OK?"

"Yes. I need to talk to you, but we don't have a lot of time, it's almost 1."

"Hey they know I'm here – it's fine. What happened?" he asked again very concerned.

"I was at the gym this morning and Rick and I were sparring and I missed a block, that's all."

"That's all? Jesus Eli- you may need stitches!"

"It'll be fine. It's what I get for not being focused. If it makes you feel better, he had to go ice his knee for my sweep and a kick that knocked him on his ass!" With that, I smiled which made me cringe because of the pain. He closed his eyes like he was in as much pain as I was. "I hate seeing you like this," he said.

"It's just a scratch, I'll be fine. I need to talk to you about last night."

"No, you don't, you need to go find out if you need stitches."

"No. I don't. I want to tell you something and you're going to stop interrupting my thought." I stared him down. "I want to tell you that I was in the wrong last night. I feel horrible about having you even remotely feel bad or nervous to talk to me."

"You don't have to do this." He said.

"Yes, I do. You didn't even need to ask how I felt about the situation, but you did and me being an ass, I overreacted. I want you to go to the dance and I want you to have a great time with your friends. ALL of your friends. I am sorry. I was being selfish last night. Our situation frustrates me as much as it does you. Can you forgive me?"

"I feel really bad, and I absolutely hate that I can't touch you right now. I don't want you to apologize. There's nothing to apologize for. I wouldn't like it either if it were switched. To be honest, I'm not too thrilled that some guy did this to you." And he waved his hand over my cheek. "I want to go kick the shit out of him."

"Yeah…not a good idea, he's a double black belt in Krav Maga, along with several other decorations, and I don't think you would stand much of a chance. Besides, I told you, because of our fight… er… argument...or whatever it was, I wasn't focused which was completely stupid on my account. I should always be prepared and I wasn't." An older gentleman was walking up to us while we spoke and disrupted our conversation. "That's my boss," Austin said as we both turned and looked at him.

"Hey, Mr. Andrews."

"Hey, Austin. Is there a problem over here?" Mr. Andrews looked at my face, "That's quite a nice shiner, my boy here didn't do this did he?" He looked concerned too.

"Oh no sir, you should see the other guy!" I cringed again due to smiling. "This man… er… boy - here delivered some limestone the other day and I found this cell phone shortly after he left, in the road, I thought it might be his." I held up MY cell and showed it to him. "He was just telling me that it wasn't. Then he inquired about my face."

I pointed to my face and rolled my eyes. "I won't keep him any longer."

"That was very nice of you to come all the way over in your condition to check that out." My condition?? What is up with men today?

"You want me to put it in the office?" Mr. Andrews said.

"No. He was the only one that day, so I'll hang on to it in case someone calls it or knocks on my door looking for it."

"Great idea! And hey – thanks for the business!"

"Anytime. Sorry to bother everyone." I said.

"It's no bother." Mr. Andrews replied, and he slapped Austin on the back as to say, 'let's get to work'. We parted and Austin turned back to me and said, "Hope your face feels better ma'am." With a huge smile.

"Thank you," I said sardonically.

I got in my car and headed for the deli in town. I ordered broccoli and cheddar soup to-go. I really wanted a roll with it but didn't think that would be too easy to bite into. I sent Austin a text,

"Hope I didn't get you into trouble. Hope you're having a better day. XO"

I knew he wouldn't reply back because he leaves his phone in the car while at work. I ate my soup when I got home, it was a little difficult because I had to move my mouth, but when I finished, I grabbed the ice pack and towel again and laid on the couch. A *PING* noise woke me again from my phone. What the hell, I know I didn't sleep well last night, but this sleeping all day thing was ridiculous. I looked at my phone, it was Austin replying to my text.

"Nah – he bought the cell phone story. Didn't think anything off. Nice cover by the way. LOL"

"You on break?"

"Lunch"

I looked at my phone 4:15. Makes sense.

"What are you doing after work?"

"Dunno. Some of the guys want to go grab burgers so I'm not sure. What are you doing tonight?"

"Not much. Just laying low."

"Want me to stop by?"

"I won't be much fun."

"Just being with you is awesome – no worries."

"If you want, you have a key"

"And I know how to use it!!! LOL"

"Yes you do!" Go eat – I'll talk to you later. O"

"XOXO – on your boo boo"

His last couple of lines made my face hurt. Maybe it was worse than I thought. Maybe I should get it looked at. I got off the couch, went into the bathroom and saw that my right eye was swelling shut, even with the Tylenol and ice. I decided to run to the local ER and have them take a look.

"I decided to get my face looked at by a "professional" not an "overreacted boyfriend." I paused before continuing to type. I wonder how that will sit, I thought.

"I'll let you know what they say."

"Good. You want me to take you?"

"No, you're at work."

"Fine. Tell me what they say. When are you going in?"

"In about 15 I guess."

"K talk soon."

As I walked in the lobby of the ER there was no question really why I was there. I walked up to the glass window, pointed to my face, and the lady smiled at me and nodded. "Medical card and Driver's License, please.

I reached in my purse, pulled out my wallet and dug both out. "Are you able to sign?" the receptionist asked.

"I drove myself here, I think I can sign a piece of paper," I said rudely. "Sorry. A little on the grumpy side I guess." I stated but really wasn't sorry. I was not in the mood for stupid questions today.

"If you could please have a seat over there, someone will be with you soon." She smiled again and handed me my IDs. I walked over and sat as far away from people as possible. I had no idea why they were there and didn't want to catch anything from them or be close enough to find out what brought them in.

"Miss Baylor" A lady in scrubs called from the doorway. She had a wheelchair and when I stood up, started pushing it my way. "you've got to be kidding me? A frickin' wheelchair?" I thought. I sat in the chair and she pushed me through the double doors. We entered a room with a bed and all the medical belongings around it, chair in the corner, counter with locked drawers with number pads on them and a sink. There was a TV mounted on the wall opposite of the bed and chair. I left the wheelchair and sat on the bed where I proceeded to lay down. Another nurse was in the room and as soon as I laid down she strapped the blood pressure cuff to me and started taking my vitals.

"What brings you in today?" The nurse said.

"Are you kidding me?" I thought. I removed the ice pack from my face and she looked surprised.

"Ahhh, I see." She started typing on the laptop that was sitting next to my bed to my right. "Are you in harm?

"What?" I said confused.

"Did someone do this to you? Are you in danger in any way?"

"Well yeah someone did this to me, but I'm not in danger." The nurse looked confused and a little irritated. "I was in a self-defense sparring match and I missed a block. No one hurt me intentionally. I came in because my eye is starting to swell shut and I want to make sure everyone is overreacting." She typed in my 'statement', looked over at me and said, "Ok it will be a few, the doctor is seeing another patient. He'll be in shortly. Just keep the ice on your face and try to relax." I looked at my phone 5:13. I wondered how long it would take. I was surprised how busy they were for a Saturday afternoon/evening. I just laid in the bed with my eyes closed. My face was starting to hurt again and the ice was just annoying me. I kept checking my phone to see how long it was taking the doctor to come in my room. So far, I had been only waiting fifteen minutes. On one of my last glances, he knocked on the partially cracked door and said, "Ms. Baylor?"

"Yes," I replied, really not wanting to move my face.

"I'm Dr. Kaiser. What brings you in today?" I removed the ice pack from my face and he said, "Well that's a beauty! How did you get this lovely scratch?" SCRATCH!!! See everyone WAS overreacting!!! I knew it! I explained that I was in a sparring match and that I missed a block. "Won't do that, again will you?" He said. I liked this guy. "You never know." I retorted. He smiled. He took a flashlight out of his front pocket and shined it in my eyes. He had me look left and right and up and down. I was asked to follow his finger and told him he was holding up three fingers. He asked me if I knew who the President was and what was the date. I thought this was ridiculous for a little scratch.

"So, we're going to send you for a little picture to see if it's superficial or worse, but my guess, being the genius, doc I am, I would go with small fracture due to the swelling of the orbital socket – eye. You wanna place any bets?"

"I'm a lawyer and I don't gamble when the odds aren't in my favor," I stated.

"Smart girl. The nurse will come in and take you to x-ray soon. Do you have a driver?" Right as I stated "No", a voice from behind the doctor said, "yes she does." Startled, the doctor turned around. "Hi – I'm Austin. I'm her neighbor, I can drive her home." I was staring at him like I'd seen a ghost.

"Great!" The doctor said. "She shouldn't be driving with only one good eye right now. Are you allergic to anything?" He was flipping through the notes on the computer.

"No."

"After the x-ray, I'll give you something for the pain, now that you have a driver. Sound good?"

I nodded my head, which hurt and he turned to walk out the door. "See you in a bit."

This was going to be a long night I had a feeling. Better now that Austin was here, but still long.

"What are you doing here?" I exclaimed.

"I wasn't going to let my girl do this on her own. That's not what *boyfriends* do." Ahh, he did catch it. It made me smile. He walked over and sat on the end of my bed. I moved my legs over to give him more room. "Eli – that really doesn't look good."

"So, I've been told."

"You cold?" he said. I nodded, "Be right back". He got up, headed out the door. The next thing I knew he was with a nurse holding what I discovered, a warm blanket. "Why didn't you tell me you were cold honey?" the nurse said.

"Sorry."

"You got a good friend here." She patted my leg and walked out.

"Thank you," I said.

"No problem." He smiled. "Can I hold your hand?"

"I don't see what that would hurt." He reached over and held my hand rubbing his thumb over the back of my hand. This must be a nervous habit he has, I thought.

"So, did you leave work?"

"No. When I got back from lunch, Bill – Mr. Andrews said that we had slowed down enough and I could go 'enjoy the rest of the day. Not going to have many nice ones left.' So, I went home, I told mom about you coming over with the "cell story" and how you looked horrible and you mentioned you were going to ER. I told her I wanted to help drive you home. She got her keys immediately and drove me up here. I texted her that I found you and she left. I can drive you home in your car if that's OK with you?"

"Absolutely!" I moaned and closed my eyes.

"What's the matter?" He said.

"My face hurts, that's all." The nurse came in with a wheelchair and Austin let go of my hand, got off the bed, and moved out of her way.

"How ya doing honey?" she said "I'm here to take you for your x-ray, take a seat. You want the blanket?"

"No. I'll be fine."

"I'll return her in a minute. You can put the TV on if you want. The remote is right over there."
The nurse indicated to Austin.

"Thank you. I'll manage." He smiled and I short finger waved at him. I closed my eyes because the movement of the wheelchair hurt my face. Once in the room, I stood up against a hard, grey board with cross marks on it. "You going to shoot me?" I said.

"It does look like I'm lining you up for a firing range, doesn't it?" The tech said. "Can you tell me your name and birthday? I regurgitated my information. "Any chance you're pregnant?"

"No," I said flatly. She placed a heavy lead apron-y vest thing over my chest, turned me around and tied it. She moved the grey board up behind my head, pressed my shoulders back up against it, and slapped a magnet 'R' on the right side of my face on the board. "I need you to put your head up against the board and stay as still as possible. OK?" She pulled a light down over my face with another crosshair on the plastic. She lined up the crosshair with my cheekbone. “You can close your eyes if you want. I know that light is bright.” I did as she said, but still saw the shadow of the cross-hair lines through my eye-lids. I heard her walk away, then she said, “Take a deep breath and hold it.” I did as she asked, I heard a buzzing, clicking sound. “Breathe.” She stated. The bright light was gone, so I opened my eyes to see her walking back to me. She must have gone in that little room with the glass window. “Now, I need you to put your left shoulder against that board and look straight ahead. She adjusted the grey board again next to me, readjusted the light, and I closed my eyes. I started to sway. “Woah there missy.” She held me by the shoulders. “Maybe closing your eyes this time not, the best idea? You feel dizzy or anything?

“Not until I closed my eyes,” I stated. It was true. I didn’t realize that would happen. Maybe it is serious. “Well, you can do this if you need to steady yourself.” And she took my left arm that was on the board, turned it so my hand held the underside of the board. “Gently though, OK?”

“K” I stated.

“Same thing- steady as possible. Deep breath when I say, then breathe … when I say got it?”

“Yup.”

We did the routine, I sat back down in the chair and she wheeled me back to my room. Austin was sitting in the chair when we returned looking at his phone. I crawled back into bed and covered up. He stood, and helped put up the cover. “Would you like some fresh ice?" the tech asked.

"That would be nice. Thank you." She left with the wheelchair. A short few minutes later my nurse came in with a long, white, rectangular pouch filled with ice. "Here ya go hon." She handed me the pack; it was heavier than the one I was using at home. I whimpered when I put it on my face, and Austin took my hand. "Doc said I could give you something for the pain once the x-ray was finished. You want something?"

"Yes please," I stated. She looked at Austin. "Are you her driver?"

"Yes ma'am."

"Well, aren't you a polite young man." She boasted. Austin blushed.

"I'm sorry, but because of your face laceration, I have to run an IV, OK?" She looked at me.

"That's fine," I said.

She went over to the counter, punched in some numbers on the drawer and pulled out a clear package. She walked over, picked up the scanner that was next to the laptop, and scanned the package. She turned around, reached into a box pulled out two gloves and put them on. She opened the package and placed the contents on my legs. A long clear hose, and some plastic connectors, and a needle with a butterfly sticky thing on it. She took a long stretchy strap and tied it very tight on my forearm. She straightened my arm felt the vein with her thumb and with a 'pop' the needle was in my arm. She covered it with a plastic bandage wrap. She hooked the IV to a saline bag. She reached into her pocket and pulled a small clear vial out. She took the scanner and scanned the barcode on the bottle. Then she went to scan my wrist and noticed that 'nurse 1' didn't put my medical bracelet on me. "Good grief!" she stated. "Can't have good help these days! I'll be right back." She took her gloves off, threw them in the trash and walked out of the room. A few seconds later she came back with a half sheet of paper, which was apparently my medical bracelet. She scanned the paper and separated the perforated lines and put the band on my wrist. She then re-scanned the plastic bag that held the IV tubing and the small vial. "Am I all accounted for now?" I asked sarcastically.

"Yes, honey. Sorry 'bout that." She pulled some liquid from the small vial and inserted it into my IV port. "Going to give you a little Morphine, OK? You will be feeling better really quick."

"OK"

She looked at Austin, "From this point on, she cannot be held accountable for the next 24 hours, OK son?"

"Yes ma'am," he said. The nurse wasn't kidding. I immediately felt a warmth all over. She was still putting it in me too. "How much are you giving me?" I asked.

"Not that much, we just have to do it slowly. People have fewer reactions to it if put in the IV slow vs quickly."

"AHHHH" I said, starting to feel the effects of the medicine.

"Doc also wrote up some others here." She reached into another pocket and pulled another vial out. "Sometimes people feel nauseated with Morphine, so this one is to help with that." She scanned that vial and then pulled liquid out of that vial and shot it in the IV portal.

"This one will cause sleepiness as well." And she looked at Austin.

"Ok, Good to know." He said.

"Ok sweetie, the doc should be in soon, you just try and relax. You want the TV on?"

"No thanks," I said, at least I think I said. It felt strange to talk like I was in a 3rd dimension sort of. I closed my eyes and felt like I was floating off the bed. My face didn't hurt that much, but I don't know if I could have actually stated where my face was located at the moment. I didn't like the effects of the Morphine, so I kept my eyes open.

"You, ok?" Austin asked.

"Not crazy about this feeling."

"What feeling? You feel sick?"

"No, just like I'm floating off the bed when I close my eyes."

"You need to tell doc."

"Mmmm K." I mumbled.

The doctor returned a while later and I was drifting in and out of sleep.

"Well, young lady, how ya doing?"

"I don't like the Morphine."

"Why?"

"Makes me feel funny." I slurred. The doctor looked at Austin.

"She said it made her feel like she was floating off the bed." He told the doctor.

"Gotcha. But how is the face pain, scale 1 being no pain at all to 10 being the worst." My mouth was extremely dry 'cotton mouth' and I had a hard time speaking. "I would say 9 still. The medicine didn't help the pain, just messed up my brain. Can I get some water please?"

"We can get you some water and something else for that the facial pain. I'm not surprised though. I have the results from your x-ray. I would hate to see what this would look like if your sparring partner *meant* to hurt you. As I guessed, you have a hairline fracture." He pulled my x-ray up on the laptop and removed a pen from his front pocket. "It's called a zygomaticomaxillary fracture (ZMC). Yours is a very small one right here." He pointed with his pen to a small, very tiny line, that looked like a hair. "This is the Anterior Maxillary Wall. I want you to call your primary on Monday and they can refer you to a specialist. Your eye might swell shut so you have to stay diligent on the ice and anti-inflammatory meds. Got it? I'll have a nurse come in with something else for the pain and I'll write you a script for pain meds and give you a couple till you get them filled."

"Ok thanks." The doctor shook my hand and Austin's hand and walked out the door. A few minutes later, the nurse came in, "I have something else for your pain, hun and some water." She pulled out another little vial from her pocket, scanned it, scanned my wrist. "What is that one?" I asked.

"This one is called 'Dilaudid'". She stuck a needle in the vial, pulled out some fluid and injected it into my port. She took her gloves off, threw them away and said, "I'll come back with your discharge papers." I was feeling the effect of this one expeditiously. "Hi" I said very loopily to Austin. He smiled and laughed a little. "How are you feeling babe?"

"I'm feeling good." I said lingering on the 'o'.

"You look like you are." The nurse came in and said, "On a scale of 1 to 10, what is your pain?"

"Umm 2 when I talk." I garbled

"And when you don't talk?"

"O" I giggled.

"Ok darling, it's time to go home tonight." She looked at Austin, handed him a handful of papers and told him, "If it's possible, she shouldn't be alone tonight. If she could stay at your house that would be a good idea." The nurse put on gloves, grabbed some gauze, a cotton ball, and some bandage tape. She removed my IV, and put a cotton ball on the pin mark, and bandaged it up.

"I'll take care of it." He claimed. I had fallen asleep by this point.

"She's going to be in and out for most of the night. If she wakes up in pain in the middle of the night, she can take one pill every 6 to 8 hours. You'll need to fill the script tomorrow. Any concerns, call us here at this number."

And she pointed to the number on the paper. "Got it," Austin replied.

CHAPTER 7

They wheeled me out and Austin hurried out before us and pulled my car around. He opened my door and I crawled into the passenger side. “Try to have a good night hon.” The nurse stated and shut my door. Austin jogged around the front and hopped in. “This is the first time I have driven a BMW before. It’s nice!!”

“It’s an M4. Thank you for driving me home.” I mumbled as I fell asleep again.

Once we got home, Austin pulled into the garage. He opened the house door and then the passenger side. I stepped out and he held my arm. I started to walk and he lifted me. “I can walk.” I protested.

“That’s alright, I got you.” He carried me into the house and walked me to my bedroom. He laid me on the bed and fluffed my pillows. “What time is it?” I was looking around the room. “For that matter, where is my phone, wallet?" I started to panic a little.

"I got them. They are still in the car. And it's 8:30."

"Hmm…K". I said with my eyes closed and my head propped up on the pillows. "I need to go shut the doors; I'll be back in." Austin started to leave the room and I swung my legs over the edge of the bed. "Where do you think you're going?" He returned next to my side.

"I have to pee. May I go pee please?" I ask.

"You think you can manage by yourself?" I think he was being concerned, but the medicine made it a little hard to know for sure.

"It's only twenty feet away. I think I can manage." He held my arm while I staggered up and to the bathroom. "I'll be right back." he said.

I wobbled back to the bedroom and Austin came in.

"Do you need me to change you for bed?" He said with a devilish grin.

"No, I think I'm just going to crash in this, well I might need help with my bra." He was more than happy to assist with the removal of my bra and might have got a quick show or feel, but I wasn't quite cognizant enough to know. I attempted to curl under the covers but was struggling so Austin came over and tucked me in. He sat next to me, "How's your ice? You need more?" I held my rectangular bag; it was still pretty solid. "No. I'm good, but I could use something to drink. I have a horrible cotton mouth."

"No problem, be back." He left to go get me some water. When he returned, I was starting to drift again. "Hey sweetie, here's your water. I'm sorry to wake you." I groggily lifted my head and took a big drink of water. Austin set the cup down next to me on my side table and sat back down.

"I want to say something OK?" I slurred.

"Anything."

"Please stay with me tonight."

"I'm not going anywhere. I already told my parents that the doc said you can't be left alone and I would crash on your couch." I attempted to smile, not sure if I did. I tapped the bed next to me. "No couch, here." A garbled sentence that sounded like a child statement.

"Anything you want." And he stood up, walked over to the other side of the bed. He took off his shoes, socks, shorts, and shirt, shut the overhead light off and crawled in next to me.

A sharp pulsating pain woke me and I noticed I was intertwined in arms. This felt nice. I tried to glance over without disturbing him. I just stared at him for a few, but between my bladder and my face, I needed to get up. I scooted softly out from under his arm and twisted from his leg. One leg on the floor, I now needed to maneuver the other. I balanced my foot on the floor and my hand on the side table and wiggled free. I quietly walked to the kitchen. The pills from E.R. were on the counter in a small yellow envelope with handwritten instructions,

Take 1 pill every 6 – 8 hrs.

I opened the envelope and there were 4 white mediums oval pills. I read the script, HYDROCODONE-ACETAMINOPHEN Generic: Norco. Good Lord! I will be loopy all week. I'll just take 3 Advil to start. I filled a glass of water and took the pills. I started the coffee and went to the bathroom. In the bathroom mirror my cheek bone was pretty swollen with a nasty 'goose egg', and a really nasty cut- scratch was peeking out behind the butterfly bandage. After I went pee, I quietly went back to the kitchen. The coffee was done, so I poured myself a cup. I added my 3 yellow packets and creamer. I was thinking that I better look at my schedule for the week because clients aren't going to want to meet with me, the 'cyclops'. I sat down at the table, pulled out my laptop which was leaning against the table chair and booted it up. Once it was up and running, I pulled up my calendar. I had a couple of meetings, but those could be rescheduled. No court times, and no traveling. Everything could be done from home. I opened my email up and shot the partners a note letting them know I would be working from the house;

Hey Guys,

I had a little accident on Saturday and I fractured my right cheekbone slightly. I will be working from the house for the rest of the week. I'll forward all calls to my cell and let my secretary know as well. Sorry for the inconvenience.

Ellie

P.S. I don't need a lawyer. LOL

I started to go over depositions and didn't feel like reading at the moment so I shut my laptop off, took my cup of coffee into the living room and sat on the couch. I didn't turn the TV on because I didn't want to wake Austin. I got up and got my cell which was next to the envelope on the counter. I sat back down and sent a text to Rick, "Hey – not mad- just FYI I have a fractured cheekbone. Seeing specialist. Calling for Dr. tomorrow. "

"Oh my God!!! I'm so sorry. Should have kept your right up huh?" Oh, he wants to be funny now???

"You're not going to sue me are you?"

"Shut up! Of course not, besides I think I signed something that says I can't. LOL"

"Hey, beautiful." I jumped.

"You startled me," I said, not realizing the vibration from my voice and movement from talking hurt.

"I'm sorry, didn't mean to. Why you up? You should be resting." He came over to me on the couch, sat down, and put his hand on my thigh. I looked at him and he kissed my left cheek softly. He was sitting in his underwear completely comfortable. Damn face injury, I could have fun with that if I wasn't hurt.

"Did I wake you up?"

"Nah., I rolled over and you weren't there."

"Would you like some coffee?" Then I paused, "Do you even like coffee?"

"Yes, and yes please." I went to stand up and get him a cup,

"No, you sit down. I'll do it. You need a refill?"

"I suppose, but no more. Not good for my face."

"What do you take with it?"

"3 yellow packets and a heaping spoon of creamer. Thank you."

"You left your ice pack in the room; you want me to get it?"

"No, I will go get it. Thank you." I watched him walk into the kitchen and I really wanted to follow and take advantage of my morning guest, damn face!

I stood up and went to the bedroom to get my ice pack and noticed he made the bed with my side folded down.

"Thank you for making the bed," I said when I returned to the living room. He put both mugs on the table next to the couch and sat down. I filled my ice pack with fresh ice and went to the couch. He was sitting long ways on the couch and reached up to me to sit between his legs mirroring him. I sat down and leaned against his chest. He pulled the blanket I had folded on the back over us and handed me my coffee mug. He sipped on his coffee and I mine.

"This is nice," I said.

"I agree. I could get used to this being my mornings."

I felt him put his mug down and then he leaned in started nibbling on my earlobe.

"MMM," I said, noticing that the pain wasn't as intense as this morning.

"Does this hurt?"

"No."

"How about this?" He slid his hand under my shirt and started to massage my breasts. I felt his erection grown beneath my tailbone. I turned around and placed my coffee mug on the table next to his. When I turned back, I slid over so I could have full access to his penis. I firmly, but gently, wrapped my fingers around his member and moved my fist up and down his shaft in a slow, steady motion. He leaned his head back on the pillow and closed his eyes. With my other hand, I rubbed his balls, softly rolling them in the palm of my hand. I used my forefinger and thumb around the base of his shaft and twisted gently. "Holy Shit Eli!!" he moaned. He started moving his hips to the rhythm of my strokes and was completely engrossed. It was so tempting not to straddle him, ride him hard and fast until we both finish with an orgasm. Man, I wanted him and I was wet and ready but decided to let him have all this enjoyment. As he got closer to release, I sped up my strokes and moved my other forefinger on the skin between his testicles and anus. "I don't think I can handle this intensity much more babe!!" He whimpered. "I'm going to cum!" As he started to release, I tugged slightly on his ball sack making him completely scrunch his eyes closed and hold his breath. I caught myself holding my breath too. When he finished, he exhaled and was panting heavily. He lifted his head and looked at me. I smiled. "Damn woman! You're going to kill me when you're 100%!" I giggled.

"I'll take it slow." I grinned. I got up and went into the bathroom, got a washcloth, ran it under warm water while washing my hands came back out and handed it to him. He cleaned himself up and slid up his underwear. He stood up, "whoa head rush." He laughed. Guess there's not a lot of blood up there!" I laughed.

"Do you need to carry you?"

"Um no. I got it. Speaking of which, you should be in bed resting."

"Yeah, that's not my style."

"I like your style so far, no I take that back, I LOVE your style! But you really need to try and heal so we can have more fun!" He had a point, this morning would have gone a lot different if it weren't for this stupid injury, but, then again, he wouldn't have spent the night, so....

"I have to get going." He said as slid his shirt and shorts on. Right as he popped his head through his tee shirt, the doorbell rang. He looked at me and I him, "I have no clue." I shrugged.

"Here, take the pillow and go throw it on the couch, make like you slept there." He grabbed a pillow off my bed and headed to the living room. I found my bra and a sweatshirt and pulled it on.

"Ouch, shit that hurt!" I thought as the collar brushed my face. I looked in the mirror, hair of a person that just got up – that'll work. Took his socks and shoes out to the living room and handed them to him. I spotted the two coffee mugs that indicated that we had been up awhile and scooted them into the kitchen. I quickly scuttled back in the living room, looked at Austin as an OK to open the door and proceeded to unlock the front door. A silhouette of a woman holding something was in the storm glass window. His mother SHIT!!! I unlocked the glass-windowed door and held it open for her to come in. "OH MY GOD Ellie!!!" She exclaimed.

"Austin said it was bad, but oh my God!" At least she saw this for herself which would void any thoughts of shenanigans. "I brought this soup over for you and wanted to see if there was anything I could do for you?" I took the large Tupperware container of soup from her and walked it to the kitchen.

"I don't think so. I can't thank you enough for 'lending' me Austin. He was such an unbelievable help yesterday, and so sweet to stay on my couch last night. In case I needed him."

"I was just heading out the door mom." He looked at her annoyed.

"That's fine. I honestly wasn't 'checking up on you', I did want to make sure Ellie didn't need anything."

She looked back at him as 'I'm the parent and will do what I want when it comes to my son!'

"Actually, there is something I could use." I looked at her to break the tension. Austin looked at me. "I am not supposed to drive until the swelling goes down, and I need my scripts filled. Austin is a minor -" indicating that I understood this point completely – "And cannot fill a narcotic. Would you be so kind when you have time today to run into town and get them filled for me?" I looked at Chelsea.

"Oh absolutely! Is there anything else I can pick up for you? Pudding, Jell-O, mashed potatoes?"

"All of those sound wonderful right now, let me look and see what I have here and I can send you a text if that's alright? I can write you a check or give you cash when I get out again, just let me know."

"Don't worry about that." She said.

"I have to get going mom, so I will see you guys later."

"Ok see you at home."

"Bye, thanks again," I stated like he just mowed my grass.

"No prob." When he went behind his mother, he blew me a kiss. I tried hard not to acknowledge it. I glanced at his mom, and she was looking at my scripts. Chelsea looked up at me motherly, "I feel so bad for you. Are you in a lot of pain?"

"A little. I was just coming out of the bathroom when you rang the bell. In fact, I didn't know Austin was still here. Little surprised by all accounts."

"Ok. I will let you get back to resting. I'll get these filled and someone will run them over later today." I was sincerely hoping for Austin, but couldn't quite 'read' Chelsea's behavior. Everything looked on the up and up -blanket disheveled on the couch and a pillow.

"If that's a problem, just leave them in my mailbox and I will go out later and pick them up."

"Oh no. No problem. Please let me know if you need anything else from the store. I can even make you some meals if it's easier for you."

"I appreciate it. I should be fine in a couple of days. Ice, medicine and rest. Doctors' orders." Chelsea turned and opened the front door, "I'll text you later in case you're sleeping."

"Thank you so much for all your help." I shut the door. I forgot to tell her my birthday so I picked up my phone to text her for the script. There was a text from Austin,

"Hey – I had a wonderful time this morning with you! You blow my mind!!! I can't imagine being with anyone else! PLEASE heal quickly!!! Call me if you need me." I smiled.

"I told your mom I was heading out of the bathroom when she rang the doorbell and didn't know you were still at the house. Thank you for staying last night. I really enjoyed this morning too! I told the partners at the firm that I will be working from home for the week. I am going to go take some good meds and ice my face. Talk later."

I almost forgot to text Chelsea, I texted her my address and birthday information and went to the living room got my ice pack, it was getting low, so I refilled it, took one Norco and made some toast. The toast wasn't so hard to chew, I was lucky. I went back to bed after I finished my toast.

I woke up to a buzzing vibration next to me. I grabbed my phone. I silenced it when I laid down. Nothing important on a Sunday let alone now. Five missed calls, Three from the partners, one from my dad and the most recent, Austin. Two texts. I opened up messenger,

"Hey, you sleeping?"

"Guess so...."

What time was it? 3:25- wow. Norco really knocked me out.... I listened to my messages, mainly 'get wells' from the partners offering help, my dad telling me to call home, don't do it enough, and Austin asking if he could come deliver my medication. When I fully digested my surroundings, I stood up and realized I was hungry. I wobbled out to the kitchen. I opened the fridge and took out the Tupperware container, chicken noodle. Not a huge fan, but I'm hungry. I put some in a bowl and heated it up. I picked up my phone and texted Austin,

"I'm awake now. Pretty groggy. Eating your mom's soup." A few seconds later he replied,

"You want company?"

"In a bit, when I finish, I need to take a shower -DESPERATELY! Give me an hour. "

"You need help with that shower?"

"Tempting. If my face wasn't jacked up possibly..." The thought was tempting if not for realistic reasons, I was pretty unstable on my feet right now due to the Norco.

"See you in an hour."

I finished the soup and headed for the shower. The water felt good on my body but when it touched the scratch it stung intensely. The pain reminded me that I needed to change the band-aid and the thought of that my stomach turn. The pain that was going to cause was not something I looked forward to. "Do I even have everything I need to change it?" I thought. Crap! I don't. I finished my shower dried off enough to text Austin;

"I forgot I need to change my band-aid. I don't have anything here to do that. Before you come over could you pick me up some butterfly band-aids and Neosporin please?"

"No problem. Are you finished with your shower now?"

"Yes. Anytime you want to stop by, front door open."

About a half-hour later the front doorbell rang. I was watching the news on the couch, why didn't he just come in? I got off the couch, walked to the door and opened it. Austin stood there with his hands full of…everything. He had a bouquet of flowers and a balloon, a couple of grocery bags, and a small pharmacy envelope bag. When I opened the door for him, I noticed a couple other flower arrangements on the front porch, must be from the partners.

"What do you have?" I inquired.

"Mom's been busy." He laughed.

"I guess so." I went outside and gathered the other flowers that were sent while I was sleeping. I went into the kitchen where he had set everything down. He turned to me and pulled me into a hug. He handed me his flowers, and looked at the others, "I guess not an original idea huh?" He shrugged.

"It's sweet, Thank you. I love the balloon." I kissed him on the cheek. "No other balloons? At least that's something. Who are all your admirers?"

"Partners I'm guessing. What all do you have?"

"Mom made you spaghetti, and mac and cheese. She put them in little containers – easy to eat or heat up or something. Here is the stuff for your face and here are your medications."

"Oh, my goodness, she *HAS* been busy. Thank you so much for doing this for me!"

"Isn't that what *boyfriends* do?" There was that word again, emphasized.

"Yes, I guess so." I smiled at him. "I do need to have you assist me with something though." He was putting away the containers and turned around. "Anything."

"It's going to show what an enormous baby I am." I shrank. He closed the refrigerator door and looked at me. "Can you help with my bandage please?" Again, my stomach flipped with the thought of the pain and fear of the cut splitting open.

"I'll do my best."

I finished unwrapping the flowers, found a vase for Austin's and when to the bathroom and grabbed some Q-tips. He joined me in the bathroom. He laid the Neosporin, band-aids on the counter along with small square gauze packages and rubbing alcohol.

"I got some gloves, just in case you needed help." He winked at me. I sat on the toilet lid and closed my eyes. I felt so sick!!! Austin touched my shoulder, "I will be as gentle as I can, but it's gonna hurt no matter what. I'm sorry." I nodded my head. He put gloves on and kissed the top of my head.

He peeled the original band-aid off as softly as possible but tears still streamed down my cheek. Once he got it off he soaked a gauze pad with alcohol and wiped around the gash. He dabbed the cut and I flinched. "Sorry babe, I know but we have to do this so it doesn't get infected."

"I know. Keep going."

Once he was satisfied that the wound was cleaned, he put some Neosporin on a Q-tip and rubbed it over the cut.

"Did it re-open?"

"Shh- a little, but you talking is only going to open it more." I heard him open the band-aid wrapper. "This is going to be painful; I have to apply pressure to get a good seal on the cut." I groaned as he applied the band-aid. When I heard him take his gloves off and start picking up the mess, I opened my eyes.

"Thank you." My head was starting to throb. "Did they give me anything for nausea?" I asked.

“Not sure. Why?”

“That was intense and I’m a little nauseous.” He helped me stand, walked me to the couch and sat me down. “I’ll take a look.” He stated. “This one says for nausea.”

“Ok, can you bring me that one and a Norco please?” He came in with a glass of water, one Norco, and one nausea pill.

“Thanks.” I took the pills and drank the water. “How are you going to the doctor tomorrow?

“I haven’t quite figured that one out yet. Guess I’ll see how it goes. I won’t drive if I am on anything. Don’t worry.” Austin got up went to the back room and came back with my ice pack. “You need to put this on.”

“Sorry. You know, you’re going to be a great doctor.” I said.

“Thanks. I hope so.” He covered me on the couch and we watched the news together. I woke up on the couch and it was dark outside. There was no Austin. I wonder what time he left? I wonder what time it was. I got off the couch and stretched. I looked at my phone 9:13. Wow. Again, out like a light. I had one message.

“Didn’t want to wake you to say bye. Hope you don’t mind, I shut the TV off. You can call if you want when you wake.”

I went into the kitchen and heated some spaghetti up. I dialed Austin,

“Hey there.” He answered

“Hi. I’m sorry I fell asleep.”

“No worries. I enjoyed watching you. I didn’t know if I should carry you to bed or not."

"I just woke up, so I guess I managed. I'm heating up some of your mom's spaghetti." The microwave beeped, so I held the cell with my shoulder.

"Ok, well I'll let you eat. Try and get a good night sleep. I'll turn my ringer up in case you need anything OK?"

"Thank you. Night." I hung up the phone and ate my dinner. This was nice not having to worry about feeding myself. After I ate, I returned to the couch and fell asleep watching a movie.

CHAPTER 8

I woke up sometime during the night and crawled into bed. When I work in the morning, I went and made coffee and dialed the doctor's office. I didn't even need to be seen, they just referred me to a specialist. They said the E.R. notes were already in the system and I just needed to make an appointment. I called the office of the specialist. I told the receptionist what happened and when and that the x-rays and report the E.R. was already in the system. She made an appointment that afternoon for 3:15. She said that way the doctor will have enough time to review the notes and go over my x-rays before I come in. I took a shower and some Tylenol. I was feeling more energetic probably due to less medication and all the sleep over the weekend. After my shower, I made a smoothie and went out for a walk. It was hard not to break into a run, but just the footsteps on the pavement hurt my face.

Only one time around. It was quiet with everyone at work and school.

Oh, school – I pulled out my cell phone and sent Austin a text,

"Hi. Sorry so late had a late start. Going to specialist at 3:15. Doing better. Thanks again for everything this weekend."

I finished my walk went in the house and started looking over files and paperwork on clients and before I knew it the clock read 2:30. I freshened up and headed to the specialist. When I sat in the car I had to readjust the seat. I remembered that I hadn't driven the car sense E.R. and Austin was the last person. The thought made me smile. The doctor wasn't that far away so I got there early enough to fill out my paperwork. The office was quaint, not overstated with calming pictures on the wall. There were a few other patients in the office waiting room. Two of them had eye patches on and another had a bandage on her face. It made me think if they were wondering about me and wanting to know if someone did this to me like I caught myself thinking about the girl sitting across from me. I looked at my phone to distract my thoughts and saw I missed a text,

"Hi. Glad UR feeling better. Heading to practice. Let me know what the Dr. says."

"Miss Baylor?" I looked up and there was a nurse standing in the doorway holding a clipboard.

"That's me." I stood up and walked to the door. I followed her to an examination room.

"Have a seat on the table, please.

Can you state your name and birthday?"

I told her my information. "Can you tell me how this happened? Are you in danger?"

Oh, good grief, not this again. I told her of the sparring match and that no, I was not in danger. "OK, the doctor will be in with you in a little bit. There is one ahead of you, but he's running on time."

"Thank you." As I waited I looked around the room, there were posters of cheeks, eye sockets, nasal bones, and pictures or before and after procedures. I wasn't nervous until I saw those. There was a large special machine in the corner and a counter with cabinets and sink, a glove dispenser and three boxes of gloves. There was a headband with a flashlight on it sitting on the counter, attached to the big machine. As I was looking at the door opened with a knock, "Miss. Baylor?"

"Hi." I reached my hand out to shake his. He had a folder in his hand. A nurse followed him in. She was carrying a laptop. She put it on the counter and started clicking on it. "I'm Dr. Hunter. Let's take a look, shall we?"

"Um OK," I stated nervously.

"I'm going to have to remove your bandage to get a better look at this laceration. I have reviewed the x-rays and will go over those in a few." The nurse was already pulling out gauze and cleaner. The doctor reached over and grabbed gloves and put them on. He started to remove the bandage and I whimpered.

"A little sensitive?"

"Just a little."

"Did the E.R. clean this up?"

"No. A friend of mine did." Why?

"They did a nice job." I felt the removal of the final stick of the band-aid. Then he pressed around the lump. He was telling the nurse medical notes and I really wasn't paying attention to his words rather the pain. I was closing my eyes trying to focus on my breathing. There was that nausea again. "Well if you keep this clean like your friend did, you should heal without a scar." Well, that was good news although the scar might have made me look tougher in court. He applied something cool and wet and my senses told me it was rubbing alcohol, the coolness made me flinch. "Almost done." He said. He applied an ointment and put on another butterfly band-aid. He put it on a little tighter than Austin.

"Ooo that's a little tighter," I said.

"Maybe a bit, but it will heal tighter – less chance of a scar. When the time comes and you don't need the band-aid, you will need to continue to put on ointment to ensure a flawless healing."

"How long until I won't need the band-aid?"

"That depends on you when you clean it you will see how it's closing. I would say when it starts looking more like a scratch and not so much tiger gash. Also, the swelling needs to come down a bit so it doesn't split open. Which brings me to that, if it does split and the butterfly isn't holding, you will need to come back and see me and I will surgically glue it closed. I don't like do that because the wound can't heal as well. So, let's hope that's not our option." He looked at me seriously.

"I know, no roughhousing or working out etc.," I said.

"Exactly. Even down to jogging or heavy walking. The blood pumping too much will cause it to split. Understand.?"

"Yes. For how long?"

"Right now, I would say hold off for at least 4 weeks. I'll evaluate on your next visit." Holy shit four weeks?!!! I thought.

"Now, I've looked at your x-ray," and as on cue, the nurse pulled it up on the laptop. The doctor pulled out a pointer from his pocket, "See here." He pointed to a 'hair looking' mark on the screen. "Here is the fracture, but it isn't a complete one meaning it doesn't go all the way through the bone where the Anterior Maxillary Wall would cave in due to lack of support. It's almost a surface fracture. You were very lucky. You will not need surgery and should heal in about 4 weeks as well. Again, rigorous movements might push the fracture, so no activity. Unless you really want me to put a splint up your nose to support the bone?" OK, I got it. No gym or anything else. Four weeks isn't so bad and the diagnosis is pretty mild, I'll take it.

"OK, I promise. I won't do anything until you give me the green light. When can I go back to work?"

"That depends on you if you are still taking the Norco, then NO driving. If you are feeling well enough, a week."

"Sounds good."

"OK, follow up four weeks, keep icing all day if you can, 15 minutes on 30 off. That will help it heal faster if you can bring the lump down. You can then take the band-aid off. You will need to change the band-aid about ever two days."

"Thanks, doctor. See you in four weeks." He shook my hand and walked out the door and the nurse smiled at me, handed me some papers, and walked out behind him. I checked out at reception and headed home. As I pulled into the driveway, I noticed no car. I looked at the dash and saw that it was only 4:33, he would be at practice until at least 6:30. I went into the house, sat down at my computer and ran through files. I read emails and saw that they wanted me back out to New York on Monday. Hey, give me an exact week people, good grief. My stomach growling told me to pay attention to the time and it was 7:43. I grabbed one of Chelsea's prepared meals and heated it up. That's odd. Not anything from Austin. I thought he would have at least asked how the doctor went… being that we didn't know if I was going to have my face reconstructed or not… I thought some fresh air would do me good so I grabbed my coat, garage door opener, cell, headphones. I noticed a few extra cars across the street and some guys throwing a football in the backyard. I put on my headphones, turned on my cell and put my 'guy hating' songs on. Looks like I would need them with the extra estrogen in the yard. Why does this piss me off so much? I have to be careful because too much on my face won't do me any good. I put the music pretty loud so if anyone was calling me, I wouldn't hear it. But then why would he? I'm the neighbor. He played his part – didn't even glance my way. I muted my music and I heard giggles and shouts, tackles and boy heckling. I tried to focus on the sun setting and taking in the brisk air. I needed to stop getting lost in this boy. I am a grown woman and up until two months ago didn't even bat an eye at this behavior. I walked back in the house, closing the garage behind me with all the cars still across the street. It was all I could do to not stare out the window to see when they leave. Normally, I would go to the gym – can't do that. I'm not used to be housebound so to speak. I decided a hot bath and a glass of wine would be a way to relax. I made a hot steamy bubble bath, poured a glass and lost myself in the bubbles. After my bath, I changed for bed. Still nothing from Austin. Well, screw that! I shut my phone off and crawled into bed.

I hadn't taken any Norco for two days so I decided this morning I would go into the office. I couldn't stand being in the house any longer. It was causing me to act like a stupid teenager. It felt good to get dressed up again and go back to my normal routine, minus the run. I did a quick walk on the treadmill. Once at the office I dove right into my files and legal mergers. Knowing that I was returning to New York I needed to get Mia's affairs in order. He must have made a decision about running or purchased a new business. I checked my phone, still nothing from Austin. This was just odd. I know he was ok; I saw him last night. I started to wonder if he's pissed about something? Then I started to panic, what if his mom took his cell…What if she read the messages…. OH SHIT! I sent him a text,

"Hey – haven't heard from you. What's up?"

A few minutes later he replied,

"Goes both ways." What the hell?

"I'm sorry. Is there something bothering you?" Now, I'm getting pissed and concerned.

"No. Just saying you haven't said anything else either."

"Ok – this is a conversation that is too big for texting. You need to call me when you have a minute. I'll answer even if I'm in a meeting."

"Meeting? Where are you?"

"I'm at work."

"You're not supposed to be at work until next Monday."

"Again – call."

I Looked at my cell, I was fuming. 9:46. Great way to start the morning. I tapped my pen on the desk. I'll do what the fuck I want! Why am I at work? Ugh, what I wouldn't give to go kick the shit out of the heavy bag- stupid face! I called Mia in New York to confirm my arrival.

"Hey Mr. Man, couldn't live without me?"

"Hi, beautiful! I requested you to come out for a meeting next week. Your partners said that you were out of the office for the week. What's going on? You never take time off."

"I had an accident, that's why I was calling you."

"An accident, oh my God Eli, are you OK?"

"I'll be fine. I was sparring with my coach and I wasn't focused and I missed a block. I have a pretty banged up cheek but met with the surgeon and I will heal without problems – if I behave."

"Behave – yeah that's not you. I'm glad to hear it's not that serious."

"I don't look the best; my right side is really bruised and I still have quite the goose egg and a bandage that takes up half my face holding a gash together. I don't know if you want me to meet with your team. I'm kind of scary right now."

"Your brain still works, right?"

"Never shut that off."

"We all have accidents; have you been cleared to fly?" I never thought about that.

"I will have to check with Dr. Hunter. I'm not allowed to do a lot at the moment. To be quite honest, I'm not even supposed to be at the office."

"Ellie, you need to go home and relax – go do something to relax and heal."

"Let me call the surgeon and I will get back to you on the flight."

"Sounds good! GO RELAX!"

"Not my style Mia- that's why I'm the best. And that's why you love me!"

"You got that one girl! Call me back."

"Sure thing."

I decided to book a spa day for the rest of the afternoon. Hair, massage, nails, the works. I was packing up my files and closing down my laptop when my phone buzzed. "AUSTIN'

"Hello."

"What are you doing at work Eli?"

"Why hello to you too. I couldn't stay in the house and do nothing all day!"

"Nothing – try healing."

"What is your problem?"

"I'm not happy that you aren't doing what you are supposed to be doing. The doctor told you to rest and heal."

"How would you know what the doctor said, you haven't called to find out anything that the surgeon said."

"Shit – I'm sorry Eli. You're right. I have been so busy with the coach pushing for the game and tons of school work. I've been so tired…"

"Yeah, I saw how busy and tired you were last night."

"Are you pissed that I had friends over?"

"No, but I was proving my point that you had time for that, but not the time to send a text or call to see what the doctor said."

"Again, I'm sorry. I wasn't being considerate. What did the doc say?"

I was so hot, I wasn't even sure that I wanted to tell him, but knowing he had limited time I should either end the conversation or spit it out.

"I don't need surgery."

"That's great! How long till it heals?"

"Everyone is different, but four weeks at least. And no grueling activities."

"Hey – I got to run to class, I'm sorry again. Can I call you later?"

"That's fine. I'm sorry too. Just don't do well being confined. This stupid accident is not allowing me to be uninhibited. Have a good day."

I hung up I felt a little better, but still coming down from the argument. When I fight in court, it's not emotional, I'm not connected, it's a job – this – this just sucks! I finished packing up my things and headed for the salon.

I arrived at the salon at 12:59.

"Good afternoon, Miss Baylor."

"Hello. I'm here for a half day of relaxation."

"It's good to see you. Here is your paper, this has the itinerary of where and when you will be seen. Enjoy!" A very muscular man in a tight tee shirt and scrubs came over to me, smiled a perfect white tooth smile, and said, "Hi, Miss. Baylor?"

"Ellie, please."

"Ellie, if you'll follow me. I'm John. I'll be your masseuse today." I followed John into a very dim lit room. There was a table bed draped in a sheet and incents on a stand in the corner. Very soft meditation music was playing.

"That's quite an injury on your face, I assume you can't lay face down?" Shit – I didn't think about that.

"Sorry, no. I didn't even think about that."

"No problem, I can work around it. No facial either then?" Double shit! What the hell was I thinking? I rolled my eyes internally.

"No. Sorry. I guess my brain isn't quite working today."

"It's no biggie. I can do wonders everywhere else." He smiled. And why am I in this relationship when I am sure I could completely get this guy unless he is gay… John handed me a robe and told me to change. Handed me a cloth bag for my belongings. "I need you to undress. You may leave your underwear on if you're more comfortable, but everything else off. Then climb under the sheets. Lay on your back. I have a rule. Cell phones OFF. Not on silent. No business in here. I want you to forget your life and focus completely on me. I'll be back in in a moment." He smiled.

I bet he could – I bet he's amazing in bed! I did as he told me. Shut my phone off and undressed, leaving my underwear on. I placed everything in the bag and set it aside placing in in the corner, out of his way. I crawled under the sheets and laid on my back, it was warm from a heating pad. The table bed was soft but firm. I pulled the sheet and blanket up past my breasts, almost to my neck. He knocked on the door and I told him to come in.

"Are you ready?"

"Yes. Make me forget my life."

CHAPTER 9

"I'll do my best. I'm going to raise the headrest for you because I don't want to much pressure on your face." He lifted the 'U' shaped headrest and immediately the blood that was rushing calmed down and the intensity slowed.

"Now close your eyes, and just try to feel with ALL your senses where my hands are and how they are loosening your muscles." Damn this guy was good! I heard him walk away and the sound of massage oil being rubbed between his hands. I smelled the eucalyptus and mint combination. I felt his warm hands start at my collarbone. His touch was gentle at first but growing firmer as he pressed. He did a circular pattern working on my upper chest. His fingers were on my chest while his thumbs started on my front shoulders, then his hand methodically moved to the right shoulder. His thumbs worked up my neck, while his hands worked on my shoulder. Then down my arm, working on my bicep and elbow, forearm, wrist, and palm. He turned my palm upright facing the ceiling and dug his nail in a massaging way. Jesus! I could completely lose myself in this guy! Then I had a tinge of regret because I was starting to care for Austin and having these thoughts didn't feel right. "Stop." He stated.

He snapped me out of my thoughts, "I'm sorry, stop what?"

"Whatever thought just came in your head- stop thinking about it." Crap he's really good.

"Sorry."

He continued he was now intertwining my fingers with his. They were slippery and he was tugging on them, pulling the blood down to the tips of my fingers. He let go and was pulling from the wrist down to the tips while kneading in a circular manner. Who knew that just rubbing a hand would feel so awesome. I tried to memorize what he was doing to me, so I could replicate this on Austin. I'm sure he would enjoy this after a football game or practice. 'Buy massage oil' I told myself as a personal checklist. He then worked his way back up my arm and back to my chest, this time going a little further south just to the edge of my breasts. Oh, I would let him massage those if he only asked. He didn't. He moved on repeating the right arm to the left arm. When he finished, he pulled the blanket and sheet up under my chin and tucked it in, then set a weighted scented neck rest thing on top. It was warmed as well and smelled of lavender. I heard him pause again and apply more massage oil between his hands. He cornered the blanket and sheet and started on my right foot. He rubbed the circle pattern at my heal and straight up my arch. It tickled a little, I tried hard not to squirm. He then branched out at the base of my toes, then similar to my fingers rubbed each individual toe pulling blood to the surface. Damn that felt good. I could let him do just this all day long! He worked his way up my leg by starting at the ankle and going to the calf, knee, thigh, and then holy shit… upper thigh! How far was he going? I tried to control my breathing and relax. As I did, he returned to my lower calf and back down. He repeated this with my left side. "Normally, I would turn you over, but because of your injury, I am going to move you a special chair." He demonstrated how I was to sit in it and he instructed me to wrap just the sheet around me towards the back. He left the room. I stood up, and wrapped the sheet around my front as instructed. I straddled the chair with my chin resting on a facial rest. He knocked again on the door. I said to come in. He walked over to me and took the sheet and tied the corners together. I felt better not being so exposed. I heard him get oil and rub his hands together. He started on my shoulders and down my arms again. He lifted them individually and placed them on the facial rest. They were so heavy; I wasn't sure I could hold them up. Then, he started working down my backbone. He concentrated on my shoulder blades then further down. When he was finished, I wasn't quite convinced that I could even stand up. He placed a bottle of water on the side table next to the door. "Please take your time getting up. Your muscles are relaxed and I really moved you around today, so you need to finish this water. I'll be outside." I heard him leave. I really didn't want to move… but onto the next stop. I got up, found my clothes along with my bearings, and got dressed. I grabbed my water and put the sheet on the table bed. I opened the door and he was standing there. "How you doing?"

"Oh - I'm good. Just wondering how many people fall in love with you on a daily basis?"

He smiled. "I get that a lot." He looked at my slip of paper, it says manicure next. He started walking and I followed him. He introduced me to a very up kept woman. "It was nice meeting you, thank you for letting me work on you today. I hope your face feels better soon."

"Thank you for working on me John!" I smiled.

"Hello, I'm Keisha"

"Hello."

"What are you thinking of doing today?"

"I was just thinking of a manicure, but John did such an amazing job, I feel so pretty, I'm thinking a short French full-set and matching toes." I wiggled my feet under the desk, where she couldn't even see.

"Sounds good." She pulled out her supplies and started measuring artificial nails to my nails. Then she buffed and sanded my nails down. She wiped them down with some alcohol and applied them with glue. When she was finished, she looked at me, held up my hands and said, "You like this length?" and giggled.

"Not unless I want to kill someone." I giggled back.

She took out scissors and cut them down. I pointed with my other finger to where I would like it filed to. "Oh, really short?" she said.

"Yes, please. I'm a lawyer, and I can't have anything too flashy."

"No problem." She took a brand-new file from a package from her drawer and filed them to my desired length. She then took a toothbrush and brushed all the dust off. She wiped them down again with alcohol and put on the acrylic gel. "I would like them really thin, please. I can't type if they are too thick."

She finished applying the gel on each finger and started filing and sanding again. When she was finished, she said, "Go wash your hands over there, hon."

I got up and washed them really well using a nail brush that was in a glass of blue fluid. I returned to my seat. "Do you want airbrush French or hand painted? Both last about the same time depending on how hard you are on your hands."

"Umm, I was thinking something like this." And I pointed to a poster on her wall. "Ultra-thin. OK. Before I begin do you want to flip through this book and look for any designs? Maybe for one or two of your fingers?" I looked at the book and there were tons of designs. I picked a butterfly design and a lace for another. She took out a stencil and a canister, airbrush I concluded. She sprayed the two designs, the butterfly one on my right ring finger, and the lace on the other ring finger. She then sprayed out the remaining white onto a towel. She added another color to the canister and sprayed on the towel until a light pink came out. She took the butterfly stencil and reapplied it, and then made a thin layer of pink shadowing the white. Wow, that was cool. She then took out some white paint and did a fine stipe at the tip of my nail. "I have a little extra surprise. – hang on." She reached into her drawer to the left and pulled out a segregated box. She then pulled out some tweezers. She reached into the box and got a tiny little clear gem. She took my left ring finger, applied a dot of glue in the middle of the butterfly and put the gem on the dot. "Just a little glitter." I liked it a lot. Who would have thought a silly little gem would make you feel so giddy? She then took clear polish and coated all my fingers. She made me sit under an ultra-blue light for fifteen minutes. When my little light went off, she rubbed each finger to make sure they were dry. She handed me her card and said, "If you break one or need repair, please only see me. I won't charge you to fix it ok?"

"Oh my God they are beautiful!! I won't ever go anywhere else! Thank you SOOOO much." I gave her a hug. What's with me? I'm not a hugger. "Your slip says hair next!! Follow me." I followed her to another room with a bunch of chairs facing mirrors. Keisha introduced me to the man standing at a chair. "This is Ramone."

"Hello. Thank you again, Keisha."

"You are more than welcome. See you soon."

"Hello Ellie girl!" he said excitedly while looking at my paper.

"Hello."

"What gorgeous hair you have. What an honor to be able to work on you!!!" I giggled.

"I was thinking of some highlights."

"OHH GIRL, are you open to things?" He said clapping his hands like an animated child.

"Some, but I am a lawyer and can't be too reckless."

"So, what do you think about a very light blonde and a very low light copper?"

"That sounds nice," I said calmly. "I used to have the thought that it was just hair and it will grow back, but I can't do that anymore."

"I will not do anything to harm your career. Are we cutting it today?"

"Just a trim, please. I like the length. But please be careful when you wash me, my face." I pointed to my face.

"Oh, honey. It will be like angels are washing your hair!" He turned on his heel and sauntered away. When he returned, he had two plastic bowls with black handles sticking out of each one. He placed them on the counter in front of me. He wheeled around a cart and grabbed a plastic cape and a towel. He wrapped the towel gently around my neck, followed by the cape. "Before we begin, would you like a glass of wine?"

"Wine?"

"Yes darling, we have white or red." He smiled enchanted.

"Do you have a Moscato?" I cringed.

"You don't need to be cringing. Of course, we do. I'll be right back!" He walked back and handed me a chilled glass of pinkish-gold liquid. I sipped it. "OOO that's good," I told him. I held the glass under the cape and he started in with the color and foils. When he was done I looked like I could pick up a television channel. "Normally I would have to sit under the heater, but I think the heat would hurt your face so, I will have Keisha work on your toesies!!" I completely forgot about my toes! I was so impressed with my fingers, that I just forgot. "Fine by me!" I stated. Ramone walked me over to the foot soaking tub and helped me in the oversized chair. I placed my feet on the outside waiting for Keisha to fill it up. "Welcome back, you didn't think I forgot about those toes, did you?"

"I did!" I laughed.

"You have a great laugh. You should do it more often." She stated.

"Thank you." I smiled embarrassedly. She put some oils and salts in the basin while it filled. It was all bubbly and smelled like Lilly of the Valley.

"Now all full, soak your feet and sip on the wine and forget about everything! I'll be back in a few." She dimmed the lights, put on calming instrumental music and left. I can completely understand why celebrities do this; this treatment is unbelievable! I had my eyes shut and head against the padded chair, she came in. She didn't turn the lights back up but instead used a lamp over my feet that was only bright to her work area. She did slight massage, and then callous remover and shaped my toenails and when she was done with one foot, she placed it back in the soothing water and did the other. When she was all done, she drained the basin, she put a towel on the edge and I put my feet on it. She dabbed the water off with the towel. She then grabbed some awesome smelling lotion and massaged each foot, but not in as much detail as John. She turned to her right and grabbed a small bottle of pink nail polish. She did one coat on my left foot then my right and repeated it. Then she took the white polish and did the small line that matched my fingers. A final clear coat and under the light. Right as the blue light went off, Ramone came in, pulled at a foil and said, “Magnifique!” Keisha slipped on some foamy slippers and Ramone helped me out of the chair. “Darling, you look divine!!!” He stated. I giggle again. The one glass of wine and all of this, ‘I’m the most important person in the world’ treatment had me absolutely elated.

We returned to the hair salon, and Ramone walked me to the wash chair. I saw that he padded the side of the bowl and had a girl standing next to the sink. “This is Clarissa. She is going to hold your head so your face doesn’t have too much pressure. Got it? Now I mean, I want you to put the complete weight of your head in her hands.... It may get heavier with the water. She is a ‘big girl’ and can handle it! Understand sister-girl?” I giggled again.

“Yes, I understand.” I sat in the chair, and Ramone adjusted the towel under my neck. Clarissa held my head immediately. I found it difficult to release control at first, but as the warm water made my head heavier, I gave in. He rinsed the color, shampooed, and conditioned. “This conditioner has to sit for five minututos. Just try and relax Clarissa’s got you, honey.” That was awkward. Sitting for five minutes with this girl holding my head. She really didn’t look like she minded at all. Five minutes later, Ramone came back, rinsed lightly the conditioner out. He put a towel on my head and Clarissa helped me raise my head. Ramone walked me to his styling chair and I sat down. I had finished my wine so I handed him my glass. He combed out my hair and started cutting. I loved the color already even though it was still very wet. He put a holding product in his hands, rubbed them around and applied it to my hair. He trimmed my hair but not too short. I had a slight natural curl so he parted to the left so my bangs swooped down across my eyebrow and almost over my bruise. Ramone dry-crunched it instead of rolling it so the curl was more pronounced. When he was done, I couldn’t believe how stunning my hair was! I felt like an entirely different woman! “You are now my Madonna!!” he boasted!! I blushed, which hurt and brought me back to my face. “Thank you so much!!!” I kissed both cheeks and headed for the front. At the front, I put on my shoes and went to the counter to pay my tab. I didn’t care how much this cost today this was so worth it. As I was finishing checking out I asked for the owner. The receptionist looked at me surprised. “Um sure Ma’am, I’ll be right back.” I finished separating the tips out and even gave one to Clarissa when I heard, “Hello Miss Baylor. My name is

André. How may I assist you today?" A man in a dark pin-striped suit with a neon pink tie and leather loafers stood in front of me.

"Can we please speak in your office?"

"Absolutely, please this way." He gestured and I followed his lead.

"Please, have a seat." And he waved to a leather high back chair across from his desk. He sat at his desk and folded his hands on top.

"I wanted to inform you that today has been one of the most wonderful days I have ever had." He smiled a smile of relief.

"I am a partner at Martin-Ross and Associates. I have a lot of clients and I would like to make you our exclusive spa. That means, send all of our clients that come in for business meetings a wonderfully relaxing environment as I experienced this afternoon."

"Oh - my goodness," he said. "That would be fantastic!"

"I only have one stipulation." He looked concerned.

"I wanted each and every client to receive the exact treatment, if not better if that's even possible." He looked relieved again. "I will draw up the contract so nothing is out of place and what is expected for cost and so on."

"That sounds excellent. I look forward to your papers and working with you in the future." I stood, shook his hand and headed for the door. Before I left his office, I took some of his business cards. When I returned to the lobby, I asked the receptionist if I could take some pamphlets. She hurried to the back and brought some up to me. She smiled and I told her, "I look

forward to seeing you soon." She looked puzzled. I turned and headed for my car. I rifled through my purse to get my cell, took my keys and unlocked the door. I turned my cell on in the car and saw that it was 5:03. I felt so good and wanted to do something nice for someone else that I had a great idea. My phone lit up with messages and emails, texts and news alerts. I now get why there is a 'shut your phone – life off' policy. I headed towards home. I'll take care of those later. When I pulled on the street I was in luck, no car. I quickly went into the house and changed into tight jeans and a mid-rise sweater with a black bra. I was still sticky from the massage oil, but I smelled remarkable. I put on my black flats, grabbed the empty food containers that I had washed and headed across the street. When I rang the doorbell, Max answered the door. His jaw dropped. "Hi Max, is your mom home?"
He sheepishly backed up and waved to his mom to come from the kitchen table.

"Hey, how are you? Come in."

"Is this a good time?

"Oh yes, please." She held the door for me and I walked through. "I wanted to return these too you. I still have a few more at the house."

"You didn't need to rush. You look fantastic!" she took the empty containers to the kitchen counter.

"Thanks, I spent the day at the spa." I puckered my lips and looked very proud of myself. I didn't want to tell her I was tired of her son's shit and he made me pamper myself to get him off my mind. That was the real reason I went.

"Would you like a glass of wine?"

"That sounds wonderful"

"I love your hair. It's so…so… just lovely." And she flicked it lightly with her fingers. "How is your face feeling? Do you need surgery?"

"No actually in about four weeks I have another check-up and should be good."

"That's wonderful." Chelsea smiled and indicated white or red bottle. "White please."

I told Chelsea about the day at the spa and what the surgeon said,

"I really can't thank you and Austin for everything that you did. I would really like to do something in return so, and you can't say no, - at least to the one thing." She looked confused. "I have an all-expenses paid for the full 'royal' treatment at the spa I attended today." She dropped her jaw. "What!? No - you didn't!! I can't accept that; I just made you spaghetti!"

"Well, it was more to me than just spaghetti and I want you to enjoy yourself as much as I did today! I really loved it and I would also like to loan my BMW to Austin for his dance on Saturday. It's the homecoming, right?"

"Right. Are you sure? Lending that car to a 17-year-old boy?"

"He took such good care of me at the hospital and home, I know he'll be just fine with my car. Would it be alright with you and your husband If I lent him my car?"

"I would have to ask Austin, but I'm sure he will be delighted.

Thank you for all your generosity."

"You are more than welcome. I'll get it detailed and have it delivered Saturday by 2:00 p.m.?"

"That's great. I know they are doing picture out front here around 4, then heading to dinner and then the dance." *They*, that word pissed me off, but I tried to hide it.

"Good wine," I said.

"Thank you." We continued to talk about generalities, I tried to focus on her job and life stalling until Austin came home. On my second glass of wine, the kitchen door opened and Austin came through the door. He saw me and stopped dead in his tracks. I smiled at him.

"Hi, honey. How was practice?" Chelsea said as she turned to greet him. He walked to his mom gave her a kiss on the head and stared at me the entire time. "Yeah, you won't win with me Mr." I thought while I smiled and said "Hello."

"Ellie came by to say hi," Chelsea announced.

"I see that." He winked at me because he was standing behind his mom. "I'm going to jump in the shower, can you hang out for a second longer?"

"Sure, your mom just poured me a second glass of wine."

"Second? Nice." He hurried into the shower and Chelsea and I continued to talk about life. A few minutes later Austin appeared in only shorts up to his pelvis, hanging off his hips, showing his very scalped abs – from lower to upper. He was not playing fair. He still had beads of water on his chest from his shower. The water was rippling down each defined ab. His hair was tousled and wet and he was drying it with a towel. He came over to the table and sat down at the end, between me and Chelsea. He put something on and he smelled incredible.

I was going to lose it at any moment. With the spa – and - wine and - now this show, I completely forgot I was pissed.

"Ellie has a surprise for you," Chelsea said.

"Does she now?" he replied as he rubbed his foot up against my leg.

"Um yeah, I guess." I was having a horrible time focusing. Get it together Eli!!! "Because you were so kind to me and helpful during my ordeal, I would like you to use my car for the dance."

"You're kidding me!?" He sounded shocked.

"No. Not kidding. I'll have it detailed and delivered by two. Will that be an OK time?"

"Oh my God! That's amazing! Thank you!"

"Now Austin" His mother interjected, "You have to be very careful with Ellie's car, nothing stupid."

"Right mom, I'm going to enter a drag race." He rolled his eyes. "How's the face feeling?" Right now, not much, I thought, as I was working on my third glass of wine with hardly any food in me.

"I guess ok. The surgeon said four weeks and I'll be good to go if I 'behave'."

"That's cool. Well, you best behave then." And he kept rubbing my leg. I couldn't stop him because it would be obvious, so I just sat there and 'took it'.

I had finished my glass of wine, "I should be going. I'm sure you guys have a lot of stuff to do." I stood to leave and could totally feel the effects of the wine. Woa boy! Good thing it's a short walk.

"I'll walk you out, let me grab a shirt." He jumped up and ran down the hallway.

"I can't thank you enough," I told Chelsea as I gave her a friendly hug goodbye. Chelsea led me through the kitchen, and by the time I got to the door, Austin was there wearing a hoodie.

"Here, just go through the garage, a little shorter…" She stated.

"Thank you."

"No. Thank you for your very generous gifts." Austin picked up on the 'fts' and looked at his mom confused. She waved him off and he opened the door for me and I walked through. The Autumn season caused the sunset to arrive earlier and it was almost dark. We walked through the side door and Austin pushed me up against the garage side. "Easy!" I said. "Watch the face buddy!" He started kissing my neck with little nibbles in between breaths.

"You smell mind-boggling! I am doing everything in my being not to take you right here, right now!" He was now in my left earlobe and fully holding my breasts under my sweater where he pulled the cups of my bra down.

"If you didn't have such tight ass jeans on, I'd make you cum in my hand again!"

"You talking like that, I might just anyway," I said winded. I grabbed his face and put it on mine and started kissing him hard and wanted. He pulled back and looked at me, "Doesn't this hurt?"

"After three glasses of wine, not really." I smiled. He continued to rub my nipples vigorously and I caressed his rippling chest and kneaded my finger through his chest hair. I was fully pinned by his weight against the garage and he was rubbing his erection up against me. I reached around to his ass and grabbed it and pulled it towards me harder and he continued to pulsate my pelvis. He picked me up, I wrapped my legs around him and he laid me on the ground.

"Here." I rolled over on top of him and I started riding him, rubbing my vagina up and down his very erect penis. He took my hips in his hands and pressed me harder into him. I steadied my hands on his chest. I bent over and kissed him, pressing my lips to his, opening his mouth wider and kissing him meaningfully. He thrust a couple of hard thrusts and let out a groan-depleted noise and froze. Apparently, he had just cum. "See, tight jeans are good for something," I said.

"I guess I'm going to need another shower." He laughed. I stood up, still feeling the effects of the wine. "I missed you," I said.

" I can't even tell you how bad I want to spend every minute of every day with you." I kissed him and ran my fingers through his damp hair. Kissing did hurt, but I wasn't going to give into the pain. He held me tight, "I don't want to let go, but I have to go inside."

"I know." I sighed.

"Thanks for the car. That was very nice of you."

"I've been told I'm a nice very nice person," I said sarcastically. He kissed me once more, "Very nice." And he let go.

"I like your hair by the way. Looks sexy, not that you can get any sexier." He grinned.

"Oh- yes, I can! I have this little black number; black sheer lace bra that barely covers my nipples, with straps that cross here and here" I pointed from my shoulder to my breast and across the other side. "A black sheer lace garter belt, and matching panties that has a thong back, and straps the cross my waist. The thigh high stockings attached to the garter. Maybe I'll show you for your birthday?" I smiled.

"You are killing me! Mentally killing me!"

"I know. Give you something to think about when I'm not around."

"Oh - you give me plenty to think about. Come here." He pulled me in for another kiss and I felt his large penis erected again. "You have to get in. I'll talk to you later. Night."

"Night." I turned and headed to my house.

CHAPTER 10

When I got home, I sent him a text,

"Did you have any explaining to do when you got in? LOL"

"No. No one was around. Gotta take another shower. Talk later."

I changed for bed, I had a long day, a relaxing day, but long. My face hurt a little as well. As I laid in bed I thought about the dance. I decided to go to New York early. I picked up my cell,

"Call me when you are out of the shower."

I waited in bed and a few minutes later my cell rang. "Hi," I answered.

"Hello. Miss me already?"

"Yes. But that's not why I wanted you to call. Have you taken your shower yet?"

"Why, you want me to do something kinky to myself?" He laughed.

"What? – NO! I wanted to talk to about something serious."

"Um Ok… I thought we just had a good time. What's up?"

"Why do you always jump to that? I loved our time together just now. I will let you know when I am pissed got it?"

"OK. Go ahead."

"So, I was thinking. I really, *really* don't want to be around Saturday. I am going to New York early. I might leave Thursday or Friday."

"What? Why?" He sounded wounded.

"I really can't see this part of your life. I hope you can understand. I know I have your heart, but in the same, I have your heart, you will be posing with a girl who has feelings for you. She will be hanging on you and looking hot because let's be honest, she is, and your family with be there taking pictures and it's just a really uncomfortable situation for me. Do you understand?"

"Yeah, I get it." He still sounded hurt. What was I going to do? I was the neighbor and coming over to watch would not only drive me literally insane, it would just be weird.

"How would you feel if you walked past the TV and saw me decked out in one of my hottest outfits draped on the arm of a hot looking guy at a charity event?" …It could happen…it has in past. I failed to mention that part.

"You're right. I would absolutely hate it and it would enrage me."

"I will still have my car detailed and delivered. I will just have Mia send a car to pick me up. I take his private jet to New York anyway. No big deal."

"Wow, nice a private jet? Who is this guy?"

"Shoe on the other foot now? He's a client, he's also old enough to be my grandfather and treats me as such. No chance of romance there, besides his wife wouldn't like it very much. Also, no pictures of Saturday either."

"I understand. I'm beat. I need to get to bed." He sounded tired.

"I wear you out that easily? Or are you just trying to get off the phone with me?" I giggled.

"No babe. I am just tired from practice. Really. We're good. Night."

I hung up the phone, feeling uneasy about the situation, however, I fell asleep.

The following morning, I did almost my normal routine, but instead of a run, I did a casual walk. As I finished coming back to my house Austin was just leaving for school. He ran over to me,

"Good morning beautiful."

"Not so much right now. I'm gross." And I was, I was sweaty and a headband. "You always look hot to me!" He looked around and gave me a quick but fiery kiss that shot straight down to my vagina. How does he do that?

"I'll be thinking of you today and teasing your nipples with my teeth!" he smiled.

"That's nice. Get a hardon right before you have to go drive your brother to school. You're not right!" I laughed.

"Baby, I'm right in all the wrong ways!!"

"You don't need to remind me of that! Have a good day."

"You too!" he turned around and jotted back to his car. By

that time his brother was standing next to the passenger side watching. I'm sure he wondered and asked questions. Back in the house I drank my smoothie and got my shower ready. I set my clothes out, not so business today, I went with casual and comfortable. I didn't have any meetings so it wasn't that important. After my shower, I tried to recreate my hair like Ramone did… not quite the same, but it looked fine. I gathered my laptop case and belongings and went to the car. When I opened the car door there was a long stem red rose sitting in the driver's seat. Now, when did he have time to do that? Good grief! He always surprises me. I set the flower on the passenger side, placed my things on the front floorboard and headed to the office.

The office was quiet this time of the morning, I set my rose in a water bottle on my desk and thought, it's quite all the time really, not like the busy firm Mia runs. Mia – I have to call him. I set up my laptop and files and picked up the phone. I started to dial when my assistant came in.

"Good morning, Miss Baylor."

"Good morning."

"I would have had your coffee and bagel, but I wasn't sure if you were coming in today."

"I'm sorry. I know I said I would be out for the week, but you know me, I can't sit still. Besides this really doesn't hurt that much…" I drifted out thinking unless you're making out with an extremely hot guy and fervently and aggressively rubbing your bodies together... I snapped out of my reverie and continued,

"…and I'm not taking the Norco so there isn't any reason I couldn't come in."

"I see." She stated but seemed really unconcerned. "Would you like your coffee and bagel now?

"That would be great. Thank you." She left my office and I realized I was still holding the handset. I hung up the handset, and picked it back up and dialed Mia.

"Good morning my lawful angel." He said cheerfully.

"Hello, Mia. How are you this early morning?"

"I am wonderful. I am just sitting next to my angelic wife drinking a coffee and discussing the plans for the day."

"Anything of interest for the day?"

"No, just the usual. About to head to the office myself. I see you called from there, so you must be back to work."

"You know me, Mia, I never leave work. Maybe the building… but not the job." Mia laughed.

"So true my young tycoon!!" He started really rolling with laughter on the one. "It rhymed; I'll have to keep that one in my brain."

"You are full of it this morning Mr. Listen. I am going to need a driver to pick me up at my house on Thursday evening and have the jet ready to go. I'll be at your office Friday morning sharp."

"Really? The doctor gave you the ok to fly?"

"He said, no gym activities. I'm not planning on jumping out when we fly over New York, so it will be fine."

"Alright. I'll have a driver pick you up at 5:00 p.m."

"Thanks, Mia. I'll plan the rest." I paused, "Hey Mia. I typically don't ask you for favors while I'm there but may I ask you something?"

"Anything. You know that."

"Are you still with Angelica?"

"Yes, she's sitting right here."

"I would like if you are both available Saturday evening to go for a night on the town. We always do dinner, but I mean really *DO* something. Dinner just the three of us, and a musical – you know a really good one, maybe a carriage ride, then walk Rockefeller Plaza" I was getting excited.

"Let me run all that past my 'beautiful' and if we have plans, will move them! They are not as important as a splendid night with you!"

"Oh - thank you, Mia!"

"For you my dove, anything. Angelica will plan the entire evening and she won't disappoint!"

"I have no doubts, sir. I will call you on Thursday when I land. Talk soon."

I had to get my mind off Saturday, and it sounded fun. They always boast about wanting to pamper me and take me out, well this is the perfect opportunity. I called my dad and we spoke briefly about current events and my job and his retirement; how mom and all her groups and clubs and crafts were going. We never got into details, because legally I couldn't and I didn't tell him about my face, that would just worry them and being that there was no negative outcome, not a necessary fact.

I picked up my cell, by this point my bagel and coffee had arrived. I sent a text to Austin,

> "It was nice to see you this morning! Thank U for the beautiful rose. Don't even know how..."

He replied quickly which means he was bored in class or between classes,

> "I have a key remember?"
>
> "Of course, I just don't know when... or how."
>
> "I'm magic. Just keep that in mind."
>
> "You already have blown my mind!" I smiled.
>
> "It only gets better! Class gotta run!"

The rest of the day was basic monotonous paperwork. Talking to a few new clients and arranging meetings with them for the future. The next time I looked at the clock it read 6:33. I completely worked the day away not paying attention to people leaving, although I had a faint recollection of my assistant asking if I needed anything before, she left. Hmm, I thought she was just going to lunch. I got up and headed to the kitchen. I looked in the refrigerator, but nothing but people's leftovers and forgotten sack lunches. Gross. I went back to my office and ordered takeout from a local deli. I almost placed my order then I remembered my face, I don't know if I can eat my usual sandwich…. What the hell, I'll give it a try. I ordered my ½ smoked turkey sandwich, on sourdough, with sharp cheddar and mayo. I also felt like a chocolate chip cookie and a bag of chips. I told them to call my cell and I would come down to the front. When I hung up the phone, I notified the security officer at the front desk I was expecting a meal delivery and that I was also working late. He was used to me working late and usually walked me to my car even though I could probably take care of the both of us.

I made arrangements for the new clients and their needs of what I knew so far and really got back into the thrill of my career. About a half hour later, my cell rang. My sandwich was downstairs. I took some money out of my wallet and went down to grab my dinner. Back at my desk I unwrapped my sandwich from the white paper wrapping and hesitated because I knew it wasn't going to be easy to bite into. I was right. I took the sandwich apart and ate each component piece by piece. Still good and filling. My phone buzzed so I picked it up. 11:13.

Wow, today has really gone by. '1 Message'. I looked and there was a circled 1 over the text messenger icon. I opened it up,

"Haven't heard from you all night. All the lights are off. RU home?"

"Oh sorry, I am still at the office. Completely got lost in my work. Why you up so late"

"Fell asleep on the couch after practice just woke up and saw you haven't called or txted. Got a little worried."

"That's sweet you worried. I'm OK. I'll leave here soon. Want me to txt when I get home or will it be too late?"

"You can, but I'm headed to my bed now."

"Sweet dreams. Night."

"Don't work too late. Night."

I stood up and stretched. I decided it was late, and I packed up my things and locked my office and went to the lobby. The night security officer, Jim, did his normal and walked me to my car. I thanked him and got in, and drove to my house.

Austin's house was dark when I drove onto the street. After I got in the house and unloaded my things, there was another rose, this time in one of my glass tumblers, sitting on the counter. A hand-written note leaned against the glass.

Hope you had a good day at work.

~A

He is really using his key, but not for what I intended it for. The thought made me blush. I grabbed a water and headed to the bedroom. I turned on the bedroom light and, on my pillow, was another rose with another note,

Hope you have a good night sleep. Wish I was next to you again.

~A

He is so sweet. I put my water on my nightstand and changed for bed. I crawled in and picked up my cell.

"You are incredibly sweet. Thank you for the roses … again. I will have a wonderful night; wish you were here too."

The next morning, I got ready and sorted out everything I needed for New York. I planned for work and play. No exercise, however, well, I might need something for walking on the treadmill… so I packed for everything. I wasn't leaving until Thursday, but not knowing my schedule rather be ready than rushing. I didn't want to hold Mia's jet. My phone buzzed,

"Good morning. UR welcome! Sorry, I fell asleep and didn't see it until now."

"That's alright. I was pretty tired as well. I love my surprises. You are very sweet!"

"I have to finish getting ready, I'll try and catch up with you later. Are you working late again tonight?"

"I never know. I wasn't planning on it last night, the day just kind of got away from me. Since I am leaving tomorrow, I might."

"WHAT?? Tomorrow?"

"I told you that."

"You said Thursday OR Friday."

"You have to get ready, call me when you have a minute to talk." This was ridiculous. I hated arguing through text. What a stupid concept. I was flustered and couldn't go to the gym so I made another cup of coffee and turned on my computer.

I tapped the table, then typed in a search, "Things to do in New York City". A ton of sites loaded, so I opened a new tab on the search engine and looked up, "Top Shows to see in New York City". Ahh, that narrowed it down a bit. I got up, found a piece of paper and started to make a list. I would give these ideas to Angelica. Then I thought, why just the evening? She and I can do girl bonding all day then meet up with Mia after for the rest! I'll have her show me her favorite shopping places, lunch, it will be fun and I assume she'll love it! I suspended my laptop, finished my coffee, and packed up for the office. Once at the office, I was excited to email Angelica my ideas. My assistant came in with a coffee and bagel for me.

"Thank you. I will be leaving for New York tomorrow. I will be working at Miachal's office. I do not have a return date as of yet, but I will let you know."

"Good morning. Thank you for letting me know. Should I forward your office line to your cell?"

"That would be great. I don't have any in-person meetings or court hearings so nothing will have to be rescheduled. But with these couple of new clients; I will have to get a meeting scheduled so, we can get their contacts in order."

"Very good, is there anything else?"

"Not right now, I'll make a list as I think of it and let you know."

Thursday morning blurred into the afternoon and before I knew it I was at home finishing my arranging. I zipped up my suitcase and when the doorbell rang. The driver is way early I thought, it's only 4:17. I opened the door an Austin was standing there.

"Hi. What are you doing here? Don't you have practice?"

"Not today, parents don't know that thought." He smiled.

"Um, k. Why not?"

"Coach said it's not good to overdo it before the game. We've been going pretty hard, gave us the night off."

"What if you're parents find out and ask where you were?"

"I'll tell them I went out with the guys…No biggie. Hey – if you don't want me to stay, I'll do just that."

"Don't be ridiculous, just come in. Wait. Go pull your car into my garage so they don't see it." He turned around and left. I heard him come in through the kitchen. I greeted him in the living room. He wrapped his arms around my waist and pulled me into a hug.

"Hi." He whispered in my ear. Everything tingled.

"Hi back," I said a little breathier than normal to tease him.

"MMM gonna be like that huh?" He kissed me on the neck. He unwrapped his hands, backed up, and lifted me up in a swift motion. I gasped and giggled at the same time. "What are you doing?"

"Spending some time with my girl before she goes and hangs out with rich millionaire guys!"

"Are you jealous?"

"Nope. Just going to give you a 'remember me' gift."

"A what?"

"You'll see." And he headed down the hallway to my bedroom. He placed me on my feet next to the bed facing me. He reached in front and unbuttoned my pants, and slowly unzipped the zipper. I looked at him intrigued. He tugged gently on my suit pants and they easily rippled to the floor. I stepped out of them and he picked them up. He folded them nicely and set them on my dresser. On his step back, he admired my bottom half. Thank God, I just happened to put on a lace thong and I had decided to wear lacy knee highs instead of pantyhose. "Damn woman!" He took me in his arms again and this time could feel that he was already aroused. He pressed his lips against mine hard and intense. He separated my lips with his and he delved into my mouth. Our tongues were intertwined where you couldn't tell who's was who's. I was starting to pant and yearn for more. He reached down to the top of my underwear and slipped his hand over my clitoris. He teased me by swirling his finger over and around for a few, then with his two middle fingers thrust them up in me. I gasped. SHIT! That was what I was craving.

"Already wet I see." He said. I bit my lower lip. He pulled his fingers in and out while his thumb rubbed my clit. He slowed down, which was frustrating me because I was thoroughly enjoying this. He pulled his fingers slowly out of me just to torment me. He pulled my under ware down to the floor and I stepped out, he brushed them aside with his foot. He lifted me up to the side of the bed and laid me down. He knelt down on the floor and spread my legs apart. OH, MY!!! I might just cum at the thought of this. He proceeded to blow soft and genital over my clitoris. I then felt his moist warm lips gently stroke me. He started soft then gradually started sucking harder and harder. He moved from that to sticking his tongue up in my vagina as deep as possible switching between sucking and licking and plunging. Oh, this was the best oral sex I had ever had!! He returned to my clit with his tongue and started fucking me with his fingers. While he was doing that, he slowed massaged my anus with his thumb. I have never had anal sex before, but open to new opportunities if it feels this fucking awesome!!! It didn't take me long to develop multiple orgasms. I convulsed for a few minutes and cried out with pleasure while pulling his hair. Not quite sure how hard I pulled because I lost time.

When I regained my faculties, I looked up and Austin was smiling down at me. "Did you enjoy that?" He said proudly of himself.

"Could have been better," I said blankly. He looked shocked! Took the conceitedness right out of him. I started full unguarded laughter.

"Oh, a funny girl now?" He jumped on top of me and started tickling me. We wrestled around the bed laughing and tickling, kissing and embracing. Finally, when we settled down and he was holding me in his arms, he said, "I'm going to miss you. I so wish you were the one I was taking."

"I know. I'm going to miss you too. Wanna know something?"

He looked at me. "That was the best oral sex I have EVER had!"

"Really?"

"Really, you seem to have a talent in that area, and I'd appreciate you only practice your skills on me."

"Well, if I'm that good, maybe I should share my abilities with the world." I started wrestling with him again, doing some holds from Krav Maga and he starts yelling, "Alright, Alright!!! You win. I'll only share my magic with you!" I scooted up put my underwear back on, straightened my knee highs, and went and put on my pants. He stood up. "I did mean it."

I looked at him confused, "Mean what?"

"I will miss you terribly." I walked over and put my hands on his face, pulled him into a soft passionate kiss.

"I have to get ready; the car will be here any minute. You may stay as long as you want. You can come and go as often while I'm out of town. Please, no friend here or parties k?"

"Of course not. No parties." When I walked into the kitchen, I saw the black Lincoln drive up the driveway. "My ride's here."

He pulled me into a long kiss. "Thank you for my 'remember me' gift. I don't think I will ever be able to forget it – ever!" I smiled at him. I'll txt when I land. I grabbed my bags and went out the garage door. He shut it behind me once I entered the car.

CHAPTER 11

My phone rang early Saturday morning, it was Angelica.

"Darling, I will be in your lobby in fifteen! Don't get all dolled up that is part of our fun today!!!"

"OK see you then." What did she mean 'don't get dolled up?' like sweats and a tee? I didn't even pack sweats and I wasn't wearing my exercise clothes. I put on some jeans and a button-down flannel shirt. I grabbed my sleeveless jacket, put my hair in a tousled pony-tail and some lip gloss… That's as crappy as I'm going out in New York City with one of the richest ladies in the country. I went to the lobby and made a cup of coffee. I was excited, today was going to be fun and keep my mind off of home. I was sipping on my coffee when she walked in. She walked right up to me and gave me a hug, grabbed me by my shoulders and sighed. Oh- my face, I forgot to warn her about my face, and Mia must have said something because she hasn't screamed. "Oh -my sweet girl!!"

"I'll be fine, it's just turning that ugly green now. It really doesn't even hurt anymore."

"I know. And I told you not to get dolled up!" She lectured.

"I'm sorry, these are the ugliest clothes I brought." I giggled.

"Would you like a cup of coffee?

"Yes please, they have good coffee here?"

"I cannot complain, and I'm a pretty picky coffee drinker." I smiled. After she ordered, we sat in the atrium next to a large fireplace surrounded by floor to ceiling glass windows. It looked out onto a garden with the sunrise warming the autumn-colored trees. "What are your plans for today?" I asked her.

She smiled. "Well, I thought we would go shopping and get a really cute ensemble for this evening's performance and afterglow." "Afterglow?" I squealed and grinned hugely; I even clapped my hands together.

"Yes, after the show I have arranged to go meet the cast and spend some time with them."

"That sounds wonderful! Sorry continue, I am just super excited!"

"We could also pick up some odds and ends if we come across any. Then we will have lunch at one of my favorite locations, then we will go get treated at my favorite spa and after the relaxing afternoon, head back to the house where I have a stylist scheduled to fix our hair and we will put on our new lovelies. Mia will meet us in the lobby of our building."

"Oh - my goodness Angelica, that sounds amazing!"

"After dinner at Terrace on the Green. We will carriage ride to Hamilton. It's supposed to be the best right now, also has a war theme I guess which will keep Mia's attention." She rolled her eyes. "And as I stated earlier, spend some time with the cast. Then drinks at Bar SixtyFive over at the Rainbow Room at Rockefeller Center. It has already been arranged."

"Well, what are we waiting for?" I stood up and she followed. We set our mugs down and proceeded out the door the suit dressed. The day was extremely active and busy. We should have had a bus with everything we bought. She spoiled me rotten. I had to stop looking at things because even if I showed interest or not, she told the personal shopper to "grab it". I was now the owner of purses, scarves, blouses, suits; pant, and skirt, sexy underwear, shoes to match every outfit, along with an entire outfit for this evening's event.

"I don't have a daughter to spoil, and I can't take the money with me when I die, and it brings me so much enjoyment to do this, so I will!" she stated. I felt uneasy about it, but at the same time was having a blast. After our lunch, we went for our pampering. I really couldn't get enough of this treatment. My nails were drying when Angelica walked in my area.

"I'm all finished, how are you doing?"

“I’m just drying, should be done in a minute.” I smiled. I was getting my nails ‘touched up.’

“I’ll just settle the tab and meet you in the lobby.” She walked out. I bet that is going to be quite a tab, I thought. I met her in the lobby and we walked to the car. Once in the Lincoln, I reached into my purse and turned my cell back on. I didn’t even pay attention to the time, just dropped it back in. My purse vibrated, so I pulled my cell back out. There was a small circled 2 over the message icon. I opened the messenger app; “Sorry you said no pics of Saturday, but I thought you wouldn’t mind this one.” The second message was a picture of Austin standing in a dark grey suit leaning against my very shiny black BMW. He was wearing a matching vest, white shirt and striped dark grey and light grey tie with a white handkerchief in his breast pocket. His hair was brushed into a messy wave and he had a 2 or 3-day facial shadow defining his chiseled jawline. He was wearing aviator sunglasses and smiling his perfect toothed smile. Damn, he looked like he just walked out of a page of a magazine or something! I loved the pic, but then a twinge hit my stomach, yeah, he looked amazing, but not with me. Some other woman – girl would be on that very sexy arm.

“Something wrong my dear?” Angelica’s voice brought me back.

“Um, no sorry. Just a text from a friend, everything’s fine.” I hope she fell for that complete line of bullshit, which it appeared she did, or at least knowing that I lied told her not to press. I didn’t send a text back and tried to set it out of my mind. We arrived at the apartment where we were greeted by a lady holding a tray. “Would you like a little snack while we get beautiful?” Angelica waved to the tray.

“That looks nice, I would like a glass of wine if you have any chilled.” Angelica looked at the lady and she set the tray on the table and turned to get the wine. She didn’t even ask what I liked; she must have been thoroughly prepped ahead of time. She returned with two glasses of rose gold colored wine. It was very sweet and crisp. “This is nice.” I said tasting the wine. A man in a suit came into the entryway carrying a lot of our belongings, “One more trip ma’am and I should have it all.” He told her. She pointed to a spot on the floor in the living room. He set the bags down but held the garment bags up. “Put those in the master suite.” She ordered.

“Do you want to get dressed? Maurice should be here soon to do our hair?”

“Yes please, after we separate our items.”

“Once we do that, I’ll have them delivered to your room at the hotel.” She smiled at me. The man dressed in a suit returned bringing an arm full of more packages. He placed them with the others. Angelica and I went through each one giggling about the day and her swooning over my selections. Once I had pulled out everything I wanted for the evening, she took her dress to the bedroom.

“Are you ready my sweet girl?” She asked.

“Yes,” I answered.

“Follow me.” I picked up my items, clutch, shoe box, nylons, jewelry, and followed her to a bedroom suite the size of my kitchen and living room. It wasn’t your typical modern Manhattan style; cold and industrial. She had decorated this room as if you’d walked into an Aspen chalet. One corner or the room was floor to ceiling windows trimmed out in oak with two chaise lounge chairs separated by an oak round table and a couple of throws draped over them. Ambient light hung by three induvial sconces. The room was divided by an enormous stone fireplace that faced the king oak sleigh bed filled with pillows of every shape and a duvet that you would melt in. Across from the chaise chairs, there was an entertainment center with a 60” flat screen television and a built-in library made out of the stones. The room was hickory flooring covered in complementary rugs and rustic ivory marbled walls. Next to the bed, was a single glass door also trimmed in Oak heading to a terrace. Angelica led me to the other side of the stone wall where a claw foot tub was next to; built in stone shelves to hold towels, soaps, and candles, which is what she had placed. On the side of the entertainment center was a wood counter with two sinks. The toilet was opposite of the tub and a walk in, multiple head cascading rain shower was carved out of lime and river stones. There was a high back chair sitting between the toilet and the tub next to the counter. A man was standing waiting for me, I assumed it was Maurice. “Thank you.” Angelica turned and left me alone in the room. I set my things on the counter and he gestured to the chair and I sat down. Maurice brushed and sprayed and twisted and placed it into a French twist up-do with tendrils cascading down. He also did makeup; he almost completely made my face look normal. You had to take a long look to even see the bruising and scratch. I was amazed on how he transformed my face into a porcelain doll. When he was finished, he walked out of the room, and Angelica returned.

"You can change in there. Your dress is hanging in here." She opened one of the oak French doors to a walk-in closet the size of my bathroom alone. The closet was lined with shelving full of women's attire; dresses, blouses, pants and a section of drawers. A make-up desk sat at the end of the row of clothing across from a large round ottoman which sat in the center. It had several mirrors and racks and racks of shoes. On the other side must have been Mia's. It mirrored Angelica's side but had men's suits and manly items. I saw my dress hanging outside the garment bag.

After seeing Austin's picture, I was grateful that I chose the dress I did. It was a navy-blue sheath gown with a beaded embroidery sweetheart neckline, low cut off the shoulders. The beading went down my hips accentuating my figure, and a slight train followed from behind. I had a matching clutch, and stilettos. A beautiful pearl choker with a blue emerald cut sapphires, surrounded by smaller emerald cut diamond enclosure. A matching ring and earrings accompanied the necklace. I had gotten a special push-up bra that enhanced my breasts and was complemented by the neckline. When I was finished, I opened the door to the living room and Angelica and Maurice's faces went pale, both jaws dropped open, and they stood frozen.

Maurice was the first to speak, "I honestly don't think I have ever seen anyone this beautiful in person my entire life. No offense ma'am" he looked at Angelica.

"None taken, I cannot agree more with you. You look like you just walked from a cloud in heaven, a living porcelain doll. Make yourself comfortable while I get dolled up!" She said winking at me.

"Before you go would take a couple of pictures of me?" I asked timidly.

"Absolutely. One by the fire place please." Angelica and Mia had a beautiful staircase so I took a picture by that. I think Maurice and Angelica had more fun taking pics on my cell than anything else. They had me pose this way and that, up close far away, I felt silly, but it was fun.

"I better get ready or Mia will be wondering what happened to us." She laughed. She handed back my phone and walked into the bathroom with Maurice. I flipped through the pictures, they really looked good. There was one of me standing with my left arm up against the fireplace looking at the fire. My right hand was next to my side holding my clutch. I opened a text message to Austin and attached that picture along with a couple others of me laughing and one a bit on the 'bustier' side. Two can play this game. I looked at the clock, he should be sitting down to eat about now.

"Heading to dinner then a Broadway show, afterglow party, and then a carriage ride to get drinks. Be a late night. Have fun. Hope you liked the pictures." A few moments later my phone buzzed.

"Liked?? NO- You are the MOST beautiful woman I have ever seen!!! I am SO lucky you are my girlfriend. Not happy I can't enjoy you in person." I smiled. I hope it worked, and I hope while he's dancing with *her,* he'll be picturing me. I found the wine and poured myself another glass. Angelica came out shortly and looked amazing. Maurice really did good work! We thanked him, grabbed our wraps and headed to the lobby.

When we entered the lobby, Mia lit up. He walked over to us and smiled ear to ear. "Why I am the luckiest man on this planet tonight!" he boasted. "Look at the two stunning women I get to spend the evening with!!" He kissed Angelica's cheek then lifted up my hands and kissed the back of my hands. I blushed. "You, my young fawn, are unequivocally breathtaking." He whispered as he looked up from my hands. "Thank you, Mia, that is very kind of you, but really it was all Angelica's work."

"She is my Angel!" he beamed. He held his arms out, one on each hip, and we both walked arm in arm to the car.

I was afraid to eat too much at dinner, because of my form fitted dress, but it was so delicious I cleaned my plate. After dinner, the maître d' announced that our carriage was ready. He assisted us out of our seats and as he did, another staff had brought over our jackets and he helped place them on. The air was a crisp fall evening but, in the carriage, there was a heater and warm blankets. We went from Central Park over to the show. I absolutely loved the ride. It was nice to see Mia and Angelica snuggling together under the blanket. Once at the theater, we stepped from the carriage and walked into the foyer of the theater. Angelica went to the window and took care of the arrangements. A man with a suit greeted us. He had a flashlight in one gloved hand and gestured for us to follow. While we were following him, a lady handed us little booklets with the cast and show information. He guided us to our seats, and I couldn't help but notice everyone was staring at us like we were royalty. I couldn't understand why, maybe they recognized Mia.

The show was exhilarating, so much dancing and music, the actors were so magnificent to watch and just extraordinary. The lights rose and intermission began, Mia asked if we would like to accompany him to the bar and I said I needed to powder my nose first. They escorted me to the restroom and continued to the bar. Once finished I stepped outside to find a group of young men waiting for me. They all smiled when I appeared. "May we join you at the bar?" One of them asked. "I suppose it wouldn't hurt." When we entered the bar, I spotted Mia and Angelica. I walked towards them with my 'entourage' and Mia smiled. "May we get you a drink?" Another man offered.

"No thank you, I'm meeting some friends. I thank you gentleman for escorting me, but I really need to attend to my friends." They smiled and walked to the other side of the counter. "Quite an attraction you've acquired," Mia stated proudly. "Yes, quite ridiculous if you ask me, like they've never seen a girl before." I huffed.

"Oh - they have seen a 'girl', they've never seen an exquisite woman before."

"Mia, you're too much." I felt giddy. The lights flickered calling us back to our seats for the final acts of the show.

Three encore applauses, I could completely understand why this show has done so well with the critics. It was unbelievably amazing. I was excited to meet the cast and praise them for the wonderful show they just put on. I was stunned when the tables turned and they just blustered over me, my beauty, and what an honor it was to be able to do this career for a living. We all had a wonderful time and ended up inviting the cast to Bar SixtyFive. I was eager and delighted to see some of them joined. They were a great group of people and we exchanged information, and I told them that I came to the city often and would contact them next time in town. When the last call was announced, we gathered our belongings, said goodbye and found our carriage out front.

I looked at the alarm clock when I returned to my room, 3:17. Holy moly I haven't stayed up at a function this late in forever. I hated to undress the magic, but I proceeded to make the green bruise reappear. I dressed for bed and fell asleep quickly. My flight wasn't until late afternoon, so I took my time lounging around my room. My hair was still pretty, so I cleaned the sleep out of it and re-pinned it up. I applied a little makeup and put on one of my new outfits. I packed all of my bags and packages, thinking about how it was nice to take a private jet with all these bags and such. I opened messenger and sent Austin a text,

"Had a wonderful time last night – can't even begin to tell. Hope you had fun as well. I will be home this evening if you want to "return my car" I would love to see you."

A few moments later, my phone buzzed,

"It was OK. I'll try, let me know when you are home."

OK? What was that? I'll try? What's up with the nonchalant attitude? I tried to ignore that text and focus on my feelings from last night, humming some of the songs and reeling from the past few hours.

CHAPTER 12

My driver dropped me off at 7:33 and helped bring in my bags. When we drove in, I saw my car in Austin's driveway. I thanked the driver and proceeded to put my things away. I picked up my cell and told Austin I was home and that I would open the garage. I freshened up my makeup, changed into a sexy bra and thong, and put on a buttoned-up cotton flannel top only buttoned to my cleavage and tight form-fitting jeans. I put on a little of the new perfume that Angelica bought and was feeling sexy. I turned on the fireplace and picked up a book, attempted to read but was anxious to see him. A few moments later I heard the kitchen door open.

"Hey you around?" he shouted.

"Yes, in here," I replied. I stood and started to head to the kitchen where he met me. He jingled the keys in the air.

"No damage, I took good care of her."

He smiled but not enthusiastically.

"Thank you. I really liked the picture of you and my car. I think I will keep that one for a while!" I smiled. I attempted to put my arms around his waist and he stopped me, holding my arms mid-hug. I looked up at him alarmed. He had never stopped or prevented me.

"What's going on?" I stepped back and removed my arms from his hold.

"We need to talk." And I could tell he was nervous.

"Alright", I walked over to the couch and sat down. He sat next to me. He handed me the keys and I set them on the table next to the couch. I looked at him, "What's going on?"

"You were right." He stated defeated.

"About what?" I asked concerned.

"Jess." My heart started racing and all the emotional thoughts came flooding into my brain. What the fuck happened at the dance? Maybe he realized she is what he wanted, maybe, all of a sudden, I felt like I was going to throw up.

"What about Jess?" I said sharply. Wondering if the actual color green was appearing in my face.

"She made a pass at me." He said staring at the floor ashamed.

"OK, I don't think, no I don't want details exactly, just what do you mean by 'pass'?" My heart was pounding so hard.

"When I took her home after the dance, I walked her to the door, and she started telling me all these feelings she's had all these years, and then she kissed me." He was still staring at the floor. I wasn't surprised, I just had hoped I would be wrong.

"Did you kiss her back?" I said closing my eyes just awkwardly awaiting his answer. He took my hands that were knotting into each other and looked me in the eyes.

"No. I didn't. I told you that I looked at her as a sister and that's what I felt when she kissed me like my sister was trying to kiss me romantically. It was gross for me." Nausea lessened, but I was still shaking. I did not want to come home to this news after such an awesome trip.

"OK. So, what happened."

"I kind of pushed her away and asked her what the hell she was doing, and I told her that I didn't look at her that way; I felt she was as close as a sister friend, but not a romantic friend. Then I told her that I had a girlfriend and that it was serious." I went from fearful panic to unfamiliar panic.

"She was pretty pissed at me. She said, "how can you have a girlfriend? I'm with you every day - all day if anyone knows you have a girlfriend it would be me! You're such a fucking liar, if you don't want to be with me you can just say so, you don't have to come up with an imaginary '*girlfriend*'." So, that really made me pissed, and our situation made me angry because I couldn't tell her about you because she *would* turn you in, not like that would 'win me over' but you know - anger and all."

"I'm sorry," I said tearfully.

"No. Don't YOU be sorry. I was stupid. I honestly didn't think she felt that way."

"What happened after…" I pushed, not quite sure I wanted this conversation to continue.

"Well, after a few minutes of silence I said, we have been friends for too long for this." And she said, "you said serious, how serious? I mean do you love her?" Austin paused and stared at me. "I told her yes. I believe I do." My heart stopped. I didn't know how to take in his words. I wanted to smile, cry, run, press rewind and delay my flight or not have gone at all. Should I have told him not to have gone to the dance? The emotional waves were tremendous.

"…because I do." He re-stated again staring at me fervently.

"Can you please forgive me; I can't even begin to tell you how sorry I am for being so very dense."

I just looked at him. I completely forgot how to form words at this point and all the emotion turned into slow silent streaming tears down my cheeks. He wiped the tears from my face with his thumbs.

"I'm scared." I hesitantly whispered.

"Scared of what? Me? I told you I have absolutely no attraction to her." He said defensively.

"No. Not of you. I'm scared because I love you too." He smiled his normal bright beautiful smile. "Really?" he sounded flabbergasted.

"Yeah stupid! You really are dense." I retorted. "I'm crazy about you!" He pulled my face to his and kissed me hard and meaningful. I kissed him back with just as much implication. He leaned into me and I laid back to let him position himself on top of me. He moved to my earlobe and was nibbling. I wrapped my legs around him and slowly pulled him closer to me, our bodies were completely interweaved, between passionate kissing, stroking, and slight pelvic grinding, we became breathless. He unbuttoned my remaining shirt and admired my bra. “This is nice. I like it!” He ran his fingers over the amplified definition. He then started kissing my chest, I reached down, pulled his shirt from the waist up and yanked it over his head. His defined chest felt so amazing pressed up against mine. We rolled onto the floor where I rotated on top of his pelvis. He reached up and undid my bra, freeing my breasts. He cupped them in his hands and squeezed gently. I flung my head back and thrust my pelvis into his erection. He pulled me down parallel to him, rolled me over and started sucking my nipples. He moved back up to my mouth and kissed me gently and impassioned. He straddled me and undid the button at the top of my jeans then slowly unzipped my zipper. I lifted my hips and he hooked his thumbs in the waist of the jeans and pulled them down. He moved to the side to completely remove them from each leg. He then caressed my underwear, “this is nice too!” He leaned down and kissed my belly button and started to move lower. He tugged on the waistline of my lace with his teeth. I moaned softly. He returned to my mouth and kissed me some more, which gave me perfect reach to remove his shorts. He quickly removed them and brushed them aside next to my shirt and pants. The sun had completely gone down and the flames from the fireplace were reflecting on our silhouettes. I felt his significant arousal under my lace panties. I gave into the yearning. I removed his underwear freeing his erection. I reached down and stroked it firm but soothing. He moved along with my hand motions with his hips. He grasped the sides of my panties and slid them down removing them from each leg. I intertwined my naked legs with him and we kissed hard and long rubbing our exposed bodies together.

"I don't have any protection." He breathily hissed in my ear.

"That's ok, I'm on the pill." I breathed back.

I separated my legs and wrapped them around his. I felt him slowly reposition himself and start to enter me. He felt so good as he filled me. He let out a slight moan and filled my mouth with his. I matched the rhythm of his thrusting, each time going deeper and more absorbed into me. With each thrust, I became closer to my release. "I'm going to cum," I whispered.

I felt my muscles tighten and my legs stiffen and my body build up then quivered with the delivery of my orgasm. He did one final thrust and stiffened, at the same time let out a mellowed groan and remained static and quiet following right after my insides were still pulsating from orgasm. He returned his weight onto his elbows and kissed me slow and with desire. He pulled out of me slowly and even though I was still reeling and slightly sensitive from my climax, it felt so good. I don't think it would take much to get going again, probably for either of us.

"That was amazing." He said laying on his side and playing with my tendrils.

"You look so beautiful, especially in the firelight."

"That was pretty special. I was going to wait for your birthday…" I trailed off.

"I'm glad you didn't."

"So… your first time, everything you thought? I questioned.

"Oh, that was so much better than I could have ever imagined." He kissed my nose. "By the way, those pictures you sent me, holy shit! You looked so unbelievable and I wanted to show everyone and say "that's my beautiful woman! So incredibly frustrating."

"I know it is. There will be a time when you can. Hey, how is it that you've been able to spend so much time over here? Won't your parents be wondering where you are? Just delivering my car…."

"No. They aren't home. They are at some charity function. Won't be home until late. Dinner didn't even start until 7, then an auction or something. I dunno." I reached the throw on the couch and covered us, now the adrenalin was coming down it was a little chilly. I snuggled into him and ran my fingers over his rippled chest.

"Can I tell you something?"

"You should know by now you can." I continued to play with his chest.

"When you sent me those pics on the phone, I got so jealous that other guys would try and hit on you."

"Well, to be honest…" he lifted his shoulder so I was now

looking at him. "…at the theater I went to the restroom, and when I came out there was a bunch of guys waiting for me."

I laughed because I found it funny, but apparently, Austin didn't.

"So, what happened?" he sounded irritated.

"You don't need to get mad. I simply walked to the bar, they followed, asked me if they could buy me a drink, I said no. I was with my friends, which I was, and I have a picture of them for you, by the way, they left and I continued to be with Mia and Angelica. If you don't know by now, after tonight, I am completely yours. I am not interested in going, looking, or being with anyone else. Understand?"

"Completely." He grinned. "I feel the same way."

"Good. Now that's over can we get over this jealousy thing?" I said condescendingly. After I said it, I wondered how he was going to handle the 'Jess' situation.

"How are you going to handle the 'Jess' thing?" I asked apprehensively.

"I don't know honestly."

"Well, you didn't tell me how it ended."

"I told her that I loved you and she stopped and stared at me, and said, "Oh I see…,"
I said that I couldn't feel bad because you really made me happy and that I didn't mean to hurt her or our friendship."

"I bet she was really upset."

I was actually feeling bad for Jess.

"She was… is… I'm going to try and talk to her tomorrow."

"Don't push her. She will need some time. She probably thought the night was going to play out completely different than it did and it's going to take a while for her heart to heal."

"That makes sense. Thank you for being understanding about this."

"I don't want you to lose your best friend, hope you don't." I kissed him.

"You are a remarkable woman and I love you."

"I love you too." It felt strange to say, but nice to say out loud.

"Did you have a good trip to New York?" he asked.

"It was wonderful. Mia and Angelica were so kind and pampered me way beyond words, I had SO much fun! Hang on…" I jumped up and grabbed my cell, hurried back and scurried under the throw. I flipped through the pictures on the phone and explained each event. When we got to the ones from the apartment and blue dress, he asked me to send them all to him. I showed him Mia and Angelica, the carriage ride, cast scenes from New York, and shared my excitement of the trip. He genuinely engaged and inquired about the stories I shared.

"I wish I could have been there with you."

"Will make our own stories soon." I smiled and he kissed me.

"I should head back, at least look like I've been home all night. Going to have to kill Max to keep his mouth shut." He stood up and I admired his very fine physique. I started to stand and he reached his hands down and helped me up. He pulled me into an embrace and his naked body against mine was warm and comforting. He reached around and squeezed my ass. “So, so, nice!” I giggle, I copied him and we laughed. I walked him to the kitchen door with the throw wrapped around me and kissed him one last time.

“Thank you for tonight.” He said.

“You’re welcome.”

I shut the garage door, headed to the bedroom after I picked up my clothes from the floor, moved to the shower and progressed into bed.

I plugged in my cell and it buzzed.

“I had a wonderful time. Thank you for being such an understanding and incredible person.” I smiled and texted back,

“You will see I’m not perfect, you’re just dense remember? LOL Luv U. night.”

“Luv U”.

CHAPTER 13

I was standing at my mailbox going through the envelopes, getting ready to head to the gym. It was four weeks and I was cleared to get back to it. "Try to avoid getting hit in the face." The doctor wisely advised. Chelsea pulled up next to me and rolled her window down. She was glistening from what appeared to be oil.

"Hi there, you're home early," I said with a smile.

"Yes, I am, I spent the entire day at a spa." She said haughtily. I laughed, "Did you now?"

"Ellie, that was so incredible, your gift was far too generous." She beamed.

"Really it wasn't. Look at it this way, if Austin didn't stay at my house that night, something could have gone wrong, and I wouldn't be standing here talking to you. So, in reality, there isn't anything I could do to repay you for that."

"Fair is fair, I guess. How about we just say even." I gave into her but being a lawyer could have kept up the fight. Also, sleeping with her son, I didn't feel like pushing it too far.

"You look like you're headed to the gym?" she inquired.

"Yes, I am actually, four weeks, had my follow up today, and cleared to go!"

"Really? Do you think that's a good idea?" she probed.

"I'll take it slow, and this time I'll pay better attention." I smiled.

"Ok, I'm going to go in and enjoy the quiet before the boys get home."

"Enjoy."

I walked into the gym and Rick radiated. "How are you, you're face looks all healed."

"I'm good! Got my four-week clearance today!"

"I'll take it slow; I mean you have been slacking this past month!" he jabbed.

We started sparring after warm-ups and it felt good to be producing a sweat. I blocked all of his swings, got out of his holds, and knocked him on his ass several times.

"What's gotten into you? I should break your face more often!"

"Not funny!" I grabbed him from behind, held him in a chokehold and flipped on my back so he had to tap out. "I'm just feeling good today," I said.

"No. It's something else. You've met someone."

He grinned which made me grin.

"What are you a shrink now? I thought you were my trainer, not my therapist."

"Alright, alright, enough for today. Warm it down and I'll catch you later."

"Bye Dr. Freud." I snickered. He put his hands up in a surrendering fashion. I hit the heavy bag for a while and then jogged to a slow pace. My phone buzzed on my arm and the voice in my earphones said "Text from Austin. To be read, press one." I unstrapped it from my arm and read the text.

"Hey hun, mom said she saw you at the mailbox. She said you were headed for the gym?"

"Yes, just finishing up. Good workout."

"You didn't overdo it did you?"

"Really?" I rolled my eyes, what's with people?

"Sorry, can I study at your house tonight?"

"Sure. You want help?"

"Anything would help, big exam."

"See you later. You want me to pick something up for dinner?"

"No. I'll need a break, good to eat."

I didn't quite understand his last text, but I assumed he meant when he takes a break, we'll go eat. I didn't bother showering at the gym, I just got my bag and headed home. When I pulled into the driveway, Austin's car was not in his usual spot. My garage door lifted, and it was parked there. I smirked. I walked into the kitchen and he had his books all over the table along with notebooks and a tablet.

"Hi there, you look like you've been busy."

"Hi. Yeah… just trying to get a jump on this. You look like you had a good workout." He smiled at me and stood up from his chair.

"It was great. Felt good to get back to the gym." He walked up to me and kissed me. I dropped my gym bag on the floor and put my arms around his neck.

He started laughing. "What's so funny?" I asked.

"You are amazing, even sweaty and gross, you still are sexy hot and smell incredible. I can't say after football practice anyone can say that about me." He said while laughing at the same time.

"I guess you're not the only 'magic' one then huh?" Not leading on to the fact that I had put some lotion on at the gym before I got in the car so I didn't stink it up.

"I am going to go take a shower. Clean my 'beauty-stink' off… care to join?" Austin groaned deep in his throat. He pouted at me, "Not fair. I have to get through this material. Rain check?"

"Absolutely." I picked my bag up and headed for the shower and he returned to the table. He was serious about studying tonight. I turned around and said, "Where do your parents think you are?"

"Studying at a friend's house. Not lying." He winked.

"You're so bad." I walked to the back of the house.

We studied for hours and ended up ordering delivery Chinese food. After he had enough, we went into the living room. I picked up the throw and laid it nicely on the floor. “Hang on,” I told him. I went to my room and grabbed the massage oil I have picked up from my day at the spa. He looked at me confused when I returned. I turned on the fireplace, and he smiled hugely.

“No. Not that, dirty boy.” I shot him down. He looked disappointed. I walked up to him and lifted his arms into the air, reached down at the hem of his shirt and lifted it off. Damn, he had a nice body, ‘I may scrap the massage,’ I thought. I kissed his articulated pecs. “Lay face down,” I ordered. He kissed me quickly and did as I told him doing a push up on the way down. I straddled his ass which was firm. I opened the bottle and squeezed some oil between my hands. I rubbed my hands together so they wouldn’t be so cold, then placed them on his outlined back. I started at the shoulders working out the tension, then over to his neck. I pushed down his arms then crawled in front of him and pulled on each arm individually, pulling the blood through his fingertips like the masseuse did to me. I returned to his back and worked down to his waist. I don’t know who enjoyed this more, I was extremely turned on just by rubbing my hands all over his well-sculpted body. When I completely finished every muscle, I moved to the top of his head, told him to turn to his back. He rolled over and I tractioned his neck, by gently pulling upwards. I laid his head on my crossed legs. His eyes were closed. I rubbed his temples with my thumbs and across his forehead. I gently massaged down his nose and across his lips like they did to me in New York. I kneaded his chin and up through his jaw. I stroked his earlobes and rubbed down the sides of his neck, back down his shoulders and arms. I put my arms around his neck, gave him a slight squeeze in a hugging manner and kissed the top of his head. He opened his eyes, bright green, I could stare at them all day. He smiled, reached up and pulled my head towards his. He kissed me soft and gentle upside down. I removed my legs from under his head, spun around and laid on top of him. I kissed him some more. He had his arms around my waist slowly caressing my lower back.

"Thank you, that was awesome."

"You're welcome. I don't want you to be too tired for tomorrow's exam." I stood up and helped him off the floor. He put his shirt back on.

"What are you doing for your birthday?" I asked as he gathered his bags.

"Hopefully spending it with you."

"I was thinking, maybe if you want, being that it's on a Friday, you could invite some of your friends over here. I'll have chips and drinks -pop...," I looked at him. "... order some pizza's you can watch sports, movies, whatever. Sound good?"

"Here? With you?" he questioned.

"Yeah." I put my arms around him and played and twisted the hem of his hoodie. "You will be eighteen and I would love to meet your friends and spend time with you, or if you don't like that idea, you can do all of that and I will just stay at the office late working. Whatever you would like."

"Hell yeah, I want you here! That sounds awesome." He pulled me tight and kissed me hard. I pulled away. "You have to go because if you start this, you won't." He grinned. "One… last... little…" and was cooing me as he got closer and nibbled on my perched lips. I giggled, kissed him then smacked him hard on the ass and he yelped and stared at me shocked. I mimicked his reaction, "You wounded me! Alright, I'm leaving!" He said amused.

"Have a good night. Love you." He blew me a kiss, got in his car and I opened the garage door. I watch him back out and pull in to his.

His birthday was two weeks away and I was already nervous. Coming out to his friends was huge. I wondered if he would invite Jess. I really didn't want her in my home, but I wanted to make his day special. I also wanted to get him something but didn't have a clue. I was going to give him me, but that already happened, this was going to take some serious thought. I didn't want to come off like a 'cougar' and pamper him with ridiculous gifts like a new car. I snorted at that thought. Then it hit me, I know the perfect gift, I would call in some overly due favors. I picked up my phone and got to work. Everything worked out perfectly. Not one hesitation from any of my contacts on my plans. He would be so surprised. By Friday, his tickets arrived. I put a sticker bow on the envelope and had it sitting on the counter. I sent him a text first thing in the morning;

"HAPPY BIRTHDAY!!! Hope you have a great day! See you tonight?"

"Thanks. You bet! I cannot wait! I'm in my birthday suit right now. LOL"

"I'm imagining what that looks like, great image for the day thanks!!"

"You know what you want yet? Movies or sports package?"

"No good games on we can get some movies on PPV."

"Sounds good, what time tonight will you be over?"

"6, ok?"

"Your party. How many guys?" I purposely stated 'guys' to see if he would mention *her*.

"4 or 5. Gotta get in the shower. Luv u"

"U 2".

I left a little early from the office so I could make sure I had everything he needed. I tried to remember my college days and substituting the liquor, I got several different pops, pretzels, chips and dips, and plates, napkins, candles, and plastic cups. I went to a couple of stores looking for something a little on the 'sexier' side, but not overdoing it. I found a cute mid-rise sweater and some ripped jeans with black leggings underneath sewn in. The rips were right under my right butt cheek, left thigh, and right knee. I stopped at the nail salon and had a pedicure and freshened up my nails. Last stop, birthday cake. I headed to the local bakery in town where I had ordered his cake. When I got home, I brought in all of the belongings and left the garage door open. I set up the chips next to the bowls, placed some of the pop in the fridge, some in the freezer, and set his cake on the counter next to the envelope. I also set the '1' and '8' on the cake. I pulled a lighter out of my utensil drawer and set it next to the cake. I looked at the clock, 5:17. I had to get ready. I went to my bedroom and changed into my new outfit. I left my feet bare, Austin loves my feet, says they're sexy. I made sure to put on my sexy underwear, light makeup, and his favorite perfume. I styled my hair down, with a nice natural curl. I was standing in the kitchen when I heard the commotion of guys banter in the driveway echo through the garage. moments later, the kitchen door opened and Austin walked in first followed by four guys. He moved out of the way so they could walk past him. I had seen some of them playing ball at his house but not up close. He walked over to me, put his hand on my waist and gave me a very romantic kiss. He pulled away slowly, "Hi." I felt his warm breath against my lips.

"Hi. Happy Birthday."

"Thanks." He just stared at me and smiled. I knew he was excited. He turned to the guys who were just staring stunned.

"This is my girl, Ellie." He announced to them. They all stared at me, some even had their mouths hanging open. I smiled, "Hi guys, make yourself comfortable." Austin proceeded to introduce them, "This is Jay, Matt, over there is Tubbs…" "Tubbs?", I looked confused.

"Yeah... you don't want to know…" Austin smiled and blushed a little. I nodded my head.

"…and that is Chris." He walked over to them and they grabbed him in a bear hug and all of them were snickering and snorting. A couple of them punched him in the shoulder murmuring, "Damn DUDE!!" I had my back to them so I smiled inwardly and assumed they were all checking me out. I turned around, "Hi. Go ahead take your coats off, just put them on the chairs. Babe, can you help with the bowls?" Austin came around behind me and smoothly ran his hand across my butt, stopping at the rip and pinching the black legging. He leaned into my ear and whispered, "I *like* the outfit." I jumped a little at the pinch.

"I hope you guys are hungry, I got five pizzas coming and we have a bunch of chips and stuff."

"Oh! that's great!"

"Starving…"

"Thanks…" Austin looked at me and just beamed.

"Austin, you know how to work the tv. Why don't you find something, or music or whatever?" He went into the living room and I stayed in the kitchen filling bowls. I opened the plastic cups and took the pop from the freezer and placed it on the counter island. I took the filled bowls to the living room and placed them around the room on side tables. Austin pulled me into another kiss and said in a low voice "you look so frickin' hot tonight, AND you have naked feet!! You know I *love* your feet!"

"Thanks." I winked at him.

We walked into the kitchen where the guys were talking and reminiscing about funny stories and Austin noticed his cake.

"You even bought me a cake?" he exclaimed.

"Yeah, can't have a party without a cake, can you?" The guys hooted. They had made themselves relaxed.

"Do you want your present now or later?" I smiled.
Austin had an enormous smile, "Is it an appropriate gift?" I smacked his shoulder.

"Of course!!"
"Sure." I was so excited; he was going to shit his pants!!! I picked up the envelope and the guys focused on him. He opened the envelope and his mouth dropped completely open. He looked at the envelope then to me and back to the envelope.

"Are you fucking joking right now?" he roared excitedly.

"Is this for real?" The guys were really curious at this point. I nodded my head enthusiastically 'yes'.

"Dude what is it?" Matt asked. Austin just stared absolutely stunned. Austin pulled me into a very kind kiss. Tubs smacked him and said, "come on man what is it?"

"She got me four sideline tickets to the fucking super bowl!!!" The roar from the guys was deafening. Austin picked me up and swung me around and kissed me again. "How?"

"I have some friends that owed me for keeping their asses out of prison. Also, you and your friends have Mia's personal jet for the trip and the hotel has already been booked."

"Are you shitting me right now??" Austin just stared at me.

"Dude – you're taking a private fucking jet to the fucking super bowl?" Chris yelled. They bellowed and thundered for what seemed like forever. I just smiled. I was so happy that I could give him a gift he really liked.

"You are amazing. I can't even begin to thank you."

"Just want you to have a good 18th birthday. And since I gave you my one gift already, I had to come up with something else."

"You didn't have to get me anything, all I want is you." I blushed. The guy howled over my gift for a while and told stories about their games. We all sat in the living room eating chips when the doorbell rang. The guys jumped up yelling, "PIZZA!" and ran to the door. Probably scared the shit out the delivery guy. They grabbed the pizzas and headed into the kitchen. I signed for the delivery and added a tip. When I shut the door, Austin was right behind me. He put his hands around my waist and kissed the back of my neck.

"You are the most amazing person I have ever met. Thank you so much for being my girl. I love you." I turned around and gave him a kiss on the cheek. "You're pretty special too. Come on let's eat."

"I want you to have one of those tickets." He said seriously.

"Are you sure?"

"Yes. I want you there with me to enjoy it. I will enjoy it so much more with you."

"You might be sick of me by then." I joked.

"That's true. But I still get to go right?"

"I poked him in his side." He bent over like I stabbed him with a knife. He put his arm around my neck and we continued to the kitchen. By the time the guys were done eating, there was a half a pizza left. "Anyone want cake?" I ask. The guys roared, we lit the candles and sang happy birthday and he blew out the candles and I cut the cake. I gave the cake to the guys and they devoured that as well. 'Boys can eat,' I thought. We all retreated to the living room and Austin found a movie that they all agreed on. Austin sat on the couch and I sat on the floor between his legs. He hugged me with his legs and I rested my head on his thigh. The guys had commentary and stories throughout the movie and at some point, Austin was on the floor behind me. I whispered in his ear, "How long do I have you tonight?"

"I can stay out until 1." I looked at the clock on the wall 11:37. I snuggled into his chest and enjoyed the banter and company. The guys chose a slapstick movie that they had all individually memorized and laughed and commented during certain parts. They gave away other parts like, "Oh wait, wait, wait, ready?" and they would say the lines with the characters then bust out laughing because of the joke. It was really like hanging out with my brothers.

The movie ended and Austin stretched, I looked over to the clock, 12:17. My heart sank. They had to leave. I stood up and helped Austin off the floor. The others got up as well.

"Thank you, guys, for coming over and spending his birthday with us."

"It was awesome," Matt said then indicated a hug. I hugged him and he smiled.

"You are a really cool girl," Tubbs said. I know it was hard for him to make a statement like that and I gave him a hug as well.

"You going to our final football game?" Chris inquired.

"I haven't talked about it with Austin yet, so…" Chris cut me off, "You don't need to come see *him*, you can now watch us amazing men!!" and he put his arms around his friends. I giggled.

"I'll see what I can do. Maybe pizza after or burgers?" They all roared again. I walked them to the door and they headed out. Austin was behind them all, "Hey I'll catch up with you in a sec." he shouted. Once we were alone, he shut the kitchen door with his foot, picked me up and put me on the island counter. I wrapped my legs around him and kissed him fervently. I could have had him right there on the counter, but his friends were waiting.

"I had a fantastic time. Thank you again."

"You're more than welcome. I wish we could consummate your birthday officially."

"Me too." He kissed me while moving his hands up my shirt and pulled the cup of my bra off. He fondled my breasts and twisted my nipples.

"This isn't helping me let you go, you know." I said while he was nibbling on my neck. He pressed his hard penis into me and I knew he didn't want to leave either. I squeezed him tight up against me with my legs and he moaned.

"I have to go."

"I know." I loosened my legs and he let go of my breasts. I adjusted my bra, and he adjusted his dick.

We both smirked.

"Night."

"Night." I watched him jog down the driveway and say goodbye to his friends. It was a good night.

CHAPTER 14

Monday afternoon, my phone rang. Austin standing by my car appeared on the screen.

"Hi" I answered.

"Hey, beautiful. You busy?"

"Not too busy to talk to you. What's going on?"

"Just wanted to talk to my girl before practice." I looked at the clock, 3:05.

"How was your day?" I inquired.

"Same old, same old. My friends couldn't stop talking about Friday night though. They had an awesome time and they can't believe I have a 'supermodel' girlfriend."

"So, word got around school about us then."

"Yeah, you could say that."

"Supermodel, I don't think so."

"I do. You're gorgeous. However, not all my friends were quite happy to hear about my birthday events."

"Let me guess, Jess?"

"Yeah… she's REALLY pissed at me now. Especially hearing about you, your party, your gift, how awesome you are by all the guys… not so good. The really bad part is she is sort of seeing one of the guys that were bragging how hot you are to the others in front of her."

"Matt?"

"Yeah, how'd you guess?"

"Just seemed like him, from what I observed."

"You're good."

"Lawyer, remember, my job. And yes, I'm good." I smiled.

"She stormed off and he continued on without her. I saw her later in class and I tried to smooth things over, but she's not speaking to me."

"She'll calm down. You have been friends for like eighteen years, right? It would be stupid for her to throw all that away. But it will take time like I said before, she probably had this entire story made up in her mind and was devastated. Start slowly. You might want to tell Matt to be more sensitive."

"See, I thought you'd be pissed for talking to her."

"No." I really wanted to say I don't like it. But that wasn't going to do us any good.

"I have to go. I'll try and stop by after practice."

"I might be working late tonight; I have a big court hearing that I'm trying to prep for.

You can make yourself at home, you know that, but I might not be there."

"K- later."

That week was extremely busy. I worked every night until at least 3 a.m. and started the next day by 7. I didn't even have time to go to the gym. Austin was slammed trying to get college applications out and everything that goes along with that. My phone buzzed Saturday afternoon,

"You home?"

"Yes."

"Can I come over?"

"Yes." About fifteen minutes a slight knock then the kitchen door opened. I greeted him at the door, "Hi sexy." He kissed me, he didn't even reply back. He assertively pressed me back with his mouth all the way to the living room, where I surrendered and he just picked me up and I wrapped my legs around his waist and carried me to my bedroom. He laid me on the bed and crawled on top of me. He kissed my cheek then moved down to my chin, earlobes, neck while running his hands all over my body. We rolled around on top of the bed for a while before he finally said,

"I've missed you this week."

"I can see that. I've missed you too."

"Want to go to the movies tonight? Maybe grab a bite to eat?"

“Yea – that sounds nice. What time you gonna pick me up?” I giggled.

“How about now?” He straddled my waist, took the hem of my shirt and pulled upward. I lifted my arms so it would slide off easier. He crossed his arms in front of himself and pulled the bottom of his shirt off over his head. He was so toned that by itself was just a turn on. He leaned over started kissing my collarbone, I ran my fingers up and down his flexing back muscles. I rubbed my pelvis up against his and he returned the gesture. I felt his penis - already hard. I reached in front of him and undid the button of his pants and unzipped his zipper. Instead of just pulling down his pants I grabbed his underwear as well, when they got to around his knees, I used my foot to push them the remainder of the way off. He rolled me over, reached around and undid my bra. He pulled me towards him and put my right nipple in his mouth and rubbed my other one while twisting my left nipple with his fingers. He slid his hands on either side of my hips and at the same time slid my leggings off leaving my thong on. He copied my movement and used his foot to pull the remainder of them off, but being so tight it didn’t work. He flipped me over and scooted down and pulled each leg off individually. “Damn you look hot!” He returned to sucking on my nipples and moved down my sternum to my belly button. Then traced the thin band of my underwear and slid his hand down my front and fingered my clitoris. I closed my eyes and ran my fingers through his hair. He slowly peeled my underwear off and slid them off one leg at a time the same way as my leggings. He bent over and started kissing and gently sucking on my clit. I moaned in the back of my throat. He came back to my face and kissed me intensely and we were twisted around each other. Hands rubbing all over fervently. We rolled over and I leaned forward, I positioned myself so his tip was touching me, I slowly eased myself on top of him. He took my hips in his hands as to steady me, I placed my hands on his chest and let him fill me completely. Man, this was deep and he felt so good inside of me. I lifted up and slid back down. I repeated this several times. He was moving along with my sequence. He was pinching my nipples at the same time which was pushing me further and faster into an orgasm. My body tightened and he thrust hard and fast and I collapsed on top of him panting hard. He rolled me over and kissed me gently.

"That was crazy intense!" He said breathlessly. I just kept my eyes closed, coming down from my orgasm. I moaned in agreeance and smiled. He nuzzled my ear with his nose and we laid next to each other while our breathing returned to normal. He softly stroked my chest and burrowed his mouth into my neck. He started nipping at my nape and the sensation immediately returned, my body started to get heated again. I turned my head towards his and started kissing him. Interweaving our mouths, he shifted on top of me. I felt he was all ready to go again. I opened my legs for him to enter me and without hesitation he did. I wrapped my legs around him and he put his hands in mine interlocking our fingers. He raised my arms above my head and pinned me to the mattress. He moved in and out intensely. "Harder, fuck me harder!" I squeaked.

He thrust further and faster-moaning enjoyment. I quickly let out a cry of release and came hard and sudden. He wasn't finished so he continued to thrust which pushed me into several more orgasms. My body literally convulsed under his. He froze and panted heavily then laid on top of me. I couldn't move and neither could he. When he pulled out of me, I pulsated and twitched a little more. My multiple orgasms made me a little sensitive. He kissed me softly. We both had beads of sweat on our foreheads.

"That was the most amazing sex I have ever had," I told him.

"Me too." He smirked. I nudged him, still too weak to do much else.

"I can't feel my legs," I said giggling. He ran his hand up my thigh and I could feel how sensitive I still was.

"I can. They feel nice."

"MMM Thank you. I said." He picked up my hand and placed it in his and played with my fingers.

"Why are you smiling?" I looked at him.

"Because I'm happy. I can't stop thinking about how happy you make me and how I am so lucky to have you, this wonderful woman who is not only smokin' hot, brilliantly smart, and fantastic in bed, and happens to love me. I mean how am I so lucky?"

"Well, you state it like that, I'd be smiling too." I laughed. He pulled me into a hug wrapping his firm arms around me and held me. The sun was starting to fade and I looked at him, kissed his jaw and told him we should be going. "Can't lay here all night."

"Yes, I can." He smiled and loosened his hold. We got cleaned up and I looked up showtimes for a movie. We had time to grab dinner before. I asked him if he wanted to drive my car?

"Hell yes. I love your car!" I smiled

"How late can you stay out tonight?"

"1 again." He looked disappointed.

At dinner, I broached the sensitive subject of informing his parents about our relationship. "When do you think we should tell them?"

"Well, mom's been asking me why I've been so different lately, I keep blowing her off. Max, I think he's figured it out a while ago, but being 13, he keeps to himself. Dad's dad."

"You should look into politics because you didn't answer my question."

"You're right, I didn't. I have never had to do this before, so I don't know."

"You know your parents obviously better than me, when and how should we tell them?"

"I will tell them over the Thanksgiving holiday that I have a serious girlfriend and I would like them to meet you. And we will tell them in person together that we are in a relationship. How does that sound." I was impressed, so young but so mature.

"Sounds good. What are you doing for Thanksgiving?" I hadn't even really thought about it.

"Well, we have my mom's side come over, all my aunts and uncles, and cousins. We have the full meal and watch football, then usually a game will start in the yard and my aunts and cousins crash overnight because the girls go shopping really early the next day and us 'kids' are usually up late playing video games and messing around. What about you? What are you doing?"

"I drive to my parent's cabin, more of a house really, about seven hours away on Tuesday or Wednesday. The entire family trickles over, my sisters and brother, aunts, uncles, cousins, nieces, nephews, everyone. They even bring their dogs." I rolled my eyes. "The day before, the girls, young and old, do the prep work for Thanksgiving, you know, pies, cookies, stuffing, that stuff. The guys usually watch football and argue on the better team, some go hunting. It's really cozy and I love this holiday and Christmas. I guess I should reiterate, I love it until the 'when are you going to settle down and meet a nice man' conversation starts." I growled.

"Well this year you can tell them you have met someone, and maybe they will get off your back." I smiled, "Yes I can."

"When do you normally come home?"

"Around Sunday depending on the weather."

"I'm going to miss you. I wish I could watch sports with you and enjoy the holiday with you."

"Well, depending on how your parents react to our news, maybe you could join me for Christmas?"

"I would love that, but Christmas is when we go to my mom's parents. It's a tradition, something we have done my entire life. I don't think, especially being my last year at home, that they will let me out of that. Let's see how they take the news and we'll come up with something."

"Sounds good. I just like the thought of snuggling you Christmas morning under the warm blankets, with the cool crisp morning air."

"You're not helping me here. Don't make me take you to the car missy!" He laughed. We finished our meals and headed to the movie.

After the movie, we headed back to my house. I told him to pull the car over into a dark parking lot. He did as I requested. "Put it in 'park' and move the seat back." He moved the seat away from the steering wheel and declined the back and released his seatbelt. I reached over unbuttoned his button on his pants and unzipped his zipper. I massaged his penis until it was hard and I freed it from his underwear. I undid my seatbelt leaned over and put my mouth on his penis. I sucked and fondled the tip with my tongue. I moved down and filled my mouth with him. I sucked aggressively and he moved in the progression of fucking my mouth. He sped up and I felt the warmth cover the back of my throat and tasted the saltiness of his release. He moaned. I swallowed and removed my mouth. He pulled up his underwear and pants and fastened them. He looked at me "what was that for?"

"I don't know, just felt like it."

"Ok. Anytime you have the urge, you just go ahead!"

"Thanks." He reached over and kissed me.

We continued on to drive back to my house. Once in the house he grabbed my hand and walked me to the couch. He laid long ways and pulled me on the couch between his legs. I leaned up against him and he enwrapped his legs around me. He grabbed the throw on the back of the couch and covered us. He put his arms around me and held me. We just laid there enjoying each other. Every so often he would kiss the top of my head and I would purr into his chest. His cell phone's alarm went off letting us know he had to go home. He unwrapped me and I stood from the couch, held his hands and kissed his lips softly. We walked to the door, and I put my arms around his waist. He kissed my forehead. "Thank you for a wonderful night." He spoke into my hair.

"Thank you. I had an amazing time."

"Me too. I'll talk to you later." He opened the door and disappeared into the dark. As I was changing for the shower, my cell buzzed.

"Love you."

"Me too." I put my cell on the charger, took a shower, and went to bed.

CHAPTER 15

Sunday afternoon when I pulled on the street and saw that Austin's car was in the driveway, I sent him a text that I was home. I put my leftovers away and my luggage. My phone buzzed, "Hey, glad you're home safe. Can I come over?"

"Sure. Come on in." A few moments later the kitchen door opened. He walked over to me gave me a huge bear hug and a soft little kiss on my lips. "I missed you. Did you have a good holiday?"

"Yes. It was nice. They want to meet the new man in my life." I smiled hugely.

"You told them?"

"Yes. Did you?"

"Actually, that is one of the reasons I am over here. I did, in fact, tell them I am in a serious relationship." I raised my eyebrows intrigued. "I told them that I wanted to introduce you, but being they already know you…kind of left it at that."

"When were you thinking of doing this?"

"Um, now? Is that ok?"

"Oh, um, yeah, I guess so." My stomach immediately knotted.

"Hey-," he tilted my chin up, kissed me, "If it goes really bad, I'll just have to move in, here, right?" he chuckled.

"Sure, that's a good back up plan," I said hesitantly. He took my hand, interlocked our fingers and opened the door. I wasn't quite sure if I was going to be able to walk, due to the shaking and numbness of my legs. "I'm a fantastic lawyer and go up against harder situations, I can do this!!" I told myself. He paused before he opened the door, turned and kissed me. "Here we go!" He opened the door, and I took a deep breath.

"Mom, dad, you around?" He shouted. Max came around the corner and saw us holding hands. Max smiled, "Oh this is going to be good!" he stated and sat down and prepared himself for what he believed was going to be a spectacle. His mom came around the corner and stopped mid step. "Oh, hi Ellie." I smiled

"Mom, can we go into the living room please?" she looked at us confused and a little perplexed. We walked into the living room and Austin sat on the couch and I sat next to him. His dad was already sitting in a chair watching television. "Dad, you may want to shut that off." Austin directed his dad. His dad looked up, shut the television off and had the same baffled look on his face as Chelsea.

“Mom, dad, I told you I was in a serious relationship and I wanted you to meet her. Well, you already know her.” He looked at me and then back to them.

“Ellie?” his mom yelped. “Ellie our neighbor is your serious girlfriend?” she looked shocked.

“Yes,” Austin replied bravely. His parents stared at each other for several minutes. They finally broke the silence,

“How long has this been going on?” His mother asked.

“I’ve been in love with her for a while, but the actual relationship, not too long.”

“I didn’t want to engage in a relationship with him because of his age.” I lied.

“How is this going to affect college Austin?” his dad finally spoke.

“I’m still going. That’s not going to be compromised.”

“I’m completely in support of whatever college he chooses,” I stated.

“The valedictorian better not quit school!” His dad stated. Valedictorian! What the Fuck?? I looked at Austin, “You didn’t tell me you made valedictorian. Congrats!” I smiled at him. I was so proud, and for a moment, completely forgot where I was.

“Sorry, I… yeah…” He looked befuddled. “Not exactly the way I was planning on telling you.” He blushed.

“Listen, mom, dad, I know you are surprised, probably shocked. But I am a legal adult now and I would like your approval on this. I love Ellie. She is so unbelievably amazing. Kind, intelligent, driven in life, not to mention she is so incredibly beautiful. She supports my decision to go into sports medicine and my medical degree. We can't tell how exactly everything is going to work out, but we won't hold each other back."

"Austin is absolutely correct; I would only push him to strive to be his best and support any decision that entails."

"You are correct about us being shocked Austin." His mother firmly stated. "She is seven years older than you. She's a professional, an attorney, you are just finishing high school, you still have eight-plus years of college and medical school, she's already done all that life."

"Mom, I understand your hesitation. We do have things to figure out and we will, right now we are just enjoying each other."

"I have noticed that you have been different this past couple of months. Is it because of Ellie?"

"Yes. She makes me so unbelievably happy." Austin looked at me, smiled, and squeezed my hand. I smiled back and tried so hard not to get teared up.

"Well, it will take some getting used to and we're not done discussing this, but when it comes down to the bare facts, your father and I want you to be happy. We feel that if you are truly happy, then the rest of this messed up world will work out for you." Austin stood up, let go of my hand, and gave his mom a huge hug. "Thanks for trying to understand." He turned and gave his dad a hug as well. I stood up and Chelsea came over to me and hugged me. "You know, I really can't think of a person that will treat our son better, so I think he picked a pretty great woman." That did it, silent tears streamed down my cheek and we both laughed at my blubbering.

"Thank you so much, I do honestly love your son, and only want the best for him." She hugged me again. "I know, I can tell by the way he's been acting."

"Can I turn my television back on now?" his dad bellowed. Max just stared astonished. We all giggled, "sure dad, go ahead." Austin looked at me, "You wanna stick around for a while?"

"I guess. I was just going to do laundry, no one likes laundry."

"I do." His dad piped up. "I do all the laundry around here." Austin nodded his head in agreement. "Yeah, it's weird." He laughed.

"Ellie, would you like something to drink? I have some wine left from Thanksgiving."

"A glass of wine would be nice." I needed something after that last half hour. At least my parents don't or won't argue on who I bring home, they'll just be thrilled it's someone. We sat around the kitchen table and talked about how we spend our holiday, what our plans were for Christmas and my birthday coming up. Austin looked at then a little pissed. His mom had gotten up from the table to make a cheese plate and he mouthed "birthday?" I shrugged. I mouthed back, "sorry."

"Will you be going to be going to Austin's final game

Friday?" his mom asked.

"I have to check my schedule; I would like too."

"If you can let us know, you can huddle with us, it's really cold this time of year."

"Thank you, that would be nice." She returned to the table with the plate, "More wine?"

"Oh, no thank you." She smiled. I couldn't tell if she was testing me or not. Under the table, Austin was holding my hand and playing with my fingers. It calmed me down. I asked what their plans for Christmas were and she said that they were flying to Florida to be with her parents, all her brothers and sisters and their families were joining.

"Oh, how nice, you must have gotten your tickets a while ago?" I shot Austin a look. He looked back confused.

"Actually, no. I haven't bought ours yet, I have still been trying to move things around with time off and school schedules, football practices and games have completely taken up my nights if not work…" This was a relief, maybe Austin could negotiate coming with me for Christmas…

"Chelsea, I know we have thrown a lot at you, but I would like to run something past you to think about, since you haven't bought your tickets yet." She looked concerned.

"I was wondering if Austin could join me for Christmas this year? It would be a wonderful opportunity for him to meet my entire family at once, rather than who knows when we're all spread out. I'm not looking for an answer right now, just something to consider if you would?"

"Let me talk it over with his father and Austin will let you know. Sound good?"

"Sounds perfect." I smiled at Austin and he just looked at me shocked. I winked at him. After we finished talking for a while and snacking on the crackers and cheese, I excused myself.

"I really should be going; I do have laundry to do and get ready for the office tomorrow. I have an insane schedule pretty much for the rest of the year, finishing cases and year-end business." Chelsea stood up with me and gave me a hug. I thanked her again for keeping an open mind. Austin walked me out. This time he walked me all the way back to my house. Once inside he kissed me passionately.

"That went pretty well," I said.

"They were cool about it. I'm still going to get drilled about sex, and all that junk, but at least they seemed ok."

"I'm very proud of you, valedictorian. Why didn't you tell me?"

"I don't know. Just never seemed like the right time and when it did, it felt like bragging…so…" He shrugged his shoulders.

"Not bragging. I am so happy for you!" I hugged him and he held me tight for a while. "You want to stay while I do laundry and go over files?"

"Yes, but I really should get back. I have some crap I have to get ready for tomorrow as well." He turned to leave then turned back around, "Birthday? When were you going to mention that?"

"I wasn't." I stared at him blankly.

"And why not?"

"Not an important day."

"It's a very important day!" he was getting heated. "If you weren't born, my life wouldn't be as wonderful as it is now." I rolled my eyes.

"Really? You don't know that. You don't know how things would or would not be."

"True. However, I do know that I am happy the way they are now, and I love your birthday because I love you!" I gave him a hug.

"I really would like you to stay but I know, for both of us you can't." He kissed me. Turned around and walked out the door.

As predicted, December was turning into an extremely busy month. Austin and I kept missing each other on the phone and days were blurring into days. I had year-end files and paperwork to get through for clients finishing up tax deadlines, new business was being held off for the new year. I had a lot of client meetings on site. I was able to leave the office for Austin's final football game. When I arrived at the field I spotted his family sitting in the bleachers. They were a few rows back from the center field. It was a cold night and I'm glad I bundled up, no sexy outfit tonight, just focused on warmth. It was nice to be out of the office and getting some well-needed air. Sitting with Chelsea didn't seem as awkward as I had imagined it was going to be, which helped calm my nerves. The boys ran out onto the fields and kick off began. It was an exciting game, both teams fought hard, but Austin's school won in the end. His family and I jumped to our feet and cheered as did the rest of the supporting crowd. We found our way onto the field, past the cheerleaders, and of course Jess. Chelsea stopped at her and gave her a hug. I kept going to Austin. When he saw me, he dropped his helmet and picked me up and gave me a sensitive kiss. His friends noticed me and all ran over and said hi, Tubbs even gave me a hug. Austin took my hand, reached down and grabbed his helmet and we walked over to his family, who was still talking to Jess. Austin kissed his mom on the cheek and she told him congrats on the final win, State Champions! Austin introduced me 'officially' to Jess.

"Jess, this is my girlfriend Ellie. Ellie… Jess."

"It's nice to put a face with the name. I've heard wonderful things about his best friend." I stated, trying hard to smooth things over for Austin. I know it had been difficult for him.

"Well, unfortunately, I can't say the same." She said coldly. I was amazed. I thought that she would put on an act in front of his family, but I was greatly mistaken.

"Jess, you don't have to be a bitch!" Austin said and his mother looked shocked.

"Jess, I'm sorry that you feel so callous towards me, but Austin has really only said wonderful things about you and hopefully in the future, you can be happy for him and get past this self-indulgent behavior. It was nice to meet you." I looked at Austin and he smiled a little smile.

"I do have to run back to the office. I have a client meeting at 7 in the morning."

"On a Saturday?"

"Yes. I'm sorry. End of year. I Love you. Call me later."

"Love you too." He kissed me a little more intense and I said my goodbyes to his family and walked to my car. Fuck the office – I'm going to the gym. Could have knocked that little bitch on her ass! I was fuming. I drove home, changed, grabbed my gym bag and headed out. Rick wasn't in, so I just put the strongest music on my headphones and beat the shit out of the heavy bag. I ran through my routines and warmed down with a decent run. As I was catching my breath, my cell rang. Austin's picture came up. I had calmed down with the workout, so I decided to answer it.

"Hello?" Not my usual answer.

"Hey, baby. I am so sorry." He apologized.

"For what? You have nothing to be sorry for, do you?"

"I didn't know she was going to be that way towards you. She's just jealous." This just stirred me up and pissed me off.

"Ok, one, DON'T apologize for *her*! It was completely her decision to act negatively towards me. Two, you CAN'T make excuses for *her*. She is an individual and chooses her own behaviors."

Austin just remained silent. “I guess you’re still pretty mad?” He finally said.

“I guess so.” I huffed.

“Well, after you left, mom chewed her ass out! It was incredible, I don’t think mom’s even ever gone off on me like that before!”

“I’m kind of in the middle of something right now, can I talk to you later?” I wanted to take a shower and avoid him at the moment.

“Sure, I guess so.” He sounded forlorn.

“Alright, I’ll talk to you later.” I ended the call. I took a shower and drove into the office. It was hard to focus at the office because I felt bad for blowing Austin off. I picked up my cell to call, but it was 4:27 in the morning. Shit. I have to get some sleep for tomorrow’s – today’s meeting. I sent him a text,

“I'm sorry too. Love U.”

When I got home from my meeting, there were a dozen red roses on my counter. I smiled but was too tired to do anything about it. I changed and crawled into bed. I rolled over some time later and there was a lump next to me. I groggily opened my eyes and saw Austin lying next to me. “When did you come over?” I mumbled.

“A few hours ago, you must have been really tired. Didn’t even hear me come in or feel me crawl in next to you.” I stretched.

"I'm sorry. I didn't get home until 5, slept an hour and was back in for the meeting. I am still so tired."

"Go back to sleep honey."

"Will you hold me, please?"

"Of course." I cuddle up next to him and he wrapped his arms around me and I fell back asleep. When I woke up it was dark and he wasn't next to me anymore. I staggered out to the living room and he was on the couch watching television.

"Hi." I looked at him. He held his arms out and I walked over. He pulled me down and kissed my forehead. "Hi back."

"I'm kind of hungry, you want to go grab a bite to eat?" I said.

"Sounds good."

"Let me go change."

Back at the house, we were sitting on the couch.

"Listen, I have to run to the New York office for our Christmas party next Friday."

"But that's your birthday weekend." He said.

"I know, that's why I was wondering if you wanted to join me?"

"In New York?" He sounded shocked.

"Yes. In New York. We can celebrate my birthday and attend the Christmas party."

"That sounds awesome."

"We'll head out after school; did you keep the suit that you wore to homecoming?"

"Yes."

"Good. You can wear that at the party. I'll R.S.V.P. two." I smiled.

CHAPTER 16

New York was lit up for the Christmas holiday. Every street light was ablaze and the tree was beautiful in Rockefeller Center. People were already ice skating and vendors were selling nuts and cocoa on the streets. We arrived by Mia's jet and his Lincoln drove us to the hotel.

"Have you ever been to New York before?

"No. This is amazing. The jet, the car, the city. I'm in awe." He smiled.

"I love having you here. This is the best birthday present I could ever ask for." I pulled his chin towards me and kissed him persuasively.

"Me coming along is my parents present to you, but not mine."

"You didn't have to get me anything. I have everything I need and *want*. I have you and you make me so happy." He just smiled an 'I have a secret' smile. After we checked in to the hotel we headed to the room. Austin was just staring at the lobby, it was all decorated with garland and lights, a huge tree was in the entry along with another tree in the glass atrium and the fireplace was going. Poinsettias were on either side of the fireplace and on every table.

"This place is absolutely unbelievable," Austin said looking around.

"I like it, this is the hotel I stay at all the time." My phone buzzed and it was Mia.

"My pilot just informed me that you landed."

"Yes. We just checked into the hotel."

"You know, we have plenty of room, again, you could have stayed with us."

"I know. But this is Austin's first time in the city and I wanted to show him around a little."

"Can we meet up with you later? Angelica is just bursting at the seams to see you and meet your new young man." I smiled, 'they just don't know *how* young,' I thought.

"How about 10 p.m., at Uptown Coffee and More?"

"See you then."

We walked into our room and Austin was speechless.

"This room is huge and amazing. It's like the size of half my house."

"It's not that big, but it is nice. I do have to admit I love the sleigh bed."

"It has two rooms and a kitchen connected by the bathroom."

"Yes, it's nice. Call your mom tell her that we've arrived." Austin looked at me then picked up his phone and called.

"What do you want to do first?" I inquired. Austin walked up to me and started kissing my earlobe. He moved down my neck and at the same time was untucking my shirt from my pants.

"Oh - so you want to go out sightseeing?" I giggled. He looked at me and moved to my mouth. I unbuttoned my jeans and slipped them off, he removed my shirt by pulling it over my head.

"You have the sexiest body I have ever seen." He smiled then ran his hands down my waist and back up. He removed his shirt without stopping for a second to catch his breath. "I can say the same thing," I replied while feeling the ripples and tight muscles of his chest and abdomen. He slipped his hand under my panties and started fingering me. I moaned a little, I was all ready to go, it didn't take much with Austin. He turned me around to face the bed and started nipping at my back. I heard him unzip his pants and them drop to the floor. He was caressing my breasts under the cups of my bra while suckling my neck. He undid my bra and removed it then played with the string on my thong before reaching around and removing it. He walked me forward so my thighs were touching the side of the bed and separated my legs apart. He gently pushed me forward so I was bent over the bed. He slid his fingers into me before I felt him enter me. I let out a moan and was surprised at how deep this felt. I could feel him completely fill me and his girth. He moved in and out, slowly at first and then sped up. I had never done this position before and I couldn't contain my enjoyment. He seemed to like this position as well as he was grunting as he thrust, more so than our other instances. I reached out and fisted the duvet on the bed as I let out a cry of satisfaction. My legs went completely weak under him and a few hard thrusts later I felt him firmly grab my hips and slam into me and freeze. He let out a shallow whine and I noticed he was holding his breath. He loosened his grip on my sides and eased out of me. I was nervous that when he let go I was going to collapse due to the weakness of my legs. I crawled on the bed and laid down to my steady my equilibrium. He crawled in next to me and kissed me passionately.

"I think that was my favorite position." I divulged when we stopped kissing. "I have never done that before and it was insanely incredible!"

"It was awesome, but not my favorite." I looked at him amazed. How could that not be? He was so deep and full in me…

"I don't understand why," I said confused.

"Because I couldn't see your face. It felt disconnected. Don't get me wrong, it was fucking hot, just I enjoy feeling your entire body wrapped around me and feeling you." I pulled him into a deep hard kiss. That was so sensitive and romantic. It didn't take long for him to get ready again and I wrapped my legs around him and inserted him into me with my thighs. This time I made sure that he could feel me, I ran my hands up and down his back, over his chest, and through his hair. He watched me enjoy his lovemaking between kissing my mouth, neck, and breasts. I tried to be more vocal to show him that I was thoroughly enjoying him. It wasn't long before we both found our release. I held on to his back as I came hard and he moaned as he did a final thrust. His body relaxed and loosened and he softly kissed me. "Now that was incredibly insane!" he stated and I laughed. "Yes, that was wonderful. I love you."

"I love you too."

After a while of lying next to each other, I wanted to show him around the city a little. We didn't have much time, so we grabbed a bite to eat before heading to Mia and Angelica.

I spotted them immediately when we entered the coffee shop. It wasn't hard, they stood out from your 'normal' crowd. Angelica grabbed me and pulled me into a 'Momma bear' hug and kissed my cheek. Mia gave me a slight hug and they were both beaming with smiles.

"Mia, Angelica, I would like to introduce you to Austin." Austin reached his hand out to shake Mia's first then Angelica leaned in and gave him a hug.

"So, you are the man who stole our little fawn's heart?" Mia examined.

"Oh Mia, Stop." I lectured. We all sat down and engaged in conversation. Austin told them his plans for medical school and working for a professional sports team. We talked about my previous visit and the evening we had and events that had been going on, outside the office, with them. Before long it was 1 in the morning and we decided with the upcoming party we should all get our rest. Austin and I headed back to the hotel. On the way back, I told him that I thought we might do some sightseeing before heading out to the party.

"What is this party going to be like?" he asked.

"Boring. It will be a bunch of corporate people dressed up, talking about how successful they are. There will be servers walking around with trays with appetizers and flutes of champaign. That kind of stuff. They'll also be a band of some sort playing music for dancing. We will eat a private meal before the large group of people arrive."

Austin was silent. "Everything OK" I stopped him.

"Yeah. Everything is fine. I was just taking everything you said in that's all." I kissed him on the sidewalk.

"You'll be fine. I'll be there." I smiled.

I crawled in bed and Austin snuggled up next to me. I curled into his chest. "What do you want to see tomorrow?"

"Everything. How much time do we have?"

"We should come back here to get ready around four, dinner is at five-thirty and the car will be here at five."

"Show me whatever you want, I'm up for anything. It will all be perfect because I'm with you." I turned to face him and I kissed him gently on the lips.

"You are an incredible man." He smiled. He sat up and turned to look at his cell. "It's 1:15. It's your birthday now."

"I suppose it is."

"I got you something." He said excitedly.

"I told you not to. He crawled out of bed and came back with an envelope and a box. The envelope wasn't 'card' shaped. It was a business envelope.

"I didn't know really what to get you, so I picked you up something I liked and I also wanted to give you this." I looked at the envelope and it was thick. The return address was embossed with New York University. I looked at him confused.

"My one gift to you is this letter, I am sharing my acceptance or rejection of my number one choice college." I just looked at him in amazement.

"I can't believe you! You are incredible! Go ahead," I sat up like an anxious child waiting for a puppy to pop out of the box! Austin opened the letter and unfolded the papers. At the top of the paper in the center was the school emblem and New York University in an embossed seal;

"Dear Austin,

Congratulations! It is with great pleasure that I offer you admission to New York University.

Your thoughtful application and remarkable accomplishments convinced us that you have the scholarly drive, imagination, and aptitude to thrive at New York University."

The letter went on to thank him for choosing New York out of all of his choices and a recruiting weekend that covers all questions in person and shows him around. I hugged him so hard.

"I am SO unbelievably happy for you!!! Thank you for sharing this wonderful time in your life as a present to me. That is so incredibly selfless!!" I kissed him and he pulled me harder into him. He stopped.

"I have one little thing more for you." I just looked at him. He handed me the long rectangle box, wrapped with a bow. I looked at him and he smiled. I unwrapped the box and flipped open the lid there was a dainty gold chain link bracelet with a pearl hanging from it.

"Austin it's beautiful!"

"I saw it and I thought it would look nice on your wrist. And the pearl is the heart of the oyster, it takes a lifetime of the oyster to make the pearl from a grain of sand, and I am so grateful that I don't have to wait a lifetime to meet my pearl." I had tears streaming down my face.

"That is the most beautiful thing anyone has ever said to me!

"Will you put it on me?" I held my wrist out and he placed the bracelet on my wrist. I fell asleep wrapped in his arms.

Later that day we were busy, I think we tried to see everything there was to see before the party. From the Statue of Liberty, Ellis Island, to the Fire station where Ghost Busters was filmed. We grabbed lunch at a street vendor and watched ice skating in Central Park. I was grateful that the weather cooperated and was quite nice. We had a horse drawn carriage ride where we cuddled under the blanket. It was the perfect afternoon.

I walked out of the bathroom in the living area, “Austin, will you zip me please?” he looked stunned. I was wearing a short black lace dress, hugging every inch of my body, off the shoulder. I had my strapless push-up bra on and black nylons that had rhinestones going up the back of the legs. Black heels that had an ankle strap with a rhinestone buckle. He walked over to me and before he zipped me up, slid his hands under the dress. I leaned my head back against his shoulder and hummed with the feel of his touch.

“You look beautiful.” He whispered in my ear.

“Thank you.” He pulled his hands out and zipped me up. I turned to face him and he kissed me. I pulled away, “If we start this now, we will never leave.” I giggled.

“I love the jewels on the back of your legs, SO hot!!”

“Well maybe later I’ll just wear these to bed,” I smirked.

“Bra and shoes too!!” he excitedly stated. I laughed.

“Bra and shoes too, sir. May I add, you look just as fine, if not more than me. All the women are going to swoon at you this evening, and I love it because you are all mine.” He pulled me to him and gently kissed my cheek not to mess up my make-up.

“All yours!” The women were going to be drooling, because besides the waitstaff, no one was this young at the party let alone this attractive.

We stepped out of the Lincoln and were greeted in the foyer. A girl took our coats and gave me a ticket. We walked in and a man holding a tray of champagne flutes approached us. I declined as did Austin. He was holding my hand and people started to notice us. It was just a small crowd of people for dinner. Mia and Angelica greeted us.

"You both look absolutely stunning!" she raved.

"If I weren't a married, happily married, man…" Mia whispered in my ear as he hugged me.

"Now don't be a dirty ol' man." I prodded back.

We walked around and I introduced Austin to colleagues and the partners of my firm. They introduced their wives or 'friends'. Austin either held my hand or placed his lightly on my back. Dinner was only a four-course meal and we sat next to Mia and Angelica. After dinner, we all left the dining area and headed to the ballroom. There were beautiful chandeliers with garland and pine sprigs intertwined. Huge Christmas trees in every corner of the room, a big band was setting up and warming instruments up, and the bar was decorated as well with garland and Christmas ornaments. The bartender had a Santa hat on and a very vibrant flashy vest on. There was a wooden dance floor in the center of the room and a stage next to the band. There were 30 round tables that sat around twelve people per table. If this was like last year, there would be a slight 'awards' ceremony for the employees that performed at the top of their field, that came with a hefty bonus. People started trickling in and before long the room was filled. Mia appeared on stage and the crowd silenced. He gave an eloquent speech about gratitude and how without people, he would be nothing. He awarded bonuses and then the senior partner got on the stage and gave another speech similar to Mia's, "This year we would like to acknowledge a partner and person that has gone above and beyond and without them wouldn't be as successful as we are. The employee of the year goes to Ellie Anne Baylor!" I looked shocked. I wasn't expecting an award. Austin hugged me tightly. I went to the stage and accepted my crystal and wood plaque.

"Along with giving her this, the partners here would also like to announce that we have promoted her to senior partner with our firm and what is a celebration without a cake? Please join me in singing Happy Birthday to our wonderful friend and senior partner, Ellie!" I was embarrassed and delighted at the same time! I looked at Austin and he just beamed back. As the crowd sang, a massive birthday cake with sparklers came from a double door carried by two men. I stepped up to the mic and thanked everyone, the partners and crowd for my wonderful surprise. When I returned to Austin after many interruptions, he kissed me softly and hugged me hard.

"I'm so proud of you sweetheart!"

"Thanks, I had no idea!"

"Senior partner that's really cool!" The band started to play.

"You want to dance?" He asked.

"You know how to dance?" I stated surprised.

"Yup. Mom taught me, thought it would help with 'football feet'." He took my hand, and I put the plaque down. Once on the dance floor, he placed his open palm on my mid-back and led me slowly to the music. He could really move! He turned and spun me and moved me around the floor like a professional. At the end of the song, he even dipped me. Once Angelica found out he could dance, she monopolized him all night. On one of his 'breathers', I cautiously asked him a question, "I really am not sure I want to know the answer, but it's on my mind, so I guess I want to know rather than not." He looked at me and took my hand.

"Did you dance this way at homecoming? Did you dance this way with *her*?" Austin looked at me. "No. I didn't even slow dance with her." I felt a charge in my throat, and a smile crossed my face before I could stop it. "Really?"

"Yeah, I didn't want to for one, but kids don't dance like this," and he waved his hand at the dance floor to the other couples still moving around. I leaned in and kissed him. He pressed into me deeper. A throat cleared and we separated. I giggled, I felt like a teenager getting busted by her parents. "Sorry to interrupt," Mia announced. We looked up at him, "I was wondering if I could borrow this young lady for a minute of your time?" And he looked at Austin.

"As long as you return her the same as I lent her to you." They both laughed. He put his arm out and I intertwined it arm in arm. We walked to the lobby and he stopped. He turned and faced me.

He pulled a long rectangle box out of his pocket and held it in his hand.

"Now I can't give you this officially because you are my lawyer and you and I work together and it looks like bribery. However, I, well, Angelica and I, looked at you as a daughter we never had and I would like to give this to you as a father-like figure. It's from Angelica as well, to be truthful, she picked it out." I opened the box and it was a beautiful diamond tennis bracelet.

"Oh MIA!!! You both didn't have to do anything like this, it's beautiful!"

"I know we didn't *have* to do anything, but it's your birthday and we care an awful lot about you." I gave him a kiss on the cheek and a long hug.

"May I wear it now?"

"I wouldn't have it any other way." I held my wrist out and as he was putting it on, he noticed Austin's bracelet. "That's a nice one as well." Indicating the one on my other wrist.

"That is from Austin. He gave it to me this morning." I blushed. "He said it took a lifetime for the oyster to turn a grain of sand into a pearl and he was glad he didn't have to wait a lifetime for me."

"He seems like quite the young man. I wish you guys all the best." We walked arm in arm and when we returned, I saw that Angelica had stolen Austin again. I smiled. Mia wasn't a 'dancer' so to speak, he would go slow with Angelica, but nothing like

Austin. She was eating him up. "Angelica really seems to fancy your beau." I beamed at him.

"You don't think he'll leave me for an older woman, do you?" I tried to look concerned – but failed.

"No, she would leave me first for a younger man." And we both broke out into a fit of laughter.

The party was a complete success. Everyone seemed to have a wonderful time, especially Austin and me. I was so exhausted from all the dancing and social excitement, not to mention all the sightseeing we did early that day, from the Statue of Liberty to Greenwich Village, that I fell asleep curled up into Austin in the car on the way back to the hotel. "El, wake up, we're back." I groggily got out of the car and Austin put his arm around me and we walked into the room. I changed and quickly returned to sleep.

"The Jet is prepared for take-off." The flight attendant stated before disappearing. Once in the air she returned asking us if we needed anything, I told her no. "We will buzz you if we do, thanks." I looked at Austin and pulled him into a kiss. "Thank you for such a wonderful weekend. I love you." I said between breaths.

"I love you too." I reached down and unbuttoned his pants. I slid my hand in and wrapped my hand around his penis. He was already semi-hard. I continued to kiss him fervently as I stroked his cock. After a while, I lifted my butt off the seat, slid my underwear down to my ankles. I pulled his penis out of his pants, moved over and turned around to face him. I straddled him. I felt him fill me and I moved up and down enjoying him. He put his hands under my shirt, undid my bra and was caressing my breasts. He lifted my shirt up and started sucking on my nipples and that just pushed me over into orgasm. He followed shortly. I smiled and returned to my seat. We positioned our clothes to normal and snuggled for the remainder of the flight. I drifted on and off. Once we returned home, Austin pulled me into a loving hug and held me tight.

"This was the best birthday I can remember. Thank you for making it so special."

"I really didn't do anything; it should be me thanking you. I had a wonderful time."

"Your parents will be so thrilled about your acceptance, as am I!" He kissed me goodbye and headed home.

CHAPTER 17

My phone buzzed and our picture of us by the Christmas tree came up.

“Hey,” I answered. I looked at the time 3:20. I wasn’t used to him being home from practice yet.

“Hi. How is your day going?”

“Fine, just wrapping things up before year-end. I had a lot of court appointments this week. Trying to get ahead before I’m gone for the holiday.”

“I have some bad news; I can’t go with you to your parents over Christmas.”

“Aww, that sucks. I understand though, and we had such an awesome time in New York, I’ll manage.” I felt bad, but also didn’t want to take him away from his family over such a special time of year.

"Are you going to Florida then?"

"Yeah, my grandpa isn't doing so well, and with me graduating and stuff. Ya know."

"I do, and I completely understand."

"I'm so amazed at how understanding you are." He said and I smiled.

"Just don't be showing off your awesome body on the beach or pool, got it?!" I laughed.

"What am I supposed to do? Go swimming in a snowsuit?"

"Nope, still too sexy!" He guffawed. My desk phone beeped and my secretary came over the speaker. "Ellie your 4 o'clock is here."

"I have to go. Don't worry about Florida, just have a blast and enjoy your family. I'll call you later. Love you."

"Love you too." I hung up and prepared the files for my client and headed to the foyer to meet them. I picked up my phone to call Austin and noticed it was 11:13. Shit! The day had completely gotten away from me. I sent him a text,

"Sorry I haven't called, didn't realize it was so late. Didn't even eat dinner. LOL When do you leave for FL?"

I wasn't expecting him to answer, but a few minutes later my phone buzzed.

"Hi there. You are working late tonight. We are leaving Wednesday evening. When are you headed to your parents?"

"Wednesday morning." That reminded me that I haven't

even gone shopping for anyone. Shit! I looked at my calendar and didn't have any meetings for the rest of the week. I decided that I would take the rest of the week off, or the next couple of days, really, and spend them shopping.

"I'm going to head to the gym, I'll talk to you tomorrow, get some sleep."

"OK be safe. LU."

"Me 2."

Tuesday afternoon, I called Austin. It was 11:31.

"Hey there." He answered.

"Hi. Are you done for the holiday; would you like to hang out today?"

"Um, I can't right now." He sounded off.

"Uh, ok?" I was taken aback.

"See, I kind of promised Jess we would hang out today, being a half day. You know, go grab lunch, and just hang…"

"Um sure, I guess. I didn't know you guys were friends again." I was trying extremely hard not to come across pissed or sour, but it wasn't easy and I'm sure I had some 'snip' to my tone.

"Yeah, she apologized a while ago and we've been working on a friendship again." For some reason hearing those words just really fired me up. Probably because it wasn't *him,* she was rude to, and it was me that was owed the apology.

"OK. Well, I'll just talk to you later then."

"I can come by after, maybe later tonight?" I didn't want to be 'Second fiddle' so I said,

"No. I don't think so. I am finishing shopping up, then I have to wrap everything, and I don't know what time I will even be home for that matter." I was pissed.

"So - I'm not going to even see you before Christmas now?" He sounded mad or dejected or something.

"I guess not." I heard a voice in the background, female, I assumed it was *her*. That really didn't help my mood.

"Are you hanging out with her now?" I asked.

"Yeah, we were just heading to lunch."

"Ok, well I'll let you go. Have a nice afternoon."

"Hey – what's going on? I want to see you before you leave." I was almost to the brink of tears and I really didn't want to stay on the phone. I knew he wasn't going to do anything; it was just I wanted the last few hours with him and she had him and I wasn't going to see him over Christmas, let alone for two weeks and the thought of them laughing and having these few last hours just stung.

"She's waiting and I should go too. I'll just talk to you sometime later. Bye." I hung up the phone. I had never ended a conversation that way but I was hot! I wasn't thrilled that he was going to Florida but understood, but her… if it was the guys, but it was her. She was such a bitch and just being friends was bull shit. She was waiting for us to fail. Which I might have just helped along. That thought really pissed me off. I grabbed my purse, keys, and headed out the door. Shopping wasn't fun at this point at all. I thought that I should have just gone into the office. I picked up things for my parents and really tried hard for focus on what I was shopping for and really make the gifts personal, but I was still fuming from earlier. I got everyone a little something and decided to go to the gym. I didn't want to go home and get my things, so I just bought a new workout outfit. My shoes were in the trunk so I bought a new towel, and some wrist guards because I was going to beat the shit out of the heavy bag today. I headed to the gym after shopping and Rick was there. He could tell I was in a foul mood and tried his best to beat it out of me. He wore me out, but I was still upset. Not so much angry at this point, more depressed. It was still early so after I showered at the gym, I decided to get my nails and hair touched up. The entire time I was envisioning what they were talking about, doing, where they were at, down to what they even ate for lunch. LUNCH – I forgot to eat lunch! I was *going* to go with Austin, but then…yeah. I looked at the cell, 8:23. Crap. Still early. I decided that I should have something to eat so I went to a local deli that I enjoyed and grabbed some dinner. After dinner, I headed to the house. I saw Austin's car in his driveway when I pulled in and I felt sick. Hopefully, he doesn't see me. I was in avoidance mode. I quickly pulled in my garage and shut the door. I didn't even stop to get my mail. I took most of the packages out of the car, dropping the wrapping paper rolls because my hands were way too full. I opened the door, and there was a small box with a red bow on it with a note next to it. I walked past it and mumbled about the 'stupid key' to myself. I put the items on the table and went out and got the remainder of the packages. When I returned, I placed the packages next to the others and stared at the note.

"Damn it!" I picked up the note.

"Ellie – I'm so very sorry I hurt your feelings today. I wanted to give this to you in person for Christmas. I love you.

~ Austin"

Fuck!

I hated this. I didn't know what to do… call or ignore? I put the note back down next to the box and attempted to wrap presents. It was like that little box was screaming at me. I picked up my phone, it was 9:15.

I texted Austin semi-hoping he was asleep,

"Home."

I went back to my presents and didn't even reach the table before my phone buzzed. Crap! Of course, he wouldn't be asleep. I looked at my phone,

"I WANT to come over!"

"That didn't stop you earlier!"

No answer. Huh, that was odd. Maybe I really pissed him off? I returned to the table and continued working on the wrapping. I heard the front door unlock and he walked through. I heard him shut the door and his heavy footsteps come towards me. When he saw me standing at the table, he assertively approached me. He grabbed both sides of my head and pulled me into a hard kiss. I dropped the scissors on the table and kissed him back. I couldn't hold the tears back and they streamed down my face even with my closed eyes.

"What's the matter?" he said pulling me away.

"I guess the entire day of being furious- just came out now with your kiss." He pulled me into a hard bear hug.

"I love you. You know I wouldn't do anything with her!"

"It wasn't that. I know that." Tears turning into wobbly voice.

"It was that you wanted to spend our last couple hours - with *her*. She's a bitch and is just waiting for us to fail so you can run to her and she can tell you she was right and comfort you…" now almost sobbing. He reached down and swooped me up and carried me to the couch. He laid me down and wiped my tears with his shirt covered thumb.

"I know she was a complete bitch to you and I have made it VERY clear to her that I am completely, 100%, in love with you and will not tolerate that behavior toward you ever!" He pulled me towards him and kissed me longingly. He laid on top of me and kissed me more.

"I'm sorry I get so emotional when it comes to her."

"Hey, I would too if it was reversed. I was so mad when you got hurt at the gym that I wanted to go kill him, but I spent the night with you and it was so much better!" I kissed him again, he pulled back and said, "In fact, that's what I'll do again."

I looked at him confused.

"Kill him?" I questioned.

“No. I’ll spend the night with you.” He smiled wide.

“Sounds good to me.” I smiled back.

“Do you want to open your present?” he asked

“Sure, I have to go get yours.” He got up and went into the kitchen where he left it. I got up and went to the spare room where I had it wrapped on the bed. When I returned, he was holding the box in his hand. His presents were a little larger and took me two hands to carry them.

I had a small box on the top of the large one.

“You first.” He said.

“Nope, not this time.” I smiled. “Sit.” I insisted.

He sat on the couch and I handed him the boxes.

“Which one first?” he asked.

“Doesn’t matter.” He opened the smaller one first.

“Oh nice, leather gloves!” He put on the soft brown leather gloves, “Fits like a glove!” he laughed. I smiled. He opened the bigger box next.

“No way!! Really?” he looked at me shocked.

“Try it on.” He stood from the chair and put on the light brown leather bomber jacket. It was a vintage looking bomber jacket with fur shearling inside the jacket. “The Hood is detachable,” I said.

“I LOVE IT!!!” He pulled me into a hug and kissed me. He looked sexy in it! He looks sexy in anything….

“Now your turn he said.” He handed me the little box.

"I hope you like it." He said nervously. I opened the little red box. I removed the fuzz filling and saw a little gold ring. I picked it up and it was a band, but instead of a solid band, it was wavy. I looked at him. He took the ring from me and held it on the side.

"I Love you~Austin" The dot in the 'i' of Austin, was a blue stone.

"See, it's my handwriting." He smiled.

"Is the blue stone for my birthday?" I asked.

"No. it's the first time we told each other we loved each other. It was in September so I chose a blue sapphire."

"Oh my God Austin, it's amazing!! How'd you even…?"

"I saw my mom looking stuff like that up on the internet and it gave me the idea. So, I went to a jeweler, showed him the website, borrowed one of your rings…" he looked coyishly. "… and I wrote on a piece of paper and he made this."

"I don't even have words for this." I just stared at the ring in his hand.

"Do you want to put it on?" he asked, semi laughing.

"Yes, yes I do!!!" I said nodding my head enthusiastically. I held out my right hand and he placed it on my ring finger. I looked at the ring and then at him. I kissed him long and fervently.

"Hang on." I left his arms and he looked confused. "Just hang on, K?"

"Um, sure…" I scurried off to my bedroom where I grabbed black knee-high nylons with the rhinestones up the back, the black push up bra, and matching lace thong and garter belt. I put on the heals with the belt around the ankle. I hurriedly changed and called him to my room. When he walked in, I had candles going and I was standing in his favorite outfit. It helped that I had just had my hair done. He stared at me not quite sure what to do.

"Are you just going to stand there?" I questioned.

"You look amazing and I was just taking you all in."

"Well, I would like to take you all in." I smiled and he approached me. He kissed my lips gently and stroked my cheek with the back of his hand. I closed my eyes and enjoyed the warmth of his touch on my face. I leaned my face into his hand and he kissed my neck. I reached over and grabbed the hem of his shirt and pulled it over his head. He put his hands on my hips and pulled me towards him. I felt the ripples of his chest muscles under my breasts. He slid his hands up my sides and rubbed my breasts, softly fondling the lace material with his thumbs. I moaned a little and he moved his hands around to my back. He reached up and slightly tugged my hair back, pulling gently so I was looking up at him. Damn that was hot, just enough pain to twinge excitement. When my head was back and neck exposed, he really started kissing and biting. A little harder than normal and it was erotic! I reached in front of him and unbuttoned his jeans. With a little enthusiasm, they were on the floor. I pushed his underwear off right after and reached over and grabbed his very erect girth. He moaned in the back of his throat. I walked towards him, forcing him to walk back to the bed. He sat on the edge of the bed. I kneeled down and kissed his inner thigh. I slowly moved my way to his balls, where I licked them, teasing him with my tongue. I sucked on one at a time before I put his tip in my mouth and sucked it down to the base. I moved up and down with my mouth while massaging his testicles at the same time. When I felt that he was close, I pulled my mouth off of him and indicated he lay on the bed. Before he scooted on the bed, he pulled me up to him and started kissing my stomach. He reached around my backside and slipped his finger under the panties and thrust it into me. He fingered me for a few minutes and the pulled out and ran his hands down the rhinestones. I lifted my right leg up and put my foot on the bed. He unbuttoned the right buckle on my shoe and kissed my inner thigh. He slowly removed my shoe making sure I didn't fall over. He then unhooked the garter latch and slowly pulled the nylon off. He kissed my inner thigh again, and I placed my foot back on the floor. He ran his hand across the top of the garter and lifted my left leg up with his hands. I put my foot on the bed and he repeated the actions again with my left. Once the nylons were off, he scooted back on the bed and propped himself up with pillows. I crawled on top of him and straddled him. I leaned forward and positioned him to have him fill me. I slowly lowered myself on him and he grasped my hips. I moved up and down and he steadied me while grasping my breast. He leaned forward, pulled the cups down from my bra which forced my breasts up and full and sucked on my nipples, nipping at them which drove me closer to an orgasm. I gently push him backward and really started to move. He gripped my ass and was thrusting into me hard. It didn't take long with this rhythm to find our release. I came hard and collapsed on his chest with his final thrust. I rolled on to my back and we both laid silent catching our breath. He reached over and was softly petting the lace on my bra.

"I'm really sorry that I hurt your feelings today. I guess I didn't look at it the way you did. It was insensitive."

"It's ok, I guess I'm selfish and I don't want to share you." I giggled.

"It is a special time of year and it was wrong of me." I cuddled in next to him and he held me tight.

"I'm sorry that I overreacted. I don't do good at relationships. I don't like to lose so I don't. I get aggressive." I kissed his bicep and he squeezed me.

"Well, I guess if we're being completely honest, she manipulated me. I am not good at relationships either, being you're my only one, and I think she knew what she was doing by wanting to hang out. She knew that it would one, piss you off and hurt you, which completely infuriates me. And second, I would spend time with her, special time that I should have been with you. Now that I say this out loud, it really makes me mad!"

"Well let's not think about her anymore." I sat up and straddled his waist. I reached behind me and undid my bra and tossed it on the floor. He cupped my breasts and I moaned. He flipped me over and tickled me and I laughed. I tickled him back and before long we were wrapped into each other kissing passionately. After a while, and a couple more rounds, Austin got up and grabbed his phone.

"Whatcha doing?" I inquired.

"Texting mom."

"Um?"

"Telling her I'm staying over tonight and will be home in the morning." That made me smile. When he finished texting his mom, he laid back down and I snuggled into him. Before long, he was asleep and I lay next to him wrapped in his arms, spinning his ring around my finger. I couldn't sleep, but I wasn't a big 'sleeper' as it was. I wiggled out from him and quietly threw on some leggings and a tee shirt and walked into the kitchen. I finished wrapping my gifts and then made some chocolate chip cookies. I looked at the clock and it was 2:25 in the morning. I decided that I should try to get some sleep.

The alarm startled me awake. Austin stretched out next to me. I rolled over and kissed him good morning. He pulled me into a snuggle hug and burrowed his nose into me. He knew every switch in my body. He had a morning erection already so I thought I would put it to good use. I slipped off my leggings and tee shirt and he nibbled my neck. Morning sex isn't as good in my opinion, not quite awake and not all the senses are fully alert, but I'm not giving sex up with him for any reason. We got out of bed and I headed into the kitchen to make coffee.

"When did you make cookies?" He inquired.

"Last night, after you fell asleep. I couldn't sleep, not a big sleeper, you know that. So, I thought you might like some cookies with your coffee or for the plane or something."

"You are amazing." He kissed me on the cheek then reached over and grabbed a couple cookies. I giggled.

"Oh, I see, you just love me for my cookies?!" I laughed.

"Woman, I didn't even know you could bake!" He retorted. I poured him a cup of coffee and one for myself and we sat at the table talking. I was dipping my cookie in my coffee and he looked at me.

"Uh, what are you doing?"

"What," I asked confused.

"Dipping your cookie in your coffee?"

"Yes… I've done it for years." I smiled which made him smile. I finished my coffee and said, "I need to take a shower, you want to join?" I already had my legs on his lap he was playing with my toes.

"You know I would LOVE to join you, but I really should head home."

"What did your mom reply to your text last night?"

"She just told me to be home early so I can pack."

"Nothing more? She wasn't pissed at you?"

"Probably, but I mean, I did just go to New York with you for an entire weekend and it's not surprising we're sleeping together…so… she's probably just getting over it."

"OK." I replied still not used to 'mother's' that need to know where their sons are. He got up and placed my feet on the floor after kissing my toes. He bit my big toe and I yelped. We both laughed and he put his shoes on and his new coat. Damn, he looked like a model stepping out of a magazine.

"You look SO fine in that jacket."

"Thank you again. And you look so fine all the time." He kissed me and held me tight.

"I don't want to go. I will miss you."

"I'm going to miss you too. But I want you to have fun and enjoy your family." I pulled away a little and looked up at him. "You know, you should talk to your grandpa, I mean really talk to him. Find out what it was like when he was a kid, and really dig deep. Really enjoy this time with him and all of them. Bury your brother in the sand at the beach and toss him in the pool. Go fishing with your dad… or mom…" I smiled. I knew Chelsea, she was a tomboy Mom more than a 'fifth avenue' mom.

"Ok. I will try. I will still miss you. I love you."

"I love you too. It's only two weeks."

CHAPTER 18

I was curled up on the oversized sofa, wrapped in a fuzzy blanket in front of a roaring fire when my phone made a funny ring sound. I picked it up and an app I didn't use very often was ringing. I pressed 'Answer'. Austin's live face came up on the screen.

"Merry Christmas!" he said all smiling.

"I see you got an iPhone for Christmas," I told him.

"Yeah, it's sweet."

"Merry Christmas. How's it going?"

"It's OK. It's nice and sunny here."

"It's cold and lots of snow. I'm curled in a blanket in front of the fire." I moved my phone around and the showed him the room. The people in the room waved and said hello. "We are going cross country skiing today when we all get around. What is on your agenda?"

"Not quite sure. Probably go to the beach hang out on the boardwalk area. Nothing open so… just relax."

"Oh, that sounds horrible," I said with a giggle.

"I'd rather be in the cold with you." He smiled back. I blushed because I knew my dad could hear this conversation. I shot him a quick glance to see if he was paying attention and I think he was because he had a grin on his face behind his paper.

"What did you get for Christmas?" He asked.

"Don't know. Haven't opened anything yet. People are still sleeping."

"Still sleeping? What?"

"Yeah, we're lazy up here in the north, hibernation with the bears and all." I laughed.

"Ok. I will let you go hibernate. Love you."

"Love you too. Merry Christmas." I pressed end on the button.

"He sounds like a nice young man." My father stated.

"He is. He has a really good head on him. He will do well in this life I believe."

"Well, I'm just glad my little girl is happy. That's all we want for *you* in this life."

"Thanks, dad." No one else interjected in the conversation. Once everyone was up and alert, the kids were begging to see what Santa brought so we all gathered in the room and handed out gifts. The sheer size of the gifts and people made it a half morning event. After gifts were exchanged the girls went into the kitchen and started on the traditional Christmas breakfast. One person did bacon, one sausage, one the eggs, one the pancakes, everyone had a 'job' to do. The men sat around the room talking or reading, some went to get firewood, while others played with the children and their new toys. It was always a special time here. I really wish Austin could have come and enjoyed this with me. It was 4:30 and Austin's phone rang.

"Hey, honey," Austin answered.

"It's not Ellie, Austin. It's her brother-in-law." A man's voice stated.

"Is she OK?" Austin sounded panicked.

"She is, but her dad is not. He is in surgery as we speak. He had a massive heart attack this afternoon when we were out skiing."

"Oh my God! I will be there as soon as I can. Can you give me your number so you can keep me updated on how he's doing?" John gave Austin his number and Austin went to work arranging an emergency flight change to his ticket and getting home to be with me and my family. "That's what you do for the ones you love - right mom?" Austin was telling his parents as he packed his bags.

After Matt drove Austin home from the airport, he hurried in the house and unpacked the Florida clothes for winter clothes, including his brand-new bomber jacket, grabbed some snacks from the kitchen and hopped in the car. He pulled into my house, went in and grabbed my laptop and some files lying next to it, a grocery bag and loaded up some more clothes, underwear, and socks. He locked up the house, set the address that John had given him on his cell phone and headed to my parent's house. On the road, John texted him and told him I was at the hospital, and how to get there. Austin found the waiting room and me as well. I looked shocked as he walked in the doorway.

"What are you doing here?" I said stunned.

He walked up to me and pulled me into a bear hug and held me tight.

"John called me from your phone and told me what's going on. I changed my fight and came as soon as I could."

"Oh my God Austin, that's amazing!"

"I love you. And that's what you do!" he looked serious.

I kissed him as tears streamed down my face.

"Have you had anything to eat?" He asked me.

"No. Not really."

"I figured. I'll be back." He let me out of his embrace and kissed my forehead. I sat back down on the padded bench and pulled my knees to my chest and hugged my legs. I couldn't believe that Austin changed his entire plans and came to be with me. That just amazed me. About a ten minutes later Austin came back with an Asiago Cheese bagel, lightly toasted with cream cheese and a hazelnut coffee, one of my favorites.

"Three yellow packets and two creams, right?"

I smiled, "You know me well." He sat next to me and placed his hand on my thigh. I devoured the bagel. I was hungry, just didn't realize it until I took a bite. John walked through the doorway and I introduced them.

"Nice to put a face to the voice," Austin said while shaking his hand. Some other family appeared and I gave introductions. We all sat, some making small talk to Austin, trying to get to know him better. My mom walked in the waiting room next to the doctor.

"He's in a room now recovering. The surgery went well. All clots removed and there was no significant damage." I smiled and got up and hugged my mom.

"Can we go see him?"

"Not all of you. Just a couple at a time."

"I'll go last. Emma and John have kids to get to so…"

I sat back down next to Austin after I thanked the doctor. My mom finalized her conversation with the doctor and walked over and introduced herself to Austin. Emma and John left following the doctor to my dad's room.

"So, you are the young man that stole our Ellie's heart?" I blushed like I was 16 again.

"Yes, ma'am, I'm sorry I had to meet you under these circumstances."

"It's unfortunate, but at least we get to meet you." My mom smiled. After what seemed like forever, John and Emma returned.

"Ready to go, mom?" Emma asked.

"Sure." She looked at me, "I'm going to go visit with dad now." I stated and gave her a hug. She gave Austin a hug too.

"We'll see you at home then. He's in room 1755B."

"Do you want me to go up with you?" Austin asked.

"Yes please."

Austin and I walked up into the room and I was shaking. It's hard to see your hero so weak and vulnerable. He had so many machines and tubes coming out of him, I felt sick.

"Remember, he's going to be alright," Austin said. I grabbed his hand. Dad was asleep so we quietly entered and sat on the elongated chair. I don't know what time it was but Austin woke up to notice my dad staring at him from the bed. I had fallen asleep with my head on his lap.

"Hello, Sir," Austin whispered. My dad put his finger to his lips. My dad closed his eyes and went back to sleep. The ruckus of the nurse coming in to check dad's vitals woke everyone up. She gave dad some meds and asked him some questions. Wrote down some readings and apologized for waking everyone up.

"Hi, daddy," I said and walked over to the side of his bed.

"Hey, Mouse." I grabbed his hand and it was cold.

"You cold daddy?"

"Nope."

"Are you in a lot of pain?"

"Being that they cracked my chest open and vacuumed out my veins… not so bad"

"They said you are going to be okay." I faintly smiled.

"This must be Austin? Looks different in person."

"Hello, Sir – again." Austin stood and walked over. He gently took my dad's hand and gave it a good squeeze.

"It's nice to meet you in person, just wish it was under different circumstances."

"Me too." My dad started to chuckle and then cringed.

"Oh, daddy! You, ok?"

"Yea Mouse. Just not ready for humor yet… I guess."

"You still pretty tired?"

"Yeah. They got me on some good stuff."

"OK, we'll let you sleep. I'll come back by tomorrow."

"It is tomorrow hun," Austin whispered.

"OK." I smiled at him still half asleep. "We'll come by later today ok daddy?"

My dad had already fallen back asleep. Austin and I walked to his car. He opened the door for me and I crawled in. The crisp air woke me up a little.

"I grabbed some things for you at your house, not sure if you wanted or even needed them…"

"Oh my God! Can you be any more amazing?" I reached over and pulled him into a very passionate kiss. He kissed me back. I could have had him right then and there but I was still pretty tired and shaken from the last events.

"I missed you a lot." He said after our kiss.

"I missed you too. It means more than you can imagine not only to me but my family that you did this."

"I love you and what is important to you is important to me." I smiled and put my head on his shoulder.

"You ready to head home?"

"Yes."

He drove out of the parking lot and I gave him directions to my parent's house. Once at my parents, everything was quiet. We grabbed the belongings he had brought with him and headed inside.

“Man, it’s quiet here.” He said.

“Yes. It won’t be for long once everyone is up and going… poor animals.” I laughed.

The inside was just as quiet as the outside. I quietly showed Austin around to the necessities, then we headed up to my room. We quietly changed and crawled into bed.

“I must say I do enjoy the tan you got.” I admired.

“Thanks. Sorry I didn’t wear a snowsuit for you.”

“You will up here.” I laughed. It wasn’t long before I was sound asleep in his arms. When I awoke later that day, I was all alone in the bed. Was that just an incredible dream I had… or nightmare? I put my robe and slippers on and headed downstairs. I heard the faint sound of people talking and I realized that it wasn’t a dream, Austin really was here. He was talking to people in the kitchen.

“Good morning beautiful,” he said as I turned on the staircase.

“Hi.” I looked sheepish. I don’t know why I was embarrassed, he had seen me in the morning before and I was an adult, as was he, so… I shook off the childish feeling, put on my “lawyer hat” and met Austin for a kiss good morning.

“You must have been really tired honey. I don’t think you’ve slept this late… ever.” My mom said.

"Must be all stress with dad what time is it anyway, mom?"

"It's almost 11:23." If I had had coffee in my mouth, I would have spit it all over the place.

"11:23?!?" I said shocked. Austin smiled at me. "How long have you been up?" I asked him.

"Couple of hours." He smiled.

"Oh, so I'm sure you got all the dirt on me," I said aggravated.

"No not really." He smiled. He kissed my cheek.

"Here, come have a cup of coffee." He placed his hand on my lower back and led me to the kitchen.

"Have you talked to dad today yet?" I asked my mom.

"Yes. He's OK. Not in a lot of pain, but then again, the doctors have him on a lot of meds. He said that he was sitting in the chair next to his bed." She said worried as she was twisting her fingers together, a nervous habit that I only show in personal anxiety, never in the courtroom.

"What time are you going up to see him?" I asked

"I don't know yet. You two?" she questioned back. I looked at Austin.

"Whatever you want to do. I'm here for you guys and to help in any way. Speaking of which, I should get some more wood for the fire." He put his coffee mug down and kissed me on the nose as he walked past. I smiled and glanced over at my mom who was smiling. After he was out of earshot she started, "I really like him Mouse,"

"I do too, and I know he's young." I rolled my eyes.

"You don't need to roll your eyes. Yes, he's young by age, but man, he's more mature than some of your brothers and a lot of men daddy's age. He's a good one." She smiled.

"Thanks, mom."

"Now I'm not saying it is always going to be easy and lovey-dovey..." She made air quotes. "…but with hard work… you know the rest." She patted my shoulder and took her coffee mug into the family room to sit in front of the fire that Austin was stoking. I refilled my cup and sat next to her on the couch.

"It's cold out there this morning," Austin claimed while rubbing his hands together and blowing on them.

"But it is sure pretty with the snow coming down soft like that," I stated back. I got up, put my mug on the table, slipped on my dad's boots that were by the door and walked outside to enjoy the quiet crisp morning air. It was very peaceful out; you could hear the soft snow falling and birds looking for food. It was like time stood still.

"You want any company?" Austin's voice startled me. I didn't even hear the door open.

"Sure." He wrapped his arms around me from the back.

"It is really nice here. And you look so picturesque with the snow falling on you."

"Thanks. Me and my messed-up hair and PJ's?" I scoffed.

"Beautiful. Are you cold?"

"No actually. Just really, really enjoying this."

“Me too.” He kissed my head and we stood there for a while longer before I heard my nieces chattering inside the house. I turned to Austin and kissed him.

“Thank you again,” I said and he smiled. “You ready for little girl torture?” I looked devious.

“Torture?”

“Yes. They are quite a handful, at least the little ones.” I smiled.

We walked in, I kicked the snow off my dad’s boots and set them next to the door, Austin followed. The girls who were playing with their toys looked up at the stranger they did not see come or go, just appear out of nowhere. I was holding his hand so he must not be all bad. The two-year-old, Molly, came up to me, held her hands up for me to pick her up. I did as she requested and she mumbled something incoherent.

“This is Molly.” I introduced her to Austin. She cooed. She reached towards him and he reached over and took her from me. He googled and cooed at her and she giggled. It made me smile to see that he was ‘kid-friendly’. They played together for a little while. I left them to take a shower. I turned to ask,

“After my shower do you want to run up to the hospital?”

“I would like a shower first if we have time.” He stated.

“Of course. I can make you something to eat while you’re in the shower if you want.”

“Nothing too heavy please.” He smiled.

After Austin finished eating, I gathered some things and put them in a bag and we headed to the hospital. When we walked into the room, my father was not there. I turned around and went to the nurse's station.

"Where is Mr. Baylor?" The nurse turned around and looked at a whiteboard with patient's names on it.

"He is out for his walk." She answered with a smile.

"OK thank you. Is it alright if we wait in his room?"

"That is just fine." We turned around and headed back. It was about a half hour later, a winded man and his nurse who was holding his arm walked into the room. She helped him sit in the chair.

"Hi, daddy." I stood up and gave him a kiss on the cheek.

"Hi." He said winded and tired.

"Have a good walk?"

"I wouldn't say good, more like long and exhausting. Who knew walking took so much effort?"

"Your father is doing very well. When it's time to go back, he wants to do one more lap." The nurse said enthusiastically.

"Do you know when he will be able to go home?"

"No honey. That's up to the Doc. But if he keeps up at this rate, shouldn't be very long." She stated.

"They say I can try eating some solid food today." My dad looked happy. His eyes lit up with the thought of food. I didn't want to burst his bubble on how gross it was going to be. No salt, no nothing… the fluids would be a better choice.

"Mrs. Baylor told me you like to play cards," Austin said. "So, I picked up a pack in the gift shop. Would you like to play after you rest for a while?"

"Hey now, that's not a bad idea." My dad perked up. Austin seemed to have done well with my dad. While Austin and my dad played cards, I caught up on files for clients. It wasn't my goal to work on the holiday, but I had nothing better to do. After hours of card playing, I shut my laptop down and interrupted their game.

"Hey guys, I'm kind of hungry," I stated.

"Alright, almost done babe," Austin stated without even looking up from the cards.

"I would like a fully loaded cheeseburger, chili fries, and a large pop!" My father announced.

"Yeah, right dad. Just imagine your meal is that when it comes. Maybe if you didn't eat that, you wouldn't be where you are now? Ever think of that?"

"Oh, look who's becoming little miss bossy?" my dad giggled. Still hurt when he laughed.

"Who's being bossy?" A female voice that I recognized as my mother came from the doorway.

"Your daughter." My father answered.

"Well, she does have some good family genes." She stated as she walked over and kissed him on the head. Right then Austin slapped down his cards and claimed victory.

"Woman, you distracted me!" my dad declared.

"Sir, I was winning before she even arrived," Austin stated arrogantly. We all laughed and my dad groaned. We said our goodbyes and started to leave when my dad said, "Don't get me wrong, I can't tell you how much I appreciate you playing cards and spending time with me, but you kids are young. Go do something tonight. Go have fun. You don't need to sit around and watch an old man heal. Besides, son, when you get going with the medical degree, you'll be so sick of the hospital, you don't need to be burnt out before you even get started."

"Okay daddy, we'll see you tomorrow."

"Or not… go enjoy this holiday. You wouldn't be hanging around me at home, don't do it here."

"Okay, okay. Love you."

"Love you too, Mouse."

"Bye sir," Austin shook his hand, and we walked out of the room and headed to the car.

CHAPTER 19

Despite the fact that my dad spent the entire visit with Austin in the hospital, we did take his advice and have some fun. We went skiing and had many romantic moments in front of the fire while my mom was up at the hospital. The rest of my family had to leave so it was just the three of us. Mom, Austin and I all went to see a movie one night and had a really good steak dinner at a nice restaurant, that my parents only visited on anniversaries. My dad wasn't very pleased to hear she went there without him, and had a juicy steak while he was eating "Food that would make the devil convert" as he called it. Mom loved rubbing our dinner in his face.

"I'm sorry I have to leave you, but school starts tomorrow," Austin said while holding me in a bear hug tightly.

"I know. I have had such a wonderful time with you, and can't even begin to thank you."

"You don't need to thank me, and I have really enjoyed spending this time with you and getting to know your family."

"I think they have fallen in love with you as well." I smiled. "They are some pretty cool people."

"Well, you better get on the road before it gets too late. I love you." Austin kissed me intensely and it was hard for me to let him go.

"I'll call you when I get home. Love you too." He climbed in his car and before long the sound of his motor stopped bouncing off the trees and it was silent once again. I went back into the house and the silence was numbing. Mom was at the hospital and I was all alone. Normally it didn't bother me, but I had been surrounded by family for two weeks and started to become used to company, it was a strange feeling for re-adjust too. My cell phone rang early evening and Austin's picture came up.

"Hi," he said when I answered.

"Hi. Everything go OK on the way home?"

"Yup. No one's here, it's strange." He said.

"I completely agree. Mom's gone so it's just me. I started to un-decorate the house. You know help her out so when my dad comes home it won't be more work for her to do."

"Any news on that, when he's coming home?"

"They said most likely tomorrow. So, I'm going to stick around until she feels comfortable then I will head home."

"Well, I am going to miss you."

"I already miss you." I caught myself blushing. "Just try and spend time with your friends. You haven't seen them for a while." Then I thought of *her* and I felt a twinge of anger. Why does she fire me up so much?

"OK. Well, I'm beat. I'm going to let you go for now. Unpack and get ready for tomorrow. I'll try and call before I go to sleep. Love you."

"Love you too." I hung up feeling sad and emotionally drained. Everything that had happened seemed to be a whirlwind of events. I tried to absorb the silence and regain composure.

The doctors released my father the following day and I had stayed for the rest of the week to ensure my mom was comfortable with 'nurse' duties. My father was able to get around on his own, slowly, but without assistance, and they had a nurse coming once a week to check his vitals. I was ready to return back to my regular life and see Austin again. I missed the battle of the courtroom and all the formal conversations on mergers and acquisitions, trying to save clients from liquidation, it was my passion.

When I pulled into the driveway, Austin's car wasn't there. My heart sank a little. I looked at the dash in my car, 5:45. He had been out of school for a while now, but it is Friday I thought, so maybe he was out with friends. I checked my mail and there wasn't anything in the box, that's odd. I unloaded my car for the first trip and noticed when I opened the door, all my mail neatly stacked on the counter. That's where it went. I smiled. Austin had been getting my mail for me. He is something else. There was a handwritten note next to the pile, "Love you … Mouse."

I sent him a text.

"Thank you for picking up my mail and only YOU and my family may call me Mouse!"

"I take it you're home?"

"Yes. Where are you at?"

"Hospital."

"WHAT???"

"Don't freak. Nothing happened. My shift ends at 6. I'll come over after and tell you about it. LU"

Shift? What in the world is he up to now? I spent the time getting ready for the 'normal' world Monday and unpacking, putting gifts away, laundry, and going through the pile of mail. I heard Austin pull up but he didn't come in right away. I peeked my head out the window and saw that he was shoveling my driveway. I decided to make him a cup of coffee to brush off the cold. The cup just finished when the door opened. Austin stomped off his shoes from the snow and smiled at me. After he removed his shoes, he walked over and gave me a passionate kiss. It was a little intense because his hands were so cold from shoveling as he held my face.

"Hi." He said when the kiss was over.

"Hi back. I made you a cup of coffee to warm you up."

"Thank you. Just seeing you warms me up."

"You are so bad." I softly smacked his shoulder. He smiled. He took his coat off and hung it on the chair and took the cup of coffee I was holding.

"That feels nice, nice and warm." He sipped the coffee. He was dressed in light blue scrubs with a white long sleeve shirt under the top.

"I'm glad you like it Dr. Austin." I giggled.

"You can call me doc." He laughed.

"So, what is this all about?"

"Well, after I got home, I realized I was fascinated with your dad's care and going into medicine, I felt that I should try and pick up some extra-curricular work towards my goals. I contacted the HR department of the hospital and told them my plans and they had a position, SCUT work, but it's a couple of hours and a little pay. I also get to learn a lot so it's cool."

"OK then." I was surprised but happy for him. At least he will be too busy to spend any extra time with *her*. That thought surprised me, but I brushed it off. We walked into the living room where we continued to talk about the things he's already learned, which pretty much consisted of getting around the hospital without getting lost. I told him about my dad and how the rest of the week went.

"The nurse is really nice, young like me, which I think made my mom jealous a little." I giggled. "With a fit, younger woman, ordering my dad around, he seemed to do what he was supposed to."

"I don't want to be rude, but I am famished. Do you think we can go grab a bite to eat?

"I'm so sorry, absolutely we can. I'm a bit hungry myself, and I haven't gone shopping for two weeks."

"Let me change, and we can head out."

"May I help you…change?"

"If you want." He smiled. I lifted the scrub top off over his head, then took the hem of his white long sleeve shirt and he stopped me.

"I was going to leave that on." He chuckled.

"Oh," I said with a pouty lip.

"But I do need to put some jeans on." He smiled.

"OHHH!!" I said with a huge smile on my face.

I untied the scrub pants and quickly pulled them down. I could see that he was already hard through his underwear. I reached my hand under and pulled out his erected penis. He let out a little moan. I gently pulled and stroked him for a few before I got on my knees and immersed him in my mouth. I sucked and swirled and massaged his nuts in a rhythmic pattern. He grunted a few times then I felt his release at the back of my throat. I swallowed, released him from my mouth and stood up. He kissed me and informed me that it was awesome and he was a little dizzy. We both laughed and he put his jeans on and we headed for dinner.

"Have you decided who you're taking to the Super Bowl?"

"Yes." He stared at me blankly.

"And....?"

He just smiled and stared at me. I loved his playful side.

"Oh, I see, not going to tell me huh? Well, I guess, if I have to, I have two options."

"And those would be?" his smirk got bigger.

"I can either one, wear one of my sluttier outfits, bat my eyes like this..." I batted my eyes flirty and pouted my bottom lip. "And I can tell the co-pilot that I will sit on his lap for the flight...or..." Austin's mouth dropped open. "...I can just get it out of you using criminal warfare..." Austin laughed.

"Really? Criminal warfare?"

"Yes. I will get it out of you one way or another." I smiled wicked.

"I'd like to take that option first." He said. My insides quivered with the thought.

"I was going to take you if you have the time and then Matt and a date Matt chooses."

"Really? You don't want to take 3 guys with you?"

"No. I've thought about it and I know I really just want to go with you, but being four tickets..." I smiled at his thoughtfulness.

"Sounds good to me." We talked over our plans and enjoyed our meal.

Time really seemed to fly once we got back into 'normal' life routine again. Austin and I really didn't spend much time together, I dove into work and him with school and the hospital. I was excited to spend the weekend with him for the Super Bowl. I had taken the Friday and Monday off of work so I could make sure all the arrangements went smoothly. My door opened at 3:05 on Saturday and Austin was standing in the kitchen.

"Hey Babe!!" I said excitedly.

"Hi, sexy." He gave me a kiss. I noticed that he didn't have a bag or anything.

"What's going on? Where is your bag?"

"It's at the house. I wanted to talk to you before Matt came over." I looked at him concerned.

"OK," I said hesitantly.

"I don't want you to get mad AND I don't want you to think I had ANYTHING to do with this." My heart started to pound harder.

"Matt is bringing Jess." He sounded upset.

"What?" Austin nodded his head.

"I'm sorry. Please don't be upset."

"How can I not be upset? She's vindictive and manipulative."

"I know. I've talked to her and warned her to behave. If she says or does anything I swear I'll handle it."

"Well, there isn't anything I can do about it, they're your tickets and I told you that you could bring anyone you like." I was fuming but didn't want to ruin the weekend or his birthday present.

"We're NOT sharing a room, and if she gets knocked up it's not my problem!" Austin just looked defeated.

"Thank you. I love you."

"I love you too," I growled. Austin bolted home to get his bag before the arrival of Matt and Jess. The car arrived shortly after to take us to Mia's jet and I was watching for Matt's car to pull into Austin's at the same time. When I saw them pull in I had a butterfly of nausea hit my stomach. How was I going to get through an entire weekend with *her*? I grabbed the remainder of my things, placed them in my bag and headed for the car. The driver got out and placed my bags in the trunk and waited for the others who were walking towards the Lincoln. The driver walked over and opened the door for me. I stood next to the door waiting. Austin looked like a dog about to be scolded for his bad behavior.

"Hi!" Matt said.

"Hello."

"I am SO excited!"

"That's nice." I tried really hard to smile. Jess said nothing to me and barely lifted half her mouth to smile and look semi-pleasant. Austin put his arm around my waist and kissed my cheek softly.

"Shall we go?" I announced. The driver added their bags to the trunk and opened the opposite door. I let Austin climb in first then I followed. I whispered in his ear after I got in, "Let's not have this ruin our weekend, OK? I love you." He looked at me and kissed me gently on the lips.

"I love you too, Mouse." I blushed. I was relieved to see Matt crawl in next to Austin then "Barbie". The driver shut our doors and we headed off.

"I've never been on a private jet before" Matt stated. He was obviously excited and really focused on talking to Austin about the teams and plans and our trip and didn't pay any attention to Jess. Austin held my hand, intertwining our fingers in a nervous fashion and barely got any words in with Matt's ramble. Once we were on the tarmac to meet the jet, the pilot and co-pilot were standing at the steps.

"Holy shit!!!" Matt exclaimed practically bouncing up and down. I rolled my eyes. The driver removed our bags from the trunk and opened the door for me. I got out with Austin following. I walked up to the pilot and went over the itinerary of the flight. He went over the safety procedures and route information and flight time. Once we were all seated in the cabin, the flight attendant shut the door. She quickly went over the emergency provisions and took her seat and then we were moving. Once in the air, the captain greeted us and gave us our flight time. Matt was still rambling on and occasionally acknowledging Jess. I figured it was going to be an excruciating weekend if I didn't at least attempt to make conversation with her.

"So, you a big football fan?" I asked pleasantly. She looked at me annoyed. Then at Matt.

"Um, I am a cheerleader." She responded snottily. For the sake of Austin, I didn't jump all over her and tell her that being a 'cheerleader' has nothing to do with actually liking the sport and that I feel that she's just coming along not only to get laid but to attend a very infamous event. I squeezed Austin's hand hard and he looked at me immediately.

"Is there anything you would like to drink?" I asked him trying to calm my irritation.

"Uh… sure… soda… I guess…" he was probably confused on why I squeezed his hand so hard just to ask him for a drink. I got up, not offering anyone else anything, and asked the flight attendant for a can of pop. I decided that I was going to disregard Jess' comment and relinquish any attempt of future conversation with her. I had a book and I would focus on that. When we landed, a Lincoln town car was waiting to take us to the hotel. If Matt got any more excited, I was going to have to start drinking.

"What do you guys want to do for dinner? What do you like to eat?" I asked, figuring "Barbie" would only drink water.

"Anything," Matt announced.

"Well do you want burgers, fish, steak, sushi?" I pushed. Austin said, "Why don't we try to find a place that has a variety of different meals."

"Sounds good." I looked at him and smiled.

At the front desk of the hotel as we were checking in, the thought occurred to me of how trusting these parents were with letting their kids fly across the county in a private jet, stay in a hotel for an entire weekend by themselves. Granted, they were technically adults, very immature adults, I guess they had the trust of their parents. Also, knowing the well-rounded, valedictorian, 'Austin' was going to be there didn't hurt. I asked the lady at the counter where a good restaurant would be for a variety of meals and she gave me directions to the location. Austin and I grabbed our bags, well, Austin grabbed our bags, and we all agreed to meet back in the lobby in a half-hour. Once in the room, it was nice to be alone with Austin. He dropped our bags and pulled me into a kiss. He then moved his way onto my neck, nipping it gently. I giggled and placed my head on his shoulder. He stopped and looked at me.

"What's wrong?" he asked.

"Nothing, just want to be in your arms and snuggle you for a moment."

"I like that. What was with the hand squeeze earlier?"

"Just trying to keep my temper." Apparently, he wasn't paying attention to her snotty comment and I wasn't going to bring it up.

"Temper? Did something make you mad?"

Did something make me mad??? Are you kidding me right now? I thought.

"It's nothing." I just smiled. "Should we freshen up and head to the lobby?"

"I would like to get dirty and head to the lobby." He smiled. Damn, I would too but Jess has totally ruined my mood.

"I'm pretty hungry, is that OK?" I looked at him sincerely.

"Absolutely fine." He kissed my nose and I headed to the bathroom to freshen up.

Dinner was uneventful, Jess talked to the boys, ignored me and I tried to appear interested in their conversations. I found out that even as stupid as Jess appeared, she actually was attending a prestigious college in the fall. She wanted to study veterinary medicine. The thought of her actually having a brain cell impressed me. But then, I caught myself and remembered Austin didn't hang out with unintelligent people. Matt wants to go into sports announcing for the NFL and was attending a top ten football college with a scholarship for his athletic abilities. He was the captain of the football team so it didn't surprise me. After dinner, we all headed back to the hotel. I was actually pretty beat from the stress of the day and really just wanted to fall asleep in Austin's arms.

"Whatcha wanna do?" He asked.

"You know, I am really tired from the day, you think we can just relax tonight?"

"You feeling, OK? You've been kind of off all day. Not that you're a talker, just seemed, I don't know, off."

"Yes, I'm fine." I lied. "Just tired tonight. I wanted to let you have some time with *your* friends." Stressing "your" because they defiantly were not mine.

"OK." He didn't sound convinced but didn't push it. I think he knew that I was completely exasperated by Jess' attendance.

CHAPTER 20

There were a lot of parties and preshow activities, we met Matt and Jess in the lobby and ate brunch at the hotel's restaurant before we headed out. While they were eating, I went to the front and asked if my package had arrived yet. They checked and a large manila envelope stamped 'classified' had been delivered earlier that morning. I walked back to the table and Austin looked up at me.

"Everything OK?" he asked.

"Yup, just fine."

When we finished, I called for the driver to come pick us up. Austin and Matt had football jerseys on and Jess and I just had regular outfits. I was wearing one of my more 'revealing' outfits, but respectable because these were clients that had gotten me the passes for the game. I just failed to mention how good of passes they were! The seats were F1-F4 right on the field and I was also given all-access pass to everything. The owner of the team is who I assisted in not going to prison, so he was more of a fan of me than I of him. He also had asked me out a couple of times, but I didn't play in the world and didn't mess around with clients.

The limo pulled up and Matt and Austin were ecstatic! Jess looked as if she rather be shopping and I was just happy to see Austin enjoy this.

As we got closer to the stadium the boys' chatter became more alive. We pulled in and went past the main gate for the cars. Austin looked at me.

"Where we going?" he asked.

"The driver knows where to go," I replied.

"Are we getting dropped at a special spot off because of the limo?"

"Sort of." I smiled. Austin looked at me. The driver went to the stadium and headed to an underground tunnel, underneath the stadium.

"Holy shit!!" Matt enthusiastically roared. Austin looked at me.

"Where exactly are we being dropped off?"

"Where the players park, in the unground garage."

"NO WAY?!?" he exclaimed. I figured now was the best time to inform them of the 'package' I had gotten.

"You see, I left some details of this trip out, well, more of the game day part." I had the full attention of everyone in the car, even Barbie.

"This car we are riding in, well it just happens to be the car of the owner of the team, and it is the owner of the team who is a client and has given me the passes." I smiled conceitedly.

"Passes?" Austin picked up on that quickly.

"Yes. Passes." I reached into the manila envelope and pulled our four lanyards with plastic credit card things attached to them. I handed them to each person.

"No fucking way!!!" Matt yelled.

"I can't believe this," Austin said.

"These are your tickets as well, so I advise you not to lose them," I stressed.

"What about the tickets in the birthday card?" Austin inquired.

"Those were fills, not real tickets." Austin flipped over the card and stared shocked at the printed numbers.

:ALL ACCESS PASS:

SEAT: 01

SECTION: F

"Section F, where is …wait… is that for Field?" He asked.

"No. No dude. That's not… NO. NO WAY!!" Matt interjected.

"Yes. That stands for Field. And the pass allows you anywhere you want to go. We can go meet the players before, after, meet the entertainers for the half-time show and all the celebrities associated with all of that." I beamed. Some days it was really cool to be me, I thought. Austin kissed me hard and thanked me.

"Hey if it doesn't work out man – I want her!!" Matt said and Jess kneed him and gave him a nasty look.

"No. She's mine. Forever." He stared at me.

Forever? Wow. That sent a charge into me. I glanced over and Jess was fuming.

"You said celebrities and players?" Jess finally found her voice.

"Yes."

"I can go meet whomever I want?"

"Yes." Jess started to look excited for once this trip. I don't think Matt could care less if she took off with one of the players or not.

"As long as you don't interfere with them. After the game, the owner has a party planned even if they don't win and we are invited if you guys would like to go or not…"

"Are you kidding me? Hell, yeah, we want to go!!" Austin said before kissing me again. The driver pulled up and parked outside of double steel doors. He opened my side first and I crawled out with Austin following. The others got out on their side. Austin picked me up and spun me around thanking me again for his present. I gave him a hard, meaningful hug and kissed his cheek. I waved my card in front of a little black box and the steel doors unlocked. We were greeted by a man in a black suit and an earpiece in his ear. He looked at our cards and scanned them and then held his hand to a wire hanging from his ear.

“Ms. Baylor, someone will be here to escort you momentarily.” The man stated. Austin squeezed my hand and I actually was a bit excited myself. A few moments later a man who I recognized, but didn’t know his name appeared.

“Miss Baylor?”

“Yes.”

“Mark is anxious to see you. Please follow me.” I figured it was one of Mark’s men, bodyguard-like guys. We all followed him down the long concrete tunnel to an elevator. He punched in a code and the doors opened. There were police and police dogs walking up and down the hallway. There was even one in the elevator.

“What’s with all the cops?” Matt asked.

“Super Bowl.” The man said dryly. Matt grunted, I secretly hoped he felt stupid for asking that question. The elevator doors opened and we walked out to a nice carpeted hallway, office like. Beige walls with nice paintings hanging from them. Well lit, much different than the basement. We walked down the hall to a pair of double wood doors. The man slid his badge in front of another black box and they unlocked. Mark was standing with some other men in a circle when he turned and saw us enter. He smiled hugely and walked towards me with open arms. I smiled back and he gave me a very large hug and attempted to kiss me when I moved my face and he grazed my cheek. I could smell the liquor radiating off of him.

"I see you brought your little brother and his friends," Mark stated enthusiastically. Austin who was clearly not amused and probably pissed by Mark's affection aggressively separated us and place his hand out to shake Marks.

"I'm her boyfriend, Austin." Mark looked surprised but shook his hand.

"No offense man, no offense." Mark held his left hand up in defense.

"Thank you very much for the tickets and the passes," Austin said changing the subject but hung on to my waist tightly.

"Yeah man, thanks! This is so awesome." Matt practically shouted. Jess said nothing.

"Well, you boys have fun tonight!" Mark stated in a condescending tone.

"Oh, we will, we will!" Matt spewed.

I tried to calm the situation down, "Mark as you've met Austin, this is Matt." I waved to the boy who was practically jumping up and down, "and his friend, Jess, or Jessica." It occurred to me that I didn't know how she liked to be introduced, and 'Bitch' wasn't really appropriate.

"Jess is fine." She reached her hand out and Mark grabbed it and kissed the back of it. Not even a spark out of Matt. Jess smiled and twitched her hips. I rolled my eyes.

"Jess is head cheerleader, Mark. You two should get along well." I smiled at him and his eyes sparkled with interest.

"Head cheerleader huh?"

"Yes." Jess giggled like a mouse.

"Well, we have quite a cheerleading troop here, have you thought about joining a professional team after you graduate…in…the…"

"Spring. This spring I am graduating." Jess finished his sentence. Mark put his hand, open palm, around her waist and led her away from us. As they turned, I heard him offer her a drink, and her mousy giggle again.

"Brother!?" Austin brought me back from my thoughts.

"Just ignore him. He's an ass and he's drunk or at least been drinking. He's the owner of the team and today's a huge day for him."

"You're making excuses for him?" Austin was pissed.

"No. I'm just telling you to let it go. You know who I'm with and who I love and you need to just let it go."

"But he made a pass at you right in front of me and everyone else." I was flattered, yet pissed at the same time. I had to spend my weekend with Barbie-slut who practically shot me fire bolts every time Austin touched me, and he sees this person every day and spends time with her every day and he's pissed at this situation?

"Time for a walk." I looked at him seriously. We left Matt ogling the other men in the room and asking them obnoxious questions. I walked back into the carpeted hallway. Once the doors shut behind us, I faced Austin.

"Listen. I'm not making excuses for him, but now is not the time to have a pissing contest. I love you and you know that. I have had to put up with Jess this entire weekend and I have because of you. Mark made a slight pass at me because he's used to women throwing themselves at his feet. I don't see him or even talk to him on a regular basis. You, however, see, talk to, and hang with Jess, and I am just supposed to let that go? Mark was a client, that's all. Jess is your best friend and there is a huge difference."

"Has he… have you…"

"No. Client!" I was getting seriously pissed.

"I'm sorry. You're right. I'll shake it off. I am the one who is being an ass now." I put my arms around him and kissed his neck. "I love you; can we just try and enjoy the rest of the day please?" I nuzzled into his neck.

"Absolutely! This is really cool!" We walked back into the office and joined the rest of the people. Austin walked near Matt and entered his conversation. After a while, with his new eye-candy, Jess, Mark asked us if we would like to go to the locker room and meet the players and the coaches?

"Yeah, that would be great!!!" the giddy little-boy Matt stated.

"Can we meet the half-time entertainers buy any chance?" Barbie batted her eyes at Mark.

"Sure darling, anything you want, just remember, you're my date tonight!" He smiled at her. She smiled back. Wow, that didn't take long for either Barbie-slut or Mark… Two peas in a pod I thought and the fact that Matt could care less. Wow. Mark showed us all off like prize-winning trophies to all the players. They were very friendly, but focused on the game and winning for their precious owner. A little too much testosterone for my liking, and being completely in love with Austin, could really care less about the man-meat in front of me. After the players, Mark walked us over to the dressing room area and introduced us to some of the celebrities and their entourage, that followed them. Girls and groupies and both Jess and Matt were lost with awe! We wished them all good luck but didn't want to linger and be in their way. Jess, Mark, and Matt all headed back upstairs while Austin and I lagged behind. I wanted some alone time to enjoy with him. I found a large steel door that had some spray-painted letters and numbers on it and decided to see where it led. It led to the stadium floor. There weren't a lot of people yet, and the employees were setting up the seats with poppers and banners and flags for the show and game. We found our seats and they were pretty amazing. I didn't even sit this close watching Austin play. Austin pulled me into his arms, looked me in the eyes, and stared at me.

"Thank you again, and I'm sorry I acted like an ass. I can't even imagine what it's been like for you with Jess this weekend."

"Can we just not talk about her while we have *some* alone time, please?"

"Sure." Then he pressed his lips against mine and separated my lips open with his. I could feel his moist breath against mine. He put his hands at the back of my neck and pulled me in harder for a deeper kiss where he maneuvered his tongue around mine.

My pulse was quickening and I felt the arousal grow inside of me. I wrapped my arms around his back and pulled him tighter into me. Man – I could have taken him right there. I didn't know where the security cameras were or I just might have. He pressed his pelvis into me and apparently, he felt the same way. I had an idea at that moment. I pulled away from him and he looked confused. I grabbed his hand and led him out of the stadium. We headed back to the elevators and up to the carpeted hallway. When we were walking, I remember seeing a women's restroom.

"Where are we going?" Austin asked as my pace quickened.

"You'll see." I reached the bathroom and was grateful it had a lock on the door. From my experiences, most executive restrooms did. I made sure it was empty and locked the door. Austin looked at me coyishly.

"Should we pick up where we left off?"

"You don't need to ask me." Austin picked me up and I wrapped my legs around him. He was fervently kissing my neck while gently tugging on my hair to pull my head backwards. He walked back to the counter where he untucked my shirt.

"Did I mention that you look extremely hot today?"

"I don't feel warm," I giggled.

"I mean sexy hot - not temperature." He pulled the cups of my bra down and twisted my hard-forming nipples in his fingers. I moaned. He unbuttoned my pants and I slid off the counter. I saw a couch in the lobby next to the dryers and led him over there. He laid me on the couch and kneeled next to me. I lifted my hips up so he could slide my underwear and pants off. Without delay, he started sucking my clitoris and maneuvering his tongue between my vagina and clit, circling it causing my climax to come close. He shifted positions which I didn't see because my eyes were closed from the enjoyable tongue fucking, I was receiving. I felt him, without hesitation enter and fill me. He thrust fast and hard causing an orgasm from both of us almost simultaneously. I immediately felt a calming release and my mood lifted. He pulled out of me and got dressed. I returned my pants and bra to normal and stood up next to him.

"That was cool," he said looking at me.

"Cool??" I asked because he had never referred to our sexual relationship as 'cool' before.

"I'm sorry, cool?" I stated surprised.

"I just mean, we're at the super bowl and we just had sex in a bathroom!!" He said laughing. I started laughing along with him and he pulled me in and kissed me fervently again. I pulled away, "I'm sorry, but we are just going to end up back on that counter again if you continue to kiss me like that." I smiled.

"Nothing wrong with that." He smiled.

"I thought you wanted to see the game today?" Austin thought about it for a while, "Suppose you did go to a lot of trouble to arrange all of this…"

"Yeah, I kind of did…"

"In that case I guess we'll leave that for later."

"Sounds like a plan to me…later, right?"

"Definitely!"

I went to the mirror to straighten my hair and not look like I was just having sex in a bathroom.

"You ready?" Austin put his hands around my waist. I turned, gave him a quick kiss, grabbed his hand and we left the bathroom. The hallway was empty and we headed back to Mark's office. I was feeling a bit giddy and in a much better mood. I was holding Austin's hand and caressing his arm with my other hand. I felt very affectionate and really didn't care who saw at this moment. Everyone was still in the same place when we returned which was just odd like time stopped. I don't think anyone even noticed we left and came back. I spotted some hors-d'oeuvres and realized I was hungry.

"You're in a better mood," Austin whispered in my ear while giving it a little nip. I giggled like a school girl and pressed my face into his, silently asking for more. I nibbled at my pizza ball while staring at him. I couldn't take my eyes off of him and it seemed mutual. This was the first function that we were 'alone' in our relationship. There were no parents for either of us, no co-workers, or business or school functions. We could completely be ourselves and enjoy being 'us'. That was extremely freeing. I placed one of the pizza balls to his lips and he bit it gently. When he was finished, he licked my fingers and lingered longer and sucked the buttery garlic off them. I laughed and leaned into a kiss. The kiss turned more passionate than I intended it to but wasn't stopping it either.

"Woah!!!" a voice bellowed from behind Austin. We pulled away but continued the gaze. We both knew by the sound of the voice it was Matt.

"Dude-man, you think you can leave your lady for a half a second to come talk to some of these guys here?" Austin rolled his eyes. I stuck out my tongue and crossed my eyes, so unlike me. Austin laughed and joined Matt as he was tugged away. I looked around the room and as I figured, Mark was now hanging on and slightly groping Jess. She didn't seem to mind, and I'm not her mama. I grabbed a glass of champagne and just tried to absorb the moment. I watched Austin laughing and joking with his friend. He was talking about the sport which was one of his passions and this could be a way to make some contacts. Another reason that just popped into my head of not engaging in a pissing contest. Mark walked over to the circle they were in and patted them on the backs asking how they were enjoying their afternoon thus far. When Mark walked away, Barbie-slut looked lost. I just stared at the fine specimen of the man who I was absolutely in love with and wasn't afraid of it anymore. I walked over and Austin lifted his arm and put it around my shoulder. He leaned in and kissed my neck and I smiled. I stared at him and he stared back. Jess walked over and stood next to Mark, I assumed she thought he was going to give her the same affection that Austin gave me but Mark was a man of many women and wasn't going to be tied, or associate, with just one. And just as that reflection entered my brain, a very leggy, brunette, that looked like she was a high-end dancer in Vegas, walked next up to Mark. Mark wrapped his arm around her waist and kissed her cheek. She had definitely been or is one of 'Mark's girls.'

"Well, Ladies and Gentleman, I suggest you take your seats for the pregame entertainment!!" A very large, athletic bouncer-like man announced from the double doors. I looked at Austin and leaned in for a kiss. We turned and headed down with the rest of the crowd. Matt was next to Austin and I could care less where Barbie-slut was. Matt was elated when we found our seat, Austin and I really didn't 'find' them but he didn't need to be told the details. The pregame show was starting and I cheered as did everyone else.

After the game, I was feeling euphoric! All of the excitement and buzz from the stadium. It didn't even bother me that Jess never returned to her seat.

"You want to go to the party?" I asked Austin

"Not unless you do?"

"Not really, I think I would like to have my own party with you back in the room." I smiled

"Sounds good to me." He kissed me.

"We should at least go congratulate Mark and maybe see exactly what's going on."

Austin, Matt, and I started to walk up to Mark's office when I was picked up and lifted off my feet in a bridal sweep. I looked shocked. One of the players was ordered by Mark to come get us, but I don't think that is quite the way he meant. I laughed and made fun of my short trip to the field. I was secretly praying that Austin wouldn't flip, but when I caught sight of him, he and Matt were right behind me laughing hysterically. The thought instantly occurred to me that they were going to dump something cold and wet on top of me, but much to my relief that didn't happen. The player put me down next to Mark and ran off to the rest of his team.

"Congrats on the win!" I shouted

"Thanks" and he gave me a hug. I spotted Jess and was slightly relieved that she was OK, for Austin's sake, of course.

"Wow, that was quite a ride you got!" Austin explained when he caught up with me.

"Are you mad?" I asked cautiously.

"No El- it's fine." He smiled. He then walked over and shook Mark's hand congratulating the team owner for the win. All the players were on the fields and carpets were being rolled out and podiums and were being placed for speeches. Matt asked Mark if he could introduce him to one of the cheerleaders and in a 'good 'ol boy' fashion, he agreed. Everyone was having a fantastic time. We stuck around 'till everyone and everything was calming down. Once Mark was done with all the sports-casters, photo shoots, and frenzy, I decided I was really in the mood to party. I knew Mark had hired some huge famous, group to entertain at the hotel and dancing and being free was something I was needing.

"Hey, buddy?" I asked Austin.

“Yes?” He responded while pulling me tightly into him.

“You wanna go dancing?”

“I’ll go anywhere with you!”

“Just for a little while, then we can pick up our own party in our room.” I smiled.

“Sounds good to me!”

I told Mark that we would see him back at the hotel and he had one of his men escort us to the limo. Before we left, Matt informed us that he was going to get a ride with the cheerleaders and meet us there. Jess was going to join Mark in his car.

Once in the limo, I pulled Austin into a passionate kiss. The car started moving so I worked quickly. I unzipped his pants and started stroking his penis. It didn’t take long for him to get hard. I unfastened my pants, pulled them along with my underwear down and straddled him. I was all ready to go. I easily slid down his shaft and he let out a groan. I moved up and down while Austin held my hips. He nibbled at my neck which pushed me over the edge and I leaned my head back and came hard.

“I’m going to cum with how intense your orgasm was.”

I could barely voice words, so I just incoherently nodded my head and moaned. With a final thrust, Austin stilled. After a few moments, I lifted off of him and pulled up my pants. Austin did as well.

“That was amazing.” He said and leaned over and kissed me. I curled up into him and he snuggled me and played with my hair.

The driver pulled up to the door of the hotel and we separated and exited the vehicle. I was grateful once inside because I spotted food. I didn't eat a lot and was pretty hungry. The performers were already on stage and playing. I grabbed a half of a sandwich from a server walking around with a tray. Austin grabbed one also. He must have been hungry too. We walked to the bar and ordered two pops. I didn't see Mark or Matt yet, but it was still early. Austin pulled me onto the dance floor with a slow jazzy number playing. He moved me around like a puppet. That was a turn on in itself. Every so often he would sneak in a little kiss or grab my ass. I would just giggle. A little while later, I spotted Matt surround by very attractive women, which I assumed were the cheerleaders and in the other part of the room, Mark was arm in arm with Jess. After a few hours of dancing and socializing, I was sweaty and hot and ready to head back to the hotel. Austin agreed. We said our good-nights, thanks, and called a cab.

CHAPTER 21

"I need a shower," I told Austin once back in the hotel room.

"Want to join me?"

"I never turn an opportunity down to see you naked!" I headed into the bathroom and turned the shower on. Austin came up from behind me and started kissing my neck. He massaged my breasts at the same time. He moved his hands down my stomach and unbuttoned my pants. He hooked his thumbs into the waist of my jeans and pulled them, along with my panties down to my ankles. He took a small affectionate nip at my butt and I yelped. I stepped out of my pants and turned to face him. He crossed his arms in front of himself, grabbed the hem of his jersey and shirt and pulled them off over his head. I unbuttoned his pants and they fell to the floor. I kneeled down and bit the elastic waistband of his underwear with my teeth and pulled them off, freeing his erection. He laughed and said, "Well that's a new one!"

I smiled at him and stood back up. He pressed his lips against mine while fisting two handfuls of my hair. He pulled me into him harder with great impetuousness. I steadied myself while holding onto his very defined back. I slowly eased away from him and he helped me into the shower. The warm water felt nice, but Austin's wet physique felt nicer behind me. He put the complimentary shower gel in his hands, lathered them, and began massaging my shoulders. Damn, that felt good! He worked his way around to my breasts and kneaded them while twisting my nipples. With one hand on my breast, he moved the other one down to my clitoris. He swirled his finger around and then into my vagina. He pulled his long index finger out and replaced it with two. He repeated this motion. I placed my head back on his shoulder. My breathing quickened and my body built up pressure like in a steam pot.

"I'm going to cum if you keep this up." I breathily announced.

"Go ahead, I want to feel you cum on my hand." As he finished the words my body released and he moved even faster to make it more intense. He spun me around, lifted me, placed my soapy back against the shower wall and filled me with his erection.

"I want you to cum again," he said determined and with each thrust, my body intensified. He was penetrating deep and purposeful. I reached my climax again and could not contain the cry from my release. I let out a muted noise that got louder the more Austin thrust.

"FUCK!" and with that, he stilled deep inside of me. I could feel him panting hard and completely lost track of how long we stood motionless under the running water. He pulled out of me and kiss me gently on the lips. I opened my eyes and stared into his. He ran his hands through my hair pushing it away from dripping down my face. He reached next to me, grabbed my shampoo, and filled his palm.

"Turn around please." He asked and I turned around. He started to wash my hair.

"I don't know if I have ever told you this, but I love my hair washed, brushed, anything really," I stated with my eyes closed and thoroughly enjoying the head massage I was receiving. He pulled me back into the stream of the cascading water to rinse out the soap. I added the conditioner while he washed his. We finished and rinsed off. Once out of the shower, I noticed the clock read, 3:45 AM. Wow. We were really up late. I dried off and toweled my hair. Austin followed and I quickly found my pajamas and crawled into bed. Once in bed, Austin snuggled into me, enveloped me in his arms and we both fell sound asleep.

An alarming sound jolted me awake. My senses finally came around and I realized it was Austin's cell phone ringing. I tried to make out the picture but my eyes hadn't focused yet.

"Hello?" I quietly answered. A muffled whimper came from the other end. I looked back on the phone cover and my eyes could concentrate a little better. There was a picture of Jess in her cheerleading outfit and 'Jess' under the picture. That woke me up.

"Hello?" lingering on the 'O'.

"Um, Austin?" A slurred voice asked.

"No dumb-ass Austin is asleep. What the fuck do you want at…" I looked over at the clock, "…4:45 in the morning?"

"Ellie, I'm so sorry." A drunken Jess whimpered. "Can you get Austin?"

I felt stupid for asking her but, "Have you been drinking?"

"Uh huh."

"No, I will not get Austin he's asleep. What is wrong?"

"I don't know how to get back to the hotel."

"Where's Mark?"

"I don't know."

"Where's Matt?"

"Left with the cheerleaders."

"Where are you?"

"I'm at the party."

"Do you see anyone there, like a server I can talk to?"

"Umm…" she paused. I could tell she was looking around. Then out of nowhere, a man's voice was on the phone, "Uh Hello?"

"Hi. Are you sober enough to get the girl who handed you the phone to a cab?"

"Yes, ma'am. I'm a waiter, haven't been drinking."

"Fine. Write down this address, call a cab for her, give the cabby this address and put her in it, please. Please hand her back the phone." The man did what he was told.

"Hi-E," Jess returned.

"Yeah, Hi. Call Austin's cell when you get here and I will see you up to your room. K?"

"OOH K." And she hung up.

Great, an hour of sleep and now I get to go deal with drunken slut-Barbie. About a half hour later Austin's cell rang. He stirred a little but didn't wake. I threw Austin's large hoodie on and some of my leggings. I met her in the lobby and she could barely stand straight. I paid off the cab and went back to retrieve Jess. I dug through her purse, found the room key and helped her up to her room. On the way there, I was praying that Matt wouldn't be having some kind of kinky sex with like five women and was grateful when we entered, it was empty. I found her night clothes and helped her change for bed. I set the timer on her phone at 11:00 AM. She was already passed out by the time I finished. I turned to leave and a muffled "Thank you El…" came from the pillow. I just rolled my eyes and headed back to my room.

I crawled back into bed with Austin and he awoke a little.

"What's the matter?"

"Nothing important. Go back to sleep.

"K – Love you."

"I love you too."

I drifted back to sleep, but it wasn't easy. I had a very restless time. I kept having dreams of drunken Barbie and the game and all of the excitement of the day.

When my alarm on my cell when off at 9:00 AM, I groaned, stretched, and snoozed it. Austin coiled around me and I felt comfy and warm in his rapture. Around the sixth time my alarm went off, Austin grabbed it and shut it off. He kissed my temple and brushed the hair out of my face.

"Good morning beautiful."

"I don't know about how 'good' it is, but waking up next to you is good." I garbled.

"Um, I don't remember you going to sleep in my hoodie last night, were you cold?"

"Nope!" Then I remembered 'the call.' "I didn't." Austin just looked at me confused.

"Jess called your cell phone last night, drunk and lost. I didn't want to wake you so I took care of it."

"Are you kidding me?" Austin sounded pissed.

"No. I needed something quick so I threw on your hoodie, hope that's OK?"

"Looks good on you! I can't believe her! I'm so, so sorry."

"Don't worry about it. Let's get some breakfast, I'm starving." Austin pulled me onto his chest and gave me a kiss.

I changed into my clothes, but kept Austin's hoodie on, put my hair into a messy pony-tail, added some light make-up and was ready to go.

"I really like this hoodie!" Even though I was swimming in it.

"Keep it. You look sexy in it. You look hot in everything…and nothing." He giggled.

"Thanks, I will!" I said haughtily.

We went down to the restaurant in the hotel and there were a few people straggling around. I saw a couch next to the fireplace with a table by it. Austin and I ordered breakfast from there while we snuggled on the couch drinking our coffee.

"So, how exactly did you take care of it?" Austin pressed. Not how I wanted to spend my cuddle time, talking about her.

"Like I said, she called your cell, I had her hand the phone to someone sober. I gave them directions on putting her in a cab and bringing her here. Once she arrived, I met her in the lobby, paid the driver, and took her to her room. No Matt by the way." Right when I said that, Matt came bounding in with a huge smile.

"GOOOOD MORNING EVERYONE!!!" Matt bellowed in the dining room. Austin and I just looked at him annoyed.

"What happened to Jess? She looks like hell?"

"What happened to Jess? What the fuck happened to you?" Austin barked. Matt just looked confused.

"You were supposed to be her date! You were supposed to watch out for her!" Austin was pissed. I wasn't sure if I should be mad because he was so concerned for her safety or if I should be pissed at Matt for ditching her.

"I think I will head up and pack," I told Austin and Matt. I gave Austin a quick peck on the cheek and departed before my jealousy got the better of me.

Austin joined me a little while later and I was all packed.

"Everything go alright?" Austin just looked at me. "You didn't punch him or anything did you?"

"No. He can be such an ass though." I rolled my eyes, 'You're just figuring this out?' I thought. We finished gathering our things and headed to the lobby. When we reached the lobby, there was Matt staring at his phone and a very unstable, sick looking Jess. The Lincoln pulled off and we headed for home.

The flight back was pretty uneventful. Jess and Matt slept, separately. Austin cuddled up to me and read a book as did I. The car ride home wasn't much better.

"Hey, you guys could at least say thank you to Ellie for taking you to an awesome weekend. I mean you were and are completely ungrateful and a couple of assholes!"

"We, well, at least I don't mean to be ungrateful. I had an awesome time!! I even came home with some of the girl's numbers!" Matt stated proudly. Jess just stared at him exasperated. I assumed she thought they would be a defined couple by the end of this trip.

"Are you even going to say thank you to Ellie, Jess?" Austin pressed. I nudged him and mouthed "Stop".

"No. I will not stop. She's being a royal bitch! I didn't have to bring her and she behaved completely horrible. She was extremely rude to you, and by acting that way to you she was disrespecting me as well. The kicker of all of it, she got herself in trouble, and you, after being treated like shit the entire weekend, went and bailed her out!" Austin lectured them both.

"Maybe you should look into being a lawyer". I laughed.

"It's not funny. I don't like the way they treated you."

"You're right I'm sorry."

The car ride remained silent. Austin just intertwined our fingers. The driver pulled into my driveway and opened our doors. I just got my bags and went into the house. I didn't even want to hear a peep from them.

"Hey Mouse". Austin stroked my back. I turned to face him.

"I'm going to walk them back to my house, I'll come back later, K?"

"Sure." I sounded defeated.

"You, OK?" He asked.

"Yes. Just exhausted from the trip I guess." Because telling him, "This is why I hate people because people complicate the shit out of things" might be a little too much for right now. He kissed my forehead, turned, and walked out the door. I went to the window and watched him follow them down the driveway. Once they got to Austin's house, he ran in probably to tell his family he was home, and he reappeared moments later. I watched as he animatedly talked to them next to Matt's car. He seemed to be chewing Jess out more so than Matt. I felt proud, but sad at the same time. Jess really needed to mature a bit. While Austin was talking, I decided to pick up the phone and call Mia to say thank you for the plane and cars.

"Hey Mia, it's Eli."

"Hiya Darling. How was the game?" Knowing completely well he hosted a Super Bowl party; he knew who won.

"It was wonderful. Thank you again for all your kindness."

"You're like my daughter, anything for you! I'm glad you called. You remember that offer I extended you?"

"About running for President?" I asked.

"Yes. That's the one. Well, I have started my campaign, and I need my right-hand legal girl next to me for the race."

"Um … OK… wow… When?"

"Can I have you here tomorrow?"

"Tomorrow? I really should check into the office, how is Wednesday?"

"Wednesday will be just fine. I will have my car pick you up and my jet will be ready to go, we'll discuss details tomorrow. You go rest from your big weekend."

"Thanks again Mia. Talk to you tomorrow." Right as I hung up the phone Austin walked in the door.

"You on the phone?" he asked.

"Um no, I just hung up." I stared off into the distance.

“Everything OK?”

“Uh, yes, I guess so. I have to fly to New York Wednesday… Mia’s request.”

“Wow, he’s not wasting any time. Why so urgent?”

“He’s starting his Presidential campaign and is hiring me as one of his personal advisors.”

“What? Come again?” Austin was shocked.

“I don’t have all the details yet. So, don’t start jumping to conclusions.” I walked over and put my hands around his waist. I needed to change the subject and quickly, “Why were you so animated when you were talking to Jess?”

“I was just trying to get out of her why she decided to act at her worse behavior of all time?” Not that I wanted to hear more on her, but it got him off of talking about topics I didn’t quite have answers for. I was also emotionally spent from this weekend.

“And, what did you say? What did she say?” I grabbed his hands and led him into the living room onto the couch.

“I pretty much just said that her behavior was unacceptable and she has damaged our friendship to un-repairable levels.” I was shocked that Austin cut their friendship off like that.

“What? You looked shocked.” He noticed my face.

“I guess I am a little, I mean, don’t get me wrong her behavior was deplorable, but you have been friends forever.”

“Well, I love you, and I am not going to let anyone treat you that way ever. You went to A LOT of trouble for this weekend and a lot of money was spent and they both acted like frat-brats. I am so sorry!"

"Austin, I love you too. I'm sorry they acted that way, but I had such an amazing time with you, I mean not only the fun of the game but our personal time as well. The executor's bathroom, the shower was amazing, it was all incredible." Austin pulled my chin to his and softly nibbled on my lips.

"Were your parents' home?" I asked.

"Yes. I can't stay long. Max grabbed my homework for me and I have some catch up from missing today."

"Alright, I guess I have some catch up to do for my trip on Wednesday."

"Please let me know what that's about when you know more."

"Of course, I will." Austin stood up, held his hands out for me to hold for balance. He placed his hands on my neck and kissed me longingly.

"I have to go."

"Alright, Love you."

"You too, Mouse." And he walked out the door.

CHAPTER 22

Wednesday was a long day; I caught the flight early and was working in the New York office all day. Mia and I didn't even have time to talk about his new venture in life. A knock on my office door startled me.

"Hey- you ready for dinner?" Mia announced.

"Sure thing. I'll just wrap this up and meet you in the lobby in a second." I smiled at him.

I locked down my laptop, placed it in the bag along with paperwork I still needed to look over. I had been working on finalizing and transferring his current acquisitions over to other members of the board where when he was finished with his Presidential race and/or Presidency, he would acquire them back. My cell rang right as I was placing my arm in the sleeve of my coat. Austin's picture came up with the Super Bowl champions.

"Hi, buddy!" I answered.

"Hi sexy, am I interrupting anything?"

"No. Just putting on my coat to meet Mia for dinner."

"Tell him I said hello."

"Absolutely! Can I call you if it's not too late when we're finished?"

"Sure. Talk later then. Love you."

"Love you too."

I hung up and felt tingling all over. He truly warms my heart. That thought made me smile. I picked up my briefcase, shut off my office light, locked the door, and headed to the lobby. When I arrived at the lobby, I noticed that Mia wasn't alone, a very attractive woman was standing next to him, of course, Angelica. She spotted me walking towards them and opened her arms wide. "There she is, there's my darling!" she vociferously announced. I smiled and walked right into her arms.

"Hello, Mrs.- GG."

"Has *he* been working you too hard sweetheart?" she shot Mia a stern look.

"No, ma'am, just doing my job." I smiled coyishly.

"Well, you just tell GG if he does, OK?" she said as if she was talking to a toddler. I nodded and she intertwined our arms and we walked to the awaiting car. The driver took my briefcase and Mia's as well and placed them in the trunk. We all crawled in and headed to his favorite restaurant.

"No unexpected guests tonight are there Mia?" I prodded.

"No. Just the three of us for a nice family dinner." He tapped Angelica's knee. I smiled and felt relieved. The familiar maître d' came up to us as we entered the threshold of the bar, "Sir, your usual?" He asked Mia.

"Yes." And he nodded and lead us to a cozy little table next to the fireplace. He pulled the seats out for Angelica, myself, and then Mia. When he pulled our seats out, he unfolded our napkins from the table and placed them on our laps before tucking us in at the table. We ordered our drinks and caught up on our lives and business. I divulged all the details of our trip to the Super Bowl, well not *all* the details. I also thanked them for the very kind basket they sent after my father's heart attack. The conversation took us all the way through desserts. They wanted to know about Austin and how college plans were going, and other life events, which I really didn't have any. It turns out that Austin has become my 'life event'. After our meal, I excused myself and headed back to my hotel room. I was ready to just relax and put legal documents away for the evening.

Once settled in my room, I picked up my cell and called Austin.

"Hello." He answered.

"Hi. Are you busy?"

"Not too busy to talk to you." Just hearing his voice made me smile. I apologized for calling so late and he said he was up studying. I told him about my dinner, my easy conversation with Mia and Angelica. I told him that they asked about him and were anxious to see him again. He told me about the hospital and school and trying to set Jess 'in her place' and how that wasn't going well. We didn't talk very long because we were both tired.

Over the next couple of days, Mia and I really started going over his Presidential plans and all my roles and duties I would need to organize. We decided that Angelica would help me look for a place to live here in the city. I thought that would be perfect because that way I would be close to Austin and work for Mia. I would work out of his New York office. I would have a lot of traveling so we discussed me not getting a place of my own, just living with Angelica and Mia.

"Our place is big enough; we won't even know you're there." Mia advocated. I didn't feel comfortable with that suggestion, even though it was true.

"A girl needs a place of her own, ya know?" I countered.

"I guess, so then let's get my 'partner in crime' started while we work." He suggested. Angelica was more than happy to help, this was her thing, shopping. Although not for apparel, housing is just as fun, according to her. I made a business plan on how I would take a sabbatical from my home office for an indefinite amount of time. I would close the current cases I was working on or transfer them to another lawyer. When I found a place, which I had absolutely no doubt would happen very soon with Angelica, I would return home and finalize and clean my office. I would also put my house up for sale and hire a moving crew to the new location. Everything seemed to be going accordingly.

Saturday morning Angelica met me in the lobby of the hotel. We went to the little restaurant and had a light breakfast.

"Are you excited?" she asked me.

"Yes."

"I have a lot of properties scheduled for us to look at today. The agent will be here shortly and we will head out then."

"Sounds good. Thank you for all your hard work on this. I really appreciate it."

"Darling, you're the daughter I've always wanted, anything you need, I will help." She smiled sincerely. We had just finished our meals, mine being a bagel lightly toasted with cream cheese, and hers, an egg white omelet when a middle aged, average professional looking man appeared next to Angelica. Angelica rose and greeted him by kissing both cheeks. She introduced me to Brian and he shook my hand politely.

"Would you like something to eat or a coffee?" Angelica offered.

"No thank you, but we should get going. We have a lot of properties to see." He stated. We paid our bill and headed out with Brian to the Lincoln car waiting for us.

We had to have seen every place that was for sale in the city. It was so overwhelming. We looked at tall high-rises with bell-men to high-end studio apartments. There was always something on each one I didn't like.

"If I could combine the kitchen from the one on 19th and the living room from Pier St…" I said. I was becoming extremely frustrated and being overwhelmed I was starting to get fatigued.

"One more. Can you look at one more for today? It's a little Brownstone." Brian suggested.

"One more, then I would like to go back and relax," I conceded. The driver pulled up to this brown brick building with Maple trees out front wrapped with black fences. Already I liked the fact it wasn't as "stuffy" as the other places we looked at. It had stairs leading up to the front entry with a black wrought iron railing. The railing had beautiful scroll work that resembled little trees. There was another twisted rod half-way down. A very nice composition and blend. There was a bay window to the left of the staircase and a garage to the right. We got out of the car and Brian led the way up the staircase. My first impression was good, however, not thrilled with walking up a flight of stairs in a New York winter. When I mentioned this point, he reminded me that it does come with a garage, and even though there would be stairs leading from the garage, they wouldn't be in snow. The front doors were tall and slender with stain-glass rectangles. Above the two stained glass rectangles were smaller stain-glass squares. The doors were covered by a beautiful copper awning that fit between corbels and below pediments. Brian unlocked the door and we walked into a little entryway foyer. The entryway was attached to the living room. The floor was a hardwood herringbone pattern, light maple color. The bay windows to my left were trimmed with a dark mahogany wood. There was a large center window that went from the floor almost to the ceiling. On either side was a frosted smaller rectangle window and then two larger side windows. At the top of each window was leaded beveled stained glass. The walls were a light ivory color. Four rooms flowed seamlessly into each other; there was a significant living room to my right, which had a mahogany curved grand staircase leading to the second story, a library lined with matching mahogany built-in bookcases, a grand dining room and a kitchen designed with white marble counters and top of the line stainless steel appliances. There was another beautiful fireplace constructed out of mahogany and marble. Another spectacular mahogany staircase was on the side leading to the two sprawling bedrooms. A small white door on the opposite side or the staircase led to a two-car garage. A half bathroom was in between the hallway and the dining room. The upper floor had a bathroom with an original claw-foot tub and a terrace facing the south. It shared the floorplan of the living area below with a curved bay window. Another fireplace painted beige resided in the center of the wall complementing the trim around the windows. It is a very bright and cheerful room that radiated harmony and calmness. The herringbone design continued on the second floor. I could see Austin and me enjoying a cup of coffee in the autumn morning or an evening glass of wine on the terrace overlooking a beautifully landscaped backyard. There was no doubt in my mind that this was the home I wanted to be in. I looked at Angelica and nodded my head. She smiled at me and said, “Brian, this is the one, lets write up that offer.” Brian guided us back to the kitchen to write up the paperwork.

“I’ll submit this when I return to the office and let you know if they accept our offer,” Brian said while shaking my hand back at the hotel lobby. I gave GG a kiss on her cheek and told her thank you for all the help today. She left and I decided I should catch up on some work for Mia. I wanted to tell Austin but was afraid how he would react.

Monday morning, I was enlightening Mia with my newest find and how excited I was about the Brownstone. I hadn’t had a call from Brian yet and was nervous that they would reject my offer.

“Angelica told me all about the new place. I really hope they do accept your offer because it’s a nice location and not too far from here.” I smiled and was trying not to get my hopes up. Around lunch, my cell phone rang and I jumped with anticipation. I looked expecting to see a number and saw Austin’s Super Bowl picture instead.

“Hello,” I answered.

“Hi. Are you in the middle of anything?”

“No. Just thinking of heading to lunch. What are you doing? Shouldn’t you be at lunch or class?” I inquired.

“Lunch break, just calling cuz I miss you.” My heart got a twinge. I felt horrible keeping this huge endeavor from him, but I didn’t want to ‘spring’ it on him all the way from New York.

"Oh. I miss you too. I'm sad that I won't be able to spend Valentine's Day with you."

"That's alright. It's just a day anyway, right?" he stated. Mia knocked on my door and I looked up. "Austin, I have to go, Mia is at my door. Love you."

"Love you too."

"You want to go to lunch?" Mia asked.

"Sounds good to me."

"I didn't mean to interrupt your phone call."

"It's fine. He had to get to class anyway." I lied. Mia and I headed out to a quaint little deli for lunch. It was a nice change ordering a half sandwich and a cup of soup. My cell rang right as I took a bite of my sandwich. It was a New York number that I didn't recognize. I attempted to answer as clearly as possible,

"Hello?"

"Is this Ellie?"

"Yes." I chewed as fast as I possibly could, I took a drink of pop.

"Ellie, it's Brian, the realtor. I have some great news for you, they accepted your offer." I practically spit the food out of my mouth.

"Great!! That's wonderful news!" I gave Mia a thumbs up.

"I will email the details; the sellers are anxious to move so hopefully we can really get this ball moving!"

"Thanks, so much Brian, I look forward to your email." I hung up the phone and tried to slow my heart rate down. Wow, this is really happening!

"That's wonderful news Ellie!" Mia said.

"Thank you."

"We should celebrate tonight; I will tell Angelica to arrange a nice little dinner because you are coming over! I won't tell her about the good news, we'll surprise her with the details!"

"OK!" was all I managed to say. "I'll just catch a ride with you then after work." We finished our meals and carried on our casual conversation. "No business talk with food" was Mia's motto. When we returned to the office, I closed my door and called my parents. I told them everything that had been going on and the good news about the Brownstone. I really wanted to tell Austin, but for some reason was still really apprehensive about how he would feel and nervous about his reaction to me leaving. I wouldn't be leaving for long; he would be joining me in the city for college soon after. My desk line rang which pulled me out of my reverie. It was the branch in Paris, while I was talking to them, I had a fantastic idea for a graduation gift.

Angelica was extremely excited when I told her of the acceptance of the Brownstone. She jumped up and down and squealed like a high school girl.

"I will help you decorate it, we will go shopping the day you sign the papers. OH!! – There is this beautiful drapery that I think would go lovely in the living quarters!!" she continued on decorating the entire place. It would be fun to live near her. Her excitement made me forget that I was even nervous to tell Austin. She had hired a professional chef to cater our meal and it was very tasty. We finished our visit and I headed back to my hotel room.

My back was turned towards the door and I was completely engulfed in the paperwork covering my desk. A knock came on my door and I yelled, "Come in!" I heard the door open but didn't turn around. I was anticipating my secretary or Mia's voice to ask a question.

"Hello, Sexy." It took me a few moments to register that the voice was Austin's. I turned around in a flash and jumped out of my seat. I jolted over to him and he picked me up and hugged me hard. I gave him a kiss and then asked him, "What are you doing here?"

"I can't let my girl spend Valentine's Day alone."

"Oh, my God, how…what…"

"Mia called me the other day and told me that he would fly me out if I wanted to spend Valentine's Day with you, so I took him up on his offer." I kissed him passionately and held him tight.

"I can't believe you are standing here in my office. Thank you!"

"I missed you a lot." He said.

"I missed you too baby." I just looked into his eyes. They are so beautiful.

"I don't want to get in your way, I can go walk around the city or something until you are finished here."

"No, I can be done in just a couple of minutes. I was just organizing these papers." I fibbed. I really needed to go through them, but Austin flew all this way so I needed to put him first. I wrapped up my paperwork and jotted down some notes on where I left off. I gathered my belongings and locked up my office and we were off.

CHAPTER 23

"I have some really exciting news." I told Austin as I was playing with his chest hair lying in bed.

"Really? Do tell." He replied. I sat up next to him.

"Well, I would really rather show you. You want to go for a ride?" Austin looked at me suspiciously. "I mean, we can do that then go get a bite to eat after?"

"That sounds nice." He pulled me back down and I giggled. I wasn't very hungry and now that I was going to show him my new house, I really lost my appetite and had butterflies spinning around my stomach. We got dressed and I called Brian to get the code for the Brownstone. It was move in ready so I wouldn't have to wait for the current owners to leave.

"You're awful quiet, everything OK?" Austin asked. I stared at my fingers that I was knotting to the point of cutting off the circulation.

"Um, yes, I'm just excited but extremely nervous to show you this."

"You're not luring me to a spot to kill me, are you?" Austin teased.

"Yes, how did you ever guess?" I rolled my eyes.

"I'm sure I'll love whatever it is you are going to show me. I support whatever you do!" He was so sweet. We pulled up in front of the Brownstone and the cab stopped.

"Where are we?" Austin asked.

"The place I want to show you." I smiled at him. We got out of the taxi and I held Austin's hand. We walked up the stairs and I pushed in the four-digit code to the black box. I took the key out and unlocked the front door. We walked into the living room and I looked at Austin. "Well? What do you think?" My voice was shaky.

"Think about breaking and entering? Not really my style and being that you are a lawyer I thought you would frown on such activities."

"We're not breaking and entering. I bought this."

"I'm sorry, you what? What do you mean 'bought this'?"

"Just what I said." I looked at him crooked.

"This place is yours?" Austin asked crossly.

"Yes."

"Why are you not coming home?" He seemed to be becoming more heated. I grabbed his hands, "Don't you want to look around a little?"

"No. Not really, I would like you to answer my question." I pulled him over to the stairs to sit down.

"I've decided to take the job with Mia. He's running for President."

"President of what?"

"President of the United States."

"Like *the* President, President?"

"Yes, I told you about this already and I am going to be on his team. I bought this house to be able to work on his campaign and–" Austin cut me off, "So how long have you known about his life change? When were you going to include me in this decision? Working for a Presidential candidate and up and buying a place across the county must take some planning? Planning that you could have easily told me about." Austin stood up from the stairs and started pacing.

"First off, I didn't really know I was going to work for Mia because he just told me last Wednesday that it was validated. Second, Angelica hired a realtor and we went looking on Saturday and… it just happened so fast."

"Don't you think that is something you want or should tell someone you love, 'hey baby, I'm up and moving and I also am taking a new job…'?" Austin was pretty pissed now.

"I wanted to tell you in person."

"In person? You had no clue I was coming here so how were you going to tell me in person?"

"...when I got home," I said mousy.

"When? When you were packing or after the For-Sale sign went in the yard?" He stormed off and out the front door. This is not what I wanted to happen and was afraid of how he was going to act. I didn't even get to tell him why I took the job and bought the house. Well, with this reaction, he doesn't deserve to know. I can be pissed too. This is exciting for me and he just shit on my good news. Asshole!

"The cab is waiting for us, come on!" he broke my trance. I looked up, "You hailed a cab? You didn't even look around at the entire place." Now, I was furious. The cab ride back to the hotel was silent. I didn't have anything to say, well, I did, but just didn't want to push it. I wanted to call him every name in the book and beat the shit out of him, so I chose silence. When we arrived at the hotel Austin went straight to the room, still not speaking to me. He's never been this mad at me before and I really didn't like it. It made me feel sick to my stomach. Back in the room, Austin was throwing things into his duffel bag.

"Are you leaving tonight?"

"No. tomorrow morning."

"Why are you so upset with me?" I inquired.

"You really have no clue?"

"I mean I have a little idea, but not entirely sure."

"You do two enormous life changing things and don't bother to even tell me!"

"So, I need your permission before I make a decision now?"

"URRGGG – NO! You don't need my FUCKING permission! But would it hurt you to share your excitement with me? You know, like, "hey, Mia is running for President and wants me to be on his team, isn't that cool?"

"You know, you didn't share that you were working at the hospital with me, I found out after your shift!"

"Not the same thing. I also told you first on which college I was attending. YOU first! Not my family!" Austin had a good point on this fact.

"Maybe this is why I didn't tell you? Maybe I thought you were going to flip out? Maybe if you even took a second to hear my entire reasoning for doing this decision you might look at the situation differently?"

"Fine. What is the reasoning for making two life changing decisions without telling me about it?" I was so infuriated that I didn't even want to tell him.

"You are such an ASSHOLE right now; I don't know if I even want to tell you!"

"ASSHOLE? ME? Are you fucking kidding me right now?" I just stared at him blankly. "I flew out here to be with you for Valentine's Day, and I'm the asshole? Am I the one who made two huge decisions and didn't tell the other? Yeah, I'm the asshole here!"

"Damn it!! You're infuriating! I can't tell you anything right now!"

"Well, you said there was more to your decision-making skills so let's hear it!" I was so mad that I screamed, "I thought I would die when you moved to New York for college. I physically got sick thinking about all the years you would be away from me in school! So, I gave up my senior partner position with the firm and joined Mia's team. I can work in the office and still be with YOU! I am moving across country away from my family- to be with YOU. I gave up my entire life, house, gym, friends, firm, to be where YOU ARE! So, please FUCKING forgive me for trying to surprise you with my news and wanting to tell you in person!" The tears started to steam down my face and my hands were shaking uncontrollably. Austin actually looked flabbergasted. He walked over to me and wiped my tears away with his thumbs.

"I guess I was being the asshole huh?" he said.

"Don't touch me right now!"

"Baby, please try and calm down. I'm sorry I over reacted…WAY over reacted!"

"I don't know how I feel right now, please don't…" Austin held me and I just sobbed in his shoulder.

"You're really shaking. Can I get you something?"

"No."

"I'm sorry again. I guess it all shocked me so much that I didn't even think."

"…I know. You didn't think. I'm going to go for a walk." Austin let go and started to grab his coat.

"Alone." He looked heartbroken. I grabbed my coat and purse and walked out the door.

By the time I returned to the room, Austin was curled up in bed asleep. I quietly changed into my night clothes and slipped in next to him. He pulled me into him and wrapped his arms around me.

"I'm so sorry. I don't like fighting with you."

"Fighting, we've never had a fight before."

"I know, and I don't want to do it again… if, that is…"

"…if what?"

"…if you still want to be with me?" I pulled out of his arms, sat up, and stared at him, even though it was dark.

"Of course, I still want to be with you. I love you – dumb ass." Austin laughed, "dumb ass?"

"I was very clear."

"Yes, you were. But you left and went for a walk."

"To clear my head and calm down so I didn't kill you." I smiled.

"Well, I guess that's a good thing. So, are we OK?"

"Yes. When you love someone, you don't give up because of a fight."

"I'm just a youngin' I don't know the ways of the world!" Austin laughed hard and batted his eyes at me.

"So, do you like my plan?"

"I was avoiding the thoughts of when I went to college and only seeing you on the holidays and breaks." Austin looked serious.

"Well, now you don't have to, I'll come to you." I smiled. "I guess that's one benefit of dating a more mature woman." Austin pulled me down on top of him and kissed my neck.

"Oh, there's a lot of benefits of dating a more mature woman!" I laughed, "I love you."

"I love you too, Mouse."

I flew back and forth wrapping up clients and files at home and doing research and legalities for Mia in New York. It didn't take long for my house to sell, and I closed on my New York Brownstone about three weeks after they accepted my offer. I didn't spend much time with Austin being so busy and it was driving me crazy. Even though we made up in New York, that fight still ate at me and made me worry. My phone rang and I looked at the screen, it was Austin,

"Hello." I answered

"Hi. How's New York?

"Lonely. How are you?"

"Lonely. I was calling because I was wondering if you are still going to go to prom with me?"

"Of course, if you still want me to go."

"I wouldn't take anyone else." When he said that the thought of homecoming came to me, and a fire burned and I felt myself getting upset all over again.

"You better not!" I attempted to joke but wasn't truly feeling my own humor.

"What color vest do I need to get?"

"You still have the pic of my blue dress?"

"It's one of my favorites!!"

"That color, navy blue."

"Awesome! You look so incredibly hot in that dress!"

"Thank you. I'll be home in time for the prom, and I'll have the limo. I'll be at your house around 4:30 PM for pictures?"

"Yeah. Mom will want pictures with us and everyone else." He sounded annoyed at that.

"I'm sorry, everyone else?"

"Yeah, you know Matt, Tubs, Jay, and their dates?"

"Oh right, I forgot that you don't go to prom solo." I felt stupid, I think I should have kept that thought to myself. Austin laughed, "I have to run, I'll order my vest after school today. Love you."

"Love you too."

Saturday came quickly. I was excited to be heading to the salon to get a full make over from massage to make up. Mia had hired a limo for me for the day, which I found hysterical for some reason. The limo picked me up early in the morning and I brought my dress and all my belongings with me. I would head to Austin's after the salon. Everything was working out perfect. I was a little nervous about attending a high school dance. I told the make-up artist not to go overboard. I needed to look younger rather than, well, older. My hair was in an up-do twist with curls hanging down, and very light make-up applied. After the masseuse helped me step into my dress, I added the small touches of the beautiful pearl choker, matching earrings, ring and stiletto shoes. I also added the bracelet and rings that Austin had given me as well. I finished it off with the matching clutch. When I walked out of the massage room everyone stared at me.

"Bella, Bella!" Ramone stated.

"Aww GIRL!!! You look amazing!" Keisha said. People started applauding. I walked to the limo and the driver opened the door for me. I waved at the entire staff that seemed to follow me out and disappeared behind the tinted glass.

When we arrived at Austin's house the driver pulled in front of his driveway, stopped the car, and then got out and opened the door for me. His garage was open and there were some other cars there. The driver looked at me and asked, "May I?"

"What?" I had no clue as to what he was asking.

"May I announce your arrival?" He said beaming at me.

"I suppose so." I wasn't use to being treated like an actual princess. The driver walked up to the front door and rang the bell. Austin's dad opened the door looking a bit confused. "May I announce the arrival of Miss Ellie Baylor, sir?" At the sound of the announcement, the others in the house came running to the front door. The driver looked at me and I took that as a clue to come towards him. Austin stepped out the door and stared at me. His jaw dropped open. My mouth could have as well. He was stunning. He was in a black tux with a perfectly matching bow tie and vest. He was wearing very shiny shoes and had his hair perfectly styled. I was torn, I wanted to rip his outfit off and make love to him right then and there, but on the other side, I wanted him to stay like this forever. He met me on the walk and smiled huge. His eyes filled with tears.

"What's wrong?" I asked concerned.

"I…I'm speechless. You are unbelievably breath taking. You are the most beautiful woman on this planet and I can't believe that I have the privilege to be allowed to love you."

"Austin! That was so beautiful! I love you too and you look incredible yourself." While we were quietly exchanging words, the boys had stepped out to witness and started wolf cries and whoops and hollers. Tubs told me that I was gorgeous and Matt lifted up my hand and gave the back of it a soft little kiss. Austin's parents had now stepped outside along with the dates of the boys. I scanned them quickly and noticed Jess was not among the girls. I didn't know if I should ask or act oblivious. The sun was starting to set and it was beautiful on the horizon. A mixture of rose gold and teal blue highlighted the black silhouette of the trees. Austin's father approached us with a box in his hand. "This arrived for you today along with a phone call." I looked at him confused, who would be calling him about me and sending this box? "Mia called me and told me to please place this on your wrist in his standing." Now my eyes started to well up. That man was amazing. I held my left arm out and Austin opened the box. It was a beautiful navy blue rose with baby's breath around it. It also had a matching boutonniere. Austin placed it on my wrist and I noticed he was shaking.

"What's wrong? Why are you shaking?"

"I am just so… so… I don't know the correct words."

"Happy?"

"Happy will do." He said. I wrapped my perfectly done fingers in his and we walked to where Chelsea was asking for us to stand for pictures. After all the pictures were taken every which way and different people, the others started to climb into the limo. Chelsea pulled me aside, "Thank you." She said.

"For what?"

"For loving my son. I can't tell you how wonderful it makes me feel to know how happy he is."

"Thank you for allowing me to love him." I smiled at her and joined Austin and the rest in the car.

CHAPTER 24

I was staring out my bay window thinking about the wonderful time I had at Austin's prom. We danced all night and the meal they served was nice. Everyone behaved themselves. I even danced with Tubbs, who surprised me, he could actually dance. With that thought, I laughed. It was hard being so far away. I realized how much I missed the comfort of looking out the window across the street and seeing Austin's car or just knowing that he was across the street. Here, in New York, I am just so far away. I picked up my cell phone and scrolled through my pictures. I was excited to see him this weekend for his graduation and party. I needed to finalize his present which I hoped that Chelsea didn't give anything away by having him get a passport. I took the last sip of my coffee, stretched, and prepared for my busy day at the office. Trying to make sure everything is legalized and proper for Mia's campaign was overwhelming, but it made the days go by quickly. As I was walking to my room, my cell rang and Austin's picture appeared.

"Hi, honey," I answered.

"Hi."

"I was just thinking about you and missing you an awful lot!"

"I must have felt you missing me because I miss you too and cannot wait to see you this Friday."

"I think it's really nice that your parents are letting me stay at your house."

"I am going to sleep on the couch and you will have my bed. They obviously know we're having sex, but they aren't comfortable with it in their house."

"I completely understand and respect their feelings."

"Hey, I just called to say I love you and to have a good day. I have to get to school."

"Thanks for calling, love you too."

I worked late into the evening every night and started meeting with the rest of the team to go over strategies and the legalese of how they can approach certain topics and how far they can attack the opponents. I didn't even have time to go to the gym. I worked out at the gym in my house which really only consisted of a treadmill and rowing machine. I would definitely take some time in finding a quality coach and gym; Rick might even be able to refer one. After two weeks, I was happy that I made the decision to be closer to Austin. I hadn't seen him since prom and missed him terribly.

Being so far away, and only talking by phone or sometimes video chat, my imagination started taking tolls on me. I was thinking about scenarios happening that weren't even logical. Hollywood movies were interjecting large rolls in my brain. I was excited to see him tonight. I shook my head and tried to focus on my day and my present to him. I went upstairs and packed my things because I was going to leave from the office. I looked through my closet and found my elegant black dinner dress. I placed the dress in my garment bag. I found a matching pair of shoes and placed them in the suitcase. I picked out one of my sexier suits, black pinstripe skirt; tight right above the knee with the matching jacket and a black camisole for tonight's graduation ceremony. I placed that in the garment bag and would change into that at the office. Crap! The office, I forgot the decorator was coming today to 're-do' my office. I sped up my selection process and found an outfit for today. I finished putting everything in the suitcase, zipped it up and called the driver. I gathered my laptop and files in my case and made sure everything was set to go, locked up, and ran through all my needs in my mind; night clothes, day clothes, make-up, underwear, perfume, deodorant…Yes, I think I grabbed everything. My doorbell rang and pulled me back to the present. I pointed out my belongings and the driver picked them up. He led the way and I locked up behind him.

Mia popped his head into the office,

"What time you heading out?"

"Around 3:00, you need something done?"

"No, I have this card from Angelica and I for him."

"Mia, you didn't have to do that!"

"Ya know, there are so few 'good ones' out there that really have great potential, I would like to support the ones I can!"

"That is really sweet, I'm sure he'll love it."

I stood up and walked over and gave him a kiss on his cheek.

"Now don't be staying too long, we need you here more than they do!" He laughed.

"Alright, I guess I'll come back if I have too." Mia smiled.

"Don't forget," I added, "I'm or we are going to France at the end of June to finalize the office there so you don't have any problems with your candidacy."

"I wouldn't dream of it!" and with that, he turned and walked out. I glanced at my clock, 1:45, damn… this day is going by slowly. I double checked that I had the tickets for Paris in my briefcase. I pulled them out and read them again.

PASSENGER

ELLIE / BAYLOR

GATE DEPARTURE BOARDING ZONE

A22 3:15 PM 26 JUNE 2018 D3

PASSENGER

AUSTIN / ANDREWS

GATE DEPARTURE BOARDING ZONE

A22 3:15 PM 26 JUNE 2018 D2

Yes, they still were the same, still looked good. I placed them back in the envelope and in my case along with Mia's card. I tried my best to focus on my work, but my mind kept drifting back to my weekend and how anxious I was to see Austin. Then I thought, what if he wasn't as excited to see me? His phone call was odd this morning, "I just called to say hi…?" What is that about? Maybe he was calling to tell me not to come, but then felt guilty when I told him I missed him… What if… "Geez Eli, stop already," I told myself. I looked at the ring he had made me for Christmas and it still made me smile. He called me. Yeah, everything is OK. I picked up my cell without even looking at the time and dialed him.

"You, OK?" he answered. I was confused by his greeting.

"Yes, why wouldn't I be?"

"You still coming?"

"Yes, why wouldn't I be?" OK now, this was getting ridiculous.

"Because you called me in the middle of class and you never do that." OH, SHIT!!!

"I'm so, so, sorry! I didn't even look at the time. You weren't in an exam or anything were you?"

"No. Those are way over; I actually don't have to even be here but I figured -"

"I'm sorry again. I am just so excited to see you that I just picked up my cell and called!" Austin laughed.

"That's fine, I am excited to see you as well."

"Are you really?" I pushed.

"Very much! Why are you even asking me that?"

I sighed, "My imagination is running wild on me, and not in a good way, and…" I trailed off.

"No reason to do that. I know it's been hard but I'll see you tonight. Are you coming in a car still?"

"Yes, I am using one of Mia's limos so the entire family can ride to your ceremony in style!"

"Really? That's awesome! Mom with love that! So will Max! Hey- I need to run, got to pick up some things and head home. It's weird being that these are my last few hours here in school. Love you."

"See you soon. I love you more."

"We'll see about that later!" Austin hung up the phone. My heart was skipping and my head felt a little better. I'm glad I called him. My desk line rang,

"Ms. Baylor, your driver is here." My secretary announced.

"Thank you, I'll be right there," I said after I pushed the little black button. I gathered my things, then realized I forgot to change – SHIT! I hurried up and took the other suit out of the garment bag, ran into my bathroom and changed as quickly as I could, I figured I could freshen up my make-up on the plane and fix my hair also. I left my outfit in the office and locked everything up. My hands were overflowing with all my bags and accessories. I felt foolish but figured I needed it all. I locked up my office and ran to the elevator.

The ride from the airport to Austin's house had me nervous. I felt like a teenager about to go on a first date… So strange being nervous. My cell phone rang, it was Austin.

"Hello?"

"Hi. I assume you landed alright?"

"Yes. We are on our way now."

"Great!! There is one slight problem." My heart sank. "What's wrong?"

"My grandparents are staying here as well."

"So., are they sleeping in your bed?"

"No. My parents', but I just wanted to make sure you're OK with that. I didn't want you to have any surprises when you got here."

"That's fine. I will be fine or I am fine with that."

"You sure, you sound nervous." How can he tell?

"I'm sure. I'm fine. I'll be there in about 45. Can your grandparents ride in the limo?"

"No. My dad is driving them separately."

"Aww hun, I'm sorry."

"It's fine."

"Do you want any of your other friends to come over and ride with us?"

"Hey, that's a great idea. Let me give a couple of them a call."

"Alright, see you in 45."

"I cannot wait!!"

I hung up the phone. Crap – I didn't even think about his family, I'm going to meet his entire family, if not today, tomorrow. Now I really had butterflies in my stomach. I also sat there thinking about how and when I should give him my gift. Tonight, tomorrow? My cell rang again, it was my mom.

"Hey, Momma."

"Hi, Mouse."

"What's going on?"

"We came back from the heart doc today." I could tell by the sound of her voice it was not good news.

"And, what did they say?"

"They said that your daddy's not healing like they want him to, and I thought since you flew in for Austin's graduation, you could come visit us before flying all the way back to New York?"

"Um, wow, Mama. Um, let me check my schedule which is on the computer and try to move some things back and around and I'll try. I don't have a way up there… but I'll figure something out. Is daddy going to be, OK?"

"No. I mean his heart was so damaged that the surgery was just a band-aid and it won't hold forever. He's so stubborn that he's not doing what the doctors say and…" she drifted off. I could tell that she was exasperated and just worn out.

"OK Mama, I'll come up Sunday."

"Thank you, Mouse. Love you."

"Love you to Mama."

We pulled into Austin's driveway at 4:45. The driver opened my door and no sooner did I step out Austin was at my door. He picked me up swung me around and kissed me with devotion. I kissed him back and melted because it felt so good to be in his arms.

"Hi." I said, but he kept kissing me, my neck and holding me tight.

"H...a...v...i...n...g t…r…o…u…b…l…e.. b…r…e…a…t…h…i…n…g." I stated. He loosened and just held me. I didn't want to let go.

"Ms. Where would you like your bags?" the driver asked. This made Austin finally let go.

"You can take them in the house sir," Austin told the driver.

"You're getting quite used to this finer class treatment." I snickered. When the driver was in the house, Austin pressed me up against the limo and pressed his entire weight against me and rubbed me with his pelvis. He pressed his lips to mine and opened my mouth with his. He kissed me hard and passionately. I felt him grow hard and wanted to take him there. I reached down and slipped my hand underneath his basketball shorts and underwear and started stroking his penis. He moaned and pressed harder into my hand. I worked fast and he leaned his head on my forehead. I continued to stroke him until I felt him freeze and he let out a slight groan and I felt him cum on my hand. I gently removed my hand from his shorts. He opened his eyes and giggled a little.

"Well, that was unexpected." He said with a smile.

"Did you enjoy that?"

"What do you think."

"I just hope my parents don't notice the change in clothing."

"I'll distract them." He released me from his pinning and I followed him into the house where the limo driver was sitting having a cup of tea at the kitchen counter. Austin was holding my hand as we walked in.

"Did you guys have enough time to catch up?" Max enquired snottily. Austin shot him a dirty look.

"May I freshen up a little? The plane ride and all…" I asked. Austin led me to the bathroom and then went to change. I smiled as he walked away. I went into the bathroom and washed my hands, checked my looks in the mirror and joined the rest of the family. Austin came out shortly and introduced me to his grandparents.

"Well, my oh my, I can see why our Aussie is so smitten!!" His grandfather said with a huge smile.

"Granddad!!!" Austin started turning pink. It was cute. I looked at Austin and mouthed "Aussie??" Austin rolled his eyes.

"It's very nice to meet you both. I have heard wonderful things about you."

"Well, you probably heard them about me, but not this old goat!" his grandmother said. I laughed I was going to get along with both of them just fine.

"Where are the rest of your family?" I inquired.

"We're only allowed six tickets," Austin stated.

"They will be over tomorrow at the hall." Ah gotcha.

"Ellie, would you like something to drink? I have wine, beer, coffee, tea, soda, water…" Chelsea asked.

"I will save my wine for dinner tonight and a cup of coffee would be wonderful." They had an individual coffee maker and she popped the cup in and brewed me a cup.

"I don't know why people can't make coffee to good 'ol fashion way!" Austin's grandfather piped up.

"Like what Granddad?"

“You know, when I was in the army, we would be out in the fields, no electricity, no fancy coffee pots, and we would put the ground right in our helmets and boil them right like that! That’s why they were made out of metal.”

“So, Granddad, you’re telling me that the United States Army made the helmets out of metal just so you guys could make coffee?” Austin prodded in a joking manner.

“Not just for that, sometimes we had to boil water for wounds or soup.” He stated matter-of-factly.

Austin just laughed, “Not for protection against bullets, but culinary means… OK, Granddad.” The entire group was enjoying this conversation. The limo driver started talking about his days in the service and then Austin’s father joined in. I asked Austin if I could speak to him privately and we walked into the living room.

“What’s wrong?” he asked while rubbing my arm.

“I got a call on my way here, from my mom.”

“Oh no, everything OK?”

“No, not really. I was wondering if I could borrow your car Sunday? I know it is really inconvenient and I hate to impose but she wants me to visit while I’m back in the same state.”

“Listen, you are not imposing on anyone, don’t ever think that. And, yes, absolutely. I can drive you if you want. I don’t have any plans. My internship ended Monday, so I would love to go with you if you want me to?”

“That would mean so much to me if you were to go! Do you need to ask your parents first though?”

"Nope. Not after I move my tassel tonight!" He smiled. I hugged him and told him thank you.

CHAPTER 25

"We would like to start off diploma presentation with our Valedictorian, Mr. Austin Michael Andrews," the guest speaker announced. Austin walked across the stage in his long black robes, golden, burgundy, white, and blue tassels bouncing with his pace. His matching cap and a golden medal reflecting the stage lights. We all stood, even his grandfather who was beaming with pride. He shook the hand of the guest speaker, assistant principal, and then the principal. He posed for the photographer shaking hands with the principal and finished his walk while moving his tassel on his cap from one side to the other. He hugged a few teachers before returning to his seat on the stage. I was so proud of him and I welled up and Chelsea had to hand me one of the many tissues she was holding on to. We looked at each other and laughed at our silly sentimental behavior. When the ceremony was over, we stood in the lobby for Austin to join us. He was told not to doddle too long because we had dinner reservations. Shortly after, he came bounding out of the auditorium arm in arm with Tubbs and Matt. They were laughing and having a wonderful time. Tubbs walked over to me picked me up and spun me around. I squealed. He set me down and I leaned up and gave him a soft kiss on his very rosy supple cheek. He turned as red as a beet and held his face. “I am never washing this spot again!” He swooned.

“Great! Then it will go with the rest of your body!” Austin teased slapping him on the back. We all hooted and snickered with this. Austin came up to me and kissed me softly on the lips and stared at me intensely. “I’m so proud of you and happy for you. I love you.” I said never breaking eye contact.

“Thank you. You inspire me to be better and try harder.” That was enough to push me over. My eyes welled up and the tears streamed down my cheeks.

“Austin, that was… stop being so wonderful, you’ll ruin my makeup!” I guffawed. He took my hand and held it.

“Let’s go eat I’m starving!!” Austin roared. We all started to turn around and Austin turned back to see what the delay was. Chelsea was giving Jess a hug. That heated me up from deep down. I didn’t like that, but then I thought, Austin might not have shared all the details and I better just keep my cool.

“So, we’ll see you tomorrow?” I overheard Chelsea say. Damn it! Why is she inviting that bitch? I looked at Austin and he shrugged. He nuzzled my ear and whispered, “Don’t let it bother you." I squirmed from the hot breath hitting my ear. I looked at him and kissed him tenderly on the lips.

"Is anyone else coming? I mean your friends from school."

"I hope so I invited a lot of people, I mean we're having the party in a hall, so…" Austin shrugged and smiled. He was in such a playful and good mood. Most of us gathered in the limo and headed for the restaurant. Austin's dad drove separately to the restaurant with his grandparents.

The restaurant was elegant. It had dimly lit lighting with small frosted glass candles on the centers of the fabric covered table. The hostess led us to a back room with a larger table. It had already been decorated with the school colors in balloons and streamers. Austin was seated at one end of the table and he directed me to sit next to him on the right. Everyone else just found a place of their own choosing. After dessert was finished and the plates had been cleared, the coffee was refilled and his mother picked up the cards and gifts and set them on a small table to the left of him. I assumed it was a 'gift table' and I was right.

"The rest of the family will bring theirs tomorrow," Chelsea told him. He opened the boxes first and one was a shadowbox frame for him to show off his robes, tassels, and medal. Another was a frame for his diploma and a couple of checks and cards from his grandparents. Mine was last. I handed him a card.

"This one's from Mia, who is so incredibly proud of you!" I beamed.

"Eli, he didn't-"

"I know." I cut him off. "He wanted to."

Austin opened Mia's card, read it, and stared stunned at it. He sat there for several minutes just staring at the gift.

"Austin? Everything alright?" I asked.

"Austin, what is it?" Chelsea prodded.

"Um, it's just a very nice gift Mr. Williams has given me and it, um, surprised me that's all, sorry everyone." Austin apologized. He folded the check and placed it in his wallet, where he didn't do that with anyone else's. I looked at him half confused and half concerned. Austin gave me a 'I'll tell you about it later' look. I then handed him my envelope.

"It's thick." He stated.

"Yup." I agreed.

Austin opened up my envelope and pulled out the paper and tickets enclosed. He read the paper then looked at me, "Are you for real?" He asked me seriously.

"Yes. That would be a pretty sick joke if it was." I replied.

"What is it?" Max shouted from across the table.

"Well, my beautiful girlfriend here has given me a trip to Europe for my graduation present!" he announced to everyone at the table. There were a lot of gasps of air and clapping. He leaned over and gave me a very nice kiss. "Thank you very much."

"You're welcome. You don't think you're going alone do you?"

"I won't go anywhere without you!" I smiled, "I wouldn't let you." I winked at him. The conversation continued about his future plans and Europe. They asked about my career and family information. It was a really relaxing night.

I stretched Saturday morning forgetting exactly where I was for the moment, Austin's bed, that's right. I snuggled into the pillow and closed my eyes. When I became more cognizant, I noticed there were already people up. I wondered what time it was. I rolled over and grabbed my cell phone, 7:47 AM. His grandparents must get up early also. I sat up turned around, put my feet on the floor stood up and tried to gain balance. I opened the door, walked down the hallway and saw Chelsea and both grandparents sitting at the kitchen table.

"Would you like a cup of coffee?" Chelsea offered.

"Yes, please."

"Austin says that you use the 'yellow packets."

"Yes, three yellow and some milk, or cream…doesn't matter." I walked over and joined them at the table. I glanced over and noticed Austin was still sleeping on the couch.

"You sleep alright?" Chelsea asked.

"Yes, thank you, he has a very comfortable bed." Chelsea laughed, "Probably from all of those years of jumping on it!" That made me giggle as well. Chelsea handed me my mug on a small plate with a spoon and sugar. "The creamer is already on the table."

“Thank you,” I added the cream and sat back and listened to the conversation going on between them. They had asked if I had ever been to Europe before and I told them that I had, and one reason I would be accompanying Austin is that I had some ends to tie up before the campaign trail started for Mia. Granddad started in on how it must look so different today from when he was over in the war and continued about his days serving. I truly enjoyed listening to his memories and it stopped me from having to talk about myself. Shortly after I started my second cup of coffee, I heard Austin rustling on the couch. I looked over and he was stretching. A moment later I felt him standing next to me. He kissed the top of my head. “Morning.” He said. I brushed his leg with my hand, “Morning.” I stood up and told him to sit. I went over and grabbed a mug that was upside down, filled it with coffee and brought it over to him. “Thank you,” he said.

“You’re welcome.” I sat next to him in a chair and picked up my mug.

“I have errands to run for the party tonight, Ellie, would you like to join me?” Chelsea asked.

“I would love to, what time do you want to get started?”

“Oh, I would say around 11:00 or so. That will get a good breakfast in us and people can have their showers.”

“That actually will be great, I need to pick up some extra clothes because I wasn’t planning on going to visit my parents.”

“You’re visiting your parents after here?”

"Yes, my mother called and told me my father wasn't doing well and she would like me to come visit being that I'm in the same state."

"Oh, I'm sorry to hear he's not doing well, his heart again?"

"Yes, I guess it's not healing like they thought it would. If the bathroom is open, I'll take my shower now."

"Earlier the better!" Chelsea said with a giggle. I excused myself and headed for Austin's room to get my things. All of a sudden two arms came from behind and squeezed me. Then one hand pulled my hair away from my neck and warm moist lips started kissing the top of my shoulder. "Hmmm," I quietly said.

"Good morning."

"Morning." I turned to face Austin. "Did you sleep OK on the couch?"

"I would have slept better next to you." He smiled.

"Yeah, like that was ever going to happen."

"No kidding. So going shopping with mom?"

"Yes. It will be fun; besides I wasn't lying, I do need at least another pair of jeans and shirts and stuff. I only brought enough for the weekend."

"You don't have to wear anything for me!!" Austin laughed.

"You are so bad!" I kissed him a little more passionately and pulled away.

"I need to take a shower, could you get me a couple towels please?" Austin let go of me and turned and headed into the hall. I grabbed my outfit and travel bag and followed him. I caught the ending to a punch to Max trailed by a "Shut it!" I just rolled my eyes and thought "boys." Austin gave me a quick kiss on the cheek, handed me my towels, and left shutting the door behind him. I quickly took a shower and hurried to get dressed. I put some light make-up on and towel-dried my hair. When I returned to the kitchen breakfast was underway. "Can I help with anything?" I offered.

"No, just relax, mom and I will call everyone when we are finished." Chelsea said.

"OK, just ask if you need another set of hands." I joined Austin on the couch. They were watching the morning news.

"You smell amazing!" Austin quietly told me. I smiled. "Thank you." We sat there on the couch for a while. "What things do you have to get done for the party?" I asked, because if we were running errands for the party, then what was it that he was supposed to be doing?

"I guess Mom wants me to get the balloons, the centerpieces, confetti, streamers, card box, and when Max and I do all that, we are to take it to the hall and that's where you guys come in to help set it all up."

"Oh, I didn't know I was in for manual labor?" I giggled.

"You don't think you can stay here for free do you now?" I looked at him and he jabbed my rib cage and started to tickle me.

"I will take you down little boy!" I squealed between the tickles. This apparently caused some attention and now Max was saying, "Yeah, yeah, take him down!!" We ended up on the floor and I was trying to focus from laughing so hard. I swept my leg around him, pinning him down but I couldn't hold him, he was too strong on the top so I needed to choke hold him from underneath. Max and their dad were starting to cheer which made this more exciting. "C'mon son! You can beat her!" his dad was shouting.

"NO! She's going to kick your butt!" Max countered. Austin did a common move and straddled me, pinning my arms above my head and sitting on my hips. I loved when Rick did this move, it was my easiest to get out of, I wiggled my hips to where Austin was straddling my thigh's, I separated my legs and caused him to split his knees apart, which caused him to loosen his grip on my wrists, I quickly scooted up pulled my legs through his, wrapped my legs around his and locked them down. I yanked my wrists free, put my arm around his neck, grabbed my other arm pulling him into me in a very tight choke-hold. I usually would flip over but I made my point, he wasn't going anywhere! He tapped my arm and I loosened my grip. Max jumped up and down and his father booed, I heard clapping from the other room and looked up and both his grandmother and mom were watching the exhibition.

"At least we know she can hold her own!" Chelsea said to her mom. They both laughed and went back to cooking. Austin and I untangled ourselves and caught our breath. It felt good to spar again, even if it wasn't the best situation.

"Did I hurt you?" I stroked Austin's wrist.

"No, maybe my pride is bruised a little, but no." I kissed his wrist and he smiled, "All better see." He held up his red wrist.

"That was fun!"

"We should spar more often on the mat," Austin suggested.

"Maybe after some lessons so I don't kick your butt every time." I snickered.

"Oh, you think you won that? I let you win so you didn't look bad!" Austin scoffed.

"Son, now come on, you know she kicked your butt fair and square." His dad interjected. I looked at Austin and shrugged my shoulders, "You heard the boss," I giggled.

"Fine. But next time…" I made an 'oh' face and stood up. I held my hands down to help him stand. He took my offer then pulled me into a kiss. I felt my cheeks warm with the embarrassment of him kissing me in front of his family. I was grateful that it was short and sweet.

"Breakfast is ready!" Chelsea called out from the kitchen. "Thank God!" I thought. We all headed to the kitchen and sat at the table.

After the breakfast dishes were cleaned and put away, Chelsea returned from her shower and was ready to go. She was giving the boys the orders of the day, "Now Austin you remember what you have to get done and what time we will meet you in the hall correct?"

"Yes, Mom."

"Hon, you know my sisters and brother and all are coming here first right and then after we get home and change, we'll all head over together, right?"

"Yes, darling. I will stay here with dad, to greet them with bells-" Austin's dad stopped in mid-sentence. "Where are my bells?"

"Oh! for Heaven's sake you are the most infuriating man that walks this planet!" Chelsea scoffed. Their dad just chuckled. And with that, we were out the door shopping, for what, I still was not clear because Austin was picking everything up that I could think of.

We just finished setting everything up in the hall and it looked so nice. The centerpieces were sitting on top of confetti and tea light candles with weighted down balloons of the school colors and gold for Valedictorian, tied at each table. The tables were covered with cloth linens and there was netting wrapped with white string lights that draped from one side to the other that looked like waves dancing across the ceiling. Over the dance floor, twinkling fairy lights suspended from the ceiling. It looked extremely magical. Hopefully, they would have some dancers, besides Austin and me, for all the trouble they went through to do this.

I caught a ride with Austin back to the house. It was nice to be alone with him.

"The hall looks awesome! You guys did an amazing job!" he said while driving back to his house.

"I just did what I was told, it was really all your mom that did everything! She's an amazing decorator!" Austin pulled off the main road onto a farm dirt road.

"Where are you going?" I asked curiously.

"Just want to be alone with you for a little while before everyone shows up and I don't get to." I smiled. I missed him also and was tired of 'sharing' him. I knew I was really going to share him tonight, and that was going to be OK. Austin pulled over into the entrance of a farm field. He shut off the car and undid his seatbelt. I undid mine. But instead of pulling me into a kiss like I imagined, he reached into his back pocket and pulled out his wallet. I looked confused. Then he pulled out the folded check that Mia had given him.

"I wanted to talk to you about this." He waved the check in the air.

"What about it?"

"Are you aware of how much he gave me?"

"No. The card was sealed when he handed to me."

"El, he gave me $100,000.00!" Austin stated flabbergasted. I looked surprised, but then I'm sure he had a good reason.

"Was there a note that explained the amount?"

"His note said that he didn't want me to struggle out of medical school so this was to help me be as successful as I can."

"Well, there ya go. He wants you to not be piled in debt when you get out of school and obviously trusts that you will put this to proper use."

"But he hardly knows me."

"Mia is a billionaire. He has a good sense of people and knows which ones to trust and which ones not to. Just write him a sincere thank you note expressing your gratitude and that will suffice."

“Really?” Austin sounded alarmed.

“Yes. Really.” I smiled. Austin put the check back into his wallet.

“Now, are you going to make love to me here in this farm field or are we headed back to the house?” I stared at him.

CHAPTER 26

The hall was even more spectacular with the lights off. All the candles and the twinkle lights just glimmered and gleamed. It was magical, like walking into an enchanted forest. I gave my wrap to the coat check at the front. I had gotten a ride from Austin's dad. I wasn't quite ready to leave when the rest of Austin's family was and it was nice to have a little quiet before the party. I walked in and looked around. The DJ was playing soft jazz to keep a calm atmosphere, there was wait staff carrying trays of drinks on their shoulders, and a lot of people already. I recognized some of the people standing in different sections such as aunts and uncles in one area than children running around, cousins, on the dance floor chasing the flickering reflection on the wax floor in another. There were a group of younger people over by the bar, where I recognized Tubbs. I started to walk that way when I saw a very attractive, girl steadfastly walking towards me. "Jess, great!" I thought.

"May I speak to you privately?" she asked in an 'I'm not taking no for an answer kind of way.'

"Sure." She led the way out of the room and into a private section of a different hall. No other parties were booked that night so it was pretty secluded.

"Listen, Jess, I don't want to fight with you anymore. I just want to have a nice time with Austin. This is *his* night."

"I didn't pull you over here to fight. After we got back from the Super Bowl, and Austin stopped speaking to me – well you know all about that ass chewing…"

"I'm sorry, I do not know about that. Austin didn't tell me anything. It would help me understand what your point is if you recapped the circumstances." I sort of lied. I did know Austin chewed her out, but it really didn't need to be recapped.

"Oh- I thought you knew; Austin chewed me out big time for the way I was treating you and behaving as his guest at the Super Bowl and …" She drifted off and shrugged her shoulders. "…He told me that I was lucky that you came to my rescue because I could have been raped or worse and to grow up! At first, I was like, whatever, but then after thinking about what he said and going back to every time I was around you, I looked hard at my behavior versus yours and I was an utter complete bitch to you. You never did anything aggressive or mean to me, even when you were putting me in my place. I just wanted to truly say that I am sorry for the way I have treated you and my behavior this past year. I had played this entire situation in my head since like middle school and I just went into shock when you came into the picture. I acted immature and disrespectful and I am sorry. Can you forgive me, please? I really just want Austin to be happy and I know that he is with you." I was shocked. The lawyer part of me was apprehensive to why she was apologizing, but, she never had even attempted to be this kind before so I would trust her just this once.

"I forgive you, and can understand." We hugged each other and went back to join the party. Austin saw us walking in together and his face immediately showed that he was not happy with the situation.

"Jess, I told you-" Austin started, but I cut him off.

"Austin, it's fine. Jess and I just had a meaningful conversation and everything is straightened up. We're all OK." Austin looked taken aback.

"You got a good woman here dumb ass, so, I suggest you don't screw it up!" Jess stated as she slapped him on the shoulder.

"I, um, uh, don't plan on it?" He stated confused. I smiled at him and gave him a kiss on the cheek. Jess walked away to join even more people that seemed to have shown up while we were talking.

"What was that all about?" He asked curiously.

"She just apologized for being such a royal bitch and asked if I would forgive her. I'm always one to forgive once, but next time I'll just kick the shit out of her." I snickered. Austin smiled at me.

"You look amazing by the way. I love this dress. I'm just mad I can take it off you tonight." He pouted.

"Well then, should I tell you what I'm wearing underneath?" Austin looked at me with his eyes wide, then he looked around. He grabbed my wrist and without a word sprinted towards the family restroom. Once inside, he locked the door, "No, don't tell me what you're wearing, show me!" I looked at him with my jaw dropped open.

"Here?" I questioned. He turned me around and brushed my hair over my shoulder. I felt him take my zipper in his hand and pull firmly down. I was so grateful that I decided on the hot lacy push-up bra and matching garter belt and stockings. The dress gently fell to the floor and Austin reached around and cupped my breasts. He started kissing me from behind while twisting my nipples. I let out a soft moan and he ran his hand down my stomach and under my panties. He fondled my clitoris before sinking his middle fingers up into my vagina. I let out a louder moan and he repeated in and out while cupping my clit and massaging my other breast. He gently bent me over the counter where I spread my hands out for support. I felt him slide my thong to the side then he separated my legs further apart. He pulled his fingers out of me and replaced them with his girth. He filled me deep in this position. I didn't even hear him undo his zipper or his pants. He pulled me onto him and immersed deeper. I had trouble holding onto the counter with his forceful thrusts. I came hard and he followed filling me with a final thrust. I paused a moment catching my breath and stability. He replaced my thong which made me giggle and I heard him zip up his pants. I walked over and picked up my dress and put it back on. He helped zip it up. I straightened my hair while he tucked in his shirt. “Amazing as always Mouse.”

“I love you, now let’s go have some fun!”

“That wasn’t fun for you?”

“Not what I meant.” I smiled. We unlocked the door, looked around to make sure no one was right outside, and we were safe.

“Well, there you are!” Chelsea’s voice came from somewhere behind us. We froze. Turned around and tried not to look guilty.

“Austin was just helping me with something” I lied.

“You have a lot of people here Austin and I would suggest you start greeting them.” She sounded annoyed.

“Right on it mom.” And we walked hand in hand back into the room. Austin introduced me to what seemed to be the entire school, a ton of people that I would never remember. He was a popular guy. There were just about equal numbers of boys versus girls. Dinner was served shortly after the final introduction was made. I sat next to Austin and all his immediate friends sat at the table with us. Others found their seats with comfortable acquaintances. After the cake was cut and passed out the DJ really started cranking out the tunes. A lot Austin’s friends got up and started to dance as did his parents and some of his family. Austin walked around and talked to family members and thanked people for coming. He told them about his goals and college plans. I was talking to one of his aunts and I saw him walking back from the DJ. Not too long after a slow melody came on and I recognized it immediately.

"May I steal her away for a moment?" he interjected. I giggled and he led me on to the dance floor. Everyone just stopped and stared at us. He was so graceful; he really could dance. He turned me and spun me. He dipped and lifted me at all the right times. Under the twinkling lights, it felt so amazing to be in his arms. It was like we were the only two in the room. At the end of the song, he kissed me gently on the lips and murmured, "I love you too." The 'too' confused me, but then I remembered in the restroom. People applauded as we left the dance floor and it filled up quickly again with upbeat music. I danced with everyone it felt like, I even danced with Max for one quick moment before embarrassment got the better of him and he ran off. Tubbs stole me for one dance, then Matt for another. I even did a slow fox-trot with Austin's dad. It was a wonderful night and I was definitely ready to get some sleep when we were headed back.

"We're here. Wake up." Austin tapped my knee. I slowly opened my eyes which felt like a million pounds. "You want me to carry you in?"

"No. I think I can manage." I mumbled. He got out and opened my car door for me. I crawled out and he helped me up. Next thing I know he lifted me up, kicked the door shut behind us and started walking in the house. I placed my head on his shoulder. I really was tired and it felt nice not to have to walk. He walked me to his bedroom and set me down. He quietly shut his door. He helped me unzip my dress.

"I can take it from here," I whispered.

"Are you sure?"

"Not that I want too, but, yes. I'm sure. I'm not drunk, I'm just tired." Austin gave me a kiss.

"Love you, baby. Sleep well."

"Love you too."

I changed quickly and crawled into bed. I was out almost as fast as I crawled in. The next morning, I was the first one up. I was dressed in my new outfit and all packed up. I was ready to hit the road. I put my things by the door and went over and kneeled by Austin. I kissed him gently on the cheek. He moaned and stretched at the same time.

"Morning sweetheart," I said.

"Morning." He smiled at me. I stood up and went into the kitchen and made a pot of coffee for everyone when they got up. Austin came from behind me and hugged me. "Why you up so early?"

"You know me, I'm always up early. I'm ready to get on the road when you are." Austin looked at me perplexed, "Mom won't like it if we just up and leave without saying goodbye."

"I wasn't thinking of that, I just meant I was ready whenever you are."

"OK, well I'm going to get in the shower then I'll join you for a cup of coffee. Sound good?"

"Sounds wonderful." He kissed me on my forehead and headed down the hall. I grabbed a cup of coffee and sat at the table. I pulled out my phone and started to go through emails.

"Up so early?" Chelsea's voice startled me.

"Oh sorry, did I wake you?"

"No, I'm usually the second one up, husband number one." She smiled. "Did you make coffee?"

"Yes, I hope that is alright?"

"It's nice. I love waking up to a cup waiting for me." Chelsea grabbed a mug and poured herself a cup of coffee.

"Austin is in the shower," I told her as if she couldn't tell. I internally rolled my eyes at my stupid statement. I went back to my emails; it seemed safer that way.

"I see you have your things already to go," Chelsea said pointing out my bags by the door.

"Yea, I guess I'm just anxious to see my parents, It was like there was something she just wasn't telling me over the phone, ya know?"

"Well, maybe there is, and she just didn't want you to worry before you had the chance to hear the entire details in person. OR…" she emphasized, "there is nothing to worry about and she just wanted to see her daughter before you left the state. You'll just have to wait and see. Whichever it is, I'm sure it will work out just fine." I smiled at her wisdom.

"Thank you," I said sincerely.

After a few moments, Austin came out and joined us.

"Morning mom."

"Morning." Austin grabbed a mug and poured a cup of coffee for himself. He walked over and joined us at the table. Man, he looked good. His hair was still wet from the shower and he smelled like his body wash. I needed to focus on my phone or I was going to get turned on sitting at the kitchen table across from his mother.

"So, you guys headed off early?" Chelsea asked him.

"I guess so, Eli wants to get up and see her parents, I guess her dad isn't doing so hot," Austin replied.

"Well, be safe, and let me know when you're headed back. When do you want to open your gifts?"

"We can do it right now unless it's a huge family thing?"

"No, now is fine, I'll grab some paper and a pen so we know who got you what." Chelsea got up from the table and got a pad of paper and a pen that was sitting on the counter next to the phone. Austin had gone into the living room and took the card box and some other boxes and brought them back to the kitchen table. I watched as he opened each card and read each word. As he read, his mother made notes. After about twenty minutes, he had gone through everything.

"I'm just going to put these in my room and pack a bag, I'll be right back." He said. And with that picked up all the cards and the few gifts and disappeared down the hall again.

"Would you like something to eat before you guys go?"

"I'm not hungry, but Austin might. Thank you." I said awkwardly. Now, I was feeling off, and I really would just like to leave, but knew that would be rude and not make any 'points'. Chelsea got up and started some eggs and sausage. She toasted an English muffin. She made him an egg sandwich 'to go' she said. Austin came out shortly and loaded our bags into the car. He took the sandwich and thanked his mom. Kissed her on the cheek and said good-bye. I gave her a hug, thanked her for her hospitality and said my good-byes.

Once at my parents my mother was extremely happy to see us. Apparently, my father's health had been declining rapidly but she didn't want to tell me so far away. "The graph they did isn't holding and there isn't enough tissue to do another one. Unless he gets stronger, they will have to go in and remove the graph before it breaks free and floats around causing a major clot."

"Why didn't you tell me all this was going on mom?" I lectured.

"You have such big plans and moved to New York, I didn't want you to give it all up just to stay with us or move back home."

"Don't you think that would have been my decision to make?"

"I'm sorry sweetie, but we can't have that on us, you giving up such a huge opportunity." My mom said with a sigh.

"Where's daddy now?"

"He's up at the hospital, they are monitoring him closely." I looked at Austin. He just put his arm around me and gave me a supportive squeeze.

A few days later after many trips back and forth to the hospital, the decision was made to remove the graph and try to add tissue from his leg to his heart valve, maybe natural will adhere better. But it would take a while to see how it's working, a while being; go home and will call you if you need to fly back. I arranged for Mia's jet to come pick me up at the airport near my parent's town the next day and Austin would drive home. It was very difficult for me to say goodbye to him under these circumstances. I was still very upset about my dad, but after surgery, there really wasn't anything I could do anyway so I might as well go back to work. I was going to see Austin in a month, which seemed like forever. I already missed him. We had such an awesome time and I never felt closer to him ever. Austin kissed me goodbye at the airport and tears streamed down my face.

"Please don't cry, I can't tell you everything will be alright, but you know I'll be here for you no matter what right?" The tears fell harder. I just buried my head in his shoulder and he held me. "I'm going to miss you so much, but it will only be a month. That gives me time to wrap things up with my friends and family, and then…" He lifted my chin up and looked me in the eyes. He was pretty blurry on my side, "…then we will have the rest of the summer together in Europe. OK?" I nodded, even though he was right it didn't help and I didn't want to let go, but I had to be strong. I let go, wiped my eyes and Austin kissed me passionately. I kissed him back just as hard.

We parted lips, "I'll call you when I land OK?"

"I wouldn't expect any different. I love you. Everything will work out the way it's supposed to, you know that right?" I nodded.

I walked up the stairs and greeted the flight crew. The pilot went over the safety instructions while the door closed. I stared out the window acknowledging my understanding at the appropriate times, but the entire time just staring at Austin. He got in his car and drove toward home. Tears fell silently down my face.

"Miss, Miss?" Someone was tapping me. I jumped startled because I didn't realize that I had fallen asleep. I guess from all the stress with my dad and such I was exhausted. "Miss, we've landed." I re-adjusted my eyes and looked out the window. We were on the ground and it was dark outside.

"OK, thank you, I'm sorry I fell asleep," I mutter at the flight attendant.

"It's alright Miss. The car is waiting for you." She smiled at me. I stood up still trying to clear my head. Once in the car, I picked up my phone and called Austin.

"Hello," he answered.

"Hi, baby. I'm in the car heading back to my house. How close are you to home?"

"Oh, I have about two more hours to drive. How was your flight?"

"I guess it was OK, I slept the entire way back."

"Well, you didn't get a lot going back and forth with your dad, so I can see that. I don't want to talk while driving so can I call you when I get settled?"

"Sure thing. Love you."

"Love you more." And he hung up.

CHAPTER 27

I was so excited! Austin was flying into New York and we were going to get on the international flight together from there! I couldn't wait to see him; I barely slept all night. I was going over my packing and things we should see and places we should go. I wanted to have breakfast one morning in Switzerland, and definitely wanted to go have a beer in Munich, then there was Tuscany and Rome, OH! And the Parliament in Budapest, the list went on and on. I barely even focused on one of the main reasons I was going and that was for closing and transferring accounts over for Mia. That thought made me giggle. I met Austin at the airport and he picked me up and spun me around I kissed him all over his face. "Hey lady! Who do you think you are kissing me?" He stated like he was assaulted. I slapped him and he kissed me back. "Hi, sexy! I missed you too!"

"I am so excited!! You remembered your passport, right?"

"As I told you last night, and the day before that, and the day before that… yes." He pulled it out, "It's right here!" I smiled.

"I just don't want anything to go wrong, that's all."

"I know. I'm excited as well. I've never been to Europe before, this is SO cool!"

"Do you have a shopping list from friends?" I laughed.

"Yes. Everyone wants something." He smiled back.

"Shouldn't be an issue. We'll just ship it if you get too much stuff." I winked.

The flight was long but being with Austin, it was enjoyable. He filled me in on what he did with all his friends over the past month and the extra shifts he picked up at the hospital. He earned a little extra cash because he was doing it to help, so they paid him for it. I didn't have much to share, my life was pretty bland getting Mia ready for the 'trail'. We fell asleep with Austin holding me which made the flight seem shorter and it was nice because when we landed at 1:05 Paris' time, we were refreshed to go out and explore. After we collected our bags, there was a driver holding up a sign, **BAYLOR**. It was nice that we didn't need to learn how to maneuver the city right off. We had a week to figure that out, unfortunately, I would have to leave Austin alone for a week to go work in the office, but I would be with him outside of business hours.

Mia's townhouse was really elegant, not surprising. I usually stayed in a hotel when I came to work in the office for him because I wasn't here this long. Austin and I put our things away and decided to go out and explore. I did pick up a map and downloaded travel guides and international maps on my cell. There was so much to see I didn't even know where to start. I told Austin there were a couple 'must dos' while we were here; we have to spend a day at the Louvre Museum, Notre-Dame Cathedral, and the Palace of Versailles. He wanted to go up into the Eiffel Tower and visit Gustave Eiffel private apartment. I wasn't keen on going up that high, but, for Austin, I would.

We walked around the block a little which seemed to be in the center of a bustling little area. We were one block from the Metro. There was a little café around the corner that had soup and sandwiches, and a beautiful park that seemed to go on for miles and ended up at the Eiffel Tower. We had a little market that carried almost everything we needed for groceries, so we didn't need to go far in that respect either. I decided that I would ask in the office, from the locals where to go for dinner. They also had really cute little shops of nick-knacks and jewelry. I could see why Angelica really enjoyed coming here. As we were walking around there was a street cart that sold crepes. I was hungry and thought that sounded good. I ordered two crepes with chocolate. It was fun watching them make them to order. We found a spot in the grass and sat down and enjoyed our snack, which turned into more of a meal because they were huge. I looked at Austin and started to giggle, he had chocolate everywhere on his face. I decided that I should help clean him up. I started at the corner of his mouth and worked my way around. He didn't object. It was so freeing to be able to show affection in public without the scrutiny of our age being a factor. He put his hand at the base of my neck and pulled me in deeper for a more passionate kiss. I leaned back and he moved on top of me. We laid in the grass for a while just kissing and cuddling. We picked out shapes in the clouds and talked about other places we would like to try and see while we were over here. It was just the first day and it was already so magical.

The first couple of days were exhausting for me. My French wasn't as thorough as it once was and we, my colleagues, ended up speaking English, which they spoke better anyway. I was almost too tired by the time I got back to the townhouse to even barely eat dinner. Some nights Austin would order out and have it delivered. He would run a hot bath and massage my back and shoulders. I would try and come back for lunches so that way we could see each other a little more. Austin was enjoying his time while I was at the office. He wasn't afraid of sightseeing by himself. One day he took a trip to Sacré-Coeur, the Basilica on the hill. He said that you could see almost all of Paris from that one hilltop. He wanted to show me before we left. He laughed because he said it was more like a white castle than a church. Another afternoon he toured the Catacombs of Paris. I was definitely not interested in that, so I'm glad looking at spooky skulls made him happy, yuck! He picked out a souvenir skull keychain for his brother. He thought that was hysterical.

Towards the later part of the week, I was starting to get accustomed to the time difference and work was lessening. We had almost everything in place and were just going over the final details. I returned to the townhouse and Austin was dressed nicely in a jacket and khaki pants.

"What are you dressed up for?" I inquired.

"I called Mia today and asked him how I should take my lady out on the town. He suggested a nice dinner and then a ballet at the Opéra Garnier, also known as the Palais Garnier." He looked pretty impressed with himself.

"That sounds wonderful, let me go change really quick and we can head out!"

The Opéra Garnier was amazing. You just felt like you walked into the Phantom of the Opera. The beautiful drapery and the ornate detail of the boxes were unbelievable. The theater still radiates the same inexplicable ambiance as in the late 1800s. Just looking around at all the detail gave me chills. I absolutely loved sharing this moment with Austin. The ballet was incredible. Even though I had watched ballets in New York, there was just something different, maybe it was the ambiance and surroundings or because I was with Austin or both. I had a marvelous time. After the performance, we walked hand in hand under the moonlit sky.

"Want an ice cream?" Austin asked. "There's a nice little cart by the tower. I don't know if he's still open, but we can check."

"That sounds perfect." We walked over to where Austin found the ice cream cart and the gentleman was still open. We ordered two chocolate cones. The cones were funny shaped, they looked like a figure eight, double cone. I think that was the best ice cream I have ever had in my entire life.

Once back at the townhouse I was tired. I changed into my night clothes and crawled into bed. Austin came in shortly after with some lotion in his hand.

"What is that?"

"I found this in one of the little shops yesterday, I thought it smelled nice." He opened it and leaned it towards me for me to smell.

"That does smell nice. It's floral but not overwhelming. I like it."

"Would you like a foot massage with it?" I just stared at him.

"Could you honestly be any more perfect?" I asked him and he smiled.

"I love you," he replied. He put a little lotion in his hand and started to massage my foot. Man, did that feel nice.

"What are you going to do on your last day at the office?" He inquired.

"Not much really, in fact, I should be done by lunch."

"Would you like to go for a picnic lunch then, when you finish?"

"That sounds wonderful!"

"Great, I will have everything ready, all you will need to do is change when you get back. Could you text me when you are on your way?"

"Absolutely."

Austin finished the other foot and I was so relaxed. He curled up next to me and I fell asleep in his arms. The alarm on my phone woke me up and I stretched. Austin was on his back sound asleep. Today, was the final business day here in Paris. After today we were going to leave the city. One place we wanted to look at was the Mont Saint-Michel. There were also a couple of chateaux, one being the Lore Valley Chateaux, that I really wanted to see. This took some planning on how and when would be the best time. We also figured out how we wanted to spend the rest of our visit throughout Europe.

When I got back to the townhouse, as promised, Austin was ready. He had a packed picnic basket and a blanket folded next to it on the counter.

"I'll just be a moment," I said as I scurried off to change. I put on a cute little cotton tank top and a matching pair of shorts. Austin wasn't dressed up, so I felt fine in the outfit I had picked.

"Where have you chosen for us to have our picnic?" I asked while we held hands walking from the townhouse.

"I thought we would eat in the park over by the Eiffel Tower. It's such a beautiful structure."

"That it is." I agreed.

Once we found our spot, Austin opened up the blanket and laid it on the ground. He set everything out. It wasn't your typical picnic, it was more of a fruit/cheese appetizer kind of meal. He had fresh baguettes and red grapes, several different kinds of cheese and some chocolate cookies. It was very tasty. I laid between Austin's legs as he leaned back and we talked about how the designer and creator of the Eiffel Tower, created the Statue of Liberty and that there was an identical one in France and we should look up finding it while we were here. The sun was shining and it was a beautiful afternoon. The park wasn't overly crowded. There were a few other couples enjoying the sun and each other's company, some men were kicking around a soccer ball and some children were playing with some balloons that a street vendor was selling down a ways. It was a very serene moment.

Austin shifted under me and reached for something out of the basket. I sat up and he wrapped his arms around from behind me. He was holding a little velvet box.

"What's this?" I said out of complete surprise.

"Open it please."

I opened the box and inside was a beautiful antique diamond ring. It was the most beautiful ring I had ever seen. It was a square princess cut diamond cathedral ring with smaller diamonds around it. It had two bands, one directly on top of the other. The top band was white gold and had small diamonds going down the shank. The inner band was yellow gold and twisted scrollwork pressed against a small little flat round diamond. It was exquisite.

"Austin it's beautiful where did you get this?" I was shocked.

"I found it in a little antique store one day while I was out." Austin crawled in front of me, kneeled on both knees and held the ring between his fingers, slightly shaking,

"Ellie Anne Baylor, will you be my forever?"

"I love you Austin. Yes. I will be your forever."

ABOUT THE AUTHOR

Katherine Nightingale first and foremost is a mother and wife. She is a graduate of Interlochen Arts Academy and has many different passions; one of them fulfilled in writing this book. Since early childhood, she has had a very creative imagination and talent that along with her well diverse life, helped her gain the courage to create the writing of The Girl Next Door.

Made in USA - Kendallville, IN
20379_9798650966043
05.17.2023 1326